Edward Kornhauser

JINCY WILLETT is the author of *Jenny and the Jaws of Life, Winner of the National Book Award,* and *The Writing Class,* which have been translated and sold internationally. Her stories have been published in *Cosmopolitan, McSweeney's Quarterly,* and other magazines. She frequently reviews for *The New York Times Book Review.* Willett spends her days parsing the sentences of total strangers and her nights teaching and writing—sometimes, late at night, in the dark, she laughs inappropriately. Visit her at www.jincywillett.com.

ALSO BY JINCY WILLETT

Jenny and the Jaws of Life

Winner of the National Book Award

The Writing Class

Additional Praise for *Amy Falls Down*

"I loved this novel—it's totally brilliant—witty and mordant and filled with these wonderful insights into the state of publishing and writing and the way we are now. I thought Willett couldn't top *Winner of the National Book Award*, but I was wrong—this one definitely does."
                                                                    —Nancy Pearl

"Willett uses her charmingly filterless heroine as a mouthpiece to slam a parade of thinly veiled literati and media personalities with riotous accuracy, but she balances the snark with moments of poignancy."   —*Publishers Weekly* (starred review)

"A smart and witty tale."   —*The San Diego Union-Tribune*

Praise for *The Writing Class*

"Willet's delicious satire savages every literary pretension imaginable."   —*The Miami Herald*

"A marvelous toy of a book, full of wry surprises and sly twists . . . extremely clever and quite enjoyable."   —*Booklist*

"*The Writing Class* is alternately funny, sweet, and suspenseful. . . . Books like this are what caused book lovers to fall in love with books in the first place."   —*The Buffalo News*

Praise for *Winner of the National Book Award*

"The funniest novel I have read, possibly ever."

—Augusten Burroughs

"Poignant and funny, mean and tender, Willett's novel is exuberantly original." —*Publishers Weekly* (starred review)

"An elegy wrapped inside a satire, a sorrowful meditation on the mysteries of sibling love and rivalry concealed within a bitterly funny chronicle of literary buffoonery. Jincy Willett is a fearless writer, capable of startling the reader into rueful laughter at every turn." —Tom Perrotta

Praise for *Jenny and the Jaws of Life*

"Exquisite . . . A great, darkly comic collection." —*Esquire*

"The funniest collection of stories I've ever read—really funny and perfectly sad at the same time." —David Sedaris

"Exhilarating. Her art has passed through anxiety and come out the other side, completely honest yet purged of the confessional whine or the need to call attention to its bravery."

—*The Village Voice*

Amy
Falls
Down
A NOVEL

Jincy
Willett

PICADOR

A THOMAS DUNNE BOOK
ST. MARTIN'S PRESS
New York

AMY FALLS DOWN. Copyright © 2013 by Jincy Willett. All rights reserved. Printed in the United States of America. For information, address Picador, 175 Fifth Avenue, New York, N.Y. 10010.

www.picadorusa.com
www.twitter.com/picadorusa • www.facebook.com/picadorusa
picadorbookroom.tumblr.com

Picador® is a U.S. registered trademark and is used by St. Martin's Press under license from Pan Books Limited.

For book club information, please visit www.facebook.com/picadorbookclub or e-mail marketing@picadorusa.com.

Designed by Nicola Ferguson

The Library of Congress has cataloged the St. Martin's Press hardcover edition as follows:

Willett, Jincy.
    Amy falls down / Jincy Willett. — First edition.
        pages cm
    ISBN 978-1-250-02827-3 (hardcover)
    ISBN 978-1-250-02828-0 (e-book)
    1. Women authors—Fiction. 2. Life change events—Fiction. I. Title.
PS3573.I4455A81 2013
813'.54—dc23

                                                         2013004051

Picador Paperback ISBN 978-1-250-05025-0

Picador books may be purchased for educational, business, or promotional use. For information on bulk purchases, please contact Macmillan Corporate and Premium Sales Department at 1-800-221-7945, extension 5442, or write specialmarkets@macmillan.com.

First published in the United States by Thomas Dunne Books, an imprint of St. Martin's Press

First Picador Edition: July 2014

10 9 8 7 6 5 4 3 2 1

For Edward T. Kornhauser, Jr.

HEARTY HANDCLASPS

To:
M. J. Andersen
Tony DiBasio
Billy Frolick
Tom Hartley
Alisa Williams Willett
Ward and Joanne Willett

And to:
The Hurt Feelings Book Club
featuring
Meagan Jennifer Knepp
Karen Worley
Kristen Amicone
Kristin Nielsen
June Snedecor

And especially to:
The Coven

'The king died and then the queen died' is a story. 'The king died, and then the queen died of grief' is a plot. The time sequence is preserved, but the sense of causality overshadows it. Consider the death of the queen. If it is in a story we say 'and then?' If it is in a plot we ask 'why?'

—E.M. FORSTER

"God damn it," said Lewis, "I told you. I'm not in the business of exposing things. I'm a novelist. I write novels. I don't go around—"

—H. ALLEN SMITH

CHAPTER ONE

❧

Accident

B ecause the Norfolk pine was heavy, and also because she was wearing house slippers, having not yet dressed for the day, Amy took her time getting to the raised garden. Her house slippers were fuzzy, oversized, and floppy, and if she moved too fast, she would walk right out of them.

She was not yet dressed for the day because she had no reason to dress until much later, at which time she'd have to dress uncomfortably, and she was in no hurry to do that. At three o'clock a reporter from *The San Diego Union-Tribune* was coming to interview Amy as part of some bogus series about local writers. Although she'd specified no current events and especially no photographs, she didn't trust a reporter who sounded on the phone as though she were eight years old and couldn't think of anything funnier than not wanting your face on public display. Imagine, her laughter implied, denying the world the chance to gaze upon you. So Amy dreaded the interview but was not actively doing so, or thinking about it at all, as she shuffled toward the raised garden with the Norfolk pine.

She shuffled past her mimosa tree, where three goldfinches clung to a thistle-seed feeder, and past her green plastic pseudo-Adirondack chairs, covered with two seasons' worth of dirt, seeds, and leaves, which she really must hose off one of these days. She shuffled closer to the raised garden, as the screen door banged behind her and Alphonse jingled past and up ahead of her, his great basset nose zeroing in on the very spot where she planned to dig, as though her trail had magically preceded her. James Thurber said that his bloodhound always seemed more interested in where he'd been than where he was; Alphonse had an uncanny fascination with where she planned to be, and a genius for thwarting her: ordinarily a sedate plodder, he could materialize in a chair just as she was about to sit down; if she suddenly felt peckish at two in the morning, he'd be waiting in front of the refrigerator, his eyes glowing red in the dark kitchen. Now he sniffed round and round the digging spot. "No!" she shouted. "Desist, you miscreant!" Alphonse feigned deafness, as though so anxious to relieve himself that he could think of nothing else, which was mendacious, as he usually slept in until midmorning and even then typically put off his bathroom break until noon. He was just messing with her head.

So she shuffled a little faster, intent on reaching her goal before Alphonse fully committed himself to his, and when she came to the raised garden, her eyes fixed on Alphonse, and lifted her right foot to step onto the low brick wall, she misjudged its elevation by perhaps a quarter inch, not enough to stub her toes and trip, just enough to throw her very slightly off-balance, the sole of her foot catching and scraping on the rough brick rather than coming straight down to meet it, and still she rose, her attention now divided between Alphonse and the heavy potted pine, her center of gravity higher than usual as she clutched it to her midriff, and then the slipper on her left foot did flop off and she did stub her left toes, or rather skinned the tops of them on the harsh edge of the brick, which really shouldn't have been catastrophic, but was, because now she was thinking about three different things, Alphonse, her toes, and the Norfolk pine, so that somehow her balance shifted forward, and certain physical forces, inertia and momentum, began to announce themselves, clearing their throats politely. All was not lost at this point, they said, but a fall was possible, and Amy, over-thinking as usual, realizing that in such a fall the *pine* might suffer irreparably, focused on cradling it in such a way that *it* would not suffer, as though she were sixteen years old and lithe and presented with a smorgasbord of landing-position selections, none of which would injure her in the slightest, whereas what she should have done was jettison the damn plant and save herself, but no, and then she had actually lost balance and was pitching forward, her legs and feet heroically striving to catch up with her upper body, so that, still falling, she gathered speed, and, seeing that all was lost, she began to twist around in order to land on her back, and then her bare left heel slammed down on a sprinkler head and she heard her ankle crunch, but felt nothing because within the time it would have taken for the pain message to arrive in her brain, she had knocked herself out on the birdbath.

CHAPTER TWO

◇

Not Drowning

When the Looney Tunes characters of her childhood got knocked out, hallucinated birds always twittered about their heads. Now as Amy began to come to, she lay still with her eyes closed and waited for the twittering to stop. She knew where she was and recalled the twisting fall but not cracking her head on the birdbath, probably because during the event-filled fall itself she'd been so fixated on Alphonse (who had regarded her sardonically, as though Amy windmilling through the air were a daily spectacle) that she'd neglected to consider the birdbath, so that the actual impact must have been an unidentified surprise. But she remembered it now, and pictured the back of her throbbing skull as an ancient crazed vase which at the slightest touch would subside into shards. The throbbing by itself might accomplish this. Not so immediate was the throbbing in her left ankle, which was actually more painful but easier to ignore, as it was so far away. As she lay still, Amy became more and more herself, except that the birds still twittered. She opened her eyes: a quartet of juncos, assembled in a line on the ground in front of her face, lifted up and out of sight, apparently spooked by the flick of her eyelids. Imagine being that tiny. Sunlight pierced her skull. She squeezed her eyes shut and began to move, rising on her elbows and twisting at the waist so she could push herself up, and her right hand encountered a puddle of warm, viscous liquid where her head had lain. Amy froze, afraid to look at so much blood.

For a full minute she hovered over the puddle with her eyes clamped shut, imagining her own reflection in a scarlet pool. She had a fractured skull, or a subdural hematoma, whatever the hell that was, and she was going to bleed out all alone in her backyard, an aging fat woman wearing a ratty chenille bathrobe and one fuzzy slipper. Then a far-off jingle reminded her she wasn't actually alone, and, heartened, she opened her eyes. Not blood at all, but basset saliva. He must have stood drooling over her inert form, waiting for her to take her last ragged breath. He was probably off gathering firewood for the hibachi, bless his heart. "Tough luck, kiddo," she called, softly, to spare her head. "Not this time."

Amy took one full hour to make it back indoors. For a while, fearful of the pain in her ankle, she crawled on hands and knees. Midway, she heard the Blaines, her neighbors, in their backyard, calling their cats and sprinkling their camellias. She opened her mouth to shout to them and then stopped. They were nice people—she fed the cats when they visited their grandchildren—and they'd be eager to help, but Amy got stuck, as she so often did, on what words she would actually use.

When she was eighteen years old she had almost drowned in the Kennebec River, not because of the pummeling current, but because she couldn't come up with a casual phrase with which to call for rescue. "Help!" was such a cliché. By the time she was willing to scream, she had no breath left, and it was just blind luck that somebody saw her gasping and floundering and pulled her to shore. "Why didn't you say something?" they wanted to know, and she said, "I'm not a screamer." "Jesus," said one of them, "couldn't you have made an exception this one time?" "Apparently not," she said.

Now she began to rehearse. *Hi there! Hello, Blaines! Say, I'm terribly sorry, but have you got a minute?* What then? The Blaines were short, small-boned people. Between them they couldn't possibly pull her to her feet, and she'd feel funny about leaning on them—or, indeed, on anyone else. In the end she kept her mouth shut and just sat up on the cement and listened to them argue about a misplaced coupon in the Pennysaver and whether they should feed their mandarins now or in February.

Above her head the goldfinches returned to their feeder, having decided she couldn't rise up and bother them. Her head, she realized, had stopped throbbing, and she felt suddenly optimistic. Gingerly she probed the back of her skull, which didn't feel particularly mushy; in fact, it was beginning to numb up. Her ankle was swollen and blue but didn't seem broken, at least not in a spectacular way. Now was as good a time as any to find out how bad it was. She crawled over to where she kept the garden tools, selected the sturdiest rake, and used it to push herself up. With the up-ended rake as a crutch, she took a step and put just enough weight on the bad foot to learn that walking, though terribly hurtful, was possible.

By the time she got inside a curious thing had happened. She felt energized, instead of fatigued, by the morning's experiences, and she was instantly giddy. She should definitely call somebody—Carla, maybe, or Harry B, since he'd given her the fatal Norfolk pine in the first place. She'd call Harry and they'd have a good laugh about it. She started to hobble toward the phone in the living room and noticed happily that the upended rake was unnecessary: she could hop almost nimbly from place to place, so cluttered was her house with chairs and tables and bookcases to right herself on. By the time she reached the sofa, though, she was terrifically sleepy, and lay down for a brief nap before calling Harry.

When she opened her eyes, the light was blinding and so was her headache, as though a migraine had joined forces with the pain from the crack on her head, which it probably had, and then Alphonse clambered up on the sofa and stood on top of her stomach, barking out the window at what had to be the postman, which was odd, because he never came before two p.m. It couldn't possibly be that late, but she had to wait for Alphonse to jump down before she could see the Kit-Kat clock on the far wall and verify that it was midmorning. It wasn't.

Something was wrong. Amy never napped. She had a hard enough time sleeping through the night. Worse, there was an important thing she was supposed to do at three o'clock. She couldn't remember what, but it definitely involved getting dressed. By the time she had hopped into the bedroom, she remembered: the damn reporter, Holly Something, and how could she conduct an interview in her present state? The thought of drawing even the loosest trousers over her swollen ankle was too daunting, and in the end she had to settle for a multicolored flowing caftan, a shapeless billowing thing she had bought without trying on and then shoved in the back of a closet crammed with other similarly unworn monstrosities. Why did they assume that women of a certain age and weight wanted to dress like circus clowns? Forcing a brief glance in the mirror, she was even more alarmed by her face and hair than by the hideous dress. She could fix her face, but her white-blond hair was long and wild, as it always was when she got up in the morning, and when she tried to comb it through, it pulled torturously at her scalp. After much hopping and drawer-rifling she located an old crimson turban she had bought for a Halloween costume thirty years ago. (Amy never threw anything away.) Once again she regarded herself in the mirror. She looked like that creature in *The Nutcracker,* the one with all the little kids under her dress. Mother Ginger, on chemo. It was 2:55.

She pictured herself greeting Holly Gigglepuss, whose name she'd written down somewhere, at the door and drawing her into her messy house, hopping pathetically, explaining that she'd fallen down, exhibiting her own sad state, and knew that this would be worse than flailing in the Kennebec. No. With dignified mien she would greet the woman outdoors, in her own front yard. Under no circumstances would she gain access to Amy's house. Amy would be waiting for her when she arrived, and she wouldn't move. She'd look very odd, but at least not pitiful, and there wasn't going to be a picture anyway.

She had a scare getting out the door when Alphonse, who as a matter of principle always tried to escape when the door opened, came very close to successfully achieving this pointless goal (he never went anywhere but across the street), almost knocking her over backward as she scrambled to close the screen between them. She had planned to position herself on the lawn in front of the dwarf apricot, but she had left the rake crutch on the other side of the door, and there wasn't time to get it. She maneuvered so she was standing at the railing at the top of the steps, and waited. She could lean against the railing if she had to. Her headache had winked out for the moment, and she was feeling positive again. This should, she knew, have frightened her, as she had no rational reason to feel positive. For one thing, now she could not remember why the reporter was coming. She felt like a cigar-store Indian. There was definitely something wrong with her head, and she'd have to deal with it later.

CHAPTER THREE

But Waving

Then, or rather now, it *was* later. The winter sun had descended, the shadow of her little jacaranda tree had moved, reaching toward the driveway, where a natty blue SUV driven by a young woman *she had never seen before* began to back down into the street. The woman rolled down her window. "That was really amazing!" she said, waving and smiling broadly. "I'll email you the pictures!" Even from this distance her teeth were impossibly white. Amy waved her off. "Help," she said softly, waving back.

CHAPTER FOUR

Unnamed Details

Amy hobbled back indoors. After much Internet searching she diagnosed herself with a "simple concussion." Many websites offered checklists; she didn't have nausea or slurred speech (although God knew what she had actually sounded like during the interview), but she certainly had headaches; ditto "mood and cognitive disturbances," the latter in spades, since she was missing a serious chunk of time. Actually, the more reputable websites, like the one for the Mayo Clinic, strongly implied that this kind of amnesia meant that the concussion was "severe." Still, she was able to juggle incoming information to make it come out the way she wanted: namely, that she would not have to go to a doctor's office and get herself looked at. Amy was aware that she was being extremely foolish, but one of the great advantages to living alone was that you didn't have to justify yourself, except to a basset. She fixed a late dinner, which she didn't eat, went to bed early, and lay awake mistrusting her own brain, a new and unsettling experience, since the object of mistrust was also its agent.

Instead of counting sheep, she tried counting the things of which she was sure: to tease out and disentangle all of the causal threads.

1. It was New Year's Day. She was sure of that. Because Amy's birthday was New Year's Eve, and because she was no longer a child, she loathed New Year's—both the Eve and the Day. Not only was it not worth celebrating: it was eminently worthy, in the Carrollian mode, of uncelebration. Sixty-plus years ago she had been a gullible toddler with doting parents and the whole world had sung drunken songs and set off fireworks displays in her honor; now it did the same things to piss her off. Amy didn't at all mind getting older, homelier, and simultaneously bulkier and less visible, but she was disinclined to memorialize the process with noisemakers. (Once, in her mid-twenties, she and Max had, at her instigation, supplied New Year's Eve party guests with air horns, on the careless theory that if anything, including deliberate noisemaking, was worth doing, it was worth doing well. The results were much more hilarious in anticipation than in actual experience, or even distant recollection. People had screamed in pain.)

2. She had this morning decided to venture into her backyard and plant the stupid pine. She remembered deciding this but could not remember why.

3. True, Carla had given her a holly bush for Christmas, and the others in her remaining writing class had chipped in for a Norfolk pine, but until that morning her intention had definitely been to let both expire on her back steps, along with all her other plants, except for an awesomely neglected, fitfully blooming mess of potted geraniums, the undead of the Southern California plant world.

4. Still, when she had picked up the Norfolk pine—no mean feat in its ten-gallon plastic pot—and shuffled down her back steps and across her cement patio, she had been headed for a specific spot, one she must have planned for ahead of time: the center of the raised garden in the northeast corner of the yard. The garden was still cluttered with late-summer debris—silvery artichoke plants, giant zucchini carcasses, desiccated yarrow, and still more zombie geraniums—but the center ground was clear, and near enough to a sprinkler head to receive ample water. Directly behind was a concrete birdbath, which would have to come out as the tree got its growth, but for now it could stay.

5. Because of 1–4, she had had an accident.

6. Because of 5, she had lost a chunk of memory. She had given an interview to, or at least done something with, a *U-T* reporter during that missing period of time.

7. Because she was who she was, she took accidents personally. Also, she hated doctors. So she definitely remembered who she was.

Other than the physicians who took her fiction writing classes, Amy had not seen a doctor for thirty years. In the first place, she had not trusted them since she was four years old and Dr. Kronkheit told her to "Look out the window, Amy! There's a pony on Pitman Street," and though she wasn't interested in ponies, she had obliged to be polite and been rewarded with a needle-stab in the arm. It wasn't so much the pain of the shot as *the look on his face* when she regarded him with mute outrage. His eyes were actually twinkling. She had read about this phenomenon in poems. Old people and leprechauns were always twinkling. What a disgusting thing to do. "You're a good girl not to cry," he said then, sounding oddly disappointed, the twinkle fading; Amy dropped the proffered lollipop into his metal wastebasket with an ostentatious clang, which was a mistake. She just got in trouble with her mother, and as she was led out into the waiting room she saw it, the horrible twinkle, brighter than before. If she had it to do all over again—and right now, almost sixty years later, she would have liked nothing more—she would have let the green lollipop slip down her sleeve, soundlessly, into the trash, like Michael Corleone dropping that gun. Maybe the old bastard would have found it later and realized she'd won; maybe he wouldn't, but she'd have won anyway. Children saw so much more than adults gave them credit for. They didn't have the words to name what they were seeing, but they saw, all right, and they never forgot. Maybe they remembered so clearly *because* they didn't have the words. Maybe there was a file cabinet in the brain for mysterious clusters of unnamed details.

Amy switched on her bedside lamp and jotted a few lines in her notebook of story ideas. *Kronkheit,* she scribbled, and *malignant twinkle,* and *observation and hypothesis—child formulates Twinkle Theory—* She had started up the journal again last year and it was filling up, though she had yet to expand on any of the listed ideas, all of which looked like gibberish in the daylight. They were often wonderfully soporific: she would use the ideas as bedtime stories, lulling herself to sleep with opening lines. She tried now to do the same with the little girl, the lollipop, the ancient insult, but when she rolled on her side, her head spun. How can your head spin in the pitch dark when you're lying down with your eyes closed? Did that even make sense? Maybe she should have gone to one of those walk-in clinics. Maybe her brain was leaking. Maybe she was "stroking out." For the first time since the fall, she allowed herself to consider going to the hospital. Instantly her heart both raced and sank.

Amy had enjoyed good health throughout her life without effort, eating and drinking as she pleased, exercising only when there was a point to it. She was in terrible shape now, overweight and sedentary, but still she rarely got even a cold. Living like a hermit protected her from germs. Until today she had never injured herself significantly, while all around her slim, gusto-grabbing women keeled over dead during marathons, fainted from salt-deprivation in the checkout lines of Jimbo's, crippled themselves with shin-splints, got gnawed on by mountain lions and mede-vaced from wilderness areas, and generally drove up health insurance rates for the chain-smoking obese who had the good sense to stay still. When they weren't endangering themselves, these medically pious types got whole-body scans and BMI reports and knew their cholesterol and blood pressure numbers by heart. How they must love their doctor visits!

Amy stopped going to doctors after Max died. She had not yet been accosted by mammogram reminders, so for the first ten years she didn't think about doctors much, except to dismiss them as useless technicians who lost interest in you once you were officially incurable. She didn't blame them for not saving Max, who was dying and did not expect to be saved. But they had been careless with his meds and heartless in treating his ratcheting pain. The problem with residents wasn't that they were overworked. They were over-young. They behaved as though dying people were an alien species, a series of problems and opportunities, and nothing to do with their own corporeal futures. Only the old doctors really saw Max. One night toward the end as she sat beside his bed, two of these old men came to check on the morphine and then just stood there at the foot of the bed, their faces somber in the dark room, and the three of them listened to Max softly moaning. They seemed to Amy to be bearing witness. Here was the enemy, triumphant, and they had failed. Or maybe they were just taking a break, but even so she admired them for their willingness to do it there, on the field of slaughter.

She was barely forty when Max died; during the next ten years she had remarried and moved from Maine to California and distracted herself with regret over these decisions, both bad. She kept herself busy not writing, not making friends, and not having sex with the stranger she had married, and it wasn't until her mid-forties that she acknowledged to herself that she was also not getting checkups. She had entered into the mammogram era, the biopsy years, she was formally mortal, but she couldn't even bring herself to pick up the phone and make an appointment. The one time she did this, in 1993, she had dutifully noted the appointment, three months hence, in her San Diego Zoo calendar under a photo of a lustrous-eyed okapi, and for the next eleven weeks not a day went by without picturing in her mind those eyes, that calendar square, the illegible name of the doctor, the all too legible time of day, 2:15, and she lived each day with the knowledge of the exact number of days remaining before she would have to drive to that office and walk in and wait in a room full of bad magazines and get weighed and measured by chirpy young pretend nurses and then take her clothes off in an empty room and wait forever in a paper gown, and she could already smell the disinfectant and see the posters on the walls, cross-sections of brains and reproductive organs, and that goddamn breast self-exam to-do list, which she had done only once when she was twenty-five and scared herself almost to death, and at some point a total stranger, invested with outrageous rights and privileges, would come into that room and touch her actual mortal body. No. She had canceled the appointment, and blocked out the square with black marker.

Now she tried again to write herself unconscious, but when she began to reconstruct Dr. Kronkheit's office she got no further than the oak desk he made her sit on and the big glass jar of tongue depressors, and these faint sketches were immediately blotted out by the garish image of her own brain, a pink corsage blossoming with aneurisms. Though she didn't know what aneurisms were, she did know that they were very bad, and she pictured them now as flowers of evil, each deepening crimson. Any moment she might be paralyzed, or worse, aphasic.

She could turn overnight into one of those people who lose control of their words. This thought was so alarming that Amy rose and woke up her computer, hoping to determine that you can't get aphasia from a concussion, but it turned out that you could. She could right now be developing any number of different aphasias, each more frightening than the next, and could by dawn be condemned to communicating through expletives and baffling gestures. That she seldom cared to communicate with anyone was really beside the point. Amy had always figured that, given a choice, she would take blindness over deafness; she would take both of these over the loss of words. She had to get help.

By three o'clock in the morning she had frightened herself to the verge of a panic attack, with her two biggest fears—death and doctors—pinging back and forth in counterpoint, so that if she turned away from one she was faced with the other, with no respite. As a last-ditch effort to calm down, she switched on the television, immersion in someone else's narrative her only hope, and when forced to choose between *Eraserhead* and some horror thing involving torture and dismemberment, she unwisely chose the David Lynch movie. Twenty minutes later, clothed in her flannel nightgown and chenille robe, she drove herself to Palomar Hospital.

CHAPTER FIVE

⌒

Hell's Anteroom

The sky was still dark when Amy got to the emergency room, which was full of seated patients, many of whom had apparently grown up there. Their savvy parents had stockpiled toys and food. "How long?" she wanted to ask, but they weren't speaking English and she spoke no other language but French. None of them sported an obvious wound; they seemed not so much unwell as profoundly patient, condemned to dwell forever in Hell's anteroom. Amy chose a seat in a corner and settled in for a long wait. Two hours? Three? She had brought her notebook along and a copy of *Tristram Shandy,* on the off-chance that she would be able to stop obsessing long enough to focus on something besides her own mortality. Already she envied her fellow sufferers their apparent ease in this awful place, especially one grade-school girl, sound asleep on her feet with her head flung back on her father's shoulder, her long fine blue-black hair tumbling down his shirt like a waterfall.

At first the newness of the place distracted in a positive way. She focused on the passage of time, playing games with the wall clock. Fifteen pages of *Shandy* should correspond to about fifteen minutes, provided she didn't read very carefully, which she was in any event not in the mood to do. She would check the clock every sixty pages, and the time would fly by.

But she couldn't sink into the novel, which famously began with the conception and birth of T. Shandy. Right away she related this to her own shortcomings as a writer and a human being. Conception and birth! Enormous events, and she'd never written about either of them, nor accomplished them in life, nor even thought seriously about doing so. She could never have had a child with Max, and she could not imagine making a new person with a different man.

A poet friend had once argued that childless people remained children themselves until death, never crossing over into adult country. As though, Amy had scoffed, there were some *river.* Exactly, the poet replied, smiling through Amy's scorn. Poets confounded Amy: they were anarchists, never happier than when disassembling the same kinds of structure that fiction writers labored to build. Where was the joy in that? And the worst part was, the poets usually hove nearer to the truth. It had taken Amy years to figure out what her friend had meant by "aging children." He wasn't talking about narcissism, second-class citizenship, unripe intellect. He was talking about mortality. Amy had seen firsthand how people with children aged differently than people without, as they pushed their expanding babies uphill like great lumpy boulders. Of course they dreaded death, everyone does, but *their* dread was mixed with acceptance and calculation. In their new minds there was an age earlier than which they must not die and after which they could. *As soon as Jason finishes college, whenever Kate stops screwing around and figures out what she wants to do, the minute Sandy's kid gets into rehab, then I can check out.*

They aged more quickly, the mothers and fathers. They claimed it was because of constant worry, lack of deep sleep, endless drudgery, but Amy thought it was that incessant recalculation, an ongoing process she could glimpse behind their eyes. A part of their brain was always humming, gathering data, assessing probabilities, all in the service of determining when it would be all right for them to die. Their humility was frightening.

Amy was humble about her looks, her talent, her place in the world, but not about her mortality. It would never be all right for her to die, especially not as the result of whatever malignant shadow she would soon fail to discern on an X-ray and be forced to take on faith. After Max was diagnosed, the whitecoats were always slapping films up on those viewing boxes. "As you can see," they'd say, pointing to something visible only to them, "there's a shadow." Just to be pleasant, Max and Amy would pretend they could see it too. Sometimes Amy thought she saw it, except it looked more like fog than shadow, like something they ought to be able to just blow away.

Would she be polite now? She imagined magnetic resonance images of her own brain, a fluorescent cauliflower in stop-action bloom. "As you can see," the bored, white-coated child would say, and she'd say, "I can't see a damn thing, and neither can you." She'd say, "Never mind that. How long have I got?" She'd say, "Who the hell do you think you are?"

At ten o'clock in the morning sun sliced across her eyes, and she closed her useless book. There seemed to be different people waiting now; the standing child had apparently been attended to. Or perhaps she was the one sitting in the corner with her baby brother. Amy couldn't be sure; all she'd really noticed was her hair, and Amy was the only blond person in the room. Any minute now, they'd call her name.

An old man came in, pushing his wife in a wheelchair. "She's having a heart attack," he shouted to the woman behind the glass. Within a minute the two were ushered into another room, behind swinging doors. What must that room be like? Carpeted wall-to-wall in deep-piled burgundy, appointed like a palace. Why was a heart attack more exciting to these people than a bleeding brain? And why hadn't Amy made more of a fuss when *she* came in? Well, because, if she'd run in yelling "I've got a subdural hematoma," they would have taken her for a crackpot.

Amy realized she was feeling a tad better. Wretched from sleep loss, but steadier. She hadn't lost any time for at least twelve hours, she wasn't dizzy, and her head hurt in a normal-seeming way, without that scary numb feeling, as though it were someone else's head. She could go home. In fact, she'd better get moving, because if they called out her name now it would be embarrassing, and she might have to pay some sort of cancellation fee. They'd taken her name and Social Security number, but surely they couldn't charge her for nothing. And the waiting room was beginning to fill up in earnest with brand new diseased families. There was coughing and bleeding.

As Amy gathered herself, a magical shopping cart full of blankets, newspapers, and empty cans and bottles pushed through the glass doors and rumbled toward her. As the cart drew closer, a very old woman emerged from behind it, parked the cart to Amy's left, and clambered up on the seat to Amy's right, grinning toothlessly. "That's okay," said Amy, "I was just leaving. Why don't you sit right here."

The woman stared at Amy, her grin freezing while she tried to figure out God knew what, and then slid down off the chair and began to rummage through her newspapers, breathing in a labored and rusty way, as though her lungs were cluttered with refuse, which they probably were. "You're that lady," muttered the old woman. She spread a *Union-Tribune* out on her chair and began turning pages, her spidery, blackened fingers surprisingly delicate. "I know you," she said, glancing up at Amy, and back down at an ad for Cal Worthington's Mile of Cars. Amy began slowly to rise and inch away. This was just a sad little homeless person, except that she reminded Amy of an old childhood nightmare: Baba Yaga, that Russian folktale hag who had haunted Amy something fierce, not because she kidnapped little kids and ate them—Amy had always had a strong stomach for grim tales—but because of that awful name, Yaga, its ugly shape on the page, the awful yawning sound it made. What a hideous word. "You're that lady," crowed Baba Yaga, "there you are!" snatching up the newspaper and presenting it to Amy like a bouquet of paper flowers, the largest of which bloomed, horribly, with a likeness of Amy herself, standing on her own front porch in that circus-tent caftan and turban, looking *exactly* like Mother Ginger on chemo, smiling for the camera and holding on to her *open front door,* and above the picture the headline, "Enchanted in Escondido."

"I'm that lady," said Amy, sinking back down.

ENCHANTED IN ESCONDIDO
Holly Mary Antoon

Longtime Escondido resident Amy Gallup, acclaimed novelist and writing teacher, patiently waits atop a shady porch swathed in bougainvillea. "Take your time," she calls to me, as I make my way to the steps of her modest gray house, from which emanate deep, throaty growls. "That's Alphonse," she announces cheerfully, then adds, "We're harmless."

A year ago, an actual murder mystery unraveled inside this unprepossessing little house. Two members of Gallup's private course on fiction writing had already died suddenly under suspicious circumstances, and after the final class, held at Gallup's home, the killer, a class member, was unmasked, drugging another class member and attacking Gallup with a knife.

"It was a filleting knife," said Gallup, in a previous correspondence, "not a butcher knife or switchblade, which I understand is why this person wasn't charged with attempted murder, but with the legal equivalent of attempted filleting." The attacker, whom Gallup insisted upon not naming in this interview although the identity is a matter of public record, was arrested on two counts of felonious assault, is presently incarcerated at the California Correctional Institution in Chino, and will be tried later this year for the two murders. "Apparently there are jurisdictional issues," wrote Gallup.

Of course, I am not here just to talk about the current events. Amy Gallup is one of my own literary heroes: her collected stories, *Monstrous Women*, was the subject of my master's thesis at Brown. When I start to tell her about it, her reaction astonishes me. "You're joking," she says, as she leads me inside, moving with a pronounced limp. I assume that once we settle in, we'll return to the subject. I couldn't be more wrong.

"I have a bionic leg," she explains, due to a terrible accident involving her basset hound and a chainsaw. "We don't like to talk about it," she adds. Fortunately, Alphonse, the basset hound, survived unscathed, and romps gaily around Gallup as she tours a living room packed floor to ceiling with books. As she points out her S. J. Perelman collection, Alphonse trips her up and a small bookcase tips over, upending three shelves full of priceless old hardbacks, but Gallup just giggles infectiously. "As you can see," she says, "he's still trying to kill me."

Gallup, author of three acclaimed novels, has not written for more than thirty years. Could a new book of fiction be in the offing? When asked again about her immediate plans, she says, cryptically, "To visit the Palomar Hospital Emergency Room." Research, perhaps, on a medical mystery? "I don't write mysteries," she says, sitting us both down in the living room.

I am, at this point, at a complete loss.

In the touchy silence which follows, I wonder how to begin. Or rather how to begin again. How to talk to, and learn from, this profoundly eccentric and fascinating woman. In our telephone arrangements for this interview—the first in a ten-part series on San Diego authors—we had not discussed specific topics, so I have no idea what, if anything, is off-limits. If Gallup, something of a wunderkind in her early twenties, has written a word in thirty years, she has kept it to herself. On the other hand, recent history beckons. Okay, here goes.

"What drove that class member to kill?" I finally blurt, shocking myself. I have not planned to do this, but the atmosphere of the room compels me. The dark little parlor, jumbled with dusty books, its walls papered with Hopper prints and old Thurber cartoons, and Gallup, flamboyant yet oddly quiet at its center, reminds me of an old fairy tale—Merlin's library, or the Gingerbread House. "Why did the rest of the class keep meeting even after two of them had died?" I ask.

As though I weren't there at all, she picks a book off the floor, opens it up, and begins, silently, to read. Time crawls, punctuated by the whir of a crooked old Kit-Kat clock on the wall and the heavy panting of Alphonse. Clearly I have overstepped. Big time.

Still reading, she reaches up and slips off her scarlet turban, releasing a breathtaking wealth of silver-blond hair that falls to her waist.

After a full five minutes, and just at the point where I'm about to apologize and slink away, she looks up at me and closes the book. "Have you ever read this one?" she asks, pointing to the spine: *U.S.A.*, by John Dos Passos. Wordless, I shake my head. "Me neither," she says. "When I was a kid, I managed to dodge it." She bends down and scoops up the fallen hardbacks, piling them on the coffee table. "I never read any of these." I peruse the titles. *Absalom, Absalom. The Idiot. The Virginian. My Gun is Quick. Buccaneer Governess.* "*Buccaneer*'s by Henrietta Mant. It was a bestseller in 1942." She opens it up, seemingly at random, and begins to read again—this time for only half a minute. She glances up at me, clears her throat, and reads aloud. "Captain McDougal's coarse chestnut beard scraped her cheeks raw as they grappled beneath the Southern Cross, and black waves slapped the poop of the *Flaming Simoom*."

Reprieved, I scan the shelves that run along all four walls. "Where do you keep your own books?" She gestures toward a haphazard pile on the floor, in front of the fireplace. The pile looks, oddly, like kindling.

"He was on some defense committee for Leon Trotsky."

"Who?"

"I have no idea," she says. She sits in contemplative silence on a blue leather hassock, her eyes closed, her devoted basset attendant at her feet, gazing at her quizzically. She could be fast asleep. She could be, I realize, the mysterious subject of an old portrait.

At last she raises her head, and the expression on her own face mirrors that of Ambrose. Alert. Engaged. "Hello," she says, as though suggesting that the interview begin again.

And so it does.

Disastrously.

"How did it feel to be assaulted in your own living room by a trusted student?"

"Why don't you tell me?" The words are confrontational, but her expression is kindly, composed, as though she actually expected me to tell her. This is one of the oddest social moments of my life. Again, that feeling of enchantment, of timelessness, as I wait for some sign, the quiet broken only by the gentle lapping sound of Alphonse's long tongue, licking her toes. Ten perfectly good toes. Was the "bionic leg" story some private joke? Was there no end to the mystery of this woman? Abruptly she stands. "They don't love us," she says. "To them we are salt licks and food gods."

Before I am even aware of it, I am outside again, looking up at her on that stoop. Graciously, given that she has just shown me the door, she lets me snap her picture there, in the orange afternoon light. I feel like apologizing, though I'm not sure why. What did I do? Where have I gone wrong? I am desperate for answers. "When you come to a fork in the road," she says, "go off-road. Stay off-road and see what happens. You'll find out."

Find out what?

"How it feels. To be assaulted in your own living room."

But, I stammer, you were the one who had the experience. You were the one who was assaulted.

"Experience is overrated. Feelings are not news. Anyone who wants to know how a total stranger feels about anything must change her life."

Does she have any final thoughts?

"Sure," she says. "We hang, every moment of every day of our lives, by a fraying thread, and that is not news. The easiest way to the I-15 is to head straight up Ninth."

As I back down the driveway, we wave like old friends. I race back toward home, intent on typing my first draft, digging up and reading my old thesis, Googling Henrietta Mant. Halfway home, I get off the freeway, using an exit I've never used before, and begin to meander homeward on unfamiliar secondary streets. It's not off-road, but it will do.

Holly Antoon's novel, The Tuning Fork, *will be published in paperback by Monarch Press in March.*

CHAPTER SIX

∽

Imagine That

The mysterious subject of an old portrait. Maybe this Antoon person had meant "the mysterious old subject of a portrait," but by whom, Hogarth? Gainsborough? Picasso? For Amy, there was no end to the mystery of Holly Antoon, who had apparently found Amy's bizarre and rude behavior enchanting. After a brief moment of panic at this public display, Amy comforted herself with the assurance that no one who started reading this article would finish it, and precious few would even start. Books and their authors weren't a big focus of the *Union-Tribune*. In minutes, Amy was able to return to panicking about her imminent encounter with a non-virtual physician.

In Borges's "The Secret Miracle," a condemned man tries to modify his fate by imagining the most gruesome eventualities, each in intricate detail. He attempts this "weak magic" on the principle that nothing ever happens exactly the way we imagine that it will. When she first read this story, Amy instantly both hated and revered it. Hated, because she wanted to have gotten there first and would have if she hadn't been so stupid and lazy, and revered, not because of the seventeen-jewel brilliance of the prose, but because, like all great fiction, it assured readers that they were not alone. She wasn't the only human silly enough to attempt weak magic tricks.

She recalled picturing all the rejection letters she would receive when she submitted her first novel, and sure enough, her rejection from Knopf was much kinder and more encouraging than any of the savage kiss-offs she had composed in her head, so that when St. Martin's took *Monstrous Women* two weeks later, she was, for just an instant, more impressed with her own arcane powers than with the prospect of publication. In the ensuing years, she imagined away brutal reviews, car accidents, dog poisonings; she singlehandedly saved the world from annihilation after the Russians invaded Afghanistan. She had even, shamefully, imagined Max's various diagnoses and prognoses and dying behavior in exhaustive detail, never sure whether she was trying to steel herself or heroically affect the future. She was out of the room when he died; it had never occurred to her to imagine that.

Now she sat on the edge of a hard gurney surrounded by blue privacy curtains and tried to forecast the face, or at least the revealed attitude, of the white-jacketed invader who must eventually pop through. Vacuous inattention, robotic cheer, feigned concern, actual concern, she tried them all, then set to work on voices, accents, timbre, pitch. She worked more on nationalities than regions of the United States. She had time to do all this and more, but still could not bring herself to imagine the terrible moment of physical contact. Her mind just shut down at the thought of a diagnostic touch. To be groped by a slavering pervert in a dark alley would be infinitely more pleasant than to be accosted by anybody in this hospital, or any hospital. By the time the curtains parted she had not even begun the heavy lifting of diagnosis, prognosis, and next steps in what was sure to be a Jacob's ladder of increasingly humiliating and expensive tests.

The resident's name was Kurt Robetussien. He looked to be in his early thirties but had the tired eyes of a much older man. Beyond that, Amy paid little attention to his physical appearance, so captivated was she by his name. Was he on track for pulmonology? In Calvary Hospital in Bangor, Maine, Amy and Max had often amused themselves with the physician registry: there was an orthopedic surgeon named Klutz; there were MDs named Bunschaft, Hartwell, and Looney, none of whom had pursued appropriate specialties. Amy and Max had giggled endlessly over the tragedy of Harlan Bunschaft, who yearned to be a proctologist but, cursed by a ridiculous name, had to settle for neonatal surgery. Max would have loved Kurt Robetussien. In more ways than one, Amy thought, noting that he was Max's type, cherubic, fleshy, his abundant brown hair luxuriant with glossy curl. He stood before her studying a file—her file, she guessed, although how there could be anything in it was a puzzle. She remembered now filling out some stupid form twelve hours ago. For a full minute he ignored her completely, which was just perfect. She held on to the moment, lengthening it in her mind, pouring into it all the joys of her pre-diagnostic-touch life. Something bad was about to happen, but *Right Now* swelled with beauty, the just-so blue of the privacy curtains, the gravelly voice of the invisible old patient to her left, the perfect thingness of the stethoscope around Robetussien's neck. What an impossibly wonderful world.

"What happened to you?" asked Robetussien.

And how wonderful that he asked this without false concern and with only the mildest curiosity. "Life," said Amy. "Life happened to me."

He passed her first test, smiling instead of calling for a "psych consult." "As it happens to us all," he said.

"How would you know?" said Amy. "What are you, twelve?"

"Birdbath," said Robetussien.

"I beg your pardon?"

"That's all you've got here under 'description of accident.'"

"I knocked myself out on a birdbath." Amy started to explain in detail, but he was already touching her, gently palpating the back of her skull. Amy held her breath, then slowly let it out. *Now that wasn't so bad,* she thought. He had touched her and she hadn't lost her mind.

"Is your heart rate usually this high?" He was touching her again, the metal disk cold against the skin of her chest. He had reached down through the neck of her gown, his hand now millimeters from her unmammogrammed breast. "Never mind, it's slowing down." He pulled up a stool on wheels and sat down. "Who's your doctor?"

"I don't have one." Amy braced herself for a brusque retort which never came; he seemed barely to have registered the fact that a sixty-two-year-old woman in obviously lousy shape had successfully evaded medical attention. She was surprised to find herself annoyed. He was older than she had first thought. There were even a few gray hairs. Had he flunked out of med school and taken another run at it?

He took something out of his pocket and shone a piercing light in her eyes. He told her to follow his index finger as it performed a series of random loops. Amy had a sudden urge to ignore it and follow an imaginary pattern instead, as if Tinker Bell were dancing from curtain to curtain. Would he ignore that too? *I was just messing with your head,* she'd say.

"What are you looking for?" she asked.

"Evidence of a stroke, which you don't have. Tell me about the memory loss."

She did, first with a truncated, two-sentence version, and then, encouraged by his attention—the first signal of genuine inter-est so far—she elaborated fully, taking him through the past twenty-four hours, from the fall to her arrival at Palomar. "See this picture?" She showed him the Sunday paper. "This was, literally, news to me."

"You're kidding." He scanned the article, taking his time. "Hey, you're the writer." His shoulders relaxed; he turned the page and continued reading, and when he came to the end, he snorted. "Holly Antoon," he said.

"Okay, but how serious is this?"

"I think it's a riot."

"But I lost hours—"

"You look pretty sharp now. How's the head?"

"Achy."

He regarded her for a long moment. "You should have some tests," he said.

"No," she said, astonishing herself. Amy never spoke without thinking first. "No blood work. No mammogram. No colonos-copy. I prefer to be surprised."

"By what?"

"By whatever kills me." Amy was being ridiculous, but at the same time she felt proud, impossibly brave. She was saying no. She had never imagined doing that.

"You're funny," he said, looking young again. "I meant you should at least have an MRI. Why would I order a colonoscopy?"

"Oh." Amy regrouped. "I have crummy health insurance. I'd have to pay a big chunk out of pocket."

"You're asking me if it's worth it?"

"Exactly. Look. *Kurt.* When I first moved into my house, an unpleasant creature named Carlo Sbiggi tried to sell me a home alarm system, some stupid thing with loudspeakers mounted on the wall in each room of the house, so that a bunch of clueless strangers could listen to me being strangled."

"You're funny," he said again.

"And when I balked at the grotesque cost, he said, and I quote, 'You can't put a price on safety.'"

Dr. Robetussien cracked up. "A vacuum cleaner salesman said the same thing to my wife."

"You can't put a price on cleanliness," they said in unison.

"Here's where you tell me you can't put a price on health," said Amy, feeling positively giddy.

"Sure you can," said her new buddy. "And sometimes you have to pay it."

"What are you telling me?"

"I'm not supposed to say this," he said, "because we push these tests, but the truth is, you look pretty strong. If you were the kind of patient who enjoyed a fine colonoscopy, I'd schedule one. And you really should get one, and a mammo too, but that's your business. I mean, we're talking about statistics here. You're more likely to have cancer now than you were twenty years ago, but it's not irrational to avoid the tests as long as you know the score. You do need an MRI, though. If I let you out of here without one and you gork out, it's my job."

Now she was supposed to worry about his *job*. She loved "gork out," though, a phrase the meaning of which was easily guessed. "What do you expect to see on the MRI?"

"Nothing. But you did lose those hours."

"How long would I have to wait before finding out the results?"

He scratched his head and glanced again at the newspaper in his hand. "Make you a deal. I'm on for another four hours. I'll come and give you the results."

"Right away?" The man was a saint.

"More or less. Before you leave the hospital."

Amy thought about it. MRIs probably weren't all that bad. Apparently nothing human actually touches you; they just shove you into a big tube. Better still, she wouldn't have to wait for days, with every ring of her telephone a harbinger of doom. Best of all, she liked this guy. "What do you get out of it?" she asked.

Kurt Robetussien blushed violently and said nothing.

Amy remembered a time when this could have meant more than one thing. "You've got a novel," said Amy, "and you'd like me to look it over."

He started to apologize, but she waved him off. "I'll give you my email address when you tell me my brain isn't leaking. It's a deal."

"Okay, but what if it *is* leaking?"

What a card. "I'll read it anyway. Unless I gork out first."

CHAPTER SEVEN

I Know Where You Live

By the time Amy got back home it was twilight, and Alphonse, galvanized by the sound of her Crown Vic, roared at her from the backyard, where she'd abandoned him almost eighteen hours ago. He'd drunk or spilled half his water and strewn a bowlful of chow all over the patio. Alphonse loathed dry dog food. When forced to ingest it, as he surely had been today, his resentment was epic, filed away forever in his box of basset grudges. Canine experts always claimed that dogs will eat healthy dry food when they get hungry enough, but Amy, who had majored in philosophy, knew that the word "enough" was enough to render this claim meaningless. "It's a tautology," she cheerfully explained to her outraged hound, who followed her into the kitchen, purposely stepping on her heels and scraping them, barking furiously, deliberately drowning her out. She heated up leftover beef stew in her microwave, just to the point of tantalizing fragrance, and spooned the lion's share into Alphonse's bowl. "It would make no sense to say, 'If dogs get hungry enough, they *won't* eat dry dog food.'"

After sniffing the steaming bowl, he glanced around at her and barked once more, getting in the last word before turning his back and inhaling his supper.

Amy's answering machine was flashing "F," which, Amy guessed, stood for "Full," although in her present euphoric state she preferred to imagine "Fine" or "Flourishing" or even "Funny," as in, "You're funny." The machine had a thirty-minute record limit; quite possibly Carla, unable to contact her after a couple of tries, had just rambled on about her day. But because Amy was feeling festive ("Festive"), she pressed the playback button. There were twenty-two calls, only a couple of which were from Carla. Four of them were from some dame named Maxine Horner, who sounded just like a Horner, her voice so strident that it stressed out the cheap speaker. "Amy Gallup, long time no see!" She must be at least Amy's age—nobody said "long time no see" anymore—and she also sounded put out, in the third message, about not having been called back. "We gotta touch base, babe," she said, before Amy cut her off.

For an uncomfortable minute, Amy worried anew about her brain (which, according to Kurt Robetussien and her gorgeous MRI, was free of death-dealing shadows). Evidently she was supposed to know Maxine Horner. Worse still, there was someone in the world who felt free to call her "babe." Then she vaguely remembered knowing a Maxine a long time ago, although never a Horner, so maybe Maxine had got married. For now, all she could recognize was that name, that string of letters, not a face or a fact. But then Maxine Something, Amy now noticed, was connected to Manhattan, because the name was now linking neuronically to Greenwich Village. In her mind, a snapshot of a leafy Village street shimmered beside that mysterious name, both evoking the scent-memory of 1970s car exhaust. What a wonderful organ was a non-leaking brain!

While hers worked on Maxine, she fast-forwarded through bot-calls and real calls—from her old students Ricky Buzza, and Harry B, and even Marvy Stokes, from whom Amy hadn't heard since his wife yanked him out of her last workshop. Her writer's workshop vets were probably planning a party. Then she saw that her neighbors on all sides had called—the Blaines, the Wards across the street, even Mr. Franz, the old man two doors down whose wife had just died. Alphonse must have been driving everybody nuts. She stopped flipping through answers and called Molly Blaine.

"Molly, I'm so sorry about Alphonse," she began.

"Why? Did something happen?"

"I was just away for a while, and that's why he was barking up a storm."

"No, he wasn't. Not until just now. So talk about hiding your light under a bushel!" Molly sounded very excited in a positive way. About what? "Frank and I had no idea! And neither did the Millers!"

"Neither did I!" Amy wanted to say, but her freshly vetted brain was now working on two puzzles, Maxine Horner and light-hiding bushels. Had people ever hidden lights this way? She pictured a candle burning underneath a hay bale, which surely was an insanely dangerous practice. Wouldn't it be safer and faster just to blow out the candle? "Sorry, Molly," she finally said. "I didn't listen to your whole message, and I have no idea what's up."

"A famous author on Jacaranda Drive! Look how many years you've lived here, and none of us knew!"

The Baba Yaga story. "Oh, *that*," said Amy. "Reports of my fame were greatly exaggerated." Amy attempted to toss off this ancient joke with an airy chuckle, which came out in the exact pitch of her own voice as a child. Neurons were firing now to beat the band: she flashed on the high-pitched prissy voice of her own seven-year-old self standing up in front of her second grade class, holding up a dime she had just fished out of her pocket, and announcing, "This extremely rare coin was minted in 1949." She had forgotten it was her day for show-and-tell, and rather than just admit this, she had just winged it, which might have worked out if the current year hadn't been 1955. Even second graders knew the dime wasn't anything special. She didn't fool them, or Mrs. Crowley either, and she retired in disgrace. The few sense-memories Amy had of her childhood generally amounted to her own voice saying something pompous. Now she was doing it again.

Molly Blaine was rattling on about what a thrill it was to live next to such a famous person. Even if Amy were actually famous, as opposed to locally notorious for a day, this made no sense. If Amy moved in next to the Clintons or Philip Roth or Carl Yastrzemski, she might feel fluttery and self-conscious for a week, but that would be it. Now she tried to talk Molly down, explaining that she was no longer an active writer, but rather dormant, probably extinct. Her money was on extinct.

"Like a volcano!" said Molly.

"Exactly."

"Well, but you could erupt at any time, like that mountain in Alaska."

"Just like a mountain in Alaska," said Amy.

"Bless your heart," said Molly, who finally hung up after volunteering to call the rest of the neighbors and fill them in.

Great. Until now, until goddamn Holly Antoon—no, until Amy cracked her skull on the birdbath—she had enjoyed the lowest of profiles in her neighborhood, giving or receiving the occasional wave, returning people's lost pets and having the neighbors do the same for her when Alphonse wandered off. Now would come hearty halloos and waves galore. Now would come book clubs and autographs, assuming that they could locate any of her out-of-print novels online. She had enjoyed her well-earned anonymity. Had she been the reveling sort, she would have reveled in it. Now that was all over.

Her phone rang and she shut it off, her mood ruined. An hour later, plummeting into an exhausted sleep, her mind played one last trick, needling her with the possibility that one of the unheard messages had been from the hospital, calling to tell her that her MRI test had gotten mixed up with a healthy person's. Furious with herself, she stumbled back to the answering machine and heard everybody out. Most of the callers were strangers, although she recognized some of the names, writers who lived in San Diego, and that local NPR radio guy. The rest were book club ladies calling from La Jolla and Clairemont and Solana Beach. The last call was Maxine Horner's fourth, and this time Amy played the whole thing.

"Hey, babe, what's the deal? I know it's been a while, but let's face it, we had nothing to talk about. All right, hand to God, I thought you were dead. This story is a riot. I don't know what you're on, but whatever it is, I want some. Call me tomorrow. I'm serious. I know where you live now, and if I don't hear from you, I'll be camping out in your front yard. You gotta come out some time."

Maxine Grabow. Her voice had dropped half an octave, from menopause or throat cancer or both, and some madman had actually married her, but there she was, just as alive as Amy, who didn't know how to feel about this, or about the fact that her old agent, whose last words to her had been "Call me when you give a shit," was back in her life. What had happened?

CHAPTER EIGHT

⟋

Maxine

What had happened was the Internet.

Amy made use of it daily in her online editorial work and regularly in maintaining her blog, GO AWAY. For someone of her generation she was unusually plugged in, because she had to be. Her cell phone was retro and she didn't mess with Netflix, but she was computer-literate. Freelancers who made their living, such as it was, teaching strangers how to write had to stay current technologically. She followed the news on the raw feed (refusing to allow it into her life through television or radio) and so was perfectly aware of the speed with which information and misinformation could spread. Still, it had not occurred to her that Holly Antoon's silly story, which she was beginning to think of as Holly's Folly, would of course be slapped up on the Net along with the local weather outlook, real-time traffic reports, cat images, the twittering of a million twerps, and the online *New York Times*.

And if the real news, whatever that was, had been focused on one or two attention-grabbing events, then the Folly would have bobbed for a few days and sunk beneath the binary waves with no one the wiser. A crisis in the Middle East, a Malaysian typhoon, a high body-count workplace shooting, even an A-list celebrity antic, and no one outside of San Diego County would have picked up the story. Maxine Grabow, for instance, wouldn't have given Amy a single thought.

But the day the story came out and the week that followed were slow, news-wise. The economy did not significantly worsen; car-bombs went off in Pakistan and Bogotá but failed to kill anyone; there was a huge wedding fire, but in Myanmar. No freakish multiple births, no devastating hate crimes, and the most newsworthy celebrities were either in rehab or home with their newborns.

Holly's Folly came out in print and online Sunday morning, and within twenty-four hours two book bloggers had linked to it. One blog was called Washed-Ups, Has-Beens, and One-Hit Wonders. Which search string, Amy wondered, had managed to snag her name? The other blog was devoted to the works of Henrietta Mant; doubtless the blogger had arranged for some sort of alert whenever the writer's named popped up in cyberspace. Neither blog explained why Maxine spent half of Sunday trying to get in touch with Amy. To find that out, Amy would have to return the call and let Maxine Grabow back into her life.

When Amy was young, beginning writers didn't need agents or even know who they were or what they did. You wrote something and sent it out and waited for a slush pile rejection. Amy's first book, a collection of short stories, had been accepted for publication in 1970, when Amy was fresh out of college and looking for something to do. She had written half of the stories as an undergraduate looking for an easy A and the rest while pretending to transcribe Dictabelts for a debt collection lawyer in Waterville, Maine. Her best friend, Max Winston, convinced her to talk to her advisor and send it out to a couple of houses, which she did with high anxiety and low expectations. When she got the letter of acceptance, she was pleased enough but distracted by more significant events.

Max was about to complete graduate school and get himself dangled in front of the Maine draft board like a frisky minnow. His lottery number was middling and he was dithering between two draft-dodging strategies: securing a 4-F deferment by admitting he was homosexual, or wedding his best friend and hoping for a marriage deferment. The marriage ploy was much riskier—it failed as often as it worked—but the year was 1970, and Max, who was openly gay before the phrase was commonly used, was still terrified of whatever would greet him when he actually showed up at the induction center for his physical. The prospect of that physical scared him more than Vietnam. This medico-phobia was just one of the many ways in which Max and Amy turned out to be brilliantly suited.

The day Amy got her acceptance letter from St. Martin's was the same day she agreed to marry Max, "just until the war blows over." And by the end of the war, Amy, happily settled into what would turn out to be the only truly fulfilling and intimate (however platonic) relationship of her life, had written and published two well-received books of short stories, the second one, *Everything Handsome,* nominated for the National Book Award and selling respectably. She was a "Young Writer to Watch," and halfway between 1975 and the publication of *Ambassador of Loss* in 1978 Maxine Grabow descended on her like some deus ex machina lowered from the rafters.

Amy remembered first meeting her at one of her own Waterville soirées, in which Max's colleagues and students generally milled about, along with whomever Max or Amy was seeing at the time. Publishing types generally didn't make it up to Maine, and after Maxine's first visit, neither Amy nor Max could figure out how she found her way into their house. Maxine was dwarfishly short with alarmingly red hair stuffed partly into a black beret; she wore a wool suit Max identified as Chanel, with a huge moth-hole in one sleeve; she smoked Tiparillos; and, like E. F. Hutton, when she spoke people listened, although in Maxine's case this was because nobody else could hear himself think. She had a voice for the theater, but not, as she cheerfully acknowledged, the talent, which was why she had ended up heading her own literary agency. An agency, as it turned out, with only one agent, but a pretty successful one. Her star client was Henrietta Mant.

At first, Amy thought she was a lesbian. She kept staring at Amy, sizing her up in a way that made Amy both curious and uncomfortable. "Wrong," said Max. "Look at how she's checking out the guys. She's not after your bod. She wants something else, though. Watch out."

Maxine finally cornered her in the kitchen. She blew whole-leaf tobacco smoke up Amy's nose and announced in a reverberating whisper, "I'm going to make you a pile of money." She whipped out a business card that said GRABOW in big letters and "literary agent" in footnote font.

"I'm not that kind of writer," Amy said, prompting a bray so outlandish that a handful of people gathered outside the kitchen to observe.

"That's what they all say, babe!"

"You know what I mean," Amy said, reddening at her own girlishness.

"What are you working on, babe?"

Amy was backed up against the stove. *None of your beeswax,* she thought. "*Beeswax,*" she said. "It's the working title of my first novel." She began to breathe more easily.

Max had taught her how to do this, to deal with threatening social situations by transforming people into fictional characters with no inner lives. "Pretend they're foils," Max told her. "Characters in a farce, and you're the one writing it." From the start of their friendship, Max had devoted himself to coaxing Amy out of her cave, partly, she thought, for his own amusement, and partly because he genuinely cared about her. "But they're not foils," she would object, "they have feelings. I don't want to deal with those." Max changed her attitude by reminding her how much she hated it when other people speculated about her own feelings. "It's so intrusive," she would complain. "So don't intrude on theirs," he counseled, reasonably, and she was still learning not to. Maxine Grabow's feelings, she reminded herself, are none of my beeswax.

"A novel! Atta girl." Maxine's small black eyes played over Amy's face like searchlights. "You can't make lunch money on short stories, especially the kind you write. You're good, but your stuff makes people want to kill themselves. Compared to you, Grace Paley is Erma Bombeck, which is why she won the NBA and you didn't have a shot. What's it about?" More smoke up the nose. "Lose the title, by the way."

Amy wasn't actually working on anything except one story that wouldn't wake up, a story she had been trying to finish since she was eighteen, and in any event she would never discuss a work in progress with anybody, even Max. And what did Grace Paley have to do with the National Basketball Association? "*Beeswax* is all about a beekeeper. The last in a long line of beekeepers. He lives in—"

"*He?* Scrap that. Change it. Gotta be a girl."

"—in Falmouth, Mass." What a horrible woman.

"And . . . what?"

"And . . . his brothers sell pasteurized honey and mead."

"What's the hook, babe?" Maxine was still scanning her face, this time rapidly, from eye to eye, as though Amy were a human shell game.

"There isn't any one single hook, per se," said Amy, perspiring freely. She never said *per se.* She hated *per se.* "It's episodic. Each chapter almost stands on its own. 'The Swarm.' 'The Hive.' Right now I'm working on 'Smoker.'"

"Fabulous," said Maxine. She grinned widely, Tiparillo jutting from her clenched teeth like the gun on a battleship.

"*I* like it," simpered Amy, preparing to slip away into the living room, already rehearsing the scene for a replay with Max.

"Yeah." Maxine's expression changed. She seemed to be really enjoying herself now. "How about 'The Big Sting'?"

"I hadn't thought of that."

"'Queen For a Day.'"

"I'm not sure about—"

"You're not working on a novel at all, are you?"

This was the trouble with treating people like foils. You had no way of knowing whether they were doing the same thing to you.

"No offense taken," said Maxine. "I'm a pushy broad. It's my job. That and making you a pile of money."

Amy got serious with Maxine. She seriously tried to explain that she was not ambitious. She didn't have that hunger to see herself in print. Writing was a challenge for her, a lark. She wrote because she could, not because she had to, or even particularly wanted to. Maxine said that was fine. "I've got enough ambition for both of us." Amy said she wasn't a novelist. "Neither is Jackie

S, and that one sells millions." In the end she extracted Amy's phone number and promised to call every Friday until one of them caved. "She must be phenomenal," Max said later, laughing, while Amy banged her head against the wall.

Within six months Amy had started *Ambassador of Loss,* and a year later it was in proofs.

Whatever success Amy had as a writer was due to the infernal persistence of Maxine Grabow. Now here they were, both still alive, and Maxine still kicking. What she wanted from Amy was a mystery, but she was, Amy knew, fully capable of literally camping out on Jacaranda Drive. On Monday evening, Amy poured herself a tumbler of cabernet, threw Alphonse a chunk of brownie, and picked up the phone.

CHAPTER NINE

Gravitas

Babe! You look like hell, by the way," Maxine rasped out before resuming a terrible cough. She must have been in the middle of it when her phone rang.

As always, Amy was taken aback. "How did you know it was me? And how do you know what I look like?"

"Caller ID."

"My picture pops up on your phone?" My god, what a world.

"No, but your number does, and you're the only writer I know in San Diego. And your face is all over the Net."

"No it's not."

More hacking. "Your picture's in that thing that girl wrote. Holly *Antoon*. Is she for real? How old is she? Twelve?"

"Everybody's twelve, Maxine. My ER doctor is twelve."

"Tell me about it. My husband was ten, in dog years. Hah! What ER doctor?"

"When did you get married?" Maxine had retained her talent for zeroing in immediately on out-of-bounds topics.

"After your time. Lasted five minutes. What ER doctor?"

Amy rubbed her eyes. "Maxine, what's up?"

Maxine laughed so hard that Amy had to hold the phone away from her ear. "Thought you'd never ask. Here's the deal: you're gonna get buzz."

Amy said nothing.

"I'm saying buzz. Internet buzz. Industry buzz. You're gonna get hot."

"Hot buzz," said Amy. Maxine had used different nonsense terms, back in the day. But if "hot buzz" meant what Amy thought it meant, Maxine's sentiment was brand-new. She had never set Amy up as a potential generator of bestsellers. "Piles of money" had translated to "enough money to live on frugally for a year," which had actually been nice. *Megabucks,* Amy now remembered, was the term Maxine reserved for money writers. "You talking megabucks?"

"Hah! *Now* she wants money." More coughing. "Listen, babe, who knows. Maybe. The point is, you're going to be hot, but for five minutes, tops."

"And then I'll be cold forever. Which was my cunning plan all along."

Now there was silence; no coughing, no laughing. Maxine sighed. "Why am I not surprised."

The tone in her voice was one Amy now remembered well: a special mixture of disgust and regret. The last time Amy had seen her, they had met in Boston, where Max, recently diagnosed with AIDS, was undergoing a battery of experimental procedures at Mass General. Maxine had joined her in a nearby cafe. By this time, Amy hadn't written a thing since *A Fiercer Hell,* published six years before. Maxine had been nagging her for months, but this time Amy expected a reprieve—that they would sip their cappuccinos and catch up on non-literary news, and Maxine would commiserate. Instead they had a huge blowup, during which Maxine accused Amy of using her husband's terminal illness as an excuse to stop writing, and Amy, instead of calling Maxine a name (she had never used the word "bitch" in her life, even in fiction), had iced up and claimed that yes, she had arranged for the terminal illness itself with that express purpose in mind, and in the end, Maxine had said, "Call me when you give a shit," and stuck Amy with the check.

"You owe me ten bucks," said Amy, offering an olive branch.

"What for?"

"Boston. The last time I saw you was the first and last time I ever ordered a cappuccino. This was before Starbucks, remember? I couldn't believe they charged four dollars for a cup of coffee."

"I was out of line," said Maxine. "But I was right."

"I knew that. You didn't say anything Max hadn't already told me, more than once. That's why I got so pissed off."

"That was you, pissed off?" Maxine hacked robustly. "You could have fooled me."

"Why do I have hot buzz, and how can I get rid of it?"

"Remember Lex Munster?"

Amy cracked up.

"I know, sounds like the Addams Family. Maybe after your time. Lex is a senior editor at Perkins, total shlump but real knack for picking winners. I think he has Asperger's. Anyway, he called me Sunday—he reads everything every day, and he has this incredible electronic Rolodex deal with the name of every writer, living or dead, who ever had an agent, living or dead, cross-referenced, of course."

"I guess we both qualify," said Amy.

"Hah! So he calls me and reads the whole damn newspaper article over the phone. I'm on the floor laughing. That weird thing with Trotsky, and the bit about Hetty Mant, there's a blast from the past, and you're sitting there like Buddha, and the girl has no clue, absolutely no clue. You played her like a goddamn violin. It's priceless, babe."

"Maxine, I didn't play anything, I—"

"Here's the thing. What got Lex so worked up was the stuff about experience being overrated, and all that, which frankly went right by me. You had me at bionic leg."

Despite herself Amy was enjoying this. It was pleasant to have somebody, even somebody named Lex Munster, pay attention to her. Lex was right: the stuff about experience and feelings not being news was pretty good. Too bad she couldn't remember saying it.

"Lex told me that the *ARB* is planning a where-are-they-now issue."

The *ARB* was the *American Review of Books*. It didn't have the cachet, such as it was, of the *NYRB,* but even Amy, who never looked at either rag, was aware of its existence and its growing popularity. The *ARB* was *NYRB*-meets-*USA Today,* another one of the many publications Amy never looked at on purpose. "Maxine, I'm way ahead of you. They're going to do a thing on great washed-up writers, and you guys thought of me."

"You got it, babe."

"But there's washed up and then there's full fathom five. I was never big enough to be washed up. I'm a little tugboat, sunk a quarter mile out and never even missed. Countless generations of tautog have spawned on my foredeck—"

"Poor you," said Maxine.

"—scup wander through my portholes, and blue crabs play pinochle on my bow."

"Save the bullshit for Lex. Here's the deal: Jenny Marzen is one of his authors, and she's one of the twenty writers who get to pick their favorite forgotten genius."

"Jenny Marzen is who again?" Amy knew perfectly well who she was. Jenny Marzen was hot, hotter than Amy had ever been, and Jenny Marzen would be washed up in ten years and didn't know it. "And Jenny is my number one fan?"

"No, but she likes you. She read your stories in grad school."

"What is she, twelve?"

"The point is, she really liked the article, and all that stuff about experience and news. Lex says she says you've got gravitas."

"That's a dirty lie. I never even had mono."

"Hah!"

Amy was beginning to feel a prickle of interest, even excitement, and it made her a little sick.

"I'm telling you, it's a done deal. Lex just asked me to touch base with you."

"Why?"

"He thinks we're still in touch, by the way. Which is now true. He also thinks you're working on a new book."

"Which is false! Maxine—"

"I lied. It's my job. The point is, when I know more, I'll call you. Look, babe. I know you. I know you're 'above all this shit.'"

"Wrong. I'm *below* all this shit. I'm full fathom five. This is totally ridiculous."

"And I knew you'd say that, but you're just going to have to go along with the gag. Trust me. You're gonna get hot. Warm, anyway. It's gonna happen."

"Warm buzz," said Amy mournfully, but at the same time she saw it, the outline of that washed-up list, her own name in new print, her old titles mentioned in a magazine that people actually read. "Okay," she said. "Am I supposed to do something?"

"'Do Nothing Till You Hear from Me,'" sang Maxine. "I'll be in touch. Hold it." She coughed for a full ten seconds. Amy wondered if she were dying and to her surprise hoped not. She liked Maxine a lot better now than she had when she was young and they had seemed a generation apart. Now it was just a few negligible years. "What ER doctor, babe? Are you all right?"

"I could ask you the same thing."

"Emphysema, but I've had it for ages. What were you doing in the ER?"

Amy opened her mouth to spill it all, the birdbath, the bag lady, Kurt Robetussien, MD, and the Amazing Fugue State Interview. "Twisted my ankle," she said.

"Talk to you soon, babe," said Maxine. "Stay off the foot."

Amy sat for a long time with the phone in her lap, trying to get a fix on what she'd just done. Why hadn't she told Maxine about the birdbath? She and Maxine could have shared a prolonged cackle over the absurd accident and its absurder consequences, and for sure it would have remained their little secret. Except the accident was none of anyone's beeswax. Amy didn't share secrets, not with anyone, not anymore.

Alphonse clicked into her bedroom and barked for his constitutional. Amy sang softly to him: "I'm a little tugboat, short and stout." He regarded her with disapproval, as well he might. "I know it's *teapot*," she told him, letting him out into the yard. "It's called poetic license." Alphonse trotted off into the dark. He knows me, she thought, better than I know myself.

CHAPTER TEN

Birdbath II

Tuesdays were Amy's day off from the online work that paid the bills, a fiction writing workshop open to anyone willing to cough up two hundred dollars a month. Until a year ago, her teaching had been actual rather than virtual, but after her last workshop turned into a real-life murder mystery and she made herself unemployable with the local university extension, she figured it was time to teach on her own terms and at her own pace, and from the comfort of her own home. Her online work started off small but by last June was steady enough so that she could quit her regular editing job, sit back, and watch the nickels roll in. This Tuesday, three days after the fall, she woke late with a plan to spend the day responsibly, reading through student work at leisure rather than putting it off until her back was to the wall, and perhaps getting started on a book review she'd been putting off for weeks. Instead she wasted half the day mousing around the Internet, looking up Maxine and Jenny Marzen and Lex Munster, and finding evidence of the upcoming *ARB* article, which was scant but there.

Jenny Marzen made millions of dollars, as opposed to nickels, by writing novels that got seriously reviewed while selling big. Amy had skimmed her first one, a mildly clever thing about a philosophy professor who discovers her husband is cheating on her with one of her grad students, and who, while feigning ignorance of the affair, drives the girl mad with increasingly brutal critiques and research tasks, at one point banishing her to Beirut, first to learn fluent Arabic and then to read Avicenna's *Al-Qanun fi al-Tibb,* housed in the American University. This was, Amy thought, a showoffy detail that hinted at Marzen's impressive erudition but was probably arrived at within five Googling minutes. Also the girl's psychotic break was contrived, mechanically predicated on a combination of overwork and crippling guilt over the betrayal of her mentor, of whose intellectual prowess she stands in awe.

People who wrote novels about universities hardly ever got them right. Max had spent his short working life untenured, but still he'd managed to be a charming magnet wherever he taught, and Amy had surfeited on faculty gossip and professorial antics and the general behavior and attitude of academics, who were on the whole no more brilliant, quirky, or Machiavellian than travel agents. They tended toward shabbier clothes and manners, and of course there was the occasional storied eccentric or truly original mind, but most college campuses—especially the older ones—functioned less as brain trusts than as wildlife preserves, housing and protecting people who wouldn't last a week in GenPop.

Jenny Marzen, like all living writers in the twenty-first century, had a web page, and it was nothing like Amy's. For one thing, Marzen surely didn't maintain her own page—she must have minions for that—and for another, the page was devoted to selling books, promoting tours, and sucking up to fans. The home page was a riot of tasteful color (Amy paused to jot down in her notebook the potential short story title "A Riot of Tasteful Color"), featuring a glamorous head shot of Marzen, who looked just like George Eliot, if George Eliot had colored and styled her hair like Bernadette Peters, stood facing a huge wall of yellow tulips, and glanced back sharply over her bare left shoulder. Surrounding the head shot was a collage of book jackets, most of which focused tightly on one section of a young female body—an eye, a hand, a furrowed brow, a buttock. There were pages devoted to the incontinent praise of critics and fans, to her three bull mastiffs, to her family and family tree. There were interview transcripts, videos, and full-length reviews from the *Times*.

Amy misspent a half hour clicking back and forth between Marzen's site and her own, which focused almost totally on words. She had included a list of her own out-of-prints but then deliberately placed it on a page that was almost impossible to find: one had to navigate through six increasingly grumpy and intrusive links: (1) *What are you looking for?* (2) *Why?* This contained fifty choices, including "I'm bored" and "Sick of porn," and so on, only one of which—"I'm looking for a list of your stupid books"— actually functioned as a link to (3) *Tell me about yourself,* again with a ridiculous list of possibilities, some of which occupied multiple paragraphs (Amy really got into these). Eventually, the exhausted explorer arrived at the puny grail:

Monstrous Women, 1971, paper 1980

Everything Handsome, 1975 , paper 1980

The Ambassador of Loss, 1978, paper 1980

A Fiercer Hell, 1981

With her reluctant permission, her old student Ricky Buzza had recently tried to brighten the page with scanned-in images of Amy's old book jackets. She had retained only one copy apiece of the first two books, and the jackets were ripped and stained with whiskey rings. *Everything Handsome* looked particularly ugly, the title bisected at a slant by a creased brown strip of Scotch tape which appeared to cross out the whole book as a lousy idea. Now Amy clicked from this page to Marzen's, trying to enjoy the contrast between crass self-promotion and ironic humility, but, as Ricky had tried more than once to persuade her, her own page was really just pathetic.

And now the thought of Ricky Buzza set off an alarm. There was something about later today, something she was supposed to do. Amy ripped last year's *ZooNews* calendar off her kitchen wall to reveal the new one, with a single penciled-in event for today, January 4, that damn potluck thing at Carla's, with Ricky and Surtees and the other remnants of the Last Workshop Gang. Her handwriting, never a thing of beauty, was now officially a liability. Apparently it was happening in either two or five hours, and she had promised to bring "Wandolf Hillel." She squinted at the scribbled line, blurring it slightly, until she was able to imagine that it said "Waldorf salad," which at least made sense. She had only a few hours to secure a red cabbage, walnuts, mayonnaise, and a bag of apples, transform them into the promised dish, feed Alphonse, and leave for Carla's house in La Jolla. She couldn't remember why she had agreed to go—only that Carla had promised it wouldn't turn into a birthday party. Reluctantly she put her computer into hibernation and prepared to venture abroad.

* * *

Amy had put off driving until she was in her late thirties and realized that soon Max would need her to take him to hospitals and doctors' offices. Until called to duty, she had been too frightened to drive. She had gotten her driver's license at seventeen, but only by learning to do a K-turn on Pushard Lane and parallel park on Rattlesnake Hill. Everybody in Augusta knew what tricks were required and where they would be performed, and everybody studied to the test, but Amy was probably one of the few who got a parent to drive her back home afterward. What frightened her was the responsibility, the fact that a moment's inattention could ruin more lives than just her own. That coupled with the inattention itself, which would settle over her whenever she got behind the wheel. Cars were gigantic then. She could never guess at their outer dimensions, even on the driver's side, and was always running up on curbs. Power steering, in its infancy, was outlandishly touchy, as were the power brakes, and sitting in the driver's seat Amy always felt like a figurehead, disconnected to the huge machine. That she was vital to its behavior must be true, but it gave her so little to do—turn the steering wheel more than a couple of inches and risk a hairpin turn, breathe too forcefully on the brakes and slam into the dash—that she grew bored and let her mind wander and drove up on grass median strips or almost ran tractor trailer trucks off the road—trucks that she hadn't even noticed, because they were in back of her. Until Max got sick, she enjoyed the passenger life. He always said she was the world's best passenger, because she never second-guessed the driver.

After the diagnosis, Amy manned up. Max's friend Carlos taught her how to drive a stick, and she took to it instantly. Cars had changed a lot in twenty-five years: they were smaller and more responsive, and shifting gears gave her something to do, a bridge to the physical world. To her amazement, she loved driving now. She loved being of use most of all, but she also loved her solitary drives. When Max was tucked in, she would drive out along the river and sometimes out into the Maine woods, exploring dirt roads, never worrying about getting stuck or lost, feeling oddly invincible. Sometimes she would put on a Chopin mazurka cassette, or a Bach, or if she were feeling particularly sad, she'd listen to Beethoven's late quartets and sob for miles and miles, and then feel so much better. Sometimes she rocked out, unembarrassed by her awful taste, cranking up the volume until she could think of nothing at all. One time she got so excited by an AC/DC tape that she wound up in a ditch. Amy had never been a teenager: driving let her turn back the clock, for an hour or two.

But now, at sixty-two, Amy didn't feel invincible anywhere, particularly in a car, whether she was behind the wheel or not. Southern California drivers and roads were better than those in New England, but under these fabled freeways there was a constant apocalyptic vibe. She was always aware of what her old driver ed teacher had called "the big picture," and the picture in California was huge: lately, especially, whenever she merged onto the I-15 she felt like a microscopic cell in the bloodstream of an enormous predatory beast. She had never felt that way on the I-95, which was more of a pinball machine than a purposive assemblage of veins and arteries. Driving here was a grim task, not a white-knuckle game.

Not long after arriving in California, she had been driving home late from her class, listening to a call-in show, when the radio doctor interrupted the caller: "Hey. Did you feel that?" and the caller said, "Yeah, what was that?" and then, "There's another one," and "Whoa. That was serious," and they went back and forth about "that" for a couple of minutes, and then, without explanation, returned to their topic. "That" turned out to be an earthquake, Amy's first, and although she went on to experience numerous rattlers and rollers, this first one, which she didn't feel at all, was the most frightening, as she drove through it alone in the dark. What *was* that? Other times she had night-driven past mile after mile of fire, flames outlining the contours of the eastern hills, her windows rolled up against acrid smoke, but on her way to teach her regularly scheduled class, knowing that most of them would show up, because it was Fire Season in Southern California and no big deal. And then in 2003, and again four years later, it was a huge deal. On this very freeway she had seen sixty-mile-an-hour Santa Ana winds lob a eucalyptus fireball the size of a garage westward across eight lanes to torch the Miramar scrub and burn halfway to the coast.

The apocalyptic hum, coupled with awareness of her own aging reflexes, contributed to a tiny sense of dread every time she drove the freeway. Now, on an early January evening, no fires threatened, the last noticeable earthquake had happened months ago, and southbound traffic was almost light, but still she was on edge. Anything could happen. Directly ahead of her, a badly loaded old wood-rail pickup hauling gigantic Mexican planters and garden statuary, its covering tarp half free and waving desperately, swerved to avoid a peeled-off tire tread, and a fist-size chunk of cement bounced out and hit the road in front of Amy, and she had time to do nothing but watch it glance off to the right and become someone else's fate. She waited for a squeal of brakes that never came, then passed the truck at eighty-five, not slowing until she could no longer see it in her rearview mirror, wondering all the while why she was so panicked. It had been a close call, but she had seen worse, everybody had by the time they reached sixty-two. She was settled down and almost to La Jolla when she realized it wasn't the truck, or even the near miss, it was what was *in* the truck. Probably, anyway. "Birdbaths," said Amy. "I was almost hit by a birdbath."

Having named it, the thing that frightened her, she calmed down and spent the rest of the drive noting the title, "Birdbaths," and spinning the outline of a story she would never write, relaxing into denial, certain she would arrive at Carla's in one piece. How was it possible, Amy wondered, to know you are in denial and snuggle into the feeling anyway? Anything could happen, any time. Now, for example, as she merged onto Torrey Pines, or now, as she slowed to read street signs in the dark and impatient natives honked and sped around her, or even now, pulling into Carla's enormous circular driveway. Her heart could explode, her brain wink out, she could trip while focusing on the enormous salad bowl in her arms and die in a pool of blood and Waldorf salad. The earth could open up at her feet.

Amy paused to look in the living room picture window: the room was too dark for her to make out details, but they were all there, no doubt, waiting for her, with candles and a goddamn birthday cake, because of course Carla had lied, but Amy stayed in the moment anyway. She was safe. She was happy to be anywhere.

CHAPTER ELEVEN

Retreat

Amy hadn't visited Carla's place, the Birdhouse, for a full year. Her last visit had been on Boxing Day, a few weeks after the Workshop Sniper, a deranged class member who had terrorized everyone in the workshop, had been identified and locked up. On that occasion, the remaining class members had not been able to refrain from discussing the Sniper, speculating on motivations, going over and over ground that Amy had already buried deep and cemented over. For months, Carla harassed her about turning the incident into gold and jump-starting her career in the process, a suggestion Amy found offensive, even coming from Carla, who never meant harm even though she routinely offended everybody. "That story is not mine to tell," she told Carla more than once, "especially in a form that will encourage readers to enjoy the deaths of innocent people." Carla eventually took the hint, calling Amy now and then ostensibly to shoot the breeze but really to demonstrate that she could be trusted never again to bring up "the thing." Still, Amy had dodged her until the following Christmas, when, in a moment of Yuletide sentimentality, she agreed to come to this small gathering. By now fewer than half of the original thirteen members remained: two had been murdered, one incarcerated, and five had sensibly returned to their lives.

Carla shared ownership of the Birdhouse with her horrible mother, and the first thing Amy noticed was how radically the interior of Carla's half had changed. Once a deep-red *Aladdin*-themed living area with keyhole-shaped alcoves and maroon velvet walls, the main room was now a jungle choked with gigantic potted plants, so that at first Amy couldn't tell who was there. Eventually she discerned Dr. Surtees and Ricky Buzza standing and chatting behind a cluster of bamboo palms. As her eyes adjusted to the low light, she eventually saw Harry B on the other side of the conversation pit, nestled among some boisterous ferns. If there was furniture in here, and there must be unless he was sitting on a stump, it had evidently been chosen to blend in with the vegetation. The room was soporifically humid. Amy set her salad bowl down underneath a Norfolk pine, no doubt kin to the one that had contributed to her recent near-death experience, and advanced toward Harry. Behind her, Carla screamed.

"No! Amy! Don't move!"

Amy obliged, not alarmed, as Carla was pretty high-strung, and this was probably her way of "surprising" the birthday girl. She braced herself against the onslaught of blazing cake and obnoxious song. Then Carla or somebody flicked a light switch, and the conversation pit lit up like a Disneyland lagoon, which essentially it was. The floor on which she had been about to step was an oval pool of black water, across which arched a narrow bamboo bridge, its rails entwined with ivy. "Check it out," shouted Carla, flicking another switch, and the water's surface began to roll in neat waves, uniformly spaced. "It's my combination lap pool and hot tub!"

"And lawsuit!" said Harry B, Esquire. Harry Blasbalg had once dreamed of writing horror fiction but now seemed content to offer free legal counsel to his workshop friends, especially Carla, who needed all the counseling she could get.

"We've all told her that somebody's going to drown," said Tiffany. "She won't pay any attention to us." Tiffany Zuniga stood next to Carla, holding a tray of tropical drinks.

She led Amy around the pool, ignoring Carla's entreaties that they take the bridge ("It's quicker!"), to an area way in the back of the room, cordoned off by man-eating vines, which housed high-end porch furniture, including a long wicker coffee table gussied up with a grass skirt. Amy sat down in a rattan easy chair so low and deep that she knew she was stuck there for the duration. She accepted one of the tropical drinks, served in a small hollowed-out pineapple whose skin scraped her palms, and within a minute the rest were arrayed around the table with her, except for Carla, who had returned to the kitchen and was yelling back something unintelligible.

"I've decided," said Tiffany, "that she's bipolar." Tiffany was a bright girl but still way too sure of herself.

"She's just a kid," said Amy.

"She's thirty-four!"

And you're in your twenties, and still living with your dad, Amy didn't say. "How much do you know about Carla?"

Tiffany sat back and knitted her unlined brow. "Just that she hates her mother and she has horrible taste."

Carla appeared at Tiffany's elbow, her approach apparently muffled by the rushing waters. "True and true," Carla said cheerfully, waving away Tiffany's flustered embarrassment. She set down a tray of mango-dotted mini-pizzas and sat down across from Amy. "Which brings us to the purpose of tonight's gathering." Carla had lost weight. She was still plump, but no longer obese; she still wore inappropriately stretchy clothing, in this case a clingy floor-length jersey thing, peach-colored and long-sleeved. Unusually, there were no sequins on the dress, but this was made up for by a gold lion pendant, the lion head the size of an alarm clock, its mouth gaping in a toothy roar. Carla was sweating profusely in the overheated room, but the shine became her. She looked happy. Amy, who liked Carla, was happy for her, but once again braced herself against the inevitable announcement of her own belated birthday.

"Ma's gone!" announced Carla. "Ta-da!"

Dr. Surtees, the first to recover from this announcement, said, "I'm so sorry, Carla. I had no idea Mrs. Karolak was ill."

"Crazy as a fruit bat!"

If not, strictly speaking, crazy, Amy thought, she certainly was a bat. If the fruit bat had ever loved her daughter, which was unlikely, any maternal feelings had dried up when she realized that her bouncy, precocious child could act and was naturally camera-friendly. Carla had once entertained Amy for a full evening with stories of her acting exploits, all of which she had loathed. Her mother made "a pantload" in a divorce from a father Carla could not even remember, and compounded that pantload with her daughter's earnings, mostly from long-running commercials, so that by the time Carla was emancipated (sort of) and ready for psychoanalysis, she had millions with which to pay for it. That she had continued to live with the woman, allowing her to occupy the east half of the Birdhouse, was a mystery to Amy.

Dr. Surtees was eyeing Carla closely. "What happened to Mrs. Karolak, Carla?"

"Monistat," corrected Amy. "Her name was Monistat." Amy knew this only because the old crone once told her that she hadn't kept "that bastard's name."

"Oh, *SNAP!*" Carla shrieked, bumping the table and spilling the pineapple drinks. "Amy, you're so funny!"

Maybe Tiffany was right. Maybe Carla actually was bipolar. Now she was laughing uncontrollably. Amy was growing tired of people telling her she was funny. "Carla, seriously. What have you done with your mother?"

"Nothing," said Carla, hiccupping. "She's gonna outlive me. But she's gonna do it somewhere else. How fabulous is that!"

Where had she put the woman? In a vault?

"Has Mrs. Monistat gone into an assisted-living facility?" asked Harry B, prompting Carla, who had begun to settle down, into another outburst of hilarity.

"Stop it, you're killing me! It's not *Monistat,* Harry. Amy was joking. It's *Massengill.* Elsie Mae *Massengill.*"

Now everyone else laughed, except for Amy, who had not been joking at all. The goof should have amused her, but she was distracted by a pinprick of alarm. Was her brain truly unhurt? How reliable were MRIs, anyway?

"Are you guys related to the Massengill feminine hygiene people?" asked Ricky. "They must have made millions."

"I used to kid Ma about that, whenever she got all up in my face about family tradition," said Carla. "I used to tell people we were the West Coast douche-bags, as opposed to the Park Avenue douche-bags. Drove her berserk. But no, no relation at all."

It turned out that Mother Massengill, the dragon lady who had haunted the Birdhouse, screeching constantly about slammed doors and car alarms, had moved back to Pittsburgh. Carla had bought out her half of the house. "Is that your announcement?" asked Amy, greatly relieved to learn that Carla hadn't done anything unspeakable to her mother. She tried a mango-mini-pizza. It was awful. When had people started putting fruit on pizza?

"It's what I'm going to do with Ma's half of the house is why I called this meeting." Carla, master of dramatic pauses, paused dramatically. When nobody guessed, she said, "I'm going to turn it into a writer's retreat!"

Silence greeted Carla, as they all turned this news over in their minds. "What does that mean?" asked Ricky.

"I'm setting up a foundation, with scholarships or fellowships, something like that, so that writers can come here and live for a while—six weeks, maybe—and do nothing but write."

"Who's handling this for you?" asked Harry B.

"You are," said Carla. "If you're interested. You do that sort of stuff, don't you?"

Harry said it would make a nice change for him. "I've been doing nonstop bankruptcies for a year." Business was booming for lawyers, if for no one else.

At this point, the rest chimed in with their financial woes. Ricky Buzza had been downsized from the *North County Times,* which, like all newspapers, was desperate just to stay afloat. Tiffany had lost her part-time job as a church secretary. "The assistant pastor claims she can do my job on her own computer, which is probably right. But really it's because I'm an atheist." Dr. Surtees complained that no, medicine was not recession-proof, and began to pontificate darkly about Obama and the looming healthcare apocalypse. Carla cut him off.

"People! You're not paying attention. Depending on what my accountant and Harry say, I can maybe offer these six-week deals year 'round. So you can live here and write and not worry about money."

"Wait a minute," said Harry B. "A non-profit foundation, which is what I'm assuming you're talking about, isn't the same thing as just throwing money at your friends. That's a gift. The tax consequences—"

"I'm not just going to be supporting my friends." Carla looked hurt. "There will be a rigorous admissions process. Which I'm sure you'll all pass with flying colors."

Amy fished her notebook from her purse and jotted down the title, "A Rigorous Admissions Process."

"Look," said Carla, "it'll just be room and board. You can rent out your houses and sublet your apartments."

Harry regarded Carla with fond exasperation. "And who is going to be in charge of the rigorous admissions process?"

Carla looked at Amy. At least she had the good sense to blush.

A writer's retreat, Max used to kid Amy, sounds like a bugle call. They would giggle over the imagined rout, Fitzgerald and Hemingway and Virginia Woolf in black-and-white uniforms, galloping frantically away from a horde of armed Thuggees as Sam Jaffe sounds the alarm. In her writing days, Amy had never benefited from peace and quiet. She had done her best writing in chaotic, noisy settings—parties, cafes, even softball games, putting down her notebook only to rise and strike out. She had written the final chapter of *Ambassador of Loss* by penlight during a Lewiston Community Theater production of *Waiting for Godot*. (Thus annoying Max, whose friend-of-the-month was playing Vladimir.) In those days, there were only a few, mostly venerable, writer's retreats; she had actually turned down an invitation to Sewanee and a residency at the Moose Watch Colony in Jackman. She was unlured by the prospect of month-long serenity, repulsed by snapshots of cloistered rooms, simple oak desks awash in pearly sunlight from a single uncurtained window, where writers were "free to inhabit and explore the quietest of spaces." This to Amy amounted to the freedom to congeal inside a Vermeer.

But she was in the minority there, and over the years, retreats, colonies, conferences, and weekend workshops had multiplied, keeping pace with a terrifying growth in the population of writers, both real and would-be. And now here came another one: the Birdhouse, in affluent, sun-blind La Jolla. Amy could actually picture the brochure, an aerial view of the house itself, whose two curved, sweeping wings mimicked a bird in flight. What did Carla want her to do? Write the brochure?

"I know you probably wouldn't want to be our Writer in Residence," said Carla.

"I have a residence in Escondido."

"Right. But this could be a permanent teaching place for you."

"I have one of those too. My home. I teach online."

"Well, will you think about it?" Carla looked so hopeful, so vulnerable, that Amy relented.

"Okay," she said. "But no promises."

"Also," said Carla, without a pause, "I'd like to hire you to vet the applicants. I'll pay top dollar!"

Ricky's face fell. "There goes that dream," he said, as if Amy weren't in the room. There had been a couple of promising writers in Amy's last workshop, but Ricky Buzza wasn't one of them. In fact, one of them was in prison.

Tiffany asked, "You were thinking of doing it?"

"Well, yeah, what have I got to lose? I've started working on something. It's not serious fiction, though."

Everybody started talking at once. Tiffany, also unemployed, was interested too. Dr. Surtees wanted in, which was ridiculous, but he said he'd like a room of his own. He was working on a new novel, another medical thriller. Amy interrupted him before he could spill the plot.

"Look, I'll do this, but only with blind submissions." No one knew what that meant. "I'll read the samples, provided that the writers' names aren't on them." Blind submissions, at least as far as this crew were concerned, were a forlorn hope: she'd be able to identify any of these writers at fifty paces. But the principle was important to Amy. There was precious little blind reviewing going on in the publishing world, which was why so much that got published was mediocre.

Amy's concession ultimately made everybody happy but Harry B, with whom she exchanged shrugs and knowing looks. Amy wasn't worried. Carla being Carla, the whole retreat idea would probably vaporize in a month or two when she was faced with legal hurdles and administrative minutiae. And even if she went ahead with it, chances are she'd just get these three "writers," and after awhile they'd give it up. Meanwhile Amy could make a few extra dollars without leaving her own home.

A few hours later, after the doctor's mojitos, Tiffany's cornbread, Carla's spectacular shrimp moqueca, and Ricky Buzza's store-bought pie, and a fair amount of pleasant non-retreat-focused conversation, Amy took her leave. Carla, obviously concerned with Amy's feelings, begged to be allowed to keep the Waldorf salad, which was "so scrumptious"—so scrumptious that nobody had actually eaten it, including Amy, who realized after one bite that she had either overdone the salt or substituted it for sugar. Just toss it, Amy said, I'll pick up the bowl some other time. Carla waved good-bye, smiling gaily, no doubt because of the phrase "some other time."

Or maybe Amy wasn't as canny about reading people as she had always believed. She would never have predicted that Ricky, whatever his creative yearnings, would have wanted to take Carla up on her offer. And why did Surtees want it? He was scarcely hurting for money and status. Tiffany Zuniga had been spinning her wheels for two years: if she had anything to say, she didn't seem eager to find out what it was. Did they all really want to keep writing? Why? Amy wasn't perplexed because of their lack of talent. Bookshelves worldwide groaned under the weight of badly written books. She was humbled by their determination, their longing. If she had a fraction of their need to express themselves in print, she would have filled at least one of those shelves by now.

Amy was halfway home before she recognized two things that had not come up at Carla's gathering: her own birthday, and last weekend's article in the *U-T,* which, according to Maxine Grabow, signaled she was "hot." She was grateful to have been wrong about the birthday but disappointed to realize that apparently not one of the five people present, most of whom probably took the local paper, had read the Sunday article. Or if they had, they remained silent on the subject. Lex Munster had been talking through his hat. There might be buzz in his little corner of the world, but there was no buzz in Muddville. By the time she got home, Amy had failed to convince herself that this was for the best.

CHAPTER TWELVE

∽

Waking Up

T hat night she woke in the middle of an old fantasy, a book
reading, where she stood at a podium in some huge important place, like the New York Public Library, or maybe the Library of Congress, and the audience too was huge and enthralled,
their muffled coughs and shuffles echoing grandly. She was mid-
sentence, always the same sentence from her last story, the one she
had never sold. "In the whole world there wasn't enough of anything to fill her up," she read, and the crowd went wild. Amy, coming fully awake to the echo of this asinine oration, had blushed
in the dark. "Despair," Max would say, "is a walk in the park. It's
hope that kills you."

In the morning, Amy arose as usual and, still in her bathrobe,
attended to her online work. But throughout those hours she
found herself distracted, pausing every so often to open up another
browser window and Google names—her own, of course, along
with Lex Munster, and the *ARB*'s upcoming issue on lost writers,
and even Holly Antoon. She was scouring the ether for even the

slightest uptick of interest in her own existence and works. This was degrading. In the past, she had Googled herself from time to time, but always in search of negative reinforcement: R-neg. Just as the tip of one's tongue luxuriates in the crater left behind by an extracted tooth, so she had soothed herself with stark, visual reminders of her own obsolescence. This had been a time-waster, but she had never felt pathetic doing it, not like now. Now she was hungry for attention. Maxine had infected her with hope.

Managing lowered expectations is easy. You can move seamlessly from a happy life to a less happy one to one that is plainly unhappy: your colors, never exactly vibrant, can fade to shades of gray, your horizons contract until all that remain are enclosing walls, and it's all good. "But what if you wake up one day and you're old and your life is almost over, and you realize all the things you could have had?" This from a *therapist,* Dr. Kappers, whom Amy had actually consulted once. Not after Max's death, but when she came to her senses, marooned in California, married to "Bob," a man she neither knew nor liked, a man so tangential that she actually ensconced him in quotation marks, even when—especially when—they were having sex. "Oh, 'Bob,'" she would say, and he would mistake her silent chuckling for passionate throes. She had been drinking too much just to get through the nights, and she lacked the constitution of a drunk. She disliked vomiting almost as much as she disliked "Bob." What she needed was a divorce. Before handing "Bob" his hat, she consulted Kappers, in the same spirit with which you'd consult a mechanic. She respected mechanics.

Amy didn't offend easily—she was offended mostly by people who went around taking offense—still, Kappers did manage to annoy her, deeply. He refused to stay on task. "You're clinically depressed," he kept telling her. If Kappers had been a real doctor and a patient with migraines had hopped into his office on her one remaining leg, he'd have spent the fifty minutes trying to convince her that she was an amputee. "The love of your life was gay. After he died you married a man you despise. You're drinking heavily. You haven't written a word in ten years. And you come here wondering if you should *get a divorce*?" Kappers leaned toward her, his face flushed. He was furious with her. Amy wondered whether this was some new therapeutic technique, a California thing, like rolfing. *Throttling*. Her smile cooled him off. Up until this point, Amy had rather liked the man, who was way too thin-skinned for his line of work. She was about to compliment him on his directness when he wrote out a prescription for Prozac and handed it to her with a canned lecture about side effects, which she cut short by crumpling the paper and dropping it, just like a lollipop, into his wastebasket. "Never mind the divorce," he called after her. "You should get a life! You should be happy!"

A few days later, Kappers actually wrote her a letter of apology. He had behaved unprofessionally, and so on. (Apparently she had really pushed his buttons.) He sincerely hoped she would connect with a more compatible therapist. He included a list of possibles. What was wrong with this man? He was clearly no happier than she, yet the constant, grim pursuit of *happiness* was mandatory, according to him and all his happy-slappy California pals. Happiness, Amy knew, wasn't all it was cracked up to be. All she wanted was solitude. Divorcing "Bob" turned out to be quite easy, especially since they were both broke and there was nothing to fight over.

But now, mooning around the Internet like a lovesick swain, noting—and actually taking heart from—a modest rise in Google hits for "Amy Gallup," Amy was acutely aware of her unhappiness. Perhaps for Emily Dickinson hope really was the thing with feathers that perches on the soul, but for Amy it was the thing with batteries, going off at three in the morning like an invisible alarm clock, and she had no option but to wait for it to wind down. She trolled the web, wondering what she was looking for. Gush from a decrepit blogger who actually remembered reading her books? Mention in some authoritative list of twentieth-century writers? Fat chance. She knew, because she had actually checked more than once, that she wasn't even in Wikipedia. Jenny Marzen was there, of course, peeking out from behind a tree like a ringlet-haired dryad. She had a two-inch bibliography and a list of awards and external links almost as long. She was married to some fabulous architect and had four daughters, all of whom she no doubt plundered in her fiction, and they all lived on some Montana ranch that had once belonged to Helen Twelvetrees. She had written her first story "at the age of six." Well, who the hell hadn't?

What other third-rate literary posers, Amy wondered, got the Wiki treatment these days? Frankly hoping for a bracing shot of R-neg, Amy plugged her own name into the Wikipedia search box, and there, impossibly, she was, in a brand-new page. There was no picture, but all the autobiographical details were accurate, ditto her list of ancient publications, her present city of address, and the fact that she was "hard at work on a new novel." This had to be Maxine's doing. At the heart of this modest entry was a sizeable chunk of that old review from the London *Times*. The one that called her, not a writer to watch, or a promising new voice, or wickedly funny ("wicked," "savage," and "ferocious" being the most overused adjectives in the modern reviewer's modest arsenal), but one of the rare post-sixties writers likely to outshine, and therefore outlive, her own generation. Amy had not looked at this review in a quarter century. She had read it only once, a Xeroxed copy forwarded by her publisher, and it had scared her to death.

None of the other reviewers had talked this way. She had been perfectly happy to be *a gimlet-eyed, toxic-witted observer,* or better *a talented writer whose relentlessly negative outlook undercuts the pleasures of her prose.* Reviews, once she had gotten used to them, had never bothered her. She tended to shrug off hyperbolic praise and take more seriously those reviewers who plainly hadn't liked her stuff. But when she read the *Times* review, she couldn't shrug it off. Far from being a credulous idiot, this critic was an older novelist whose work she quite admired. What had gotten into him? She accused Max of having rigged it somehow—Max knew people who knew people—setting off a rare argument. "If you're dead set on failure," he had shouted, "you're just going to have to work harder at it." And leave me out of it, he had added. As if he hadn't been every bit as unambitious as she. As if a desire to coast through life had not been one of the many things they had in common.

The reviewer had said not that she *was* great, only that she *could* be, thus burdening her with responsibility for which she had no appetite. She had torn up the review upon the first reading and successfully avoided it until now. Did Maxine Grabow actually know her well enough to do this to her on purpose? The woman was brilliant.

It was time, Amy decided, for real R-neg, so she brought out the big gun: her black-and-white-speckled notebook, christened in 1968, the only notebook she had ever kept. Most writers keep, or claim to, voluminous notebooks, at which they pause at daily intervals to jot down precious thoughts, observations, overheard dialogue. Amy could never see the sense of that, or indeed of jotting itself. If something was worth writing down, it was worth writing down in full. And she had a horror of lists—grocery lists, Christmas card lists, and most grisly of all, to-do lists. Lists, like appointment books, were nails driven into the future. She knew this was an odd objection to be raised by a person whose daily life was utterly predictable, who never threw caution, or anything else, to the winds, who never packed light, because she never packed at all. Still, the future was a sleeping monster, not to be poked.

So in the first half of that notebook were mere fragments, an anti-list, the beginnings or middles of ideas for stories and novels, written in penmanship so poor they were practically illegible, baffling whether you'd dashed them off an hour earlier or forty years ago. She opened it at random, studying a line that asked "what if nobody came" and answered "winner—Morton—clams," or perhaps "winter—mortar—damp." This may or may not have been the germ for "Husbandry," her first successful story, which did contain a throwaway line about littlenecks, but really there was no way to tell.

In the days when she was actually writing, the mere act of scribbling a line of gibberish in the dark—she had always gotten these fragmentary ideas at night—was all she needed. The fragments list was just a way of clocking in. She had not written in the first half of the notebook for twenty-five years.

There were lists in the second half, also non-threatening. Names of characters and titles of stories. The name list was quite long and mostly pointless doodling. Victorine Gould. Blenda La-Croix. Plethora Harpootlian. Ebony Hornbuckle. Tarquin Fogg. Brooklyn Muckle. Bartholomew Osteen. They were cartoonish, each name deliberately chosen to forestall any imaginative use. She added to this list quite often, because it was so safe.

The list of story titles was, as they say in the creativity biz, a

Work in Progress. Toward its beginning were titles she had actually used: "Battle Fatigue." "The Turnstile." "N.O. Means No." Her method, in her writing days, was to take them down when they came to her—always in the daytime—and surf them later for inspiration. These titles, like the names and the midnight hieroglyphs, were cryptic messages from her subconscious. Of the three, she tended to trust the titles. Night dreams and the messages from them did not impress her that much.

If we all go to the same place when we dream—and Amy thought this was probably true—then we're likely to come back from this place laden with kitsch and ordinary bits and shards, like beachcombing children who spread out their shells and pebbles, lately so glistening in the sand, only to find them drably colored and in all other ways unremarkable. Daydreams, on the other hand, do not take us to common ground. Amy had learned that while her conscious mind found a phrase amusing enough to put down on paper, her subconscious might have its own furtive agenda. She might *think* she was memorializing something because it was funny, but she could be wrong about that. Perhaps it meant something deep. Perhaps it was key. Amy, straitjacketed since birth with a cautious, analytical, R-neg mind, secretly loved to be wrong.

Now she surfed her latest title entries.

"Malignant Twinkle"
"You're That Lady"
"Shadow"
"Right Now"
"You're Funny"
"A Riot of Tasteful Color"

"Birdbaths"

"A Rigorous Admissions Process"

"Blushing in the Dark"

And there it was.

She had written it down when badly frightened, desperate to distract herself with rage. Even if she hadn't remembered writing it, the shiny pencil grooves would have given it away, summoned up antiseptic scent, ugly light, blue curtains, the soft moans and harsh laughter of strangers, on the day they found out he was dying. Summoned up in turn a deeper memory, that demented old woman down the hall from Max's last room, shrieking for her mama while they tried to cut her fingernails. The suffering place. Fear so sharp and clean it was beautiful. What if you wake up one day and you're old and your life is almost over, and you realize all you could have had?

Amy sat back down at her computer, opened up a fresh Word file, named it "Shadow," and began to write.

CHAPTER THIRTEEN

Walkies

Over the next three weeks, Amy wrote at what was for her a white heat, finishing one story and immediately beginning another. She had never before focused so deeply. Even in her youth, a good writing day produced at most a page and a half. When not working or writing, she walked Alphonse, or tried to, up and down the mild gradients of nearby streets. Dickens got his inspiration from nocturnal walks down the smoky byways of Manchester; Amy tried walking at midnight, risking the alarm of all the fenced dogs in the neighborhood, as well as Alphonse, who just wanted to go to sleep. Alphonse hated walkies. Amy had once loved to walk, before her muscles began to atrophy and her joints to sing and not in a pleasant way. But the exercise cleared her head, fed it in some mysterious way, so that when they got back home, she would sit at the computer for another hour or two, mostly thinking.

Amy's nocturnal strolls ended the night they encountered a pack of coyotes. Single coyotes weren't unusual in the neighborhood—they sometimes strolled through Amy's front yard at high noon—but on this occasion, she and Alphonse rounded a corner and came upon five of them standing close together, their ears straight up, their eyes bright with hunger. They spread out slowly in a semicircle around her, not blocking an exit, which seemed odd until she remembered that running away was supposed to be the worst thing you could do under the circumstances. They wanted her and her morsel to run away. Fat chance of that, thought Amy; neither of them had run anywhere for years. Alphonse stood close beside her and growled low, bristling. Amy wasn't afraid for herself: clearly they were focused on Alphonse, who probably looked like a family banquet and was no threat to them except in his own mind. Amy straddled the basset, raised her hands high and began to wave broadly, stiff-armed, making herself as large as possible, which, she had read, was the thing to do when confronted by carnivorous mammals. Two of the coyotes actually sat down to watch, as though she and Alphonse were doing dinner and a show. She tried slowly backing away but couldn't get Alphonse to budge. Of all the times to be stalwart. She would have to make some noise.

Not for the first time, Amy felt the real pull between survival and social embarrassment. Almost as desperate to avoid waking her neighbors as she was not to be savaged, she whispered, as loud as she could, "Buzz off!! Get lost!!" Their ears twitched with interest, just like a dog's, but they didn't buzz off. Instead, they moved closer, lazily, as though they had all the time in the world. They moved like pool hall toughs in the old movies, ambling toward their target. It was time to break somebody's thumbs. She waved and whispered again, this time putting some throat into it, but not enough to stop them. She was going to have to shout.

At just this moment, all the neighborhood dogs, who shared

keen hearing with the coyotes if not keen pack instincts, went crazy. The ones who were outdoors awoke and threw themselves against their fences; inside sleeping houses, little yipping dogs scrabbled at windows. One of the coyotes, the smallest, mangiest one, joined them, howling to its cousins, and the barks turned to howls in response, building a magnificent chorus. Alphonse threw back his head and bellowed, his basset howl low and gravelly. *Aroooo.* The coyote pack did not exactly abandon the hunt but paused in their tracks as if to boost the treble, perhaps in response to Alphonse's bass notes. The animals were singing. The chorus was improvised but polyphonic, true music, and in that music Amy could hear joy and longing in equal parts. For a moment all thought was banished. This was nirvana for Amy. Then she heard footsteps behind her, and Carl Ward from across the street, a nice guy who managed the local Arby's and hunted elk every winter, was at her side with a loaded rifle which he fired once into the air, and the coyotes melted into the darkness at the top of the hill. "Beautiful," he said. She knew he meant the song.

Amy was too good a neighbor to ever repeat the midnight stroll, but this one time was enough to start her on something new. Now she had three stories going at once. She felt like a conduit. Not that characters and plots were pouring out of her—this had never happened and never would—but she had moments now, almost daily, of hyperawareness, as though she could see the web of delicate causal filaments all around her, radiating out into the neighboring streets and farther into the world. You turn a corner and beasts break into arias, gunfire erupts, waking a hundred families, starting a hundred different conversations. You crack your head open and three thousand miles away a stranger with Asperger's jump-starts your career.

Causation was intrinsic to the engines of plot; and because plot had never been her strong point, she had created narrative pull in her stories and novels through character, which worked well enough but made for slow movement. *Something has to happen,* her publisher would politely suggest. *Readers expect it.* Until now, for Amy, a glacial change in a character's perspective, a tiny realization of some portion of the truth, had been, more often than not, the thing that happened in her fiction: the change that made the story worth telling. She had thought this was part of her diehard aesthetic, even though her favorite novelists—Dickens, Melville, Tolstoy—hardly confined themselves to tiny snags in the fabric of life. Now she began to suspect that she had just been writing what she knew, which was all interior. Until she hit her head on the birdbath and all hell broke loose.

Maxine called. "What do you think?" she asked.

"About what?"

"The *Enlightenment* piece. Carmen Calliostro. My god, you didn't read it?"

"I've been busy." *Enlightenment* was an online rag, more bookish than *Salon,* less huffy than the *Huffington Post.* Amy's online reading was mostly confined to the *Onion.*

"Calliostro did eight paragraphs on you. Look it up."

"Maxine," said Amy, "I'm writing again." She felt like a fool sharing this with anybody.

"Fabulous!"

"It's stories, Maxine." Amy held the receiver away from her ear. She could have heard Maxine's obscenities from across the room. "Stories, Maxine," she yelled back. "Live with it. At least I'm writing."

"How am I supposed to sell stories? Read the thing." Maxine hung up.

Carmen Calliostro's thing was titled "Bionic Leg." In keeping with the standards of modern journalism, most of it was about Carmen Calliostro. She began with a yellowed verbal snapshot of her own lithe undergraduate form (litheness could be deduced from her byline sketch) supine on a sward in Ithaca (Carmen was way too shy to come out and say Cornell), thumbing through the stories in *Monstrous Women* and "falling in love with words for the very first time." Next came a whirlwind tour of her literary education, during which she confessed (actually using the verb "confess") to throwing Amy over in favor of a succession of trendier writers. "I was embarrassed," she said, dimpling verbally, "to have been seduced by writing so old-fashioned. It was the fiction writer's mission, I was sure, to intuit and interpret the spirit of the times. Amy Gallup was old news: the least zeitgeisty of writers." (Apparently Carmen's love affair with words had ended badly.)

"I was wrong," she wrote, in a dramatic one-sentence paragraph.

Holly Antoon's story, upon which Carmen stumbled in some unexplained way (Amy guessed at a Munster connection), reawakened her interest in Amy's fiction. After pausing to note that Antoon reminded her of her own girlish self (over the moon with the English lexicon?), Carmen finally—practically at the last minute—arrived at her ostensible subject. Like Maxine and the rest, she assumed without reflection that Amy had been in full charge of her own faculties during the interview and had invested every line of dialogue with cunning foresight. Like Antoon, she was crazy about the brilliant "going off road" metaphor, but what really knocked her out was the bionic leg. Aside from the gut-busting hilarity of the "meta-joke," she was delighted by Amy's "deliberate use of a lie to celebrate the über-truth of fiction."

What an idiot.

Amy was still laughing when she got Maxine on the phone. "That's two minutes out of my life that I'm not going to get back," she said, "but it is pretty funny."

"You don't get it. This is how it starts."

"The apocalypse?"

"I got three emails this morning. Nothing solid yet, but a feeler from NPR. I've got a call in to Lex. I'll get back to you. Just keep writing, and send me whatever you got."

"I thought you couldn't sell stories."

"Sure I can. I don't want to is all. And hey, maybe stories aren't such a bad way to go right now. I got some ideas. See ya."

That day she finished a second story. She now had two to offer Maxine: "Shadow" and an untitled one about a fatal bus plunge. A group of seniors, on their way to a production of *Our Town* at the Lamb's Players Theater on the island of Coronado, swerves to avoid a Weber grille in the westbound right lane of the Coronado Bridge and plunges into San Diego Bay. A young reporter for the *U-T* begins a series of investigative pieces on the lives of the twelve passengers and driver, detailing how each one of them happened to be on that bus on that day. The series starts out poorly, every observation a cliché, but deepens as it goes and its author begins to see her subjects as complex beings, each the product of an unlikely train of events. In her last piece, titled "What It All Means," she rises to a level of analysis and passion that frightens and excites her. It all means absolutely nothing, she writes, beyond the catastrophic loss of thirteen living souls and the grief of those who mourn them. The fatal accident was horrible and stupid. This sets off a firestorm of calls and letters from Christians, and the reporter is canned.

Amy wasn't crazy about the story. First, she never wrote allegories. For another thing, it wasn't even her allegory. Surely she wasn't the first writer to riff on *The Bridge of San Luis Rey*, which was itself a sort of riff. Since Thornton Wilder had gotten there first, the story was hardly necessary. The third-person narrative voice was impassive, authoritative, and rather off-putting, at least to Amy. And it was less a story than a sketch for something larger, like a screenplay. She didn't do screenplays. All in all, she feared it was a cheap shot. But it had practically written itself, which meant that her subconscious was largely responsible, and she was inclined, as always, to trust the director.

"Shadow" might be the best story she had ever written, or the worst. It was certainly close to the bone, scary to write. After Max died, she had for twenty years refused to consider a direct fictional assault on that topic, and since all other topics paled, she had refused to consider anything else. But something had changed. Although she would never use *his* experience, however deeply imagined, in a story, she was ready now to use her own. His death belonged to him; her grief was hers to use or abuse. An agnostic man learns that his wife is dying. She is still recovering from surgery, unaware of the news. He stumbles into the hospital chapel and down through a series of craven prayers. As he prays he regards himself with loathing, first at his own hypocrisy, and then at his inability to ignore his self-aware natterings and focus on the task at hand, which is nothing less than the production of a miracle from the common dirt of need. If he could just focus cleanly on this task he might affect her fate. The chapel, formerly brightened by sunlight streaming through a high round stained-glass window, suddenly darkens, prompting his armor to fall away, and his need rises, shining, powerful, too powerful, piercing the walls around him, and for what seems like endless time he sees his own puny beacon engulfed by the brilliance of constellations, swallowed up in freezing clouds of gas and dust, clouds with terrible shapes, crab, rearing horse, mutant eagle. Outside the hospital, the sun emerges from a much smaller cloud, the chapel fills again with light. Next to him, an old woman fishes in her purse, hands him a tract from the Jehovah's Witnesses. "Bless you," she says. Under the picture of a naked old man suffering on his knees, the question, "Where were you when I laid the foundations of the earth?" He waits for her to leave and then places the tract on the seat behind him. He sees that others have come into the room, each sitting alone. In their faces and the set of their shoulders he can see they are all like him, waist-deep in a river of suffering. He has never seen this river before, but he knows it is as real and ordinary as the chapel itself. Dust dances in the sunbeams.

Maxine was really going to hate these stories. Amy attached them both to an email and clicked *Send*.

CHAPTER FOURTEEN

Hypothetical Promises

After some weeks, Maxine called. "KPBS-FM wants an interview." KPBS was the San Diego public radio station.

"About what? You mean they want an interview about an interview?"

"What they say is they want to catch up with you, given that you're a local writer who's working on a new novel—"

"Not." Amy had an unsettling thought. "Maxine, they'll want to get me talking about what happened last year, with the workshop and the murders."

"I'm way ahead of you. I already told them that it's off-limits. I said you wouldn't even discuss it with your oldest friend, so you're certainly not going to spill the beans on the radio."

"Who's my oldest friend?"

Maxine snorted and hacked. "You cut me to the quick."

*   *   *

Carmen Calliostro's "Bionic Leg" had not exactly ignited a firestorm of Amy-centered articles, but in the first few weeks after the accident Amy counted five, four online and one in actual print, an opinion piece in *The Boston Globe,* mailed to her without comment by Maxine. Most who wrote about her claimed familiarity with her fiction, pleasure at her having resurfaced, bemusement about her eccentric behavior during the Antoon interview. Two of the pieces had "redux" in the title, two were called "Going Off-Road," and the best one, from the *Globe,* highlighted her pronouncement that "Feelings Are Not News." The male writer, probably Amy's age, took the opportunity to reminisce about the days when televised evening news, confined to fifteen-minute talking head segments, was more informative than the 24/7 news of today; when local newspapers investigated local events; when poll results were not the centerpieces of news reports; when feelings were not news.

"Ms. Gallup," he wrote, "remembers a time when competent reporters would never dream of asking people how it felt to lose their job, witness a schoolyard shooting, or have their life savings wiped out in a Ponzi scheme. Competent reporters were too busy collecting and verifying facts. Competent reporters and their editors assumed their readers were bright enough to figure out for themselves how catastrophic events feel. They feel bad. What readers needed was information: What happened? Who was involved? Where, when, how, and why did it happen? That was all they needed from us. We haven't given it to them for thirty years. We've been doing such a rotten job that now even the novelists are complaining. How do I feel about that? Lousy."

The "even the novelists" crack was childish, but Amy didn't mind. Like a lot of journalists, he probably looked down on writers who made stuff up. She had worked with a few of them over the years, reporters and columnists who imagined they could write novels if they just had the time. They were professional writers, after all, so how hard could it be, when you don't have to do any legwork? Often they demanded that she tell them "the rules." The rules for what? Leads. Paragraphs. Objectivity. She learned that laughing gaily and telling them there are no rules just made them paranoid. The rule is, there are no rules. The rule is, if it works, it's okay. Journalists either dropped out of class in disgust or, in a couple of cases, learned how to write fiction. Because they were professionals, they could take criticism: the best of them were hungry for it. Successful crossover journalists surprised her: before working with them, she had always assumed that the ability to imagine a good story on paper was a gift that one either had or lacked. They taught her that it could be learned. So she didn't mind a backhanded compliment from the Boston curmudgeon.

After receiving that *Globe* column, Amy got in the habit of checking online for news follow-ups, and over the next month, just as Maxine had predicted, each day or so there were new listings for her, growing at what appeared to be a modest exponential rate. As though there were a hand-packed snowball with her name on it, slowly rolling down a gentle winter slope. It wasn't exciting exactly, but it was interesting. Newspapers in Providence, both Portlands, Seattle, Sacramento, Iowa City, Baton Rouge, Indianapolis, and Pensacola all picked up the Boston column. Readers responded online, many disagreeing vehemently, as in, "You and A. Gallop are heartness snobs in the first place in the second place you don't have any felling's to begin with. Shame on You!!!"

Two weeks later, the Knoxville *Record* ran an original op-ed by some columnist named Aunt Bette, scolding both Amy and the curmudgeon, while spelling both "heartless" and "feelings" correctly. Amy's full name was used three times in the column. Aunt

Bette had apparently tried to slog through *Everything Handsome* once on an overnight train to New Orleans and had found it "the kind of novel *The New York Times* trumpets, where you have to keep a dictionary handy just to get through each sentence, and when you come to the end of the book, you just scratch your head." Clearly, argued Aunt Bette, feelings don't mean much to intellectuals, but regular Americans read with their hearts as well as their heads. Amy, who read with her eyes, wondered whether this column would be picked up by other papers too.

It was. In fact, the number of papers running Bette's column was almost double that of the first bunch. Amy, whose literary fame had come and gone in the pre-Internet era, found herself with over fifty hits on Google News.

So now Amy was going to Do Radio. She would have to drive into the city for an interview at the station, on the campus of San Diego State. "Couldn't we do it over the phone? And really, what's the point of this, Maxine?"

"The point is to get you out there. Baby steps, remember. At the very least, you'll reach thousands—okay, hundreds—of educated, book-buying San Diego citizens. And there's always the possibility of the interview being picked to run nationwide."

For an instant Amy imagined being on NPR talking to Robert J. Lurtsema, but then remembered he was dead. Alphonse, who always sat at her feet when she talked on the phone, sighed and rested his chin on the floor. "That's not going to happen, Maxine. I'm old. I'm yesterday's news. I wasn't even news yesterday."

"You've got the brains and the voice for it, plus you don't give a damn, which will keep you from being nervous. My money's on you. If it doesn't work out, you haven't lost anything."

Only after she had hung up did Amy realize Maxine hadn't said anything about the bus plunge story and "Shadow." She must really despise them. Was she playing mind games? If Maxine thought Amy was going to bring them up first, she had another think coming. Amy didn't care whether Maxine liked them, or even if she sold them. Resuscitating Amy's career was Maxine's bright idea. The hell with Maxine.

Two mornings later she found herself in an unpopulated room at the radio station, waiting for "Brie Spangler," whatever that was. She had been expecting high-tech gadgets, chrome boxes and booms and cables. Instead, the place was practically empty and preternaturally quiet. She didn't even see a microphone, unless the mike was behind a delicate disk of gray netting, like a robot's hairnet. There was a comfy chair and a set of headphones and silence of a quality she had never experienced. Not just the absence of sound, but positive, warm, burnished silence. The best part was that she was all alone. There was an adjoining room behind glass, for the engineer or something, but no one was there either. What a wonderful room.

Eventually a plump pink rabbity-looking young woman entered, introduced herself, and sat down next to Amy, in front of her own hairnet. She seemed flustered. "I'm Brie Spangler. Actually Britahnya Spangler," she said, avoiding Amy's eyes. "Isn't that stupid? We're on in five."

"Seconds?"

"Minutes."

What a strange little person this was. Amy felt, in a good way, as though she'd fallen down the rabbit hole. "Isn't what stupid?"

"My parents," she said, and then interrupted herself. "Look, do you know how to work the headphones and mike? Should we go over what we're going to do?"

Amy thought about it. "Surprise me," she said. The technology looked child-simple; she assumed the rabbit would tell her if she talked too loudly, or too softly. "What about your parents?"

She snatched a glance at Amy and looked quickly away. "They didn't want to call me Brittany, because it was too common, so they named me after the French province. In French."

"Oh! *Bretagne!* I misunderstood you." Amy became aware that she made *Bretagne* Spangler self-conscious. Either this was her first interview ever, or she cared what Amy thought of her.

"Everybody did, from preschool on. I've spelled my name out loud five million times. The studio calls me Brie."

"Isn't that better?"

She sighed. "It's a cheese."

"Like Camembert," said Amy, sympathetically.

"Which sounds nice too, but it's a cheese. My parents' generation was all about how it *sounds*. I had a friend who had a friend whose mother named her Derriere."

"You're kidding."

"We're on in thirty."

"Seconds?"

"Uh-huh." She spread out a loose-leaf binder and did something to both mikes.

"Remember," said Amy, with five seconds to spare, "don't mention the murder." Amy couldn't help herself. She was having too much fun.

"*What* murder? Oh, *that*. Don't worry, we'll—" Suddenly Mary Martin was singing into Amy's ears: "If They Asked Me, I Could Write a Book." After the first verse, and with pitch dropped half an octave, the rabbit spoke. "This is Brie Spangler on KPBS-FM. It's time for 'On the Shelf,' our weekly spotlight on writers. Today we're privileged to have in our studio . . ." Amy was impressed. She sounded nothing like she looked. She sounded voluptuous and intellectual at once. Amy snaked her little note-pad out of her purse and jotted down "voluptual" at the same time appreciating that Brie was listing all her titles without error and quoting from her best reviews. She'd done her homework. Amy also appreciated that she apparently cared little for workshop-murder gossip and was all about the books.

For the first fifteen minutes they chatted about her early writing life, and Amy's favorite novels, and then Brie's. Amy asked as many questions as Brie; they were comfortable with each other. Brie was settling down. This was fun: Amy was less anxious here in this quiet room than anywhere else, except her own home. Even when teaching, or visiting Carla, she always felt unsettled. Here was the equivalent of a warm hearth on a cold night.

"In a recent interview," Brie said, "you listed all the books on your shelf you haven't read yet."

"Well, not all of them. That would have taken too long."

"And I loved that they were great books and not-so-great books, and you just jumbled them together. William Faulkner and Mickey Spillane."

"And why not?"

"And why not! But nobody ever does that. Nobody ever talks about F. Scott Fitzgerald and Jackie Susann."

"And John Cheever and O Henry—"

"And Agatha Christie and—"

"Doris Lessing—"

"Yes," said Brie. "And why is that?"

Amy thought. "It's probably not that nobody reads all of those writers. I mean, I've read a lot of them, and I can't be the only one. It has something to do with the old highbrow-lowbrow distinction and the need for people to label themselves. They say they're too heartland for Orwell. Too devoted to Shakespeare to read Stephen King. Or so they say."

"Or too wrapped up in movies to read at all." Brie turned to face Amy, her notebook forgotten. "Do you think we're all going to stop reading? Is this the end of the age of books?" She looked dewy and anxious and gazed at Amy as though Amy were some sort of sibyl.

Don't ask me, Amy wanted to say, but of course she *was* asking her. Apparently that was the point of an interview. "It's the end of the age of something," she said. "Words are running wild and free on the Internet. Nobody knows what's going to happen. That isn't necessarily a bad thing. Suppose the publication of new books were interrupted for ten or twenty years, while publishers merged and diversified, thrashed and sank. Suppose there were a de facto moratorium on the brand-new printed word. Suppose all we were left to hold in our hands and read were the books that were already out there."

"Wouldn't that be terrible?" asked Brie.

"Why? For the first time in a hundred years, readers would have time to read all the books they'd been meaning to get to, and the tens of thousands more that they never even heard of. Nosebleed-inducing farces. Horror stories guaranteed to rob us of sleep. Pulse-pounding page-turners. Sprawling, sumptuous histories. Best of all, those books that the critics have told them were essential to our lives. Insightful novels of intoxicating ferocity. Intoxicating novels of ferocious insight. There's a million of them, each one 'compelling.'"

"I've never understood that adjective," said Brie.

"Me neither. But maybe if we got a chance to read them all, we'd find out."

"But meanwhile, what would happen to all the writers?"

Amy smiled. In her utopia, she said, most of them would give up and turn to meaningful employment. By the time the presses started rolling again, the ratio of readers to writers would have returned to its ideal proportions. The sort enjoyed by Dickens and Twain, and even Hemingway and Dreiser.

Brie asked if in Amy's utopia everyone would be forced to read highbrow.

"Absolutely not. There'd be something for everyone. Just not so much of it. And when we finished reading a book, we'd have a real shot at finding someone else who read it too, and discussing it with them."

"Well, isn't that what bestseller lists are for? So that we'll all— okay, I take it back." The rabbit blushed, annoyed with herself. "I hate bestseller lists," she said.

"Good for you."

Brie's eyebrows knitted. "What's the ideal proportion? Of readers to writers?"

Amy paused, as though calculating. "Ideally, there should be more readers than writers."

Brie studied Amy's face, clearly unsure whether Amy was kidding.

She was a bright girl, but young. If she'd been in one of Max's classes, he'd have already used the Irony Klaxon, an old bicycle horn he always kept handy when lecturing. "They're not wired for irony yet," he explained to her, "so I have to help them. Your brain must be fully developed before you can cope with a straight-faced joke. They think you're serious unless you're smirking." Max hated to smirk, although he was quite good at it. Amy didn't know how.

"Look," she said. "There may still be more readers than writers, but surely we're approaching some kind of catastrophic tipping point." Amy had no idea if this was true, but she liked the sound of it. A world choked with writers, like an echoey room crammed with chatterboxes, was an enervating thought.

Brie was quiet for what must have seemed like a long time to anyone actually listening. She turned back to her notebook. "In that recent interview, you were asked how a particular event felt. I won't go into the event here, because the important thing is that you challenged the reporter to tell *you* how it felt. Your point, if I understand you correctly, is that she should have been able to imagine those feelings for herself. That we all should. You didn't come right out and say, 'That's a stupid question.' You were nice about it. But I think that's what you meant. You said, 'Feelings are not news.' You said, 'Experience is over-rated.' Could you explain what you meant by that?"

"I can explain what I think I meant. After all, the interview was some time ago, and it all came and went pretty quickly." Amy wondered why she was bothering with the truth, or at least some technical version of it, at this stage. "I think I meant, for one thing, the obvious point that news should confine itself to what actually happened and why and who was responsible and how it could be avoided or repeated in the future, depending on whether it was a bad event or a good one. It's my business if somebody hits you over the head and steals your wallet, because the same thing could happen to me. It's not my business how you responded to it emotionally.

"The other thing I may have meant is this: Feelings are not news, but they are the rightful province of art. If you want to know how it *feels* to be a young black man watching another black man being tortured and lynched, read 'Big Boy Leaves Home.' If you want to know how a poor boy *feels* when he's trapped and yearning for a beautiful rich girl, read *An American Tragedy*. Fiction, when it's done right, does in the daylight what dreams do at night: we leave the confines of our own experiences and go to common ground, where for a time we are not alone. Where we don't have to ask how it feels, because we feel it for ourselves." Amy sat back, happy about what she had just said, although she wished she had come up with some more examples. She hadn't thought on her feet like this for years. Perhaps ever. Explaining what you said when you were not in your right mind was a challenge.

"Common ground," repeated Brie. She was about to say something else when Mary Martin warbled again, signaling the end of the interview.

Afterward, vigorously shaking hands with Amy, she reassured her that they'd be doing this again "soon." She seemed sincere—she seemed downright eager—but Amy didn't take her seriously. This was Southern California, where all promises were hypothetical. I'll call you Monday, if I remember to. We'll do dinner, if I ever feel like it. I'll drive you to the hospital for your cancer surgery, unless my boyfriend wants to take me to Laughlin.

When Maxine asked her the next day how it had gone, Amy said fine, nothing special. A week later Maxine told her NPR was running the interview on *All Things Considered*. "You're a hit, kid," she said. "Keep writing, by the way. *The Atlantic* bought 'Shadow.'"

CHAPTER FIFTEEN

Blind Submission

It had now been almost three months since Amy cracked her head on the birdbath, and in that time, and as a result of the accident, she had completed two and a half stories, been interviewed on radio, and gotten her first acceptance from *The Atlantic,* which had played tag with her decades ago but never before consummated an adult relationship. Like the kraken, and with that creature's formidable reach, her old agent had risen from the deep, bringing with her another mythic creature, a Munster, with the power to thrust Amy into the literary limelight, or what passed for the literary limelight in the early days of the twenty-first century. Amy awoke most days feeling perky, for her. While she did not actually look forward to the day, she was curious about what was going to happen next.

She was so pleased by the *Atlantic* thing and so wrapped up in her third new story that she completely forgot about Carla and her writer's retreat, so it was a genuine surprise when she got an E-card in her email inbox, inviting her to a "Virtual Gathering."

This turned out to be an online chat thing involving the old workshop gang (Carla, Ricky, Dr. Surtees, Harry B, and Tiffany) and three prospective new students. When Amy called Carla up to beg off she was met with spectacular whining and pleading. One of the prospects was a doctor, Carla said. Amy said that Surtees was a doctor too, and so what. "Another one's a journalist," said Carla. "Think about it. I just advertised the retreat a week ago, and we've already got two professionals."

"Carla, I said I'd read their submissions, and frankly, I wish I hadn't. I didn't promise any virtual get-togethers. I'm busy. Just have them send me their stuff."

"Okay, but remember, you promised to aid in the admissions process."

"Yes, the rigorous admissions process."

"So I'll be sending you six stories. There are the three new people, and three of us, but I won't tell you who."

"And how many of the six can your retreat accommodate?"

"Three, for now," said Carla.

"So, just to get this straight," said Amy, "you're expecting me to reject three of the six?" This didn't sound like Carla at all. It didn't even sound like Amy. Her workshops, virtual and otherwise, were always first come, first served. She never excluded anybody because of an obvious lack of talent. For one thing, she'd go broke, and for another, talent wasn't all it was cracked up to be. Stamina, perseverance, and hunger for criticism were much more indicative of future success.

"Well," said Carla, "right now I'm limiting it to three. Do your worst!"

"You can plan on it," said Amy.

* * *

Amy planned to read the submissions as quickly as possible, giving them much shorter shrift than she would if they were actual students in her course. All she had to do was pass/fail: she wouldn't need to explain herself. For a moment she felt absurdly powerful. This must be how editors felt, the paid readers at the gates of magazines and publishing houses, who got to chuck unsolicited manuscripts in the bin at the first sight of a cliché or misplaced modifier. Of course they were paid execrably, but then so was Amy, and editors had benefits.

Planning to race through the six manuscripts in an hour or so, Amy glanced at each. Per her instructions, these were blind submissions, all double-spaced in Times New Roman 12, with not a name in sight. Still she was unable to avoid identifying a submission by Tiffany Zuniga, which was virtually identical to a piece she'd submitted over a year ago, in Amy's last workshop. Twenty pages in which a young woman named Maggie, who has lost both job and lover, lolls in bed, loath to rise and face another miserable day. If Amy's memory served, Tiffany had added a whopping page and a half to the original manuscript. Now it was clear that Maggie didn't even live in her own place, but sulked in her childhood room, even though she was twenty-five years old. The writing was clean, intelligent, observant, but there was even less narrative pull to these pages than there had been before the latest addition. Over a year had gone by, and she still hadn't even come up with a title. Amy tossed it on the floor.

She had expected to identify Surtees in a heartbeat, and in fact she did, but she was surprised, in a quick once-over, to see that three of the manuscripts, not just one, were about hospitals. *Womb to Tomb* had to be the Surtees one. It was yet another stab at political suspense, or whatever the genre was called, the sort of thing they sell out at airports, with red, black, or silver covers and graphics that lean heavily on cross-hairs and the silhouettes of submarines and bombers. In *Womb to Tomb,* no doubt the logo would be a caduceus entwined by twin cobras with dripping fangs. His last effort had been an anti-HMO novel. Now he was apparently going to do for Obamacare what *Code Black: A Medical Thriller* had done for the whole notion of managed healthcare: zilch, if Amy had anything to do with it. A brief once-over of these twenty pages showed Surtees planned to bludgeon his readers with medical and health insurance jargon, then jangle their nerves with government conspiracies. True to thriller form, the opening chapter focused on a hapless old woman awaiting a routine pacemaker upgrade, drifting into a terminal Propofol haze while her local Death Board signs her exit papers. *Womb to Tomb* joined Tiffany's piece on the floor.

Next was the outline and first chapter of another novel, *The Driver,* focusing on a romantic sad sack in Revere, Massachusetts who stumbles into participating in a robbery that goes horribly wrong. The writer had deliberately chosen an ordinary working-class character, not very bright but with a sweet streak. His best friend, an unemployed meth addict, talks him into driving him to a convenience store and then, at the last minute, tells him he's going to rob it. The driver, unable to stop his friend, starts to drive off, when he hears gunfire. He rushes into the store to find his friend wounded by an armed clerk; he goes to drag him away when his friend takes out a gun and kills the clerk. The driver and his friend are both arrested and charged with felony murder. Throughout this chapter, the writer stayed firmly within the driver's point of view, so that events which could have been rendered simply lurid were dreadfully sad. This one was a keeper.

The second hospital novel was going to focus on a plain, middle-aged, divorced oncology nurse. Amy would have given it a thumbs-up even if it had been poorly written, simply for the quixotic choice of protagonist. Happily, the nurse was mordantly funny, both about herself and about working at Hope Memorial, which she and the other nurses refer to privately as Abandon All Hope. Chapter 1 focuses on a dying child, a deeply unlikeable teen whose only remaining pleasure in life is guilting his distraught, frantic mother. At the scene's close, the kid drives his mother away with the line, "That makes two of us" (the mother having cried out, "I'd give anything if this were happening to me, and not you"). He looks at Ernestine, the nurse, and asks, "You think I'm a creep, don't you?" and Ernestine says, "Yes." Taken a little aback, the kid says, "Well, excuse me, if I didn't have terminal cancer, I might have been a nicer person," and Ernestine says, "We'll never know, will we?" and leaves. Amy put it with *The Driver*. All she needed was one more.

And it wasn't going to be *Skinny White Chick*. Above the title, the writer had typed: "To Whom It May Concern: This is most definitely NOT chick-lit! It's Bitch-Lit, if you will. It is a rueful, humorous, sometimes bitter, often raunchy look at the plight of the modern American career woman. I promise no happy endings." Amy threw it on the floor and then, sighing, picked it up again. She'd give it three out of twenty pages and then quit with a clear conscience. A brief scan of these pages revealed the words "mascara," "strappy," "chardonnay," and "yeast," which she jotted in her notepad for later use. The writer was literate but furious: a fine combination if you're writing a polemic but deadly if you're going for frothy wit. The skinny white chick, Margot, when she isn't writing "brilliant, headstrong short fiction" that never gets published, edits children's books by day and cruises upscale bars by night, picking up "bad boys." The walls of her bedroom are plastered with rejection slips and temporary restraining orders.

The last of the six entries wasn't a chapter at all, but a twenty-page outline, professionally typed and developed. Amy had heard of these, though she'd never written one, because she'd never had to. She'd gotten her start in an era when all you had to do was send your stuff in and wait for it to come back. Now, unpublished hopefuls needed agents just to get their foot in the door, and in order to get agents, they had to pitch themselves like Slice-O-Matics.

The outline for *Caligula's Scalpel* was impeccably formatted and error-free; each chapter was described in such detail that it was possible to read the entire novel in ten minutes, which Amy did. Its eponymous hero was Dr. Caligula Denton, which told Amy that his creator had to be too young to know what Dr. Dentons were. Could this be Ricky Buzza?

Caligula Denton is a "brilliant Boston brain surgeon" who diagnoses himself at a young age as a sadistic psychopath. He devotes himself, in his off hours, to the extensive study of his own condition, which he determines is organic in origin. Not that he has many off hours, since his days are spent mastering neurosurgery "at Olympic levels" and his nights killing people in vicious ways, earning himself the moniker of Hieroglyph because of the symbols he either carves into his victims or displays via arrangement of their body parts, or both. The Boston cops, aided by the lovely Clara McGee on the faculty of "Harvard University's Department of Criminology," soon are hot on the trail. All this happens in the first three chapters.

Amy rubbed her eyes and watched Alphonse root at the reject pile, which shouldn't have smelled inviting, as there were no grease spots or food stains on the printout. Still, after circling the pile and stomping on it with his great basset feet, he lay down on top of it, rolled on his back, and began to writhe ecstatically, crinkling and ripping the papers, making that nasal "ong-ong-ong" noise he always made on his back, which apparently felt divine.

He couldn't be scratching his hide, since the paper was smooth. He displayed great abandon whenever he did this. All dogs were famously attracted to garbage, but only Alphonse could sniff it out in print. She really needed to clip his nails, but the clawing and shredding were immensely satisfactory to witness.

What bothered Amy most about *Caligula's Scalpel* wasn't its ludicrous, derivative plot. Serial killers had buzz these days—and while old-genre serial murderers acted that way because they were just nuts or rotten to the core, the new ones were driven as much by the need to puzzle as by lust for torture and slaughter. In fact, most of them were way too cerebral to be lusty. Their killing floors were cathedrals dedicated to their own genius and depth of erudition. Of course Dr. Denton is an amateur egyptologist. Of course he arranges for the Harvard professor to play Holmes to his Moriarty, so he can spar with someone on his own intellectual level. The whole idea was stupid, which was why Amy was so annoyed with herself for not being able to stop reading the outline. What was it about the most hackneyed plot that kept most people, including her, flipping pages? *Caligula's Scalpel* was every bit as bad as *Skinny White Bitch,* yet she was going to persevere, just to find out what happened next, while she could not have been paid enough to see the skinny bitch through to her solitary, rage-fueled, self-affirming, masturbatory predestination.

What happens to Caligula is that he gets lonely and bored. He pines for the company of his own kind, so he sets out to create an extended family. Following a Byzantine selection protocol, he picks ten of his scheduled surgical patients for experimentation, and after a few mishaps he learns how to alter each patient's thalamus, limbic system, and prefrontal cortex, whilst simultaneously removing clots, tumors, and other humdrum detritus, and to do this without other operating room personnel noticing. Not only does he turn men, women, children, and infants into serial murderers, but he also implants some sort of Rube Goldberg time-delay for the trigger so they don't all go off at once. Before long Boston is hip-deep in Hannibals, and it's a race to the finish between beautiful Clara and the wisecracking detective to stop Patient 10, a United States senator, from eviscerating the Committee on Homeland Security and Governmental Affairs and arranging to feed their giblets to the Supreme Court. Amy stopped reading before the last page. She didn't want to wreck the surprise when she read the actual draft.

Carla called her within hours of receiving Amy's terse email, anxious to divulge the identities of the lucky three. Ricky Buzza really was responsible for Caligula. Good for him. Amy cut her off before she could tell her more. "You need to check with these people, Carla, and make sure they're still interested."

"I did, and they are. Surtees isn't going to take up residence, of course, and Tiffany—"

"Wait. Are you saying I voted for Surtees and Tiffany?" Amy was dumbfounded. She couldn't have mistaken Tiffany's chapter, and who but Surtees could write *Womb to Tomb*? Not for the first time, she wondered if that Robetussien character had mixed up her MRI results with those of somebody with a perfectly healthy brain.

"Actually," said Carla.

"Actually what?"

"Actually, I changed my mind about the maximum number. I *can* take all six, especially since Surtees and—"

"Damn it, Carla!" Amy never swore, but this was too much. "You just wasted three hours out of my life." Now she was lying, but Carla deserved it.

"Look, they're all really excited. Grahame Troy is dying to meet you."

"Who's he?"

"She's a friend from my yoga class. She's going through a rough divorce, and this is just perfect for her."

"Skinny White Bitch."

"For sure. She can't weigh a hundred pounds sopping wet."

Amy sighed. "Nobody's going to meet me, Carla. We had a deal. If they want to work with me online, that's fine."

"Oh, they're all signed up for that. I just thought we could all—"

"No."

"—maybe once a week, or twice a month—"

"No."

"Okay. We'll talk about it later."

"No."

"Don't you want to know about the other two newbies?"

"No."

"One of them you already know. It's Brie Spangler, from KPBS-FM."

"Oh." That was a pleasant surprise.

"The other's an ER doctor, from Escondido. His name is Kurt Robetussien. Isn't that a riot?"

Amy stared at Alphonse, who was staring back, head cocked to the left, as he always did when she talked on the phone. Robetussien must have written that oncology nurse thing. How interesting. "Am I supposed to know him too?" she asked, genuinely wondering. "Did he say I did?"

"I don't think so. How would you know him? He works at a hospital."

* * *

After hanging up, Amy sorted out her feelings about Robetussien following her all the way into the workshop retreat. Okay, he had pleasantly threatened to send her a manuscript in exchange for that speedy MRI, and now he had followed through, and it was a pretty good one, at least so far. And yes, he was a likable guy. Still it bothered her that he had turned up like this, mingling with people she already knew, and it wasn't until later that night that she understood why.

Amy was writing again; she was getting published again; she was on the verge of being rediscovered, and it was all on account of her bizarre behavior during a few lost hours, behavior that meant absolutely nothing if it wasn't purposive. Kurt Robetussien was the only person in the world besides Amy who knew the truth about it. He was legally forbidden to share medical information about her, but did her accident qualify as medical information? If Robetussien were a character in cheap fiction (*The Case of the Baneful Blurb*), he'd try to blackmail Amy into pushing his book and she'd have to kill him.

Well, that wasn't going to happen. Still she was vexed, and for a time lay awake wondering why. Maybe it was just the loss of privacy. It was one thing to recognize yourself as an unsightly slapstick victim, splayed out on the ground like a circus clown. It was another to be seen that way by strangers. She wouldn't begrudge their laughter, but their pity would more than sting. The accident was none of their beeswax. If she ran into Robetussien again, she'd have to have an awkward word with him.

Amy drifted into deep sleep, coming awake again only just before sunrise, in the middle of a sex dream involving her much younger self and Anthony Hopkins in footy pajamas. Not for the first time, Amy blushed in the dark.

CHAPTER SIXTEEN

Croatoan

The NPR *All Things Considered* broadcast of her radio interview happened while Amy was putting the finishing touches on her third new story, "You're Funny," about a dying woman who makes people laugh. She begins as a humorless child, chronically disappointed by human behavior and the natural world. While adults exhort her to gape in wonderment at rose petals, rainbows, and the grasping fists of newborns, she has never been moved past mere curiosity to transports of gratitude and joy. She smiles so seldom that her parents, egged on by know-it-all friends, begin to worry. One Thanksgiving, at the age of ten, she surprises her family with a spontaneous smile. (The dinner table, which her father compulsively calls "the groaning board," actually groans rudely when he sets down the huge turkey, and she permits herself a moment of private delight, which is visible to all.) Her mother notices the smile, and then her aunts, and in seconds the entire gathering is transported to gratitude and joy, which annoys the girl. Remembering what women always say when infants smile, she shoots them all down. "It was probably just gas," she says. After a long moment of shocked silence, the group bursts simultaneously into laughter and applause. "You made a joke!" crows her mother. She has done nothing of the kind, but instantly understands what has happened: she has said one thing and meant another thing, and apparently this is hilarious. She has discovered irony years ahead of her time. Although she doesn't understand *why* it's funny to say one thing while meaning something quite different, she finds that presenting an ironic perspective to the world is a kind of gateway to social acceptance, and social acceptance (which she does not otherwise require) is itself a gateway to being allowed to live as she likes. All goes well until she comes to the end of her life—a life spent as a professor of economics, the dismal science; a life spent ironically. She has achieved solid academic success and accidental acclaim as a deadpan wit, the sort who are routinely quoted at parties and to incoming graduate students. One December day she slips on wet ice and, in an otherwise unremarkable fall, drives a pine needle into her wrist. The wound instantly becomes infected. Within hours she is fighting for her life in a hospital bed. When asked for her symptoms, she can manage only, "Terror. Agony. Regret," and the last thing she hears is the chuckling of an old nurse. She has time for an epiphany— *I meant what I said*—but no time to share it with the nurse.

"You're Funny" was uncomfortably close to a fable. In fact, all three pieces, Amy could see now, might come across as lessons rather than stories. But she wasn't at all sure what the lessons added up to, and so comforted herself with the notion that they weren't lessons at all, because they didn't provide answers. Perhaps they were questions in narrative form. This sounded pretentious, but still it was how she meant them. Or how she thought she meant them. It always bothered her when critics praised writers for being "in full control of their craft." You were, or should be, in full control of your sentences, but you had no more control over your stories than a sailor does over the weather. And if you do control your story, the weather isn't real: you're sailing a toy boat in an old MGM tank.

She had just sent the story off to Maxine when her phone started to ring. Carla, Surtees, and the Blaines next door told her that she had just been on NPR. This put Amy in mind of that old joke about the guy who put a dead horse in his bathtub, just so when somebody told him there was a dead horse in his bathtub, he could say, "I know." Amy said "I know" to all three callers, and again later that night to calls from old friends in Maine. She didn't fill anyone in on the coming publicity explosion, because she was just beginning to believe in it, and it frightened her. Still it was pleasant to say "I know" in an offhand tone, as though being broadcast nationally on radio were no big deal. She jotted down "I Know" in her title list.

A week later came a frantic call from Carla. "We've got twenty new applicants for the retreat," she said.

"So what? You don't have room for more than three, or six, or whatever it was. Just turn them down. And stop saying 'we.'"

"But people really want in, because they heard you on NPR."

"There's a way we can make this work," said Harry B.

Amy stared at her phone. "Is this a conference call?"

"Amy, I know you don't want to teach. But they're lined up around the block—"

Carla was exaggerating, but Amy wasn't surprised about a modest ratcheting up of local interest, since the same thing had happened on her teaching blog: an uptick of people wanting to take her online course—eleven since the NPR thing, so that for the first time she had a sizeable number of people on her waiting

list. Amy told Carla this, explaining that she was already dealing
with the fallout from the interview and had no time to do anything else, even if she had been inclined to, which she wasn't.

Predictably, Carla started to whinge, but Harry cut her off.
"We're not asking you to run a workshop," he said.

"Wait! Yes we are, Harry!"

"Unless you want to," said Harry. "We're calling for two reasons. One, we can make money on this thing. Not the residence-
retreat part, which is basically a giveaway, but the twenty new
people who want to take classes here and they're willing to pay
three hundred a pop."

"What's a pop?" asked Amy, still uninterested, but curious.

"The usual. Six-week course, three hours a week."

"How is that possible? Don't they know we're in a recession?
Harry, the locals who take these courses are dead broke. They're
living in upside-down houses. Half of them must be unemployed
by now. Writing workshops are hardly recession-proof enterprises."

"I'm surprised too. Some of them may be spending Christmas
money, but the rest are all attracted by your name."

"Yeah!" said Carla.

"But we've got a couple of people lined up to teach in your
place. Actually, we've got enough money to pay three people, these
two and you, as a consultant. If the newbies know you're consulting, and if you agree to deal with them online from time to time,
we'll probably keep them."

What two people? "Who are the two people?" asked Amy.
"They suck."

"Carla, put a sock in it," said Harry. "One is Marva Leaming."

"I hate her," said Carla.

So did Amy, although she had never actually met her. Marva
Leaming had been a local creative writing guru for at least as long

as Amy had lived in California. She was teaching at the Extension when Amy first started there, and she still taught multiple classes for them. Her classes had filled reliably, while Amy's were always touch and go. She had a following.

None of this would have bothered Amy, except that every now and then she got one of Marva's disciples in her own class, with noxious results. They badgered her for exercises and thought experiments. She compiled a few of these, just to fend the students off. *Write a story backward, using bulleted lists. Write an action story entirely in dialogue. Describe a recent outing, then go back and excise all modifiers.* Amy didn't really see the point of these, and neither did most of Leaming's disciples. What about freewriting? they would ask. What about metaphor-building? Inevitably, Amy drove them away when, frustrated by their demands, she would break into a rant. How much freewriting do you suppose Charles Dickens did? How about Herman Melville? Has anybody uncovered Shakespeare's surefire remedy for writer's block? Amy's own surefire remedy was to kick out any student who, having contracted to bring in a piece of fiction on an assigned date, failed to do so. It generally worked like a charm. Deadlines were the only cure she knew.

Every childbirth drama Amy had ever read in workshop had been written by a Leaming disciple. Amy often considered posting a list of verboten topics (nursing home life imagined by eighteen-year-olds; stories that begin with alarm clocks going off) but never did, because it would have been mean. But because of Marva Leaming she learned to warn during the first class that stories about childbirth were cliché minefields. There may have been a time when obstetrical events were shrouded in mystery, but that time was long past. This never deterred the Lemmings, as Amy privately called them, who defiantly wrote at excruciating length about water breaking all over expensive new shoes, dilating cervixes, pushing and not-pushing, and that delirious moment when the baby emerges and all agony is instantly forgotten, though apparently not forever, since the stories, most of them barely disguised memoirs, generally focused on flamboyantly described pain and the central character's heroic ability to transcend it. No matter how gently Amy criticized these pieces, their authors remained unchastened. "Marva says we should write what we know," they would say. Amy would try to explain as kindly as possible that this was exactly what they hadn't done. They weren't writing what they knew; they were writing what they'd already read a million times before. They weren't seeing with their own eyes, not at all. Occasionally a Lemming would understand her point, but to no avail. "Marva says writing is communal." In what universe?

"Has Lemming agreed to do it?" she asked.

"Leaming," said Harry. "Yes, she has."

"But only if you don't want to," said Carla, while Harry muttered in the background.

"You said you had two," said Amy. "Who's the other?"

There was a two-beat silence. "It's not exactly a teacher," Carla finally said. "It's a writing coach."

"A what?"

"A writing coach. You know. She's a motivational speaker, like a life coach. Actually, she's a life coach too."

"Oh my God."

"Holly Hamm," said Harry.

"She sounds like a Christmas entrée."

"You can Google her," said Harry. "It's not important. Our point is, the point of this call, really, we do have a proposition for you that we think you'll like."

Amy had already Googled Holly Hamm, whose professionally constructed website was listed first on a page full of holiday recipe sites. Holly, while not exactly porcine, resembled a festive Christmas ornament, with a megawatt smile and springy brown hair. She looked like a prep school gym teacher on speed. One of her college degrees (from "Beauchamp University") purported to be in physical education. She was also a licensed practical nurse, and she was a diplomate, whatever that meant, in "dietetics," "human psychology," and "therapeutic choreography." Though the page promoted her as a writing coach, she was experienced in all sorts of coaching, including, as Carla had mentioned, the coaching of life itself, for which she was also "certified." She had presented writing seminars internationally, most recently in Rangoon. Her site claimed that she "wore many hats." She was equally proficient at fencing, storytelling, and dressage.

"This is horseshit," said Amy.

Carla gasped. Amy never swore.

"It says here that her weekend-long coaching seminars 'show aspiring writers how to turn their experiences into fiction that sells.' How can you even think about hiring this person? She's a con artist."

"I see your point," said Harry, "but she fills rooms. She can help us widen our base."

"Amy," said Carla, "I don't like Marva Leaming either, but Holly's the real deal. She can put butts in seats."

"How very inspiring," said Amy. "Look, I have work to do. I'd wish you luck, but that would be immoral. If my name appears in any of your ads, please remove it."

"Wait!"

Amy hung up. For the next few minutes she tried to shrug the whole thing off, and then laugh it away, but the laughter was hollow and the shrug plain embarrassing. No one was watching. She dragged Alphonse out of a deep sleep and out into the street, force-marching him uphill while she talked to herself. They passed the coyote spot and kept going, all the way to the big rock at the summit of the cul-de-sac. There she came to the gross realization that her feelings were hurt.

How could she have spent so much time and energy on these people and have them come away knowing so little about her and what she valued, exercising such awful judgment, willing to do business with characters like Leaming and Hamm? Carla and Harry were, she hated to admit, her friends, and they didn't know her at all. This was what hurt: not the hiring of her old rival or the idea of paying a charlatan to milk the suckers, but the fact that they hadn't realized how offended she would be. Nothing she had taught them had stuck. She had imagined herself real in their minds—not deeply understood, as only Max had understood her, but still distinguishable from other people, unique, not quite a cipher—and all the while she had had only two dimensions. Just a name and a shape and a cluster of attributes. She was the writing teacher, the eccentric with the dog, the Sniper's nemesis. She was a flat character, and while she had never aspired to more from the world at large, she had apparently expected more from her friends. How humiliating. How childish.

By the time Alphonse dragged her back indoors, she had formulated a plan of action. There were six messages on her answering machine, all of which she erased unheard. Obviously they were craven apologies. She had hung up on them, and even Carla and Harry could not have mistaken her anger for anything else. She called them back. Carla picked up on the first ring.

"Amy, I'm so sorry! I never meant—"

"Here's the deal," said Amy. "Hire whoever you want to work

with the twenty new people, the people *lined up around the block,* assuming there really are twenty new people lined up around the block, assuming there really is a block, but go ahead and give them Marva Leaming, Coach Hamm, Mahatma Kane Jeeves, whoever the hell you want, I really don't care, but the rule is, they are to have no contact whatsoever with the six retreat people: Ricky, Surtees, Tiffany, Robetussien, Brie, and that Skinny Bitch person, although I'd love to throw her to the Lemmings, and if you can figure out a way to do that, go ahead. I'll come down once a month and do a workshop with those six alone. The rest of the time, we'll work together online. I want half of whatever money you take in. If the Lemmings get their mitts on even one of my people, the deal's off, and I'm gone, with half the money anyway. Take it or leave it."

"And your name on the brochure," said Harry.

"Absolutely not. I won't have my name on the same piece of paper with those clowns." Amy was beginning to breathe normally. Briefly she wished Maxine could hear her. She'd be so impressed. Half the money! Amy had never demanded money in her life.

"How about two brochures," said clever Harry. "One for the retreat; one for the ongoing workshop/seminar/motivational thing. Your name will be on the retreat brochure, right under the title."

"Which is what?"

"We're thinking of 'Something Colony,'" said Carla. "Amy, I'm really, really sorry."

"Like a penal colony?" asked Amy. "Devil's Island?"

"So far," said Harry B, "all we have is Birdhouse Writers' Colony."

"Too wordy."

"That's what I said," said Carla.

"Exactly," said Harry. "We need one word, like Breadloaf."

"How about Meatloaf?"

"She's still pissed off," said Carla.

"Cheese Log."

Harry laughed.

"I'm all right, Carla," Amy said. She had indeed calmed down, partly because she felt "empowered," an icky word but useful on the fly, and partly because she was distracted by wordplay. "How about Croatoan?"

"That sounds familiar," said Harry.

"It's a mystery word carved into a tree in Virginia in 1590. An entire English colony went missing and left only the word behind."

"So we'd just call it Croatoan?"

"Yes. With the subtitle 'The Missing Writers' Colony.'"

"I like it," said Harry.

"So do I," said Carla, "although won't some people think it's just a joke?"

Amy said nothing.

"Oh, I get it!" said Carla. "Amy, you're so funny."

"Bye," said Amy.

"I'll send you the paperwork," said Harry B.

Later that day, Amy wrote down "Croatoan" and "You Don't Know Me" in her notebook, briefly touched base with Maxine, who said something new might be in the works with NPR, and fed herself and her dog, all the while thinking about Harry B and how competent and efficient the man was. As soon as she read him the riot act about what she was willing to do and the terms under which she would do it, he came up with the idea of two brochures, neatly separating her from the other two people on their payroll. Later still, she recalled that before she had slammed down the phone on the two of them, Harry had mentioned a proposition, one he was sure she'd like. She'd forgotten all about it. What had it been? she wondered. And why hadn't he countered with it, when she presented her list of terms?

She looked over at Alphonse, who was busy cleaning his front paws. She loved to watch him do this, how his long tongue would curl delicately around and in between each toe, over and over. Sometimes he did this at night in the dark, waking up to do his ablutions, as though prompted by conscience, the licking sounds soft and comforting to hear. He must have had a great mother. "You're a good dog," she told him. He rewarded her, as usual, with a mordant gaze; his version of "I know." "Hey, there's another dead horse in the bathtub," she told him fondly, and simultaneously realized the truth: that Harry, and possibly even Carla, had herded her into that list of demands. No, not Carla, she wasn't that clever, but Harry was a trained mediator. No wonder he was ready with the "two brochures" solution. Harry's proposition was the very thing she came up with herself. Maybe not all of it—maybe he hadn't planned on giving her half the money. Maybe he'd planned on giving her more! "Sonofa*bitch*," Amy said. Alphonse raised one eyebrow and turned back to his paws.

Harry had known she would never work with Marva Leaming or a writing coach. He had let Carla worry about that possibility, thus adding to the verisimilitude of the whole telephone conversation, which, she could see now, had amounted to a kind of stealth negotiation. Still, the more she thought about it, the less outraged she became. He had also known something else about Amy: that she cared about the students she already had. That she would never abandon them to the ministrations of these people. Harry knew her, a little bit. So, in her own juvenile way, did Carla. Amy hadn't been wrong about them after all.

She lay awake for a time thinking about that, and how, after Max died, she had neither wanted nor needed to be known by anyone. He had known her as well, Amy guessed, as it was possible to know anybody; he often said that she was the only person in the world who knew him, and she had no reason to doubt him. He was fond of his lovers, some of them, but that was all. She couldn't remember the names of hers. Sex was best between strangers. Love was possible only through knowledge. Or perhaps knowledge only through love. In the beginning, it was *I know what you're up to. I know what you did. I know you like that guy.* And then *I know you feel like hell. I know you can do better than that. I know your childhood stories, your most embarrassing moment, what frightens you more than anything. I know what makes you laugh.* Their friends banned them from charades. She'd get up there and signal "book title" and "three words" and he'd say *"Appointment at Appomattox."* "I know you," he said at the end. "I know you so much."

What did it mean that now, after all these years, she wanted to be known again?

CHAPTER SEVENTEEN

The Wheel of Tide

Amy had been working so hard on new fiction that she'd paid less attention than usual to her blog, GO AWAY. She had kept it for years without making regular entries in it: months might go by before she thought of a new posting idea, or a new list to include, to supplement the original lists. The lists were never intended to be anything but amusing. The list of lists included:

FUNNY LOOKING WORDS (like "disembosom")

FUNNY SOUNDING WORDS (like "phlebotomy")

HYBRID TITLES ("Arms and the Man Who Came to Dinner")

ODD HEADLINES ("Man Eating Catfish Displayed in Memphis Aquarium")

MOST INTRIGUING OPENING PARAGRAPHS OF REAL NEWS STORIES INVOLVING PEOPLE SMUGGLING THINGS IN THEIR PANTS

WORDS THAT ARE THEORETICALLY INDEPENDENT BUT ACTUALLY ONLY EVER USED WITH ONE SPECIFIC OTHER WORD ("trove")

ADJECTIVES THAT ONLY EVER MODIFY ONE THING ("tumescent")

NOUNS THAT APPARENTLY CAN ONLY BE PLURAL (examples included "fantods" and "tongs")

TITLES OF BOOKS PUBLISHED TEN YEARS AGO THAT YOU CAN NAME OFF THE TOP OF YOUR HEAD

The previous December, a few weeks prior the Birdbath Incident, Amy had begun a new list:

REALISTIC NOVEL PLOTS

under which she included storylines from writing exercises she had once used:

A devoted couple suffers a devastating car crash from which only the man recovers, the woman dying at the scene. He is crippled by grief and guilt. At night he scans the skies, as though she might suddenly appear to him. "Where are you?" he demands. But her voice does not whisper in his ear, nor does her ghost appear in dreams or mirrors, nor does he even spot, out of the corner of his eye, passersby whom he mistakes for her. Memories of her inevitably fade away, until he needs to look at a picture in order to recall her face. The end.

A poor but innovative and talented boy enters a hot air balloon construction contest in which all other contestants have access to expensive, high-tech equipment. The boy has only rudimentary materials: bagstring, paraffin, and Mylar scavenged from Dumpsters and painstakingly assembled and glued. The other contestants snort with derision when they see the finished entry and even try to get him disqualified, without success, since the judges both like and pity the boy. On the day of the contest, his patchwork hot air balloon comes in last place, receiving a hastily composed honorable mention which is accidentally misspelled as an "Honorable Memtion." The end.

A boy and girl meet in college, date, fall in love, and break up senior year. They go on to marry other people and raise families, but neither is truly happy. They meet again at their twenty-fifth reunion. He has been divorced for five years; her husband has been unfaithful to her throughout their marriage, and she is in the process of obtaining a divorce. Initially, they do not hit it off. She finds him stiff and prematurely aged; her bitterness turns him off. But over the next two years they find excuses to call or email each other, and ultimately they find themselves deeply in love—which, they admit, they had not been when they were young. Their marriage is a low-key affair, but they splurge on their honeymoon hotel in Marrakesh. On the second night, their wing of the hotel catches fire, and they both die horribly. The end.

As was her custom, Amy had posted the list and then forgotten about it. When, while recovering from her injuries, she looked in on GO AWAY in the New Year, she was disturbed by the number and tenor of comments it had prompted. She was used to pleasant, often thoughtful, seldom snarky comments and suggestions. Occasionally other writers would visit her page and chime in, adding to her lists. In this case, though, the list was a bomb. Readers misunderstood her purpose. Comments included: "I must say I never took you for a proponent of 'sick humor.' Remind me never to read another one of your books"; "These are cheap shots, Amy"; "What's your point? Are you allergic to happy endings, or what?"; "This would be precocious if you were twelve years old. As it is, it's just very sad." The most discomfiting comment was: "WTF!!! LMAO! GFY AimEEE!" She understood the first two acronyms but had to consult Carla for the third. "It probably means 'Good for you,'" she said. "Or it could mean, you know, 'Go do something to yourself.' But I'm sure not."

Amy didn't mind criticism but bristled at being misconstrued. This particular list had been culled from one of her old workshop teaching notebooks, and it was supposed to be all about a perennial workshop issue: real life vs. fiction. When beginners were criticized for unconvincing plots, they often objected, "But this is based on a totally true story! This really happened!" As though facts trumped anything. She would explain that it was the writer's job to make the events plausible, which, in their case, the writers had not done. We don't read fiction to learn facts; we read it to make sense. While their eyes glazed over, she would talk about the fictional universe as opposed to the actual one, becoming caught up in ideas that evidently fascinated only her. The fictional universe is *knowable,* she would say. The fiction writer is god. She creates people whose lives actually *cohere.* But what if the writer is an existentialist? a wise guy would ask. What a terrific question! Well, then, that fictional world is meaningless, and the reader can *know* that, because that's how the writer has set it up. Amy herself wasn't sure what this last claim actually meant.

To aid in her lectures she had worked up a series of models for her students—plot lines that no publisher would buy into, for stories no one would want to read, and for a variety of reasons, none of which was because such things never happened in the real world. The last one in the list—the one about the happy couple who die in a fire—was the one she most often revised. She used various smoothly flowing plots, dramas, romances, comedies, and abrupted them with plane crashes and natural disasters.

One alternate was about a young girl's fraught relationship with her mother and how that relationship deepens in complexity over the whole of the girl's life, as she comes to know her mother as a person as mysterious as any other. Through years of misunderstandings and estrangements they have always loved each other; toward the story's end, they begin to *like* each other, the daughter particularly admiring her mother's refusal to go soft in old age. (The residents and keepers at her nursing home peg her as "negative.") The daughter makes arrangements to bring her mother home with her, renovating her own small house to accommodate them both. A few days before the mother is to be transferred, a serial killer, posing as the cable installer, attacks and strangles the daughter. The end.

Perversely, Amy added this particular variation to her blog list, prompting more outcries. The fact that these plots never worked well as pedagogical tools probably should have dissuaded her from airing them on the Internet, but she dug in her heels. She didn't have a large blog readership, but it was much larger than the average class, so somebody was bound to understand her. One in a hundred was all she needed to set her mind at rest. Toward that end, she added an example with an ending that was not depressing or horrific.

A young girl is killed (murdered, perhaps; or slain by a hit-and-run driver), and her older brother becomes obsessed with finding out who killed her. Police leads peter out; years go by; he joins the Air Force, intending to make a career out of it, but, haunted by his sister's death, resigns his commission, returns to college, and becomes a crime scene investigator in Cincinnati, his hometown. He marries and begins a family, but his spare time is mostly spent investigating the murder/accidental death of his sister. He narrows down the suspect pool to three men, one dead, all local. He doesn't yet have enough information to get the attention of the local prosecuting attorney, but signs are that with continued persistence he will prevail. His wife, who has been patient with his obsession, gets pregnant for a third time and, faced with an overload of domestic worries, sits Peter down and explains that things have to change: that if he values his life with her and his daughters, he must let go of the past and devote his attention to them. They stay up all night talking. He agrees reluctantly to try. He finds this difficult at first but surprisingly not impossible. He has, he sees, a hope of happiness. After awhile, he no longer glances toward the file cabinet where he keeps all his carefully gleaned evidence. He never finds out who killed his sister and eventually stops wondering about it. The end.

The day after the NPR interview aired, Amy checked in on her blog and found ten full pages of comments, some from well-wishers weighing in on the interview, but most in furious response to the list that nobody liked, which she now retitled "THE LIST THAT NOBODY LIKES." There were new voices among the comments, some loutish, some learned, and as usual everybody misunderstood her. She was particularly disheartened by a comment from SamLWeiss, who obviously knew something about how fiction was constructed:

These plots are ridiculous. I see your point, but no writer worth his salt would, for example, junk up a lit-fic novel—a book about a man finally understanding what his wife means to him—with all that crap about crime scene analysis and suspect lists. I mean, you might mention the early trauma and his obsession with his sister, but you'd do this in the context of the larger story, the story about his growth. This is a character-driven novel derailed by a cheap plot device.

Amy was eager to get back to a new story idea of her own, but she could see that NPR was bringing out the torches and pitchforks, and she was afraid that if she didn't stop and explain herself, things would get out of hand. As Maxine said, and whether intentionally or not, she was building "a base." She posted a frigid response to SamLWeiss:

I'm not sure you see my point at all, which is my fault, as I neglected to signal with a festive "LOL" or smiley face that I was joking. My point was pretty much the one you've just made: that successful fiction isn't junked up with ill-fitting events. On the other hand, actual lives are. Ask any biographer. Part of his job is to ignore or somehow morph the stuff that doesn't fit. Our narratives are incoherent, at least until we recollect them in story form. The lives of many of us, most of us, do not follow classic narrative arcs, SamLWeiss. Some have competing arcs, going off in all directions, like bad flower arrangements. My own arc probably looks like a polygraph readout. So far, I guess, I'm character-driven, but I'm pretty sure I don't lead a genre life—not even a lit-fic life. Do you? And I know, and so should you, that at some time in the future my arc, and your own, will be derailed by a cheap plot device. Perhaps I'll put that on my tombstone.

After a pause, she decided to change the name of the list once more, and for the final time, to:

THE ACCIDENT-DRIVEN LIFE

A week later, as Amy was wrangling with Carla by email about setting a date for her first retreat appearance, Maxine called. "You've really done it now," she said. "You've teed off the Christers. This is brilliant, babe."

At her urging, Amy checked out GO AWAY, now teeming with hundreds of comments, most of which actually said (or boiled down to) "You are not an accident!" In fact, so many said just that, no more, no less, that Amy suspected they had been assigned by an organized cabal of pastors. "Accident" and "luck," Amy learned, were the dirtiest words in the Fundamentalist lexicon. The Anti-Accident Brigade wrote to cheer Amy up, to assure her that everything happens for a reason. They often said just that: "Everything happens for a reason!" The Brigade was divided into two general schools: those who allowed that terrible, inexplicable things ("things *we* call accidents") happen in real life, but they're all part of God's mysterious plan; and those who claimed, against all evidence, that God would never allow for such terrible things in the first place, at least not the way Amy had described them. One of them, Betty1986, wrote:

> You've left out the most important parts of these "plots." That loving bride and groom perish together, their arms around each other, uplifted by the certain hope of heaven. The murdered daughter has time to show her faith to her murderer: to face her martyrdom with joy. Who knows, she may have started this lost soul on the path to

his own redemption! None of these plots are accident-driven. They
are purpose-driven, and the purpose is often not ours to know.

Some of the lengthiest comments came in the form of testi-
monies, personal true stories of "so-called accidents" that had enlightened their lives, or turned their lost lambs from the crooked
path. They wrote about being "blessed" with cancer, heart attacks, paralyzing strokes; worse, of never experiencing the full-
ness of God's love until their own children were taken from them
by some ghastly—and literal—deus ex machina.

Jackinthepulpit91 posted the entire first verse of an old hymn,
"It Is Well with My Soul," famously written by Horatio Spafford,
a businessman who, upon learning that his four daughters had
perished together in a winter crossing of the Atlantic Ocean,
penned the undying words

When peace, like a river, attendeth my way,
When sorrows like sea billows roll;
Whatever my lot, Thou hast taught me to say,
It is well, it is well, with my soul.
Refrain:
It is well, with my soul,
It is well, with my soul,
It is well, it is well, with my soul.

Apparently he had written the hymn as he voyaged east to join
his grieving wife, when his ship's captain pointed out that they
were sailing over the very spot where the *Ville du Havre* had gone
down, at which point Spafford had (in Amy's imagination) dashed
in unseemly haste to his stateroom, inked a pen, and started to
write. Jackinthepulpit91 also included a link to a page where Amy

could actually hear his own entire family singing this hymn, along with many other favorites.

Amy had been raised in a Congregational church and could remember singing this very hymn, a pretty one, without knowing its history—a history which she now could not help finding less than inspirational. What father, beholding his children's watery grave, is immediately moved to assess the health of his own soul? How about giving a thought to them? How were their souls doing there, in the freezing water, as their heavy garments tugged them down? She did some quick research on H. Spafford and found that the posted facts were true though incomplete. Spafford was no stranger to what heathens call "accidents." He lost his infant son to illness and then all his money in the Great Chicago Fire. Spafford's hymn was set to music by Philip Bliss, a gospel singer and composer, who himself died three years later, along with his wife, in a catastrophe trifecta (bridge collapse–train crash–fire), which the spectacularly terrible poet Julia Moore memorialized as the "Ashtabula Bridge Disaster":

Have you heard of the dreadful fate
Of Mr. P. P. Bliss and wife?
Of their death I will relate,
And also others lost their life;
Ashtabula Bridge disaster,
Where so many people died
Without a thought that destruction
Would plunge them 'neath the wheel of tide.

Amy pasted this stanza into her posted reply to Jackinthepulpit91, without explanation and attribution. Let him figure it out. She called Maxine back. "Why is this *brilliant*?" she asked. "I don't have time to argue with these people. And I don't want to be mean to them. If their faith sustains them, it's not my business. I just want them to go away. Hence the title of my blog."

Maxine coughed up a lung. "Don't you see what you've got going here?"

"Where? On the Internet? It's an amusement, Maxine, mostly to me, and to a few other people. That's it. That's the only reason I started it."

"Not anymore," said Maxine. "You're getting attention. What did I tell you? They're coming out of the woodwork."

"That's supposed to *excite* me? Is this my new readership category? Things that come out of the woodwork?"

"Settle down," said Maxine. "We're not just talking readership anymore. Mostly readers, okay, but you're on the radio now. Who knows what's gonna happen next? It's a new world, babe."

"I was on the radio *once*."

"Trust me, that was just the start. They're interested in doing another one next month. Maybe a regular thing."

"A regular thing about me?" Amy's heart began to race. "I can't be a regular thing, Maxine. I don't have that much to say. This isn't funny."

"Of course not just you. You and a couple other writers. You know. Shooting off your mouths about stuff."

"Maxine, I'm not sure I like this." Things were happening too fast. Amy felt buffeted.

"Which is why I wasn't going to tell you until we worked out the kinks. Forget it for now, okay? Don't worry about it. Have a drink."

Amy put the phone down to pour herself some wine. "Back to the blog," she said. "Tell me again why it's a good thing to be attracting woodwork creatures to a site devoted to idle reflection, most of it of interest mainly to me."

"Give me a second." Amy could hear the click of a lighter. Maxine took a drag.

"Are you still smoking?" asked Amy. "With those lungs?"

"Here's the deal. You're not gonna understand it, but you are gonna have to trust me. You're not just a writer now. You're a package. In case you haven't noticed, writers don't just write, babe. They package themselves, or they have people do it for them. People like yours truly."

Amy held her tongue.

"Shut up," said Maxine. "You think Charles Dickens wasn't a package? You think Mark Twain wasn't a package? Edith Wharton? Hemingway? Fitzgerald, there was a package! They were all great writers, sure, but they were also commodities. They spent as much time in the spotlight as they did staring at the old blank page. The only difference today is every idiot who writes a book expects to be a brand name."

"Like Jenny Marzen," said Amy, in spite of herself.

"Exactamento."

"Maxine, tell me something I don't know. I've looked at their stupid websites. I've seen their head shots. I've watched them on C-SPAN. Hell, I was trapped one time in an elevator with some silly girl who thought I should know who she was because she had written some excrescence about saving your marriage with sex toys."

"I know the one you mean. She got on *Oprah*."

Amy took a deep breath. "Maxine, I'm not going on *Oprah*."

"You are a very eccentric person," said Maxine.

"Because I don't want to be on *Oprah*?"

"This is what I'm trying to tell you. You're what my pop used to call an oddball. You've got talent and smarts and you're funny and you're not like anybody else out there. And you're not afraid of anything. You can do radio. You're a natural. Who knows, maybe you could do Charlie Rose."

"Heck, why not?" said Amy. "Let's schedule that while I'm convalescing from my lobotomy."

"What I'm suggesting just for now," said Maxine, "is that you let this blog discussion do its thing. Nudge it along. Give it its own page, its own subtitle. Make it all about them and you. Get a little back-and-forth going with these people. You don't have to rain on their parade unless you want to. Pick out the letters that interest you; there must be some. You could set it up as a kind of advice column—"

"Absolutely not!"

"Not advice, then, but a dialogue. If you disagree with somebody, go ahead and explain yourself—your own ideas. You're good at that."

"But then I'll have one of those wretched opinion blogs. They're a dime a dozen, Maxine. Everybody's online disgorging about politics and animal abuse and their innermost fears and what they just had for breakfast."

"Yes, and they're all talking to themselves, or to their own circle of friends. But you're not. Not anymore."

Amy was silent. She was certain Maxine was wrong, but if she went along with the gag for a week or so and nothing happened, and all the unwanted visitors drifted off, then Maxine would get off her back. "I'm not going to spend any real time doing this," she said. "Just a few minutes here and there. All right? All right? Can we just not talk about this anymore?"

"You got it, babe," said Maxine. "I'll call you in a few."

"Maxine?"

"Yeah?"

"You've got me all wrong, you know. I'm afraid of everything. I'm afraid of spiders, and planes, and doctors. You name it. I'm afraid of the dark. The dark, Maxine."

Maxine laughed and coughed. "Yeah," she said, "but you're not afraid of failure, and you're not afraid of success. You really don't care much either way. I've never met another one like you. We're gonna use it. You'll see."

CHAPTER EIGHTEEN

Case Studies

After a couple of days of sulking, Amy took Maxine's advice and set up a separate page on her site, entitled I KNOW YOU ARE, BUT WHAT AM I? and tried to fix it so she could organize combative comments and appropriate responses according to topic, alphabetically. But she couldn't figure out how to inform blog visitors of this new page or what system to use when they got there. Ricky Buzza had, she remembered, learned from his brother how to monkey with websites and was picking up extra cash freelancing, so she called him for advice, hoping he could talk her through the steps on the phone, but the process was too complicated for that. He showed up at her house with a pizza and ended up camping out for most of the night. If Amy had known this was going to happen, she would have stopped it, which would have been a shame. Instead the night unfolded quietly, beginning with an awkward chat, proceeding through an efficient rehaul of her website, and from that to the sort of occasion Amy hadn't experienced in thirty years: a pleasant evening spent in the company of another human being.

Carla had of course told him that he had been "selected" to attend her retreat. Although he scrupulously avoided thanking Amy for the selection or discussing *Caligula's Scalpel* directly, he talked about how much he was looking forward to April, when he could spend his days doing nothing but writing. Amy couldn't resist asking why he wasn't already doing that, since he had been out of work for most of the previous year.

"Steady work, yeah," he said. "The *North County Times* cut me loose. But I've been doing stuff like this, picking up odd jobs, to help my dad with the mortgage. He never asks for it, but I know he didn't plan on me moving back home. When I'm living at Carla's, I can just hand the stipend over to Dad."

Amy didn't ask how much the "stipend" was. Knowing Carla, it was generous.

Amy had not had a visitor since Holly Antoon, and before Holly, since the last class meeting of her final non-virtual workshop, which had famously ended in mayhem. Visitors—even cable guys and computer repair people—always brought out a stillness in her house, as though it were holding its breath until they left. With no other model to go by, it seemed to impersonate some decrepit roadside museum, like *The Thing?* Having Ricky there made her conscious of its drabness and clutter, a state with which she was ordinarily comfortable.

For instance, the maple bookcase that Alphonse had knocked over during the Antoon interview two months ago had not been righted, nor had its spilled books even been picked up and piled on the floor or coffee table, since Amy never spent time in the parlor. While Ricky finished with her website, Amy raised the bookcase and began to shove the books back inside, all the while annoyed with herself for being shamed into doing it.

"Can I give you a hand?" he called.

"I'm fine," she said, but he asked more than once, and then, magically, by two o'clock in the morning, they had polished off almost two bottles of Syrah and rearranged Amy's entire library. Either Ricky had grown up a lot over the last year or Amy had not paid him enough attention in the past to get an accurate read. She had basically dismissed him as a juvenile lead, born to pine after Tiffany Zuniga and curse his fate when she shooed him away. He was actually a bright and funny guy who knew more about the world than she had at his age, probably because of his experience as a reporter. He had worked for only five years, but he was wise to the ways of school boards and other low-level politicos. Before he was let go, he had finally gotten some experience on the crime beat. As the two blew away dust and began to set up category stations on the coffee table, he entertained Amy with the Double Bubble Laundromat Murders, which took place in Rancho Bernardo and involved a trapezoid of wife-swappers, a violation of ground rules, lots of hurt feelings, and a dead patent attorney stuffed into an industrial-size clothes dryer.

"His body was discovered by a divorced dad who'd come in after midnight to do his kids' laundry. He called the cops and then hung around. When I interviewed him, he wouldn't shut up. He told me that when he opened up the dryer and saw the guy in there, 'Right then,' he says, 'I suspected foul play.'"

She had very few books that had been published in the last ten or fifteen years. She almost never bought them, and when sent review copies, she donated them to the Escondido Public Library, even when she had liked them, because she knew she would never look at them again. Most of her books were old and seriously bunged up, some of them missing a front or back cover. There were few first editions, most of them gifts from Max's friends. She had once chanced upon an underpriced first edition of the *Spoon River Anthology* at an AAUW book sale and for a short while been excited by the find, but really, it was a book, like any other book. A good book, readable, in one piece. She didn't understand the allure of first editions.

"You're a collector," said Ricky, surveying a four-foot pile. "I've never heard of most of this stuff."

"No reason you should have," she said. "They just mean something to me, or most of them do, or they did once. I've never seen the point of collecting things, especially books. If you collect things, you have to worry about them and put them in boxes or covers or behind glass, and you never actually use them."

Ricky doled out morsels of pizza crust to Alphonse, who would shadow him throughout the evening, never taking his eyes from his right hand. Dogs, Amy had discovered, made an intense study of human hands. The only way Amy could ever convince him she had no food cruelly secreted about her person was to show him her empty palms.

"My granddad has this one," Ricky said, holding up a copy of *The Handbook of Skits and Stunts.* "I never understood why. It's not like we ever did anything with it. It's got the lamest bunch of party games in it." He thumbed through the book, which Amy hadn't opened since she was in her twenties, having inherited it from Max's father. "Listen to this stunt: '*See the Weenie.* Raise your hands up to eye level, put the tips of your forefingers only nearly together, and focus on a distant object. An illusion of a frankfurter, floating in space, is created.' Can you imagine what would happen now if you walked up to a kid and asked him if he wanted to play See the Weenie?"

"In the first place, these games were intended for adults. Also the handbook was published in more innocent times," said Amy, as she tried to see the weenie through her own forefingers. It didn't work. "What's the publication date?"

"Nineteen fifty-three."

"We were still saying 'only nearly together' in 1953. It sounds so much older, like something from *Little Women*. Now we would say 'close together.'"

"So why," asked Ricky, still laughing about the weenie, "did your father-in-law and my grandfather have the same silly book?"

"Probably everybody had it. Probably it was a moneymaker in 1953. I can remember lots of books like that, books that everybody had. *By Love Possessed. Kon-Tiki. Power of Positive Thinking. The Egg and I.*"

"The fifties," said Ricky, nodding sagely as he opened a new bottle, "were a time of great conformity."

"The fifties," said Amy, "were a time when they weren't publishing two hundred thousand books a year. If you were a reader, you didn't have that many choices. Are you saying we don't live in a time of great conformity right now?"

Ricky, his back up, retorted with lists of choices—pop music, TV channels, movies, blogs—arguing that there can hardly be *widespread conformity* with so many niches from which to choose. Amy replied that *niche* was a marketing term: that the whole point of a niche was the *fit*. "If you *fit*," she said, "what difference does it make whether you're fitting into an alcove or an auditorium?"

By this point—close to midnight—all the hardbacks were on the floor, with man, woman, and dog happily swimming among them, clearing out spaces for kneeling or starting a new category or, in Alphonse's case, for lying on his back licking pizza sauce off his teeth. In the beginning there had been just two categories, fiction and non. Now castles began to form: Reference books. History. Poetry. Humor. Literary Analysis. Science. Ricky could not persuade her to divide fiction into subcategories.

In the Reference pile were three editions of *Merriam-Webster's Collegiate,* three visual dictionaries, books of synonyms and antonyms, and a ragged pamphlet entitled *World's Worst Metaphors,* which distracted Amy for a quarter hour, so happy was she to have rediscovered it. There were useless but entertaining single-volume encyclopedias. There were four copies of *Fowler's,* one of which she set aside for Ricky, who wanted to know the point of visual dictionaries. "They're indispensible," she explained. "For instance, you're in the middle of a scene, and you need to show an angry, disappointed man, alone in his house, deserted by his wife and children, taking stock of his life, noticing the shabbiness of the furnishings, the ugliness of the prints on the wall, and he's trudging up the staircase and sees that termites are actually eating away at one of the posts that support the handrail."

"Wait—there are termites *inside* the house? Why would there be termites inside the house?"

"I don't know. The point is, you need to find the word for 'post that supports the handrail.' So you get out your trusty visual dictionary—"

"Sweet," said Ricky.

"And you find a picture of a staircase, with arrows and labels for the parts—and there it is: *baluster.*"

Ricky thought for a moment. "Realistically, though, how many readers know what a baluster is?"

"Not the writer's problem. They'll either figure it out from context or just make something up and keep going."

"I'm totally getting one," he said. Amy put one of her visual dictionaries in a grocery bag along with the *Fowler's*, to send home with him.

The Reference castle developed its own surrounding villages, with guides to reptiles, birds, butterflies, spiders and insects, mammals, plants, seashells and fish, and books on carpentry tools, masonry for hobbyists, chicken-sexing, how-to manuals. *Build That Gazebo! Renovate That Stoop!* There was a locksmith's bible. There was a series called *Peeps at Many Lands,* written near the turn of the previous century, offering simple-minded glimpses of Egypt, Australia, and Italy.

The oddest book in the pile, if Ricky's goggling reaction to it was anything to go by, was a huge primeval medical text entitled *Constipation in Adults and Children,* published in 1897. Someone had found it in his attic and shown it to Max, who thought it so amusing that he often read from it at parties. Max taught Romance languages, but his hobby was the history of Western medicine, or the Cavalcade of Quacks. He and Amy may have shared a phobia of hospitals and doctors, but he eased his fears with investigation and ridicule, whereas Amy was way too squeamish to comfort herself in this way. She had kept the book for sentimental reasons, which now struck her as inadequate. As Ricky opened the book Amy said, "Don't. You'll be sorry if you do."

"Why?" Ricky glanced down at what Amy was sure was one of the book's copious illustrations. "Oh my god. What was wrong with these people?"

"I told you not to look."

"What *is* all this? There are all these exercises and instruments. Here's *the Atzperger Apparatus.* Listen to this: 'I have seen very good results in building up a broken-down nervous system, from a properly arranged hot-air bath of very short duration, followed by the cold rain-bath or the Scotch douche.' What's a

Scotch douche? Didn't they have Ex-lax? What was the big deal about constipation? Oh my god. *The self-acting clysopump.* There's a whole chapter on 'flatus.' What's flatus?"

"Look it up. You're sitting right next to a dictionary." Amy had located her old copy of Richard Krafft-Ebing's *Psychopathia Sexualis* and was thumbing through it, remembering how, as a child, curious about sex but unwilling to sacrifice her privacy, let alone her dignity, by consulting an adult, she had discovered this tome in the desk drawer of a maternal uncle and swiped it, staying up nights to school herself in the ways of love. It was a miracle, she later realized, that she hadn't been ruined for life. Assuming that she had not. The case histories alone implied that the human race, with which the child Amy was not familiar, was unredeemable. It had been published a few years prior to the constipation book. What a jolly age that must have been.

On the positive side, these old books assumed an impressive level of erudition from their readership. Krafft-Ebing, apparently out of concern for propriety, would break into Latin at the drop of a hat. "Listen to this," she said. " 'He would often stuff long gloves with wool or some such material to make them resemble arms and hands. Them he would make *tritus member inter brachia talia artificiala* until he had achieved his object.' " While reading Amy saw that she chose this passage precisely because she figured Ricky wouldn't understand Latin. She and Ricky did not know each other that well, nor would they ever.

Still she had to explain the book to Ricky, who, half listening, continued to pore over the one he was holding. She did not explain how she had come upon the book, or why. Max had adored it. She remembered him reading out the Latin passages, gravely and with perfect pronunciation, as though reciting the Odes of Horace, and everybody laughing, including her, secure in their derision, enjoying their twentieth-century superiority. *What was wrong with these people?* Whatever it was, it certainly wasn't wrong with *us*. Now, reading with fresh eyes, she was diverted by the idea of homemade sex toys, since that's what the stuffed gloves must have been: the last resort of the Victorian deviate, who had no recourse to specialty shops and catalogs, no support groups, no one to lobby for deviant rights.

On the one hand, the lonely perch of Mr. Z of Case Study 122 (a clinically diagnosed "kid-glove-fetichist") was pitiful. Imagine if your therapist was kindly Dr. Krafft-Ebing, who described almost all of his patients as witless perverts of heavily tainted ancestry. Still, she admired the patient's ingenuity, his can-do spirit. When, at the age of twelve, she had read about Mr. Z, she had fixated only on his "fetich," trying to figure out what in the world he was doing with those stuffed gloves, and why whatever it was "brought him to the verge of despair and even insanity." Now she noted with pride that Mr. Z, unlike most of the patients, was American. Of course he was! Mr. Z saw a problem and devised a solution.

"Listen to this," said Ricky, still reading. "The *Kammigriff.* The Application of the Wet Sheet. The Psychrophor. The Row Boat of Ewer. Goodyear's Pocket Gymnasium. What the hell?"

"'A man had an inamorata,'" countered Amy, "'who allowed him to blacken her hands with coal or soot. She then had to sit before a mirror in such a way that he could see her hands in it. While conversing with her, which was often for a long time, he looked constantly at her mirrored hands.'" Amy had had childhood nightmares about severed hands. She tried to remember whether they started before or after she rifled through her uncle's desk drawer.

Ricky burst out laughing, though not at the mirrored hands

story. "This guy thinks it's a fatal mistake to read in the bathroom. He calls it a pernicious habit. He says we shouldn't try to do two things at once. What's a Cloacina?"

"Cloacina was the Roman goddess of sewer drains."

"He says, 'Cloacina is very exacting, and demands the full concentration of the mind.'"

Amy was about to retort with Max's favorite case study, the one about the man for whom sexual performance was possible only in the presence of an ugly old woman wearing a nightcap, but again her thoughts wandered, Ricky's words reminding her how, as a child, even while being terrorized by Krafft-Ebing, what frightened her most about the sexual act was the probability that she would not be able to read while it was going on. Again, she declined to share so intimate a fact with her visitor.

"Can you picture," said Ricky, "what life must have been like for these people?"

"With ease," she replied, rising to place *Psychopathia Sexualis* on an outlying Reference pile.

"Amy?" Ricky closed his book with reluctance. "I know it's weird, but could I borrow this constipation thing? I think I could use it with Caligula. The gross names of those devices—"

"Ricky, you can't *borrow* it, because I don't want it back. It's yours." Amy placed it in the grocery bag.

"Is it strange," he asked, blushing a little, "to want to use this stuff in my book?"

"Why do you think I'm drowning in all these books, you silly person? We write fiction to make sense of the world. That requires research."

By tacit consent, they turned back to their task, pausing now and then just to check out a cover, or retrieve something that had drifted out of the books and onto the carpet. No love notes, pressed flowers, or faded ribbons slipped from these pages, but over the next hour they found four letter envelopes, which Ricky discreetly handed to Amy without reading, and which she set aside for later examination.

By one thirty they both had wine headaches, and Amy was particularly fatigued, but the castles and villages were all complete, and all that remained was to place each category and subcategory into an appropriately sized case or shelf. Into the bedroom bookcases went all the fiction, novels separated from short stories and both separated from dramas. She included her own books with them, alphabetically filed, between Lisa Fugard and John Gardner. One narrow maple bookcase was just the right size for her poetry collection. History, ancient and modern, lined one wall in her office, with a surprising number of biographies—she had not realized that she owned so many—filling up a row of pine shelving against the other wall, along with her disaster books, about the Hartford circus fire, the Mount Pelée Volcano, the San Francisco Earthquake. "Wow, you really like this stuff," said Ricky, and indeed she did, if by "stuff" he meant "cautionary tales about things that can go terribly wrong and could actually happen to me," because underneath the Disasters was a shelf quickly bursting with true crime books, five of them on Lizzie Borden alone.

The handsomest shelves she owned, a set of antique oak bookcases with glass doors, she and Ricky dragged from storeroom to parlor and filled with humor, mythology, philosophy, essays, fairy tales, and the children's books she had inherited from her mother and father and of which, of all the books she owned, she had actually taken good care, so that their faded covers were intact. To these books she gave pride of place, eye-level center. The very last book she shelved was her father's *Mother Goose Nursery Rhymes,* with the Arthur Rackham checkerboard cover, a sinister Mother

Goose wearing a black hat and riding the goose as though it were a broomstick.

Ricky offered to help with the remaining mess, but she made him drink a mug of coffee and bundled him out her front door. "Thanks for these," he said, hugging the full grocery bag. He would not let her pay him for anything—not the blog work, nor his heroic labors in her Augean stables. "I know," he said, as he backed down the porch steps, "that Carla strong-armed you into teaching us at the retreat."

"Just once a month," she said, "and I wasn't strong-armed."

"Hey, I know Carla, and I also know you have your own work to do, and your own life. This was my pleasure."

"Watch out," she called to him, "for the self-acting clysopump."

"And Winternitz's Device!" he called back.

What a good boy, she thought as he drove away. And he hadn't asked her once what she thought about *Caligula*, or what his chances were of selling the book. She felt a pang, tiny but sharp, as the rear lights of the car disappeared around the corner. She felt as though their good-bye had weight. This was odd. It must have been that phrase, "good boy," popping up stupidly, as though she could take pride in him, as though he were hers to let go. As though he were her son. She had never felt that way about anyone. She must be getting sentimental in her dotage.

She closed and locked the door and wandered from room to room. How pleasant to have them all arrayed like that, bundled up and spiffy. Tomorrow she would visit them in daylight. Tomorrow, and the day after that, she would spend a little time with some old friends. She turned out all the lamps except for the two in the parlor, where she sat and looked through those letters that had floated free. There were an ancient bill from Calvary Hospital and an equally old letter of inquiry from her French translators.

There was that obnoxious letter the extension people had sent her last year, letting her know she would work for them again when hell froze over. The only treasure in the bunch was an unopened letter from "Bob," postmarked in August of 1991, telling her he was sure he had left his Cornell class ring next to the bathroom sink and enclosing two dollars worth of twenty-nine-cent tulip stamps. She kept the stamps and threw the rest in the trash, and then, for no reason she could imagine, fished out the old hospital bill, folded it twice, and stuck it in her notebook, where she also scribbled three additions:

"Calvary"

"A Time of Great Conformity"

"The Drawer"

The only real mess she and Ricky had left behind was a litter of tiny scraps on the parlor carpet. The oldest books had shed the most, brittle shards of yellowed paper arrayed in little mounds, like the chips of winter leaves. She would vacuum in the morning. Amy turned out the lamps and shuffled off to bed. Just like leaves, they crunched beneath her feet.

CHAPTER NINETEEN

*

Molluskeena

A month later, on the first of April, Amy awoke to exactly the sort of day she despised: a day with appointments, not just one but two, the sort where she had had to use a *calendar* and pencil in events, each for a particular time and place. This was how most of the world lived. Most people planned meals, outfits, leave-takings, homecomings. Penciled in reminders to drop off or pick up dry cleaning. Most people thought nothing of leaving their dog alone for hours. She didn't know how most people stood it.

At eleven she was due at the Birdhouse for her first class with Carla's retreat people. She would have to keep them occupied for the entire afternoon, at the end of which they'd sit down to eat together. Getting together with Ricky, Tiffany, and Dr. Surtees would probably be pleasant enough, but she was not looking forward to meeting Grahame "Skinny White Bitch" Troy, and she had no idea what it would be like to make small talk with Brie Spangler. Then there was Kurt Robetussien.

Even worse, before the retreat marathon, at nine in the morning, she had to be back at the KPBS studios for an NPR hookup. Maxine had given her the news in stages: first it was just the date and time and place of the interview; then the fact that she wouldn't be the only writer talking. That it would be some sort of "round table discussion." When Amy had resigned herself to that, Maxine had made a third call, a *Babe, I forgot to mention* call, and what she had forgotten to mention was that there would be an assigned topic: Writing as Ritual. Amy hadn't picked up a Maxine call for two full days after that. Maxine tried to leave a message on her machine, telling her who the other three round table writers were, but she erased each message before the names. If she knew who they were, she wouldn't be able to resist looking them up, and she really didn't want to get bogged down doing that.

The KPBS parking lot had only two cars in it besides Amy's Crown Vic, which Amy thought was odd, until she was once again alone in that wonderful quiet room with the ethereal microphone and the comfy office chair and realized that the others weren't coming. Apparently they were scattered all over the country in different PBS stations, and she would not have to deal with them in person. Her mood lightened. Brie Spangler popped in, offering Amy a cup of coffee, explaining that, with her headphones on, she would hear some sort of lead music and then the interviewer's voice, and it would be clear when it was her time to speak. As soon as Amy had the headset on, Brie waved good-bye and popped out again.

Once again the music was "If They Asked Me, I Could Write a Book," this time sung by Peggy Lee. The invisible interviewer, whose name was Tom, began by reading a passage from Susan Cheever's book about her father, who would leave the family apartment every day dressed in a suit and tie as though on his way to the office, and journey by elevator to a storage room in the basement to spend the workday in a dark, airless room alone with his typewriter. Tom then threw open the discussion to his panel of writers, including, along with Amy, Hester Lipp, Constance Lent, and Jenny Marzen.

Well, of course, thought Amy, and no wonder Maxine had tried to prepare her. Marzen, who had nominated Amy for Best Washed-Up Writer in that *ARB* feature that had yet to run, had probably suggested her as a fourth for today's round table. Disinclined by nature and principle to compare herself to other people, Amy was uncomfortably aware, for just a moment, of her low rung on the hierarchy of this small group. Constance Lent, whom she had actually read, was a popular, literate writer of mysteries, the sort that focus more on the why of crimes than on the who; many of her books had been turned into movies or BBC TV series, and while she wasn't a household word like Marzen, she was, as they say, ensconced. Amy couldn't place Hester Lipp, but she must be well-known, since Amy knew instantly that her name was spelled with two *P*s. A memoirist, apparently, as that's how Tom described her, at which point Amy tuned out, doodling *M*s, large and small, all over one page of her notepad. Amy was the last to be introduced. To her dismay, Tom did this by reading from that haunting old London *Times* review, the one that had threatened her with destiny: "One of the few writers destined to ignore, outshine, and outlive her own booming, blustering, disappointingly conformist generation." Two seconds of dead air followed Tom's pronouncement, before Amy cleared her throat and rasped, "Hello."

Immediately the rest began to chime in with their thoughts about writing rituals, and their own habits. Constance Lent, who Amy had always assumed was British, had a New Jersey accent.

Amy liked her right away. "I don't have a ritual. I just have a couple of spots where I think about what I'm going to write next, and another spot where I usually write, and that's about it." Good for you, thought Amy. Tom tried to draw her out. "And is there a particular notebook, or typewriter? Do you write at an appointed hour?" "No," said Constance Lent, who was rapidly becoming Amy's hero. "So, you write when the spirit moves you?" asked Tom, sounding just a bit anxious. "I guess so," said Constance Lent. "Are all these spots in your house?" asked Tom. Amy laughed, forgetting that the mike was on. "Sorry," she said. "It's just beginning to sound like Twenty Questions." Only Constant Lent agreed. "Yes," she said. "He's getting warmer!"

"When I'm writing memoir," said an unamused Hester Lipp, "I like to work in my kitchen." Hester had a strong Yankee drawl—she sounded more like Vermont than Maine—and spoke very slowly, with a slight lisp. "I have a small oak table for my laptop, next to a window with a bird feeder on the other side. When I'm having particular difficulty, I—this is going to sound odd, I know—I always like to have a glass colander full of sugar peas nearby. I find that stringing the peas and popping them into a bowl really frees my mind."

"That is so interesting!" said Jenny Marzen. "And it makes perfect sense. The act of creation requires nutrients."

"Where do you write, Jenny?"

Jenny Marzen ate up the next five minutes with a fulsome description of her writing process, from meditation, which took place on horseback "on my old rundown ranch in the Montana hills," to first drafts, always written on a long yellow legal pad using a number 2 pencil from her father's old stock of Eagles. "The Eagle," Jenny pointed out, her voice low and urgent, "was the only pencil used by Thomas Alva Edison." "Puts a new spin on that cartoon about 'light bulb inspiration,'" said Tom, chuckling uncontrollably, along with Jenny and Hester Lipp, who must have felt left out, because, before Jenny could spill the beans about where she typed her final drafts and what large animals and comestibles were involved, Hester brought up the topic of "different rituals for different projects."

"As I said," continued Hester Lipp, "I write memoir in the kitchen, but if I'm working on a novel—as I am now, for the first time in my writing life—I find that I have to write curled up in my bedroom window seat."

"Fascinating!" lied Tom.

Hester must be pretty thin to be able to curl up in a window seat and stay put for hours. Amy pictured her as rangy and rawboned, like Kate Hepburn, without the looks. Because Tom had clammed up, Amy opened her mouth. "Hester," she asked, "why do you suppose you write fiction and nonfiction in different rooms?" She wasn't at all interested; she was just trying to shut down Jenny Marzen.

"I must say I don't know," said Hester Lipp, her voice distinctly colder than before. "I'm new to fiction—to *making things up,* as opposed to *laying out, brick by brick, the facts of my life.*" Instantly, Amy realized who Hester Lipp was, and why she had known how to spell her name with two *P*s.

Hester Lipp had written *Where the Sidewalk Starts,* an inexplicably acclaimed book of memoir, recounting—in severe language and strange, striking imagery—Lipp's childhood and adolescence on a leafy suburban street in Burlington. Her house was large and well-kept, her schooling uneventful, her family—the members of which she described in scrupulous detail—uniformly decent and supportive. *Sidewalk* was blurbed as a devastatingly honest account of what it means to grow up middle class in America. Amy, who forced herself to read the whole thing, thought the book devastatingly unnecessary. Amy had forced herself through it because *The New York Times* had assigned it to her for a review, and she stomped on it with both feet. Amy's review of *Sidewalk* was the only mean-spirited review she ever wrote.

She had allowed herself to do this, not because she was tired of memoirs, baffled by their popularity, resentful that somehow, in the past twenty years, fiction had taken a backseat to them, so that in order to sell clever, thoroughly imagined novels, writers had been browbeaten by their agents into marketing them as fact. All this annoyed her, but then Amy was annoyed by just about everything. She beat up on Hester Lipp because the woman could write up a storm and yet squandered her powers on the minutiae of a beige conflict-free life. In her review, Amy had begun by praising what there was to praise about Hester's sharp sentences and word-painting talents and then slipped, in three paragraph steps, into a full-scale rant about the tyranny of fact and the great advantages, to both writer and reader, of *making things up*. She ended by saying that reading *Where the Sidewalk Starts* was like "being frog-marched through your own backyard."

Amy had allowed herself to beat up on Hester Lipp because *Sidewalk* had already gotten a number of raves, so one slam shouldn't damage her, even if it did run in the *Times*. She probably wouldn't even notice. Well, clearly that was not the case. Hester Lipp had apparently memorized the review, quoting from it just now with frosty accuracy.

Amy was aware of dead silence. "Amy," said Tom, "are you there?"

"Pardon?"

"Would you share your own writing rituals with our listeners?" Amy guessed he was saying this for the second time.

"Actually," said Amy, and stopped. She had planned to say something about writing down story and novel titles at random and taking her cue from them, but she was preoccupied by Hester Lipp and that book review, and then by book reviews in general, whether they were an honorable way to make a few bucks, and why not just leave the reviewing to the real critics, the ones who get to wait until a writer has died leaving behind sufficient evidence of quality and variety to warrant the spilling of more ink, the death of more trees. On the other hand, maybe she had bullied Hester Lipp into writing a good novel. Maybe she had done her a favor. Or not.

"Actually, Tom," said Amy, "I have a number of intricate rituals. I write my first drafts in indigo ink on dozens of small Moleskine notebooks. I type out the second drafts on a green Olivetti Underwood. I shuffle the pages together five times and leave them for a full week on an unfinished rosewood table in my fruit cellar."

"Fascinating!" Amy pictured Tom stretched back in his chair with a cold compress on his forehead.

In the background, Amy could hear someone either wheezing or giggling.

"The act of reassembling those pages gives me the time and the impetus to visualize the finished draft, which of course I always accomplish with my ancient Compaq PC, using the most basic of word processing programs."

"You don't use Word?" asked Jenny Marzen. "How does your publisher handle that?"

"I type my final draft in html code."

"Wow!" said Tom.

"Why do you do that?" wondered Jenny Marzen.

"It's obvious," said Constance Lent. "Like driving a shift, instead of an automatic. Right, Amy?"

It was interesting how you could tell, just from a person's voice, that she was smiling. "Exactly," said Amy. "It brings you so much closer to the road."

For a couple of minutes, Amy and Constance Lent batted the metaphor around, improvising upon it, playing monkey in the middle with three monkeys. Constance was particularly adept: she managed to equate "the road" with "the underlying truth of one's novelistic effort," sounding so serious that for a dizzy moment Amy wondered if she had misread her intent. Tom and Jenny Marzen moved in tandem through confusion into positive excitement (Amy at this point guessed that they shared the same studio; Jenny Marzen wasn't all by her lonesome in a minor city radio station). "I guess I'm going to have to learn html code!" said Jenny.

"They're making a joke," said Hester Lipp, even less amused than before, but at least the woman wasn't an idiot.

"Oh," said Tom, and then, after a beat, "I guess the html code should have been a tipoff."

"Tom," said Amy, "the *dozens of Moleskine notebooks* should have been a tipoff. Do you know how much those cost? We're novelists. We can barely afford three-ring binders."

"MollusKEEna," pronounced Hester Lipp.

"I beg your pardon?"

"The notebooks. The name is pronounced 'mollusKEEna.' Did you imagine they were made from the skin of moles?"

"I guess I did," said Amy. "I mean, I didn't think about it much. I noticed the *e* at the end but thought it was silent. Thanks for the information, though." Amy meant this. *Molluskeena.* What an odd word.

"So we're split down the middle," said Tom gamely. "Two of

you value certain rituals in the creative process, and two of you do not. I wonder if we've hit on a significant statistic."

Hester Lipp wouldn't let it go. "You thought people were buying notebooks made from rodent hide? How peculiar."

In the background, Constance Lent was laughing helplessly.

"It's not that I don't have writing habits. What we're calling *rituals,*" said Amy. "Of course I do. I just can't bring myself to—"

"Share them!" said Jenny Marzen. "I totally respect your reserve." She went on to joke that she had done so many interviews lately, in preparation for the upcoming publication date of her newest novel, *Blahblahblah,* that she had lost all sense of privacy. "I envy you your intact boundaries," she said.

"I was going to say that I can't bring myself to talk about them, because they're so boring." Jenny Marzen started to assure her that her rituals must be remarkable, because her work was so brilliant, but Amy cut her off mid-condescension. "I mean that all writing rituals are boring, especially to the writers themselves. Or at least to one of them."

"Two of them," said Constance Lent.

"So why, I wonder, did you agree to come on this program?" asked Hester Lipp. My god, the woman was angry.

"To sell books," said Constance Lent. "And actually, in my case, also because I wanted to meet *you.*"

"Well, and of course, I wanted to meet *you,*" said Jenny Marzen. "This is a fortunate opportunity to meet all of you."

"I meant I wanted to meet Amy Gallup."

"I am not here to sell books," said Hester Lipp.

Tom, who had been lying doggo, jumped back in, drowning out poor Hester. "There's no reason we can't change topics," he said. "We've never done a show on the business end of novel-writing, and it occurs to me—"

"What a terrific idea!" said Jenny Marzen. "Although for another time, surely. We have only a few minutes left." Shouldn't Tom have been the one worrying about time? What was she, Big Ben? Amy couldn't believe how much she was letting the woman tick her off. She felt like she was in high school. She hated high school.

"And I was going to propose," said Tom, "such a show in the very near future. You would all participate, I hope?"

Somebody sniffed. Amy assumed it was Hester Lipp.

"I'll do it," said Constance, "if everybody agrees to discuss what advances they got for their books and how well they've done in royalties."

Amy said that was a great idea, because it sort of was. Jenny worried that their publishers might object, and besides, "Isn't that just talking shop?"

"Yes," said Amy, "and so is schmoozing about your prewriting ceremonies, but I'll bet our listeners would be much more interested in dollars and cents. They are avid readers, most of them, and many of them would be surprised to learn what we get paid."

"And Jenny," said Constance, "what do you care about offending your publishers? They wouldn't mind. Your advances aren't exactly a secret. The only writers who don't publicize theirs are the ones who aren't getting six figures."

"I'm sorry," said Hester Lipp, "but I'm not comfortable talking about money."

Hester Lipp wasn't comfortable talking about anything. Amy was feeling bad for her and so sorry about that frog-march wisecrack in the *Times*. By now she was picturing her as a creature made entirely of clichés, an angular, goose-necked, razor-lipped type, so overgrown that her thin white cardigans rode up in back. She hadn't really grown up in that perfect suburban house. She had *festered* there, tormented by her loving and supportive family, who kept trying to push her out into the light. She probably had a giant mole in the middle of her face. "What is six figures, exactly?" asked Amy. "I always get confused. Six figures to the left of the decimal point? If so, my first advance was barely four figures."

"Mine too," said Constance Lent. "I do all right now, but just all right. A lot of my mysteries just sell to libraries."

"No kidding!" said Amy.

"We're down to the last few minutes," said Tom, "and I'm wondering if you all have any final thoughts."

"I think," said Hester Lipp, "that the rituals we use in approaching our work reveal much about us and the wellsprings of our art."

"I could not have said it better," said Jenny Marzen. She drew in a breath as if to say more, but apparently checked herself.

Constance Lent said, "I think our writing habits have as much to do with chance as anything else. Morning people probably write in the morning. Your favorite writing spot is probably dictated by the architecture of your house and the size and age of your family. If you're a superstitious type, you may rely on special pens and all that—and if you're not superstitious, you'll write with anything."

"Amy?" asked Tom. She had to hand it to him: he was a real pro. His genial tone had not changed over the entire interview, which had been, thanks to her, sour, disjointed, and raucous, and not in a good way, and here he was, sounding eager to hear from her yet again.

"I don't know anything," she began, "about the writing habits of Jane Austen, or E. M. Forster, or Shakespeare, or Thomas

Malory, or Mickey Spillane. Do you? In fact, I don't remember reading about writing rituals at all until I read how Nabokov wrote his novels on index cards. It was about then that writers started to become celebrities and gurus. This was probably the same time I learned about Cheever taking that elevator to work, and I agree that's a nice story, but the truth is, I wish I didn't know about the index cards and the elevator. I don't want to read *Lolita* and think about index cards. If I'm curious about someone's life, I'll read biography." Amy had never felt, or been, less articulate, but she kept going. "And most writers just aren't that interesting. They spend their time writing, which is not a spectator sport. We don't write in order to be admired, or emulated, or wondered about. Especially wondered about! We don't need the spotlight, and we do nothing to deserve it anyhow. We don't save lives. We don't tap-dance. All we do, we take what's in our heads and try to get it down on the record. We can call it art or entertainment, it doesn't matter. Communication is all. The leaving of a mark. The books we write . . . they're the best of us. That's what you should be looking at. What does it matter how the words got on the page? There they are."

Tom let a second go by before thanking them all by name. Peggy Lee began to whisper, and Amy took off the headphones and left the building, dodging Brie as she went through the door. "I'll see you in a few," Brie called to her, but Amy had driven ten miles north on the 15 before she really heard her and remembered that she couldn't go home.

She would have to turn around and go to La Jolla and spend the rest of the day at the Birdhouse. Her cell phone crowed, literally, a bantam rooster crow she had downloaded expressly to let her know when Maxine was calling. She shut it down. The hell with Maxine and her big plans and her damn buzz. By the time she got to Carla's, she was in the foulest mood she could remember.

CHAPTER TWENTY

∽

The Great Wazoo

She was late. She had lost her way in La Jolla and then driven around forever looking for a drugstore to get some ibuprofen for an incoming headache. They were all waiting for her in Carla's Jungle Adventure Lagoon Room, although it wasn't immediately clear who was there, or how many there were, since most of them were obscured by vines and tree trunks. Here and there she thought she could discern a shoulder, a lock of hair, but everyone was camouflaged. Were they all slathered in green mud? Maybe someone would pin her with a blow-dart and put her out of her misery. "It's Amy!" Carla exclaimed, and magically faces and bodies emerged from the forest. There was Ricky Buzza, standing next to Tiffany on the wooden bridge aslant the brook; Brie Spangler and Dr. Surtees were sitting facing each other in a pre-Colombian swing-set; Kurt Robetussien, instantly recognizable even without his hospital blues, had been buttonholed in front of a huge mossy boulder by a slim blond woman in yoga pants; and of course Carla was out in front of everyone, advancing on Amy like a half-time band. "Carla," Amy said, "how did you get that boulder in here? Did you knock out a wall?" Carla was in many respects a child: often you could stop her in her tracks if you distracted her with just the right question. Not this time, though.

Carla proceeded to introduce Amy to the entire group, which was stupid, since everybody but Yoga Pants already knew her, and then launched into the usual inordinate praise. "Where do you want me to stand," Amy asked curtly. She was being rude, but that was just the price Carla would have to pay for conning her into doing this in the first place. In the end, they dragged a primitive wooden throne over in front of the boulder and sat her down in it. The chair was studded with pastel-colored beads that dug into her spine. Carla explained they were fashioned from tagua nuts, gathered from the floor of the Amazonian rain forest. She gave Amy a pillow and began to pass out more pillows for the class to sit on. "Oh, for goodness sake," said Amy, "I don't want you all sitting at my feet. I feel like the Great Wazoo."

"Oh, Amy, you're so funny!"

"I'm not kidding," Amy said sharply. "Put them in chairs."

Carla, chastened, did her best, and soon Amy was facing a line of hunched, frightened people. Under normal circumstances, this tableau would have cracked her up and lifted the mood. Half of them were sitting on fake tree stumps, the fake brook was babbling robotically, and they were all looking at her as though she might go off, which was absurd. Amy never went off. But Amy, like Hester Lipp, was not amused. "Why do you want to write?" she asked them, sounding, even to her own ears, like an angry mother pointing to a mess and asking who did it.

She had given very mild versions of this speech many times before, often during first class, the object being to make students confront their own expectations and preconceptions and to enter into the spirit of a workshop with a reasonable attitude. She had often touched on the difficulties of getting published, the heartache of rejection, the letdown if and when you do get something in print. But now she piled it on thick. "Everybody knows someone who brags about papering her walls with rejection slips, or keeping them in a scrapbook, or displaying them under glass like matchbook covers, or making them into a hat. That's nothing to brag about. That's not admirable bravado. It's foolish. If you're getting lots of rejections, that just means you're sending your stuff out there. That's what you're *supposed* to do. Get over it." When she had finished blunting their keenness for the task at hand, she moved on to the publishing industry, the superabundance of books, her old song about how we should all stop writing and read instead. She described in obscene detail how out-of-print books get pulped. Some of these people had heard this before, but she made them listen to it again.

She ranted to drown out her thoughts about Hester Lipp and Jenny Marzen and the shameful pleasure with which she had prodded and poked at them, lobbing spitballs like a little kid. She had never acted like that in her life. Hermits don't engage. She could have made exactly the same points in a civilized manner, but no, she'd wised off about Moleskine and fruit cellars. She continued hectoring and simultaneously heard the echo of that last speech, her national radio swan song, prattling about leaving your mark and "communication is all," for god's sake, she'd sounded like a moron. Maxine was going to kill her. "One more thing," she said at last, reaching into her bag for notebook and pen. "We're here to discuss writing. *Not publication.* Do not ask me about agents. Are there any questions?"

Amy's cell phone crowed wildly. She must have nudged it back on when she grabbed the notebook. Amy reached into her bag and shut it down without looking, keeping her own expression stony, daring anybody to laugh. Kurt Robetussien took her up on it. "You got chickens in there?" he asked, pointing to the bag, and Ricky said, "Or are you just glad to see us?" and the rest held their breath while Amy decided how she felt about that. "I'm always glad to see you," she said, and to her surprise, she was.

She would have been much gladder to be home alone with her dog, but she was calm now. For the next hour she let them talk a little about their six projects and then give one another feedback on what they'd read so far. They had by now shown one another the chapters Amy had read (during the "rigorous admissions process"). Amy planned to devote twenty minutes to each piece but got some extra time from Tiffany, who admitted that she hadn't submitted enough material for them to chew on and bowed out of the discussion. No one, not even Ricky, disagreed with her, so they moved on to Dr. Surtees and his Obamacare thriller. If he had hoped for a pass from his fellow physician, he must have been disappointed, since Kurt R shredded the first chapter of *Womb to Tomb* while the rest watched. "What you're describing here," said Kurt, "is medical malpractice. It has nothing to do with socialized medicine. The old lady's cardiologist is such a jerk that he doesn't catch the pacemaker snafu, doesn't take her family's calls, and basically ignores her to death. She wouldn't be circling the drain in the first place if he had done his job." Dr. Surtees attempted to laugh off the criticism in a collegial way, as though it were all about politics rather than aesthetics, and had Amy been teaching a real class she would have called him on it, but she let it pass.

Grahame Troy, the blonde in yoga pants, did a five-minute paean to Kurt's novel, the brilliance of the scene between the oncology nurse and the dying kid, how enlightened it was that a doctor was writing from the point of view of a nurse. Surtees asked him why he made that choice, and Kurt said nurses were more interesting than doctors. "I see," said Dr. Surtees, who seemed more annoyed by the general praise of Kurt's chapter than the drubbing his own had gotten.

Getting them to talk about Brie Spangler's stuff was difficult, perhaps because it was already so polished, but more likely because Brie had apparently made up a whole world rather than confining herself to home base, as had the two physicians and Tiffany. Amy admired Brie's ambition and reach: she wasn't writing about a female journalist. She was dealing with an uneducated petty criminal who accidentally helps murder somebody, and it was clear from the tone of just the first chapter that the novel would be dark and tragic. Amy made a promise to herself that she would, in the coming weeks, pay special attention to Brie.

Sighing, Amy announced it was time to discuss *Skinny White Bitch*. "That's 'Chick,'" said Yoga Pants, clearly put out, and Amy apologized, but she went on to make the same mistake twice more in the ensuing discussion, so that by the end of the segment Yoga Pants plainly disliked her with Lippesque intensity. If this had been a real workshop, rather than workshop-lite, Amy would have bent over backward to assure her that the fault was her own. (Actually if Yoga Pants hadn't made such a big deal out of the mistake, Amy wouldn't have kept making it.) She would have joked about her aging brain and failing eyesight. She would have stopped Ricky from riffing on *chick* vs. *bitch* and "Seriously, what difference does it make?" She would have reined in the class, not one of whom had anything positive to say about the stupid thing. Even Carla was dismissive: "I'm really sorry," she said, "but if this isn't chick-lit, I don't know what is."

Amy left the discussion of *Caligula's Scalpel* until the very end, figuring its lurid subject matter would generate a lot of talk just at the point where class energy is apt to flag, but even she was impressed by the general surge of enthusiasm. Carla and Tiffany, who usually disagreed about everything, both said it was brilliant and creepy. The doctors found it entertaining; even though Caligula's plan to create serial killers through brain surgery was science fiction, it was *fun* science fiction. This surprised Amy, as she had thought the plot was just silly, but as she listened to them talk, she found herself agreeing, at least about the entertaining part. Ricky's language was still rather self-conscious and stilted, but even in this early chapter he was loosening up, enjoying his absurd creation. Only Yoga Pants disliked it, calling it "formulaic," prompting a mass eye-roll so spontaneous that it seemed synchronized like a wave cheer, and Amy had to look away to keep from laughing. This was a good group; she was almost sorry that her involvement with them would not run very deep. Again she felt that pinprick, that odd pang that had accompanied Ricky's leavetaking the other night, and now could begin to narrow it down; it was some form of sorrow. Again she put it away.

For the next hour she walked around the lagoon, balancing a plate of food, touching base with the people she knew, acknowledging a wave from Brie Spangler, who was locked in a phone call across the room, listening politely as Yoga Pants, who probably thought Kurt Robetussien was single, bragged to him about how she had folded all *her* rejection slips into origami swans. She remembered then that the fictional skinny white bitch chick had also plastered *her* walls with rejection slips. No wonder Yoga

Pants resented her. Amy had unwittingly singled her out when she was ranting at them for wanting to be writers. She would never have done such a cruel thing on purpose. She was not a cruel person. Not before today anyway.

"It comes in a kit," said Carla passing by, spooning pineapple chunks on her plate, and Amy was just fine with not having a clue what she meant. A half hour later she was back with a mug of hot green tea, plain, just as Amy liked it. "The inside is styrofoam, and when you get it in the house, it's glued in layers, but you can't see the seams."

"The boulder," said Amy. "That's how you got it in here."

"You can get kits for anything," said Carla.

Amy reached up and patted Carla's shoulder, surprising herself with voluntary human contact. "I'm tired," she said. "I think I'll go home."

On her way to the door, Kurt Robetussien startled her, stepping out from behind an adolescent Norfolk pine, which she identified as such at the same moment he spoke her name. She was so distracted by the plant that she missed what he was saying. What was so riveting about a Norfolk pine, she wondered, then recalling the small one she had been carrying when she brained herself on the birdbath, eventually resulting in an encounter with this very doctor. A doctor with whom she was now forced to have a cringeworthy word about medical discretion. Coincidences, she told her students, must occur much more sparingly in fiction than in the real world. He was smiling at her, awaiting a response. "You're doing good work," she told him, hoping that answered his question. She didn't want to seem dotty or scattered to a man who had stuck a stethoscope down her blouse and listened to her heartbeat: a man who had seen behind those blue privacy curtains. If he asked her if she'd scheduled a mammogram yet, she would lie.

"So are you," he said, and she smiled back and reached for the doorknob. "You were fantastic this morning. I was rolling on the floor. Don't worry, it's my day off, I wasn't rolling on the floor of the ER!" Again, she was wrong-footed. Even allowing for hyperbole, he hadn't laughed helplessly during class, and in any event Amy had never been less hilarious in her life. "I didn't know," he continued, "that you were a radio personality."

Oh god, she thought. "Neither did I," said Amy, attempting a smooth recovery, horrified to realize that people, at least one person, had actually heard the broadcast. She hadn't thought of that. Assuring him that she'd see him in a month, reminding him that he could email her anytime about his fiction, she turned to get away before he could inquire about her colon, breast, or brain, or worse, about her radio hijinks. But then she remembered: she couldn't make her getaway just yet.

She leaned in a few inches and lowered her voice. "A word," she said, "about the . . ." About the what? Birdbath? Last night she had tried rehearsing this moment and had found even the rehearsals too uncomfortable to pursue. With the careless confidence of a child, she had imagined the phrasing would come to her. *This extremely rare coin was minted in 1949.*

"Novel?" asked Kurt. "Don't worry. I can take criticism. I'm not even sure I'm serious about the thing. This is my wife's fault, really—she insists it's pretty good. She's a writer herself, actually—"

"Birdbath," said Amy.

"What?"

"The accident. My accident. The ER. The MRI." She had to

keep feeding him clues, because obviously he'd forgotten about the whole thing, and great, she had now managed to remind him. "I'm so sorry," she said. "I was just worried about . . . you know . . ."

"Have you had any more episodes of amnesia?" His expression had changed instantly to one of professional concern, tinged with just a hint of disappointment.

She had managed not only to remind him of the accident but also to present herself as a freeloader, one of those people who sidle up to physicians at parties to ask them if a skin tag on their underarm is anything to worry about. "No, no, no," she said, "I'm so sorry, no. Completely different issue."

"What are your symptoms?"

"I don't have any symptoms," she said. "I'm talking about my . . . Listen. That silly accident I had, the one I met you about—" Amy had not been this inarticulate since she was eight years old, if then. For what seemed like hours she explained about the accident's aftermath, and the fact that she was getting critical attention from which she was continuing to benefit and hoped to continue benefiting. He kept looking at her closely, quizzically, no longer annoyed but also not getting her point, which forced her into a vivacity which probably looked as grotesque as it felt. She laughed, she gestured airily, she actually touched him lightly on the arm, as if she were the type of woman who touched people, and still he waited for her to come out with it. "Look," she said. "You're the only person in the world who knows that I gave that interview *non compos mentis*."

His face relaxed. "Got it," he said. "Hey, no worries. Your secret is safe with me. Everybody's secrets are safe with me. I'm a doctor."

"Except now I've insulted you by implication," she said, "and I am so sorry."

"Tell me honestly," he said. "Is my stuff as awful as *Womb to Tomb*? I thought I'd be the only doctor here."

So much for Amy's Shameful Secret. Kurt's was that he wasn't there just because his wife pushed him into it. "Are you kidding?" asked Amy. "I never met a doctor who didn't want to be a novelist. But you're the first one," she was happy to tell him, "that could actually make it. Just don't tell that to Surtees."

She left him smiling, happy, oblivious to the gimlet-eyed approach of Yoga Pants.

Amy was just getting into her car when Brie ran out of the house. "Is your phone off? Because Tom Maudine has been trying to get you for hours."

"Who's Tom Maudine?"

"The interviewer!"

"Oh. *Tom*." Was she supposed to call him back so he could yell at her? Maybe she should. Maybe that would make her feel better.

"Also Constance Lent called a couple of times, and also Eliot Riyad." She handed Amy a piece of paper with numbers on it. "He's one of the producers. Of NPR. In Washington."

She was such a nice girl. She kept adding information in discrete dribs, careful not to insult Amy's intelligence, just as Amy had done with Kurt. Brie needn't have worried. "Producers of what?" asked Amy.

"NPR. They have a million of them."

Amy sat down in the driver's seat, staring dully at the piece of paper. "Am I supposed to call these people?"

Brie leaned down, propping her elbows on the car door. "They'd like it if you did," she said, "but if you want to call them back tomorrow, that's fine too. And if you don't, I'll bet they keep trying."

Amy looked up at her. "Why?" she asked.

"You were good," said Brie, smiling. Then she grinned. "Boy, Jenny Marzen made an ass out of herself, didn't she?"

"Is that why I was good? Was I good at making other people look bad?"

Brie thought for a minute. "Only in comparison," she said. "Not on purpose." She closed the door gently. "See you in a month!" she said, running back into the house.

Amy drove down to the cove and parked, rolling down the window, just listening to the cries of the terns and gulls. There were no bathers today. Out in the water she could see a fin. A dolphin maybe, or a shark, depending on your mood. If Brie was right, whatever Amy's fall had set in motion back in January was still steaming along. She hadn't derailed it. Not that she had meant to. She had left her house today almost looking forward to that radio interview, that quiet room.

Max was wrong about her being dead set on failure. She wasn't dead set on anything, and all her life she had been content with that. She had regarded ambition as a flaw, or something close to it. Ambitious people thought they could see into the future, and worse, loved what they saw. They called it "potential." They drew up blueprints, laid foundations, planned expansions. They were deluded, of course, and if they lucked out, they never admitted their luck. Their success had been foreordained. Their visions realized. Now Amy for the first time could sense the future, that sleeping monster, stirring, waking, lumbering upright. Looking straight at her.

Before leaving for home, she got out her notebook and wrote the titles

"Rituals"

"You Can Get Kits For Anything"

"Privacy Curtains"

"Your Intact Boundaries"

There was plenty of daylight left, and she needed to write, to clear her head, to put the rest away. She would not be calling anyone back today.

CHAPTER TWENTY-ONE

No Goggling

A my became a weekly fixture on Maudine's show, driving down to the KPBS station each Friday morning for a new "round table." She had agreed to do this providing that no topic be set ahead of time. She and the rest of the writers would come up with something spontaneously. Maxine said they were worried about dead air. "So the worst thing that could happen is a few seconds of silence?" said Amy. "Tell them to take the long view." "What are you," asked Maxine, "a Buddhist?" But Amy prevailed, and although some weeks were better than others, the discussions were lively and often very funny. Whenever a writer would get momentarily self-conscious, Amy would say, "Nobody's listening anyway. It's just us," and the speaker's tongue would get untied. Maudine sputtered about this a few times but before long decided to go with it, and the title of the show, which had been "Writers Speak!" became "Just Us."

"Everything you touch," complained Maxine, "turns to bronze."

Maxine had called with news. "The Munster piece is running this Sunday."

"Munsterpiece!" Startling herself into a laugh, Amy choked on an apple slice, holding the phone away from her ear, and when she put it back, Maxine was saying something about Constance Lent. "Maxine, I thought the *ARB* story was dead in the water, what with my radio antics with Jenny Marzen. Wasn't she the one who put me up for the list in the first place?"

"You don't listen," said Maxine. "I just said." Maxine really sounded put out. "Not only is Marzen still in your corner, but there's a bunch more, including half the writers you've been talking with on the radio. Munster's cutting the list from ten to five, giving the five writers-to-rediscover more space, and you're going to lead off the list, so you'll get top billing and more space than everybody else. This is huge." When had people started using "huge" like this?

"Huge is the new awesome," said Amy. "What about the five who got cut? That's it for them, then?"

"God damn it," said Maxine. "I knew you'd do that. I just handed you the keys to the El Dorado and you're worrying about the poor saps you trampled over on your way to the top. Excuse me. The pathetic losers flattened by your inert carcass as I dragged you—"

"Mixed metaphor."

"Kiss my ass," said Maxine, and hung up.

When she didn't ring right back, Amy called to apologize. She couldn't remember Maxine ever being this touchy.

"For your information," said Maxine, "and not that I believe for a minute that you're really all that worked up about it, the other five writers will get space two weeks from now in the *ARB*'s next issue. You didn't hurt anybody. You know, I really do feel like I'm pushing a truck uphill. And those are the good days."

When the mid-June *ARB* edition came out, Amy didn't buy it or read it online. Neither apparently did anyone else in San Diego, so she wasn't pestered by awed calls from well-wishers. In fact, of the few California people she knew—her neighbors, Carla and the gang, and the retreat people—only Brie Spangler had ever picked up on evidence of her chelonian ascent, and that because she actually worked for a radio station. No one had ever even mentioned Holly Antoon's story, which meant that no one had ever read it—except for Kurt Robetussien, in the ER. And he was the only one who had actually heard her on the radio. Kurt was busy saving lives, and Brie was a wonderfully discreet girl; she wasn't surprised that neither contacted her about the *ARB*. The secret of Amy's burgeoning fame was safe with them.

But the East Coast was a different story. Days before the hard copy came out, her phone went off at seven in the morning, Roofy Mehnaz identified herself ("This is Roofy Mehnaz calling from New York") and threatened to make Amy "a crapload of money." Amy hung up. The phone rang again. "Sorry," said Roofy Mehnaz, "I know it's early there, but I wanted to get to you first." Amy hung up again, then lifted the phone off the hook so the signal would be busy, only Roofy Mehnaz, having not hung up in New York, kept going, listing the titles of movies and books with which she had had some sort of connection. "I know you're with Grabow, you don't have to tell me, but I can do a lot more for you. Maxine's old school. Also old." Roofy Mehnaz, then, was some sort of agent. Amy wanted to ask her about her name and how she spelled it, but she restrained herself. "Send me an email," she said, and when Roofy started to ask for her address, Amy told her to call Maxine, and hung up. Immediately the phone rang again.

This time Amy stumbled to the bathroom to get her glasses so she could see who was calling, and sure enough, it was a 212 number, and not Maxine's. Maxine knew better than to call her at seven a.m. anyway. The call went to voicemail, and while that was happening Amy turned down the volume so she couldn't hear her own voice and that of whoever was calling. Five minutes after the call ended, the phone rang again. Amy spent a half hour, pre-coffee, hunting down the instructions for her damn phone, so she could turn off the ringer, which she did.

She knew it wasn't entirely rational to treat these harbingers of success as though they were physicians calling with biopsy results, but she had other things to do. She was working on two new stories, the first of which, "The Drawer," was practically writing itself. Amy rarely wrote about either sex or childhood, but this was a freebie. It was the sort of story she had always cautioned her students against. "Nobody cares about the facts of your life. Use experience as a jumping-off place, not an end in itself."

She could remember the ozone-scented air, the cold raindrops on the window of the bedroom, on the day she had discovered Krafft-Ebing in Uncle Fred's house; she could see the pattern on her bedspread when she first flopped down to start reading. A lavender bedspread stamped with gold fleur-de-lis; she would think it hideous now, but she remembered picking it out when her mother took her to the Sears in Portland and tried to get her to go for white chenille. Such sensory details were ordinarily lacking from her memory, whether recent or ancient. There must be a part of the brain devoted to sex memory. Maybe that was what they meant by the lizard brain. Anyway, she could remember everything, and shaping it into a story took only three days. *Curious bookish girl explores the mysteries of sex, gets wildly misinformed, struggles ensue.* Years later she figures out that the answers aren't in books, but she never gets the hang of trusting her own body, which she regards from a suspicious distance. The end. "The Drawer" was slight, funnier and less dark that her usual stuff, but she knew Maxine could sell it. She had just sold the Coronado bus plunge story, "What It All Means," to *Harper's.*

"Calvary," the other story, was a mess. Now that she had decided to deal with Max's death, she was having a terrible time finding her way in. The title was grandiose and would have to go: the fact that it was the actual name of the hospital where he died, of other hospitals where tens of thousands die, was no excuse, but for now she left it in place as, day by day, she tried anew. She had begun to think of the project as an assault on some outlandish mountain peak, the sort so popular with moneyed adventurers that their freeze-dried corpses littered the slopes like candy wrappers. Most of her own assaults ended ignominiously. She would break a new trail and at some point realize that the going was all too easy, that she had slipped without realizing into a slick groove.

The trouble with big themes wasn't that the big boys and girls had gotten there first—they'd gotten to everything first, including sexual curiosity in overly cerebral children—but that they had landed on those themes with such great feet that their imprints were deep and almost impossible to avoid. Even as Max lay dying, Tolstoy intruded on what ought to have been the rawest and most immediate experience of her life. *He screamed unceasingly . . . It was unendurable . . . Oh, what I have suffered!* And oh, how Amy had wished, still wished, that the lines were her own. She could play with emotions—anxiety, terror, the demise of hope, that constant awareness of inadequacy—she could bring them to life on the page as effortlessly as she had the lavender bedspread—but to what end? To explore the awfulness of death, of loss, of grief? What did she have to add to what was already known?

Well, she had her own sorry self, her own story, the snowflake of her life, but even as a child she had been unimpressed by the breathless adult observation that no two of these were exactly alike. In the first place, she had thought, how does anybody know that? And in the second place, so what? The snowflake factoid was, to the child Amy, the first instance of a formal invitation to goggle. "No two snowflakes alike!" was impressed upon a child in order to cultivate "wonder." But she wasn't literally supposed to "wonder" about the snowflakes, since wonder invited curiosity, which in turn should prod a person into learning and thinking deeply. No, she was supposed to goggle at them. Also at the contents of aquariums and the patchwork farmland thousands of feet below her airplane window on the last time she would take to the skies. Her earliest memory of her father was when he lifted her up to the apartment window at nighttime, saying, "Look, there's our shadow on the moon." Later she had gone alone to her bedroom window and made rabbit shapes with her hands. She was then disappointed in her father, who had obviously lied to her; he had just wanted her to goggle.

Of course, in that instance *she* was wrong. Children have such literal minds: long before you need an irony klaxon, you must have everything *spelled out*. Still, what a pill she had been. Even at the time, Amy wondered what her parents saw in her. Clearly they loved her, and she them, but the whole thing was a mystery. Amy set "Calvary" aside and began work on "Snowflake."

Only to be distracted by the flashing light on her silent phone, and now Maxine was insisting that she go to Los Angeles. Amy had lived in California for twenty years and never been farther away from Escondido than San Diego. She had never even been to Tijuana. Now, horribly, Maxine had lined up two gigs for her up north: one at an independent bookstore in Pasadena, and one at KYJ, an AM radio station. "Absolutely not," said Amy.

"Which one?"

"In the first place, I don't do bookstore readings. The last time I did one was fifteen years ago. They mixed up the nights, and I got a big crowd for Leonard Nimoy. They were not happy."

"Nevertheless, Vroman's wants you, and they guarantee a crowd."

"To what end? In case you haven't noticed, Maxine, I'm out of print."

"So? The people who bought your books kept them, and they're going to want them signed."

Amy was flummoxed. This was not at all like Maxine. Nobody would earn a penny from this enterprise, which sounded like a sentimental schlep down memory lane. "I'm not doing it," she said.

After a long silence, Maxine said, "Fine. Knock yourself out. But you are doing KYJ."

"Why can't I do it from here?" Amy was already starting to bargain with Maxine. This was not a good sign. Maxine was making her feel guilty.

"It's KYJ," said Maxine. "Their shows are syndicated nationwide."

"Then they must be syndicated here, and I can just go—"

"Wrong. Chaz Molloy wants you in the station with him."

Even Amy had heard of Chaz Molloy. He was a national talk radio figure, not as big as Rush Limbaugh, but on a par, in more ways than one, with Schlesinger and Savage. Chaz Molloy was an anti-intellectual pseudo-populist blowhard who regularly took on what he called Cultural Fatheads ("Icons for Idiots"). He called his show "The Petri Dish." Amy hated that she even knew this much about Chaz Molloy. She never even went to the movies, never mind listened to talk radio. She hadn't deliberately heard pop music since she was thirty. But she knew what an iPod was, and texting, and tweeting; she knew who Baba Booey was, and which celebrities were adopting African children and which were gay; she knew what "chick-lit" meant. None of it had anything to do with her, but she had absorbed it anyhow. It occupied precious space in a brain that was by now becoming choked with information. Some starlet went out in public without underwear and presto, Amy lost the first names of the Dashwood sisters. Had humanity ever before experienced such fact pollution? Surely not in the days when all societies were manageably tiny, technology was limited to the plough and the sword, and history was essentially personal. Not that Amy was a Luddite, but there must have been a time when the sheer quantity of available information was optimal, and it wasn't now. If the universe, as one old philosophy teacher had argued, was the sum of what there was, then there was just too much. "Why?" asked Amy. "Why does Chaz Molloy want me in his radio station?"

"He needs a writer, to keep the 'cultural' thing going. He mostly gets C-list celebs. You want an honest answer, you weren't at the top of his wish list. The last writer he tricked onto his show was Maya Angelou. Now everybody knows what a Molloy interview is, and nobody who's anybody will put themselves through it. I'm talking about writers, of course. Betty White, Sally Struthers, Rod Blagojevich, they can handle it. Politicians and show biz people have thicker skins. They'll do anything for their causes, or for publicity, or both."

"Throw him Jenny Marzen," said Amy.

"She wouldn't do it."

"Hester Lipp."

"She's not big enough."

"And I am?"

"Just barely," said Maxine.

Amy had an awful thought. "Maxine, tell me the truth. Did you approach this man? Is that what it's come to?"

Maxine, who coughed so much that she could actually convey a wide variety of emotions, coughed derisively. "Give me a little credit. I wouldn't *approach* a clown like Molloy. He called me. I'm as surprised as you are."

"I'm not surprised," said Amy. "I'm sick."

"Somebody must have tipped him off about the *ARB* list. Lex doesn't deal with California people."

Amy wrangled with Maxine for what must have been a full hour. She could not understand how Chaz Molloy's market and her own, assuming she even had a market, could possibly intersect. At the height of her career she had hardly been a household word, and she was not and never had been politically active. And how would allowing some idiot to insult her on syndicated commercial radio do her or Maxine any good? It wouldn't, said Maxine, so don't let him. In the end, when Amy gave in, she did it sullenly. Remember, she had told her, this was all your idea.

Amy lay awake all that night trying to understand why she had let Maxine bully her into going. She knew even while it was happening how Maxine worked the con, throwing out two gigs with every expectation that Amy would refuse to do the bookstore and then feel pressured to comply on the other one. Eventually she realized that underneath all the outrage she was mildly curious. Not about Chaz Molloy, or the radio station, but about what she would do when she got to LA. She had no idea what was going to happen; apparently this was enough to get her there.

CHAPTER TWENTY-TWO

The Road to Shambala

Amy drove north. Over the past two weeks, she had not completed one thought about the interview and was unworried about it now, since she expected to die before she got halfway to Hollywood, where, according to Google Maps, the radio station was. Having lived for twenty years in San Diego, Amy had neither driven to Los Angeles nor planned to do so. She had relied on Maxine, who had promised to set her up with a train and taxi. Maxine called her up thirty-six hours before the radio interview, swearing impressively about "so-called public transportation" in Southern California. "The train will deposit you three miles from the station," she said, and when Amy said fine, I'll cab it from there, Maxine said no you won't. "Cabs are useless. I tried to get you a limo at the station, but it was too late." In the ensuing marathon yelling match, Maxine admitted that for a thousand dollars Amy could have door-to-door limo service, at which point Amy, caught between the Scylla of the I-5 North and the Charybdis of grotesque luxury, settled on the six-headed beast. "Look," said

Maxine, *"I'll* be paying for the limo, not you." Amy said nobody should pay for a limo. When did ordinary people started taking limousines? It was the principle of the thing. She hung up while Maxine tried to change her mind. Whether she was taking pity on Amy or genuinely worried about a twenty-car pileup, Amy didn't care. She and Maxine were apparently becoming like family, with that familial raising of the rudeness threshold. She printed out three separate map directions and programmed her handheld GPS while trusting none of them.

Amy hated to go anywhere she had not been before. Max had found this hilarious, along with her dislike of untasted foods and general mistrust of all new experiences. But then Max was not a New Englander by birth. There were excellent reasons for fearing the new. Getting lost was one of them. She had such fear of losing her way that last night she had come close to calling Carla and asking her to drive up with her. She knew Carla would drop everything to do it: she'd insist on doing all the driving too. Pride, Amy had always thought, was more virtue than vice. In this case it prevented her from taking advantage of a nice girl who must have better things to do.

After a sleepless night, Amy filled Alphonse's bowls and se-creted various snacks around the house, just to keep him amused. She had arranged with the Blaines to check in on him and let him out a couple of times. She took out of the freezer a giant beef bone she had bought at Ralph's. It was the biggest bone she had ever seen, an uncut femur longer than her forearm, to which a few strips of meat and fat still clung. She had been saving it for a dog treat and now she placed it in the raised garden in front of the bird-bath. Alphonse could decimate ordinary bones in an hour; this one would keep him busy for at least a day. Bill Blaine, avid gar-dener, would be up tomorrow with the mockingbirds and sure to notice if her car wasn't back yet; by nightfall, they'd sound the alarm. The Blaines surely would care for Alphonse during her prolonged hospitalization; if she died in a fiery crash, they would find him a good home.

If you had to drive the freeways, Sunday morning was probably your best shot. Traffic, while not exactly light, was not intimidating. But as she pushed through Irvine the road grew sinister, older and more decrepit. She was heading into the oldest snarl of cloverleaves in the most extensive highway system in the known universe. Past Anaheim, the 5 took on the dull patina of antiquity. Amy tried to distract herself imagining the cracks, crumbles, and roadside detritus as artifacts from some ancient world. Archaeologists would devote months to resurrecting and restoring a single billboard, then quarrel for years over its significance. A bikinied blonde, jacknifed into a half-full martini glass, might be evidence of anthropophagy, or perhaps a minor deity, the goddess of potable water. Maybe the ancient decadents drank only wine that had been sat in by virgins.

Amy did pretty well until she had to merge onto the I-10 and then begin obsessing about upcoming exits. At this point her GPS, an inexpensive little device the size of a bar of soap, began taunting her with what she would have to do in the near future. The voice was a woman's, maddeningly upbeat, and she liked to work with odd fractions ("In nine-tenths of a mile, *take exit on left*!") but cunningly avoided specific details ("*Take ramp ahead, then bear left, then stay right*"). If Amy took the wrong exit, the woman would start babbling urgently and forcing Amy into endless, nightmarish loops. Amy had not bought the model that actually spoke the names of the streets because it was too expensive, and anyway its computerized speech, while more entertaining than the chirpy obnoxious female, sounded like the vocalization of space aliens.

Whenever Amy was forced to go somewhere new she could not bring herself to listen to music, not so much because it might make her lose track of where she was (she never actually knew where she was anyway), but because she was haunted by the thought of ironic music streaming from the crumpled, smoking wreck of her death car. Now for the same reason she gripped the steering wheel, fighting the instinct to shut off the damn thing. She imagined herself trapped, paralyzed, dying, listening to *Recalculating! When you can, make a U-turn! Then, bear right!*

By the time she pulled up to the station, all her muscles ached from having been clenched for the last ten miles of a journey which had, of course, been wholly uneventful. There was no great relief, no gratitude mixed in with the exhaustion. Phobic episodes always ended with a vague sense of anticlimax, even disappointment, as though underneath all the terror she had been hoping for the very worst to happen. A Platonic catastrophe.

The first floor was a streamlined, white, unpopulated place. After wandering around looking at elevator signs, Amy realized that more was housed here than just the radio station. There were law offices on the top two floors, kept busy perhaps by lawsuits threatened by interviewees such as herself. When she arrived at the KYJ floor, the elevator doors opened onto a thoroughfare, its walls covered with posters of grinning, mostly male faces, its blue carpet worn and scuffed by scurriers loaded down with bags, boxes, newspapers, and coffee. She found a reception desk and discovered she was almost a half hour early.

The receptionist was of indeterminate age and species, the first cosmetic surgery victim Amy had ever seen up close. She was blond and tall and looked as though a crew of thugs had starved her, forced her to break rocks in the blazing sun, inflated her breasts, and punched her in the mouth. They hadn't gotten into her eyes, though, and in their depths Amy thought she glimpsed a desperate human captive.

"I'm Shambala," she said. "Who are you here for?"

Amy went blank. Shambala's parents had to be her own age. They must have had her at the last minute. Poor Shambala, a love child named for a Three Dog Night song. "I'm here for someone whose name escapes me."

"Gotta either be Chaz Molloy or—"

"Molloy, that's it," said Amy. "Are you from Boston or Providence?" Shambala's accent humanized her, surprising Amy into an uncharacteristically personal question.

"You can tell?" Shambala was crushed.

"Well, it's nothing to be ashamed of!"

"My so-called dialect coach is a gyp," said Shambala, ushering Amy into a small room that smelled like flop sweat and ham sandwiches. "This is our green room," she said, fluttering her fingers at a row of complimentary water bottles.

"What's he like?" asked Amy.

"Chaz is a real good guy," said Shambala, but her eyes said something more nuanced. She went to leave, then turned back. "Danvers, Mass," she said. "You from around there too? *You* don't sound like it at all."

"Maine," said Amy. She thought about explaining that she didn't sound like Maine either, because in order to pick up regional dialects, your parents have to have them, or else you need to spend your formative years outside of your own head, but Shambala shrugged, smiled, and left before Amy could decide how to say this.

Amy rummaged through her carry bag, into which she had thoughtlessly thrown a few of her books, her notebook, and a box of Kleenex. The *ABR* piece, which had apparently occasioned the interview, was not there. She remembered intending as recently as this morning to print it out and read it here, just prior to the interview, so it would stick in her mind. And she had printed it out. She just hadn't brought it with her. Perhaps it was time to start keeping to-do lists.

Amy called Maxine but the call went straight to voicemail. She tried to think of who else might have read the piece, but the only numbers she had were Maxine's and Carla's. By the time it occurred to her to ask Shambala if she could access the Internet somehow, a potbellied young man in a brown T-shirt poked his head in the green room. "You're Amy, right?" he asked, looking briefly her way, and he told her to follow him. He sounded stoned.

The design on the back of the T-shirt invited her, with words and a big white arrow, to "kiss this." To keep up with his long strides she would have had to jog, but she had no interest in doing either, and when she arrived at what must be Chaz Molloy's studio, he was holding the door wide, his posture slumped and aggrieved, as though she had kept him waiting for hours. "Thank you," she said, which seemed to annoy him further. As she walked, Amy realized that the thoroughfare wasn't really all that busy: the number of people rushing around did not approximate the number of desks and office doors. This was Sunday, after all. Not exactly rush hour at KYJ.

Molloy's studio was small, bright, loud, and ugly. A glass partition divided it down the middle, with a large desk on the other side and two big microphones hanging down like banana bunches, one for a plump, balding, red-bearded man shuffling papers and snapping his fingers at the T-shirt stoner, and one apparently for her. This must be Chaz Molloy. Wordlessly T-shirt Guy pointed her to her seat, then shuffled out of the room. "Real Coke, John," Molloy shouted after him, "not that diet crap." As she rounded the partition and sat down, Amy felt invisible and okay with that. Clearly these people were not going to waste her time with rote pleasantries.

"Amy . . . *Gallup*?" said Chaz Molloy, not looking up from his papers. When she didn't respond, he glanced up, at which point she nodded to him, smiling politely. "Know how to use the mike, Amy? Know the drill?" Amy nodded again. She assumed the drill couldn't be too complicated. Molloy shuffled some more, then looked at her speculatively. Amy looked back. Molloy pressed a button and said, "We need a voice check. Raul? Voice check?" and in after half a minute yelled at Raul, who ran in, fitted Amy with cold headphones, and asked her to say something in her normal voice.

"This is my normal voice," said Amy.

Molloy smiled at her, crinkling the corners of his eyes to simulate warmth. "Are you nervous? Would you like John to bring you some coffee?" When she shook her head, he put headphones on himself and spoke directly into her ears. "Okay, dear, we're on in ten." His radio voice was a gorgeous low baritone; his undertones had undertones. He sounded like an attractive man with a full head of hair. He was calling her "dear" because she was old. If she were younger, he'd call her "babe." Amy hardly ever took offense at this sort of thing, but thought she could make an exception in his case.

Molloy was a bully. His show of courtesy had been delayed by a calculation as measured and deliberate as those eye-crinkles. Amy had not dealt with bullies since middle school, and even there they had not threatened her because they mantled nothing she wanted. She viewed them, as she did most people her own age, as through a telescope. She saw the damage they did to kids who wanted to fit in. She wondered why these kids didn't simply shrug off the taunts and insults and appreciate society's cold shoulder for what it was: the fortifications of an enormous blocky prison. Outside those gray walls she was free. She wasn't alone—in the distance she could spy other individuals, grazing. They would nod gravely to one another in passing.

"Aaaand we're back," said Molloy. "As promised, in the studio with me this fine Sunday afternoon is *Amy Gallup.*" He pronounced her name as though it were a curiosity, some strange billboard glimpsed from a late-night highway. "Who is *Amy Gallup,* you ask? Well, Amy Gallup is, according to *The New York Review of Books,* a writer to be reckoned with. And *The New York Review of Books* should know. Right, folks? I mean, *The New York Review of Books*! Amy Gallup, welcome to the show." Molloy crinkled at Amy, displaying an expensive set of blindingly white teeth.

"American," said Amy.

"I beg your pardon?"

"The *American Review of Books.* Not the New York."

Chaz Molloy made a droll face. "Oh, my bad. We certainly wouldn't want to confuse the two, would we? No, of course, it was the *American Review of Books.* Now that we've got that straight, Amy Gallup is the author of six highly acclaimed feminist novels, the latest of which, while it sold less than four thousand copies, was nominated for the National Book Award. Congratulations, Amy! Tell us, Amy, what constitutes a feminist novel?"

Oh, god, thought Amy. They got me all the way up here for *less* than nothing. This was just like the Nimoy snafu, only worse. "Actually," she said, "I have no idea, because—"

"Now, *come on*! You write them, you gotta have some idea."

"There's been a mistake," said Amy. "I don't know who you think I am, but I've not written a feminist novel, nor have I been nominated for a major award in decades. I'm sorry," she added, idiotically, as though this were all her fault.

Molloy looked closer at his papers. "It says right here you wrote—no, wait a minute—okay, madam, you are one hundred percent correct. My crack team of screw-ups went and highlighted the wrong section." Molloy glared out at a distraught middle-aged woman who had poked her head in the door. "Nice going, *Leslie Carnahan*," boomed Molloy, using the woman's full name right on the air in front of everybody. The mistake probably hadn't even been Leslie's, who at any rate did not deserve public humiliation. Still, Amy was greatly relieved, as she had begun to wonder if the *ARB* article, rather than Molloy's crew, had been responsible for the confusion, which would have been even worse.

"So you *don't* write feminist novels," said Molloy, marking time while he scanned his material again.

"Is that going to be a problem?"

"Says here you wrote a novel called *Monstrous Women*. Catchy title!"

"That was a collection of short stories," said Amy.

Molloy shot her a panicked look. "Well, were *these* novels? *Everything Handsome? The Ambassador of Loss? A Fiercer Hell?*"

"Yes, those are novels."

"Amy, I'm so sorry about this," said Molloy, who was now going to have to fill time discussing material with which he was completely unfamiliar, as opposed to material with which he was glancingly familiar. He looked more mortified than apologetic. "This has never happened before."

Still, Amy summoned up fellow feeling. "I believe you," she

said to him. "Happens to me all the time. The last time I gave a reading, they thought I was Leonard—"

"Says here," said Molloy, "that you're 'A talent ripe for rediscovery.' What does that mean, exactly?"

"Search me," said Amy. "I didn't write the article. I had no idea what it was going to say until it came out." Actually, she still didn't know what it said, but if she told him that, he'd probably lose it. *A talent ripe for rediscovery*. What baloney.

"Come now," said Molloy. "If I said that, oh, I don't know, *Robbie Williams* was a talent ripe for rediscovery, you'd know what that meant, wouldn't you?"

"I might, if I knew who that was." This came out snottier than Amy had intended.

"Says here," continued Molloy, whose expression was no longer mortified, "'Amy Gallup is a fearless writer, unaffected by literary trends.' Says your work is unflinching and mordantly funny. What's your take on that, Amy? Are you 'unflinching'? *Unflinching*," he repeated, in a mock-thoughtful tone. "I'm just riffing here, but it's my understanding that people *flinch* when they're being shot at or menaced in some way. We flinch to avoid being hit. In 1962, during the Cuban Missile Crisis, the Soviets flinched and we didn't. I'm just wondering here how a writer, or a novel, can be unflinching. I mean, can a novel actually flinch?"

So much, Amy thought, for fellow feeling. Still she couldn't summon up anger at this person. He was overbearing and contemptuous, but no Jenny Marzen. What an odd thought. Now she decided to pretend that they were having a civilized disagreement, just as though in the United States this were still possible. "Fiction, a poem, any work of art can shy away from the truth, for one reason or another, often because you can make more money with a lie, but sometimes because you're just not good enough."

"Okay," he said, obviously unengaged by what she thought was actually a promising topic, "but isn't there a difference between shying away and flinching? What does fear have to do with anything? In what sense are you a fearless writer?"

"In no sense," said Amy. "There are certain terms, like *fearless* and *unflinching* and *compelling* and *luminous,* that are used so often and so promiscuously that their original meanings have gotten lost, assuming that *compelling,* all by itself, ever had an original meaning. On top of which I think you'll agree that not flinching from the truth on paper is quite different from not flinching when faced with a firing squad."

"Bless your heart, madam, you're a human thesaurus!" Molloy gestured toward her like a supplicant, palms up, then crooking his fingertips at her, as though summoning a waiter. He was trying to communicate something, like *Hurry up!* or maybe *Come on!* Baffled, she shook her head and shrugged. He looked back down at his notes. "So you don't think that you're fearless and unflinching."

"That's correct," said Amy. "In fact, I've never bought into the concept of moral courage, as comparable to physical. When people say artists are fearless, they're attributing moral courage to them, which I think is spurious, really. To me, courage is significant only if it involves a physical threat, or at least the perception of a physical threat."

"Huh." Amy counted three seconds of dead air. Had she put him to sleep? "Folks, we're going to take a break, but don't go away, we'll be right back with *Amy Gallup,* today's guest artist, who is not a fearless writer."

Molloy whipped off his headphones and stormed out of the room. Through the closed door she could hear his muffled bellowing in the hallway. All she could make out was *What am I supposed to do with this, Leslie? You're useless, Leslie!* He stalked back in and with a strained smile asked Amy if she had copies of her books with her. Sorry, no, Amy lied. Clearly he had planned to read aloud and ridicule sections of that feminist novel. Molloy didn't frighten her, but she wasn't about to let him get his paws on her books. She wondered why not.

He was even unhappier after he put his headphones back on than he had been when taking them off. He apologized to his listeners that, because of his *bumbling assistant Leslie Carnahan,* he would be unable to read any of Amy's work on the air.

"That's okay," said Amy. "My stuff isn't ideal for that anyway. It's rather dense. Plus, really, unlike poetry, fiction is best read on the page."

"And if our listeners want to read your books, I'm sure they can buy them online. Can we go over the titles again?"

"Actually they're all out of print," said Amy.

Molloy rubbed his eyes. "Out of print. All of them."

"Yes," said Amy, "but that's what libraries are for."

Molloy stared at her in what looked like unfeigned disbelief. "Yet, according to this very article, your novels are, and I quote, 'necessary to our lives.'"

"You're kidding," said Amy. "Does it actually say that?"

"Yes, it actually—wait a minute," said Molloy. "Am I supposed to believe that you haven't even read this thing?"

Maxine was going to kill her. "I was planning to," she said, lamely, "but I've been busy."

"*'Necessary to our lives,'*" he said again, drawing out this ridiculous phrase, "and I've been trying to imagine just how *necessary* your novels could be. Especially since they're *out of print.*"

"Again," said Amy, "you're asking the wrong person. I—"

"Do you think your novels are as necessary as, oh, I don't know, the Constitution?"

"Certainly not."

"Are they as necessary as the Bible?"

"They're not even as necessary as the menu at Olive Garden," said Amy. The difference between Molloy and Jenny Marzen, she decided, was that Molloy was wretched. He didn't adore himself, and while he probably had fans, they didn't love him. Pack animals didn't love their leaders. It was impossible to take his dislike personally, and not just because he had nothing she wanted. Chaz Molloy hated everybody. Marzen's cheerleading was much harder to endure than Molloy's contempt.

Molloy slumped back in his chair with a martyred expression. He must be John's role model. "Are you criticizing the person who wrote this, I must say, very generous and complimentary article about you?"

Who *had* written it? God, Amy thought, I hope it was no one I like. "I am *sympathizing*," she said, "with the person who wrote this. Pieces like this, book reviews and the like, are written to deadline. I write them myself occasionally. It is much harder to think originally, to express your ideas clearly without slipping into cliché, when you're so limited in time and you're given so little space for discussion. It's easy enough to know that you like something; it's much harder to decide why and then say so in six hundred words."

Molloy held out a warning finger, said, "Back in a minute, folks," flipped a switch in front of him, glared at Amy, and said, "Lady, you're giving me nada here. How am I supposed to fill fifteen more minutes?"

Amy actually looked around to see if anyone were standing in back of her. No. He was apparently talking to her. "Why are you asking me?"

"Sweetheart, this is 'The Petri Dish'! This is KYJ! This is not an effing literary salon!"

"Then why did you invite me? What were you expecting?"

"Somebody with a pulse," said Molloy. He said it under his breath with his head turned away from her, but had to know she had heard him. He blushed. Amy could see the heat flashing up his neck. "Don't mind me, dear," he said, avoiding eye contact, "it's just been one of those days." He shouted into what Amy assumed was an intercom, "Where's my goddamn Coke?" and donned the headphones, welcoming his listeners back on for the second half of the show, and inviting them to call in with any questions. "I don't usually open the lines until the final segment, but I'm going to make an exception in this case, folks, since, frankly, I've run out of material." A full second of dead air followed, during which he snapped his fingers in the direction of a mirror on the opposite wall, behind which there must lurk some production crew with a bank of phones or something.

"What do you do," asked Amy, "if nobody calls?"

"Never happens," said Molloy through gritted teeth. There would be no more crinkling.

A third voice arrived in Amy's headphones. "Chaz? This is John from Fontana, first-time caller, long-time listener." John's voice sounded familiar. "Chaz, is this lady for real?"

"I assure you, John, she is absolutely real. Exceptionally so, in fact."

"So she's like somebody we're all supposed to read? What's that all about?"

"You tell me, John. I'm out of ideas at this point."

While John and Chaz agreed about something at length

without actually articulating what the point of agreement was, Amy recognized John's voice. John was John the T-shirt Guy. *This* was what they did when nobody called. Amy considered ratting him out but decided not to. In their place, she would probably have done the same thing. Of course, before being in their place she would have taken the gas pipe, but the principle was the same. She wondered how old the expression "take the gas pipe" actually was. Her grandfather used to say it a lot, and it always made her laugh. She heard "John" use the terms "Vocabulary Nazi" and "cultural fathead," and Molloy's unconvincing demurrer. Amy assumed the script required callers to "convince" Molloy that his guest of the week was an Icon for Idiots. "Take the gas pipe" was, Amy guessed, about the same vintage as "Pull a Brodie." Old slang expressions were so much more energetic and colorful than most of the current ones, which seemed designed more to obfuscate than to paint an indelible picture.

"Amy," Molloy was saying. "You can jump in any time now."

"I'm sorry," said Amy. "Was there a question for me?"

Both men laughed. Molloy was cheering up a little.

The next caller was female. "Chaz, this is Kaitlyn? From Apple Valley?" Shambala sounded like she was reading from a prepared sheet. Molloy cut her off when she referred to today's guest as "Ed Begley Jr."

"Chaz, this is Laverne from Burbank, first-time caller, last-time listener." Maxine's gravelly voice was unmistakable. "What's your point, exactly? You're all over this woman like a cheap suit!"

Molloy cut Maxine off. Few of the callers who weighed in during the next five minutes could conceivably have been real. She had no idea how Maxine had arranged it, but her shills kept duking it out with Molloy's, and for a while Amy sort of enjoyed it, but eventually she let her mind roam. What if she had told

Carla, or Dr. Surtees, or Kurt Robetussien about this show. Would they have called in to defend her? She was annoyed with herself for even thinking such a thing. At the final commercial break, Amy asked Molloy, "Is this the way it usually goes? Do you even *have* listeners? Or is it like professional wrestling?"

Molloy sighed. "No, this is not like professional wrestling. Pro wrestling is *big*. Pro wrestling makes money. What this is, this is *Sunday*. All the true callers are at the beach, at the game, at the goddamn zoo with their goddamn kids, that's what this is." "John from Fontana" brought Molloy his Coke, for which service he got called an ugly name, unbefitting even to "John from Fontana."

"We're on in thirty," he told her. "Look, you seem like a nice lady. The mix-up's on me. Well, not me per se, but, you know"—he waved at the mirror on the far wall—"you get what you pay for. But now I'd appreciate it—America would appreciate it—if you'd jump in and say *something*. Okay? Anything? In case someone's listening?"

Amy thought about it. What she thought was, what the hell.

In the first place, no one *was* listening, and in the second place, even if somebody was, she had already gotten all she was going to get from the birdbath interview, and it was plenty, more than she deserved: she was writing again. She was writing damn well, better than ever. Why had she been so worried about the truth coming out? Why not spill it now? She would make a gift of it, a small carcass Molloy could drag back into his cave. Amy suddenly felt light, energized. Fearless.

"Aaand we're back," he said, reintroducing Amy as "a human fireball with an impressive vocabulary whose works are necessary to our lives. Amy Gallup, let's wrap this thing up. How'd you get to be a cultural icon?"

"By accident," said Amy.

"Well," said Molloy, "that explains a lot!"

"I fell down and knocked myself out on a birdbath, and then I did a newspaper interview when I was not in my right mind, and one thing led to another, and here we are."

"Good one," said Molloy. "Seriously, why were you picked for this *American Review* gig? You're out of print. Nobody reads you. Except whoever wrote this article telling everybody to drop what they're doing and discover this great talent that's been lying around under their noses since, what, 1982? How'd this happen?"

So much for her grand reckless gesture. Why didn't he believe her? Why was he so fixated on her bit of praise from the *ARB*? Was he a failed novelist? Did everybody in North America have an attic chest full of rejected manuscripts? She'd given the man an actual scoop for God's sake. "Listen to me," she said to him. "It was an accident."

"Tell me something, when you're writing, when you're writing *ripe, necessary* novels, do you do more than play with words? I ask, because, let's be honest, that's mostly what you do, isn't it?"

Amy took a beat. When she wrote dialogue, she sometimes took a beat in order to emphasize a line or vary the rhythm of the conversation. Now she took one to check her temper. "I've never *played with words* in my life," she said.

"Intellectuals love to talk about *accidents,* don't they? Everything's an *accident*. The Big Bang's an *accident*."

"Do soldiers play with bullets? Do carpenters play with wood? Wordplay is for writers with nothing to say. When I have nothing to say, I don't write."

"The Big Bang, the origin of human life, it's all a big fat *accident*. No divine plan, no cosmic design, if we get hit with a comet tomorrow, it's just a great big custard pie in the kisser."

"You don't listen," said Amy.

"Tell me, how many government grants have you taken so you can continue not writing?"

Amy relaxed. The hell with Chaz Molloy. "I really can't remember them all," she said.

Molloy's shoulders instantly relaxed, and he leaned back in his chair, stretching out his arms, rolling the kinks out of his neck muscles, talking all the while. "There we have it, folks," he said. "Your tax dollars in action. The Enn Eee Ay. The same chowderheads who paid Robert Mapplethorpe to stick bullwhips up his fanny."

"Oh, not just the NEA," said Amy. "Also the USCWA, the SSWC, and the NCN."

"NCN?"

"National Consortium of Novelists."

"I never heard of it."

"Nobody has. You have to be a novelist to know about it."

"Are you serious?" Molloy was not a stupid man, but already relief, even joy, were overwhelming his innate skepticism. "How much money are we talking about here?"

"Conservatively? For me alone? Over a lifetime? In the high six figures."

"And for what? If you don't mind my asking. What did we—excuse me, the NCN—pay you for?"

"Basically, anything I wanted to write. Of course, you have to apply, you have to click the right boxes, line up the right references, you have to jump through hoops, but if you know what you're doing, you're a shoo-in."

"So if I wanted to write, say, a romance novel about young nurses in love, or some chick-lit nonsense, or a coming-of-age memoir about growing up gay in Cleveland—"

"No," said Amy. "Too mainstream. Nobody submits work that isn't way, way out of the mainstream."

"Mainstream," Molloy repeated, leaning forward. Goggling.

"Well, think about it," she said. "If you're writing pop stuff, it's going to sell, it's going to make you money. Who need grants when you've got profits?"

"Who indeed!" said Molloy. "So let me get this straight. You can write anything you want, as long as it's guaranteed not to sell."

" 'Guarantee' is such a scary word," said Amy. "Every now and then an NCN book will fall through the cracks. One of my own novels actually made a few bestseller lists." This much was true. For some reason, her books had always sold well in Albany, Oakland, and Columbus, Ohio.

"Amy," he said, addressing her this way for the first time in the interview, "what does *out of the mainstream* really mean? Could you give us an example?"

"Well, Chaz," she said, knitting her brow to simulate thought, though careful not to overdo it, since, however gullible the man was at the moment, surely he had a working BS detector. "It's not as though there's a checklist or anything. It's more about what doesn't fly than what does. Genre fiction's out, of course, unless you turn it on its head. Omniscient narration is out, unless the narrator is, you know, severely autistic or whatever. What's out, frankly, is clarity. That's the deal. What you have to aim for is obscurity."

"Obscurity," said Molloy, who by now looked like a little child on Christmas morning.

"Yes, because the thing is, if the work is obscure, then it needs to be explained. And that's where the Academy comes in!"

"The Academy?"

"Yes," said Amy. "That's the ultimate goal. That's the gold

standard. To write a novel so profoundly obscure that it must be taught. Then college students can be forced to buy copies, you see! If the same courses are taught year after year, you have a captive market."

Amy had no idea if this was true, but it had a certain appeal. Actually, she was suddenly veering dangerously close to a point of likely philosophical agreement with Chaz Molloy. It was time to wrap things up. "And of course, once you've got the Academy involved, you've got a closed loop, financially speaking, politically speaking. And ultimately, that's what we're talking about here, right? Politics?"

"Meaning—?"

"Meaning that no matter who's in charge, regardless of prevailing political winds, regardless, let's face it, of *the will of the people*"—Amy furnished air quotes and a tone of amused scorn—"we can keep churning out arty-farty ivory-tower left-wing anti-gun ACLU tree-hugging lesbian atheist fetus-hating garbage, and you can keep paying for it."

"There you have it!" announced Molloy triumphantly, his mouth getting ahead of his brain, because she could see on his face the rapidly dawning understanding that he had been had.

He opened his mouth to retrieve his mistake, to shape it into a save, but a blue light was blinking over that mirror on the wall, and there just wasn't enough time. Too bad.

"I never took a penny from the government," Amy said, "and I have never *played with words*. You colossal ass."

Molloy, his face flushed, opened his mouth and shut it again. For the first time since she'd gotten there, Amy heard music. "Bolero," scored for heavy metal guitar. It sounded like an air raid. "That's all, folks," he shouted, "tune in next week when our guest will be—*Leslie?* Who's on for next Sunday?" The door remained closed. "There you have it, folks! Our guest will be *Some! Random! Cultural! Fathead!* Stay tuned now for—" The blue light and music went off simultaneously, and Molloy threw his headphones at the wall and charged off cursing.

Amy could hear him walking down the hall screaming imprecations, but she couldn't hear anybody answering him. In the muffled distance, a door slammed. She looked toward the mirror and waved. "Is anybody in there?" she asked. "Is it all right for me to leave?" The mirror disappeared, and in its place appeared a brightly-lit roomful of people—Leslie Carnahan, Raul, Shambala, and John from Fontana—waving gaily back at her. They all looked genuinely happy. Her new friends. She'd actually connected with somebody. Well, at least it hadn't been a total loss.

Cars were like hounds: they always knew their way home. Driving home she felt expansive, nearly content. She turned off the GPS lady, found Oscar Peterson on the radio, and let her car nose its way to harbor. For the first sixty miles she basked in the modest glory of her performance, which she really owed in its entirety to Chaz Molloy. First, he had prodded her into an honest confession, which in the end had relieved her conscience and cost her nothing. And if he hadn't pushed her too far with that wordplay insult, there would have been no performance at all, just a waste of time and gasoline. Her NCN riff had been pretty inspired. Also, as obnoxious as he was, she had not blamed him for the feminist icon debacle. He had no way of knowing she had been dogged by such misapprehensions since childhood, starting with when she had been chosen for some all-district poetry award and gotten pinned with a medal for "excellence in athletics." Her birth, marriage, and publication dates were often way off, and her name in print had invariably been misspelled (with an *o* instead of a *u*), once on the inside cover of a first edition. Amy attracted these little muddles the way some people won door prizes. Molloy had dealt with it gracelessly, but she couldn't hold that against him, especially in light of how inappropriate an interview subject she turned out to be. Surely if he had known anything about her—whatever there was about her to know—he never would have agreed to have her on in the first place.

Which led her to wonder, about the time she was passing through Costa Mesa, how Maxine had gotten her the interview in the first place. Had she lied? Surely *she* hadn't deliberately confused Amy with that feminist writer. Amy tried to remember how Maxine had explained it. Molloy, she said, needed writers to interview, to balance out the "celebs." Jenny Marzen, Amy now remembered, refused to do it. Had Marzen contacted Maxine? Maybe, but that still didn't explain how either of them convinced KYJ she was punching-bag material. She worried at the problem for a few miles, then gave up. Amy, who would have made a hopeless engineer, had never really been driven to understand the how of things. However it had happened, Maxine had gotten her on the show, and that was that, and thank god it was all over with anyway.

Except . . . why? Why had Maxine done whatever she did to shoehorn Amy into that ridiculous spot? Even if Molloy had exaggerated his lackluster audience numbers, surely the people who actually listened to him were not in Amy's demographic, assuming that she actually had a demographic. Can a demographic fit into a telephone booth? Maxine always had her reasons, whether Amy agreed with them or not, and now she couldn't imagine what had possessed her to inveigle a minor, long-forgotten writer, all buzz aside, into such a pointless quest. Why, unlike how, was always worth pursuing.

But not now. She thought about "Snowflake," and then about how badly she had wanted to see the shadow of a rabbit's ears on the surface of that full moon. Sixty years ago! That young moon.

She would have made great time but lost a half hour when the smoking wreck of someone else's life backed up traffic north of Oceanside. She turned off the engine, took out the notebook, and wrote

"True Caller"
"All Buzz Aside"
"The Deal"

Tomorrow, she'd turn her phone back on, and once Maxine calmed down, she'd tell her all about it, and Maxine would tell her all about why. Oscar Peterson played "Hymn to Freedom." Amy just loved that tune.

CHAPTER TWENTY-THREE

Ants

Alphonse stayed mad for two full days. The Blaines had apparently left him out in the yard, which he hated with a passion. Not the yard itself—a pleasant enough place for postprandial strolls—but the very idea of roughing it for long periods of time. The intense inland summer heat had come early, confining him to treeshade. All of Amy's trees were surrounded with dirt, except for a huge pine tree growing at an acute slant behind the raised garden, but Alphonse didn't like pine needles either. The basset was happy only when sleeping on deep wool pile or upholstered furniture. So when Amy returned from KYJ and threw open her back door, he barreled past her without a welcoming grunt or even a dirty look.

Amy knew he'd get over it. Still she was grateful when, by nightfall, having spent a full afternoon gnawing on that giant bone, he was back to his old self, gracing her with an occasional sidelong glance, coming to her at bedtime so she could stroke his neck and ears.

* * *

Amy intended to spend the next day profitably, attending to her online workshop, where student fiction had begun to pile up. In order to get to the workshop link, she had as usual to go through her blog page, which she hadn't actually looked at for weeks, and this time she saw a warning flag on the Comments feature. Apparently her blog had gagged on comments.

She had to check them out, since the last time this had happened her spam-catcher had failed or been hijacked or something, and her website had become a bedlam of misspelled obscenities. Sure enough, today her pages were contaminated by links to Spanish Prisoner scams, plight cons, pornography, and genital enhancement products. She had to download and install a newer battlement plug-in. Still, an hour later, after she had waded through and deleted all the junk, the warning flag still flew because *legitimate* comments continued to overwhelm her site. The garbage she had just cleared away only revealed the truth. Actual human beings, as opposed to bots, were flocking to her website. What was wrong with them?

At first she thought they were still fulminating about "THE ACCIDENT-DRIVEN LIFE." Glancing through some complaints, she found no new arguments for compulsory happy endings. If anything, there seemed to be a charge in the opposite direction, led by people with names like Stabby Appleton and truthierthanthou666, supporting Amy's right to generate fiction that made people miserable and anxious. In fact it soon became apparent that most posters were complaining, not about her, but on her behalf.

In fact, when she backed away from the screen a little and caught sight of the design of the comment queue, Amy realized they were all part of a single thread which had begun on the third of July, entitled "Chaz Molloy Epic Fail." The poster was Stabby Appleton, who provided an audio link to the entire KYJ interview. Stabby advised that "The real carnage begins at 26.06.11." Amy worried at this number, trying to figure out if it was some kind of terrorist code. When she gave up and clicked on the link, she saw it referred to times: Amy had unloaded on Chaz Molloy, feeding him all that baloney about the National Consortium of Novelists, at about the twenty-six minute mark of the thirty-minute interview. Listening to herself do this was shamefully enjoyable, the ostensive definition of a guilty pleasure.

Amy remembered the first time she had ever heard herself on the radio. She had been fifteen and chosen by Mrs. Gormley to be Longfellow Senior High's representative on a local radio show. The assigned topic was something like "The Twist: Threat or Menace?" Mrs. Gormley had adored Amy, who had in turn thought Mrs. Gormley a dumb pushover. Even though Amy had zero interest in geopolitics, she had steered the conversation elsewhere—to Cuba and the Peace Corps—since she had never been on a date and couldn't have cared less about dance crazes. What she really wanted to talk about that day was the Flying Wallendas, a high-wire act that had just endured a catastrophic fall in Detroit. She had that morning stared at a terrifying newspaper picture, snapped at the very moment when, for the Flying Wallendas, everything had come undone after their tightrope pyramid collapsed and all seven became the playthings of gravity. The picture had both thrilled and unhinged her: the thrill, she knew, even at fifteen, especially at fifteen, was wrong, almost dirty. She had wanted to make out the expressions on their faces as they tumbled, and she had wanted even more not to, and was still trying to figure out what this meant as the oleaginous JAB radio host, Leo LaMotte, swooned over her use of the word *mesmeriz-ing*. Didn't people have dictionaries? Didn't they read? Amy dominated that radio conversation without meaning or even registering a word of what she said, so that later on, when she caught the evening rerun of the show, she had recoiled from her own fatuousness. She had sounded like a pretentious child, which, she instantly realized, she actually was. On top of which her voice was at least a half-octave higher than she had ever imagined. There would be no point in asking her parents if she really sounded like that. They would just tell her what she wanted to hear.

Now, listening to herself spar with Molloy, she was more pleased with the pitch of her voice than with what she was actually saying. For women, aging was mostly a process of subtraction, of loss, except that their voices became stronger and deeper. Amy had noticed that men paid more attention to her when she lost her looks and had assumed that was because they were no longer distracted by desire, but it occurred to her now that words spoken in a lower register simply sounded more significant. Surely Mark Antony had not been cursed with a high, piping voice. Perhaps all young girls should receive voice-deepening instruction, as they once had learned how to iron men's white oxford-cloth shirts and walk with books on their heads.

The problem with being a smartass was that it only worked in an unfair fight. She had tricked Molloy handily. She had been clever and fast on her feet. But now, listening, she didn't approve of her own behavior. Once she had settled into his pitiful kingdom, making a fool of Chaz Molloy was no challenge. He was a fool already. According to her blog posters, though, she had been "totally brilliant." They quoted and misquoted her, providing as evidence for her brilliance her "arty-farty ivory-tower left-wing anti-gun" rant, the vulgarity of which now made her cringe, and the fact that she had called Molloy a colossal ass, which, accurate enough, was hardly witty.

To Amy's sorrow, at least half of the pro-Amy brigade had misunderstood her. Pro- and anti-Academy splinter groups formed, each arguing on the premise that the Academy was real. Well, it was, in the sense that there really was a community of academics whose literary judgments were taken seriously, at least by that community and its most prominent cadets. But the anti-Academy posters assumed Amy had been championing genre bestsellers, ridiculing works that you had to have an "MBA" to understand, and the rest somehow thought she was skewering mainstream fiction, whereas all she had intended to do—all she had actually done—was lasso a buffoon and smack him around.

As always, Amy responded more positively to negative criticism. A particularly thin splinter group, comprised of 46&Wondering and Ranty Ravingsworth, jabbed at her for taking a gig on KYJ in the first place. 46, who claimed to have read everything Amy had written, seemed grief-stricken over the fact that Amy was "reduced to midget-wrestling." (It was a tribute of sorts to Amy's blog that she didn't attract people inclined to jump all over the word *midget*.) 46 and Ranty had a good point, so good that Amy decided to respond, posting her own comment below theirs:

I agree with you. Participating in that sort of show is feeding the beast.

Amy started a sentence about her agent pressuring her to do it, then backed over it. It was uncomfortably close to "sharing." No, it *was* sharing. Where had that odd impulse come from? Besides, ratting out Maxine in public was just wrong: she owed

Maxine a lot more than she did 46 and Ranty. Deciding it was no one's beeswax why she had fed the beast, Amy hit "publish" on her comment page, closed it out, and began a new story, "True Caller."

By now Amy was used to her modestly active new writing life, one in which story ideas actually burgeoned, more often than not, into stories. "True Caller" was apparently going to be about a college dropout living in his parents' basement who spent his free hours calling radio talk shows. He made enough money at In-N-Out Burger to afford his own Internet connection and some professional-grade voice-changing software. Amy had to do some online research to discover what technology was out there, which turned out to be alarmingly impressive. Voice-changers were Google-flogged as though they were party accessories like karaoke machines: buyers were encouraged to have endless hours of fun with their friends. The non-fun-focused were assured that the software could be used for "business purposes" and for "creating a stimulating conversational ambience," which, Amy guessed, was the closest the ads could legally come to the essence of a technology allowing phone stalkers to scare the hell out of women in the middle of the night.

Her True Caller, though, whose name eluded her, aspired to drive call-in DJs mad and ultimately to bring down the monstrous rotting structure of radio talk-show culture. He called them all, the right-wingers, conspiracy seers, preachers, celebrity mongers, advice gurus. He created distinct personalities, male and female, each with its own dialect, pitch, and backstory. Typically he would agree with the host, opening with copious, breathless praise, proceeding to share an illustrative story promising to support whatever point the host was making on that particular show, and at some point the story would begin to veer off into the ether. At first, he just made the stories nonsensical: one minute he'd be talking about the damn wetbacks and how his Uncle Delbert couldn't get a job to save his life and the next he'd be yelling about tarantulas in his hat. Later he tended to stay focused, taking the host's message on race, Area 51, the Founding Fathers, or whatnot and stretching it out to its darkest imaginable reach, forcing the host either to repudiate what he'd just been saying or go on record as agreeing that we should repeal the nineteenth amendment or perform live autopsies on environmentalists. The story bogged down as Amy wrestled with technicalities, mainly about how the Caller always managed to dupe experienced screeners, and she wasn't sure it would ever amount to anything, but she enjoyed— actually enjoyed—creating all those personalities and took care to elevate each, however slightly, above its cartoonish beginnings. At the very least, "True Caller" was a great writing exercise.

So when Maxine interrupted with a call, Amy was feeling expansive—expansive enough to pick up the phone when she heard that low raspy voice. Expansive enough to hear Maxine out as she spun a most preposterous tale, of Munster and Marzen, of buzz and dish, of Manhattan and round tables. As Maxine droned, Amy grabbed her battered copy of *Le Morte d'Arthur* and opened to the end, the dog-eared page where Guinevere refuses Launcelot and walls herself off in the nunnery, and Launcelot says, "Sithen ye have taken you to perfection, I must needs take me to perfection of right. For I take record of God, in you I have had mine earthly joy." She had loved that speech since childhood, the shining steel greatsword of the old language. She had loved it even more than the astonishingly evolved notion of the round table itself, which surely was located somewhere in the British Isles, not the island of Manhattan, and what was Maxine going on about? "The big agencies," Maxine was saying, ". . . publishers, journalists, PEN, CNET, the usual suspects. It's a weekend deal and it will be televised."

"Okay, well, remind me when it's on and I'll watch it."

"You don't listen," said Maxine.

Amy put the book away. "I'm listening," she said, her good mood evaporating.

"You're not keynote," she said, "but you're important. They've got you on at nine p.m. on Friday."

"On what? Maxine, what are you—"

"Your assigned topic is 'Whither Publishing—the Writer's POV.' Sorry about that. You're on with Marzen and somebody else, I don't know who, but believe me, you'll be the icing."

Despite her growing alarm, Amy laughed. "That's the stupidest title I've ever heard," she said. *Whither* was a silly word except when used by the ancient dead, like Malory. No one could use *whither* unselfconsciously. *Here I am using "whither."* "You of course said no," she said.

"Basically all you have to do," said Maxine, "is riff on what you've been saying on the radio. The NPR rants are really strong, but you'll probably also get asked about the Molloy massacre, which isn't really on point, but remember, they'll be drinking."

"Are you talking," Amy asked, her breath quickening, "about some kind of Skypy thing, with me on a giant screen? You know I don't have the face for that. I have a radio face. I have a radio body. Tell them no."

"There's a business class ticket ready for you, both ways. They're paying for everything."

Amy was instantly light-headed, light-bodied, weightless. She didn't feel safe in her chair. "Give me a second," she said, navigating to her bed, falling into it like a rickety invalid. She closed her eyes against the spinning. She was as frightened by this physical reaction as she was by what Maxine was saying, and she had to tune her out to understand why. All she had to do was say no. She had been saying no her whole life, half the time to Maxine, who knew better than to even hint at Amy getting on an airplane. Why was she doing this now? "Business class what?"

"You know what," said Maxine, sounding like the voice of God.

"No," said Amy faintly.

"I tried to do Amtrak, babe. I've been online all morning and on the phone, trying to come up with a way to get you out here in two days, but it ain't happening."

"Two days??"

"I told you. You don't listen. Day after tomorrow, nine o'clock. Well, you're supposed to get there for dinner, but I already told them you might not make it."

"Wait a damn minute." Amy rallied, sitting up in bed, the blood beginning to return to her extremities. "Two days means I'm an afterthought, a last-minute sub. Toni Morrison backed out. Joyce Carol Oates has to wash her hair. They went through ninety names and finally got to mine. Well, tell them to stuff it."

Maxine coughed and hacked for a solid minute. Anybody can cough. It's not like a sneeze. Maybe there was nothing wrong with her lungs at all, and she was trying to wheeze Amy onto that plane. Amy waited her out. "Okay, I lied," Maxine said. "I set this up two weeks ago. I just forgot about booking a train. I'm sorry." More coughing.

"I don't believe you," Amy said, the tension between them

suddenly thick, bringing memories of that morning in Boston where they parted ways over uneaten bagels and bitter old coffee. They were right back there again. Max was dying, Amy was turning to stone, and Maxine was about to throw down a napkin and tell her to call when she gave a shit. All Amy had to do was hang up. She listened to the silence and knew Maxine was listening too, and as it lengthened, it changed somehow, took on a perceptible quality, a color. She had read about people tasting sounds and hearing colors and dismissed synesthesia as a rare example of science bumbling out of its proper zone, but now the absence of sound, which had been a black smudge, was lightening into blue. Amy lay back and closed her eyes. "Maxine, what aren't you telling me?"

Maxine lit a cigarette in response. Amy heard a metal lighter flick open, clang shut. Hearing, she could smell steel and lighter fluid and charred cotton wick.

"Is that the old Zippo?" asked Amy. "The Reddy Kilowatt Zippo?"

"You got a memory," said Maxine.

"I miss Reddy Kilowatt. Whatever happened to him? The energy crunch, I suppose." Reddy Kilowatt's act was encouraging people to light up every room in the house and turn night into day. "At Colby we had a house mother we called Reddy Kilowatt behind her back, because—"

"It might as well be lung cancer," said Maxine, "but it's not. Pulmonary shitstorm. I'm not gonna die tomorrow, but I'll probably miss the Mayan calendar deal."

"Are you alone?" asked Amy. "Who's going to help you out?"

"I'm all set," said Maxine.

There was another long silence between them, paler blue. Alphonse clicked into the bedroom and, in a rare display of fellow feeling, stood next to the bed so that Amy could lay her hand on his great warm head.

"I really did forget about the train," said Maxine. "I was going to set you up with a sleeper through Chicago, and then stuff happened. I messed up. And then this morning I tried to fix it, but I can't. You'll have to fly."

"I know," said Amy. What had frightened Amy from the start was that she knew she was going to do it.

Maxine said she'd email instructions about the plane and the hotel and they said good-bye.

Amy lay unmoving until night began to fall. She didn't think about Maxine, sick and dying, and what that meant. She didn't think about the plane, the speech, all those goddamn people, the cameras, the plane again. She didn't think about her own mortality. There would be plenty of time to do all that on the plane. For a while she didn't think of anything, and then, gradually, she began to puzzle over timelines.

If Maxine had set up the round table thing two weeks ago, then she had known about it since before Amy's schlep to KYJ. This had to mean that her epic throwdown of Chaz Molloy had nothing to do with the invitation. If her blog comments were at all significant, then the KYJ interview probably increased awareness of her among the Whither people, but they already knew who she was.

Baby steps. That's why Maxine forced her to go to LA. She had understood that in order to get Amy on a plane she first had to dislodge her from her chair, her house, her town. Having journeyed to that far-off radio station, Amy couldn't tell herself that travel was out of the question, that she wasn't that kind of writer, that kind of human being. And *of course* she had waited to spring the New York trip on Amy at the last minute. Amy didn't have enough time before boarding to make herself crazy sick. Maxine had planned all of it, and what humbled Amy now was the realization that Maxine actually knew her. Perhaps she had known all her clients this well. Perhaps she knew Henrietta Mant like the back of her hand. Perhaps this was simply a business skill. Amy didn't take it personally, but it moved her anyway.

At midnight, when the dishes were done, when she'd sent word to all student writers and Carla about her imminent departure— telling everyone when she'd be back, doing the grown-up thing, as though she believed she would survive the trip—she sat in her darkened parlor waiting for Alphonse to pound at the back door. He was barking out there in the yard, which he didn't often do this late at night, and she might have to go get him in a minute. His bark was basso and, as barks go, easy on the ears, but still her neighbors needed their sleep.

Amy marveled at her own calm. When she was young, she had lived in the future: looking forward to some events her greatest happiness—the anticipation always more thrilling than the thing itself; dreading other events a full-time job. "How about right now?" Max would ask her. "Right now is excellent," at which she would claim that of course she lived in the present, in the here and now, who the hell didn't, she just wasn't zen about it, and eventually she would pretend to concede his point, but she never understood it, or indeed how any sane adult could revel in the moment if there was something serious right around the corner. It was a preposterous notion, like setting up camp in the mouth of a bear cave, because "Right now, they're hibernating." But here she was, at peace, and in less than forty-eight hours she would be locked into a whining metal coffin, and she would just deal with it then. She was profoundly incurious about how ineptly she would do this. When she was young, she would have driven herself mad rehearsing.

His bark was getting louder, even deeper, outraged. Something was infuriating him and he was not about to let it go. Amy stood on the back steps and peered out onto the raised garden, where she could just make out his shape in the discreet light of a waxing crescent moon. He was standing his ground there, tossing something big into the air, grabbing it again after it landed with a thump, over and over, growling and barking continuously, berating it. Alphonse never killed things—he wasn't bred to, and it wasn't in his nature anyway, so the object couldn't be an animal. When Amy got closer she could see it was the giant beef bone from Ralph's. "What's your problem?" she asked him. He threw down the bone and barked at it full-throated, rhythmically, his whole body shuddering with each bark. One bark per second; you could set your watch. Amy shined her flashlight on the bone. "Look," she started to say, "it's your own damn bone, for Pete's sake," and then she saw it was covered with tiny black grease ants, swirling about its surface from top to bottom in smoothly shifting patterns. It looked like they were trying to spell out a rude message. No wonder he was angry. Any other dog would have shrugged it off, but not Alphonse. Alphonse had the attention span of Boris Spassky, and he never forgave an insult.

Amy grabbed his collar and tugged him into the house. "I don't blame you one bit," she said. "Tomorrow we'll wash it off and leave it inside. Tomorrow I'll still be here." He muttered something under his breath and went to bed. What a wonderful dog he was. Barking at ants in the moonlight, and she allowed the thought, just for an instant, that this would someday be a memory. That all that remained of this stalwart, irascible creature would be this image, which would disappear when she died, along with whatever random memories of herself remained extant, and that she had no say in who remembered her, and that in no time at all, no one would. But right now he was immortal. Right now was excellent.

CHAPTER TWENTY-FOUR

Storyteller

The next morning Maxine FedExed her a twenty-DVD Conquer-Your-Fear-of-Flying course, the running time of which was over one hundred hours. Since Amy would be airborne in thirty-six, she called Maxine to complain and was told that DVDs numbered 19 and 20 represented a crash course. "Is that supposed to be funny?" Amy asked.

"I hate it when you lose your sense of humor," said Maxine.

"Well, then, stop sending me to my flaming violent death."

"They have DVD players onboard. You can watch it while you fly."

"And change my ticket to one-way," said Amy. "I'm taking the train back."

"What makes you think I bought a round-trip ticket? You're booked on Amtrak sleepers from Penn Station to LA."

Amy hung up rather than thank Maxine for her thoughtfulness. She really couldn't manage that on the day before her flight. She spent the rest of the day cleaning her house and throwing away most of her clothes, outfits she hadn't worn for years and didn't want strangers rifling through with pity and alarm. By the time she was through, two drawers had been completely cleaned out. Alphonse frolicked in her half-empty closet. Since she would be gone either forever or for only two days, she made ordinary arrangements with the Blaines.

The night before, she slept like ice, dropping off without preamble, and woke up the same way an hour later. She spent the rest of the night at her computer. At dawn, just before she turned it off, she erased her search history, depriving anyone who came in after her death to mop up the spectacle of her search strings:

plane crash statistics

plane crash statistics by company

why do planes crash?

jet engine failure

what happens when you burn to death?

breathing at 30,000 feet

falling from 30,000 feet

jet crash survival rates

fear of flying

acrophobia

agoraphobia

claustrophobia

pteromechanophobia

airport security

cattle handling

heavy-duty squeeze chute

max winston

amy gallup

Having numbed herself with facts and images and secreted two capsules of Klonopin in her change purse, Amy stayed frozen through the drive to Lindbergh and the two-hour check-in procedure. Docile passengers trundled single-file as though actually confined by narrow cattle chutes. Though some of the livestock were white-faced, exuding fear, most were nonchalant or downright happy. Eventually they were separated into shorter lines, one for breeding, one for slaughter. Many carried infants, kept their older children close, reassuring them with pats, corralling them with firm yanks. In her head, the slaughterhouse threatened to morph into Auschwitz, and Amy shut the movie down and would have blushed in shame had her blood been warm enough. It was so odd how the same mind could entertain competing narratives simultaneously. In one, she shuffled to her death; in the other, right alongside it, she sneered at her own self-indulgent terror. What a ridiculous woman. Amy took off her sandals, placed her pocketbook in a gray feed bin. A distinguished elderly Frenchman was led off down a special third chute, swearing about his *souliers*, apparently refusing to take them off. Good for you, she thought, as she submitted to an outrageous X-ray strip search, *Aux barricades!* But by the time she took her seat on the plane, he was two rows behind her, being laughed at by his American wife.

The hackneyed phrase "in the belly of the beast" had entered her mind at the moment she entered the plane, which was a good thing, as it annoyed her and dulled the horror of the moment. Belly indeed. The plane was no whale, no Questing Beast. It was an ugly place crowded with uniform objects all shaped like blue and white lozenges, no sharp corners or edges anywhere. Lozenge chairs, lozenge windows, lozenge compartments, the whole thing like a giant box of Sucrets. Amy was now encased neatly in dread. There was no wildness to it, though, nothing she could not handle. The first thing she did after getting settled was to take out her notepad and jot down "Manageable Dread." This was a hubristic act, not to mention a crap title, but what the hell.

When to take the Klonopin? If Amy dry-swallowed them now, she would with luck be affected for the full duration of her direct flight to New York. She read the instructions, which Maxine had folded around the pills when she'd stuck them into the DVD package, and according to these she should take only one Klonopin, because more than one could cause "drowsiness, alterations in mental status, confusion, coma, and respiratory arrest," all of which sounded promising. Except perhaps confusion. If she were confused into imagining she was home with Alphonse, fine, but might she turn into one of those creatures who become shrieking Jeremiahs and have to be pried off the emergency exit door at 30,000 feet? Or worse, what if she became voluble, spilling her guts to bored neighbors, swiping their drinks, groping them, sniping at photos of their grandchildren? Loss of control, Amy knew, lay at the heart of pteromechanophobia. She knew this because she'd read up on it a few hours earlier. She had known it anyway, since a monkey could figure it out. All forms of public transportation involved handing over control of life and limb to strangers; flying called on Herculean feats of denial in sentient, earthbound animals. Put them both together, and full-blown panic is the most rational of responses.

All around her, as they waited for takeoff, people fiddled with their seatbacks, leafed through magazines, stared out the window with unfocused eyes. They were thinking about the people and places they were leaving behind; in a few hours, they would anticipate disembarking, hugging relatives, hailing taxis. They took so much for granted. Amy, who seldom envied anyone, envied all of them and wished mightily for a stupidity pill. *Stupefaxopram. Panglossonil.* Something that would leave her inhibitions alone and just crank up her denial mechanism, which she pictured as a frozen set of gears in the back of her brain, rusted from disuse. *Pollyannazam.* The first-class cabin was warm, the seats swiveled, and her neighbor's seat was over a foot away. She thought of offering him her window seat—Amy could not have cared less where she was sitting when everything went south—but he was already settled in, setting up his laptop on a tray. There was a television screen in front of her. Apparently she could download and watch two hundred fifty movies. That might be more distracting than the pre-flight safety demonstration, which was accomplished (after the attendant announced she was about to do it) entirely in pantomime, some bits of which were apparently intended to be droll. She indicated exits as though voguing; she demonstrated the use of the safety belt by first wrapping it around her head and then wagging her finger *no.* Passengers ignored her, in marked contrast to the raucous stomping and applause emanating from the economy section, whose attendant was apparently rapping. Max, who loved to fly, would have hated both performances. No one has the right, he would say, to perform anything before a captive audience. He suffered his last hospital stay in a room with two other dying men, both of whom slept through full-blast broadcasts of *Night Court, My Two Dads,* and *Mission Impossible.* Amy always shut it off, and the next day it would be on again. The night before he died, Amy unplugged the TV and twisted off one of the prongs with a pair of pliers. He managed a smile then, and a thumbs-up, but Amy couldn't forgive herself for not doing it earlier.

Having hours ago researched the soothing effects of biofeedback, she elected to remain physically calm during the runway taxi: her breathing stayed slow and shallow, even at the moment of liftoff, even during the climb. She of course ignored the window. She swallowed and swallowed to ease her protesting ears, and so far it all seemed to be happening to someone else, someone who, though unhappy to be there, was disengaged with the plane's behavior, disinterested in her own fate. Perhaps *this* was denial: she had willed herself into it, and now she pretended—successfully—to be engaged in a thought experiment, a virtual flight. That was it: she was virtually on this plane. How clever of her stomach to register virtual weightlessness. As a thought experiment, this was going brilliantly, but she trusted it wouldn't last. She flagged a passing attendant, scored some sparkling water, and popped one of the Klonopin.

This was in fact her third flight. Her first, a round-trip flight from Boston to Trinidad in 1971, had been pleasant enough. She had been newly married, and she and Max had settled on separate honeymoons—he flew to Madrid and she visited a couple of lovers, one in the Islands, one in the Navy. She had actually enjoyed most of the trip, despite the absurd route (on the way home, on top of the planned stopover in Pensacola, the travel agency had arranged for her to change flights in Atlanta and New York City), and despite the fact that a landing-gear light had at one point malfunctioned, forcing passengers to assume the crash position just in case. Now she could remember the general hilarity on that Eastern flight when the captain told everybody not to panic and a brand-new stewardess, in the middle of describing the crash position, began to shake and cry, her voice rising in volume and pitch, and was wrestled into a seat and strapped in by two burly sailors. Amy had giggled along with the others, imagining, even before the plane touched down, how she would describe the scene to Max. "I was really afraid," she later told him, "which is probably why the whole thing was so funny." But she hadn't been really afraid. She had been twenty-four years old. She had experienced only virtual fear.

Seventeen years later, flying to Rochester, Minnesota, with a desperately ill Max, she did not even register the journey out, because they were on their way to Mayo, the Lourdes of the New World, where Amy had convinced herself that Max could get on some experimental program and magically prolong his life. She had focused so grimly on this outcome that when it didn't happen, when the doctors there were as clueless as they had been at Mass General, as hopeless as Calvary, she, not Max, had broken down, without warning enduring a full-blown panic attack as they lifted off the icy runway, and Max, all skin and bones by then, no muscle tone at all, had held her still by force of will, preventing her from doing something that, he kept assuring her, she would never live down. All the way to Logan he held her, hectoring, cracking jokes, singing songs. He spun scatological tales about the Clinic personnel; made up a silly show tune called "Hold the Mayo"; he dug the *Chanson de Roland* out of his carry-on and read the whole thing to her in French. The plane's interior was a poor illusion, a fragile construct, willed into being by all the happy idiots around her, and only Amy could see through to the truth, that there was just this pitiless void, and the two of them inside it, tiny, withering, and Amy shook herself apart almost, and hid her face, herself, in Max. "Now," he said as they shuffled off the plane in Boston, "don't you feel silly?"

Now Amy began to relax just a tiny bit. They had been airborne for an hour, and she had admitted and made peace with those terrible airplane sounds, the hum and whine of machines, the insectile chirpings of the pilot, and with the artificial air, and the rhythmic mumble of far-off conversations. There was nothing out the window to frighten her. She took out her notepad again and wrote "Barking at Ants." She was about to put it away, but then kept writing. This never happened to her—she always let a title settle into her head before fooling with it—but now she was anxious to get started. It would be easy enough to weave Alphonse's midnight windmill-tilting into a larger story. She was three pages in when she realized that the larger story was trite, a stupid thing about a pathologically even-tempered family with a chronically outraged dog who sniffed out suppressed anger and then for some cartoonish reason took it all into himself. The family—Downtrodden Dad, Frustrated Mom, Warring Children—was terrible, but the dog was great, and Amy tore up the pages and started again. She would write a dog story. Jack London had gotten there first, except that he hadn't, because his dog only needed to keep his person *alive*, not *happy*. He hadn't had to grapple with human neurosis. Because she stayed in the dog's POV, the family (unchanged, as boring as ever) became background noise, like that engine whine, little tin food gods, which would have been fine with the dog, except that they expected some sort of daily interaction with him, and the shorter ones couldn't be counted on to let him outside often enough. He tolerated the gods but hated the house, especially the doors. The house was a metaphysical obscenity. That the gods loved the house was plain, as was the fact that they appreciated that the house was set down and shut off from a larger place. "Outside" was one of their favorite words, along with "inside": they were always saying them to him in a high pitch, and when he was younger he would bark wildly, knowing that this would get them to open the door, but the aging dog knew better, that outside was no different from inside, and Amy stopped writing because the whole thing was collapsing into some dreadful eco-fable. Also the passenger to her left had snapped his laptop shut and leaned toward her. "Excuse me," he said, smiling widely, showing her all his teeth. "May I tell you a secret?"

His name was Patrice Garrotte and he had a number of secrets, foremost of which he spilled immediately. "I recognized you right away," he said, his voice at once honeyed and reedy; he sounded like Dan Duryea making a prank call, and his Bette Davis eyes were milky brown. At first, he batted his lashes like a belle, but as he honed in on her, he stopped blinking completely. "I've read each of your books. Of course I was hesitant to disturb you." His breath smelled bright green, as though he had just been chewing parsley.

Amy focused on these sensory details in order to disappear into the experience of Patrice Garrotte and so spend precious seconds, perhaps even minutes, doing something besides poke at her dormant pteromechanophobia. Besides Maxine, nobody living had read all her works. Garrotte was old, but younger than she. Besides, how had he recognized her? Was he some sort of plant? Had Maxine sent him?

"You are much lovelier than the photograph on your Facebook page," he said.

"I don't have a Facebook page."

"Actually, you have three, but only one looks authentic, and they all use the same picture. The one in which you're standing in front of your house."

What picture? What Facebook page? The authentic one must be Maxine's work.

Telepathic Patrice Garrotte had already reopened his notebook, typed an imprecation, and now showed her the Facebook page, with Holly Antoon's hideous snapshot splayed across the upper left corner. On her profile page was an Amy Gallup Photo Album with JPEGS of her old book covers. There were regular posts about scheduled radio interviews and a big stupid thing about the televised CNET show, which, Amy had to remind herself, was due to take place in a few hours. *As if.* According to this page, Amy had 713 friends, all strangers.

"I take it you're en route to the Whither Publishing Conference."

"Unfortunately." Amy had decided to continue this conversation, in part because she was almost curious, in part because the plane had begun a series of midair hiccups. Passengers walking the aisles grabbed seat backs and righted themselves, pretending— she could see the pretense in the set of their shoulders—that the hiccups were perfectly normal. Amy's many doomsday scenarios had never included the plane disintegrating without the aid of lightning, a bomb, or another plane, but of course that could turn on a dime, and Patrice Garrotte offered her shelter, slowed her heartbeat. Maybe he would produce a weapon. A little one, incapable of penetrating the skin of the plane. A knife. After all, she had had a knife pulled on her before, and that hadn't worked out badly.

"Are you in . . . publishing?" she asked him. She already had him pegged as an unpublished writer trolling for connections, or perhaps for a sympathetic ear. Perhaps he had a wrinkled, parsley-stained manuscript secreted about his person. Perhaps she would actually read it.

He laughed, so sharply that a little boy in front of Amy peered over the seat, stared fearfully, and popped down out of sight. Patrice laughed without closing his eyes or taking them off of Amy's face. How did he keep them moist? Amy found herself wishing for Internet access—which, in fact, she could achieve in seconds through the laptop port before her, only she couldn't very well search right in front of him for "blink reflex" and find out whether protuberant unblinking eyes were a sign of some organic mental disease. "Not at all," said Patrice Garrotte. "I am merely a dedicated reader."

How dedicated? Amy wondered.

"In the most literal sense," he said. "I am a sponge." His eyes twinkled, or rather did the parched equivalent of twinkling. "As opposed to a sandglass or strain bag. Sadly, I am not a mogul diamond. Unlike you."

A sponge, a sandglass. Who was he quoting? Amy had the distinct impression that she had better remember, although she kept speculating about the twinkling mechanism. How do eyes twinkle, anyway? She should definitely write that Twinkle story, the one about her pervy pediatrician. Garrotte's had the dull satin sheen of dolls' eyes. Stony eyes, she thought, that in the moon did glitter, and then she got it. "I'm afraid that these days I'm more of a strain bag than a diamond. I'd be content to be a sponge." Samuel Taylor Coleridge had categorized readers into types. The sandglass reader just reads to pass the time; the strain bag retains only the bits of pulp that haven't slipped through the net. The sponge was obvious. She couldn't remember what the mogul diamond was, except that it was the best.

"You're too modest," he said. "I've been following you on NPR. Your words are an inspiration."

"I wasn't aware," said Amy, "that I was putting myself out there as an authority on reading. In fact, I don't read much anymore."

"Precisely! You've told us all to put down our books. You're an inspiration," he said again.

The captain interrupted with an unintelligible speech about the right side of the plane. He sounded breezy, so probably there wasn't anything amiss with the right side of the plane, the side that Amy was on. Still, the damage had been done: she had been reminded that she was on a plane.

Patrice Garrotte leaned toward her, extending a spectral arm in front of her face, pointing out the window like the Ghost of Christmas Future. "Look down," he said. "Look at that."

Whatever "that" was, Garrotte was pleased about it, but this was hardly reassuring. Something was outside the window, and that was bad. They were six miles above the earth. Nothing should have been outside the window. Against every instinct, Amy faced the window.

"Look down," said Garrotte again.

Some immeasurable distance below, the width of Amy's thumb on the pane, a trail of black smoke exactly paralleled the flight of their own plane, like an underline, italicizing them. "What is that?" she asked, though she knew what it was. It was why she never flew.

"It's a contrail."

"Contrails are white," she said. Beneath her feet, the floor felt like exactly what it was, the skin of a tin can.

"They are white," said Garrotte, "when viewed from the earth."

"But isn't it steam?" Amy struggled to keep her voice low.

"It's frozen smoke," he said.

"From what?"

"Jet exhaust."

So another jet had flown underneath them, inches away, in the opposite direction.

"The skies are mobbed, you know," said Garrotte.

Was he trying to drive her insane? "Mobbed," not "crowded," which would have been horrible enough.

"I have a confession to make," he said.

She could feel, in the soles of her feet, the palms of her hands gripping the armrests, the rumblings of a panic attack, her first since Max died.

"I too am on my way to the Whither Publishing Conference." As confessions go, this was way too puny a diversion. "I am the managing editor of a small independent publishing house, the Big Reveal Press." Garrotte shrugged and shook his head. "The name was recently forced upon us by our backers, all of whom are under forty. Its original name was Epiphany Press. Basically, we publish offbeat books for intellectuals. Skeptical science, general debunking, but now we want to branch into out-of-print fiction." He apparently took Amy's stare for curiosity. "I'm sure you can guess . . ." Garrotte blushed, instantly, as though a switch had lit up his sympathetic nervous system, his cheeks and neck turning a shade close to magenta, too much blue in the red to be healthy, but he rallied and persevered. "I'm sure you can guess my mission here, and I only hope you're not offended by being approached directly, rather than through Ms. Horner."

Garrotte's big reveal was that he wanted to secure the publishing rights to all her books. Amy tried to focus on his words, his demeanor, anything but the antics outside her window and the fading surfaces, shapes, and colors of the plane's interior, that all-too familiar sensation that the construct would not hold, that the ravenous void was pushing against it. She should never have looked. That voids by their nature have no power to push was not enough to interrupt or even slow her freefall. It had come on her so quickly. She could not stop it.

Garrotte lost his dry-eyed serenity as he fumbled with dollar figures, apologizing before and after each suggested offer, as though the market value of her old books would make a bit of difference in a few seconds, when she would cease to be. Amy reached for the second Klonopin in her change purse, but in her shaking hand it danced free of its Kleenex nest and fell to the floor, the non-floor, the anti-floor, and when she went to reach for it, she could already feel icy wind at her fingertips.

Garrotte swooped gracefully and snapped it up, placing the little tablet in her hand, then disappeared and returned with a sm... bottle of Evian, opening it for her. "You should probably take that with a bite of something," he whispered. "What would you like? I'll order it for you."

Suddenly parched, Amy tipped the bottle to drink, water sluicing down her trembling wrist, and when she looked at the tablet, it was halfway dissolved. There it goes, she thought, watching the little puddle in her palm turn milky, there it goes, and was not startled when Garrotte mopped up the puddle with a white linen handkerchief. Touching her. As though they had known each other for decades. Anything was possible now.

"It's just as well," he said. "That might have knocked you out. You don't want that."

Loss of control twinkles naughtily at the heart of pteromechanophobia. This sentence formed in her mind so clearly she could see it all at once and wondered if she had spoken it aloud. She was stretched evenly between two losses, loss of reason, loss of dignity.

Loss of life didn't even enter into it. Did she want to spend her last moments outside of her self, flinging off memory, history, identity, and flailing in the Now like a crazy person, handing over her shell to uniformed children, making it their mess? Or would she expose herself to the stranger on her left, this grotesque miracle of discretion who was plainly ready and able to minister to her pitiful needs? Could she let him hold her? No.

"Snakes, fog, thunder, and bees," Patrice Garrotte was saying, his voice low and companionable. "*All* winged insects, really, but especially the ones that buzzed and stung. Heights, needles, children's balloons . . ." He smiled wistfully. "I was her only child," he added, as though they had been talking at length about his mother and not the publishing needs of Big Reveal. Perhaps they had. "My father had no stomach for it, but I got brilliant at arranging and anticipating. I was a magician of misdirection. Once I got her through three consecutive days without a phobic incident. But I couldn't foresee every trigger." He paused and leaned toward her. "Moonlight," he confided, "on a white bedspread." He pretended to see on her face an expression of sympathetic understanding. She could see him do that. "Really," he said, "I was not an unhappy child. Not at all. Just a busy one." Again he disappeared from view, again returning in a flash, this time with a tray of food that he placed in front of her.

"They look rather excessively imagined, don't they?" he said, still pretending that she was engaging in their conversation, that she had just gotten off a light remark about the contents of the tray, which was littered with what looked like doll food, arranged whimsically in tiny inappropriate containers. There was a shot glass half full of crimson foam topped with a rose blossom of artfully folded prosciutto. A cone of Emmenthaler secured a spray of shaved asparagus around a cube of some kind of raw fish on a stick, like a lollipop. What looked like a cup from a little girl's tea set held a placid, pale yellow broth, and in its depths either a quail egg or a human eyeball. The tray was mobbed with edible nonsense. "It's the amuse-bouche assortment," he said, arching his sketchy eyebrows.

We are not amused, thought Amy, except that she must have said it, because she could just make out her own croaky voice over the apocalyptic hum and whine.

"I'll take it away," said Patrice, preparing to stand.

"Leave it," she said. Of course it had to be an egg, but she decided to believe it was an eyeball. Gazing down at it had a calming effect. This didn't make sense, but she was so grateful for the calm that she embraced it fully. "Tell me more," she said, without lifting her eyes to him. "Tell me more about your mother. About your magical ways."

"She was a wonderful storyteller," he said, "which was a good thing, since she was a very poor reader. My earliest memories are of her reading to me from picture books, beautiful books she got from the library, but in truth she was fabricating. Her stories always went along with the pictures. She made them up on the spot. When I got a little older, I began to correct her, because the stories were always changing, and children don't want that. They want them to stay exactly the same. So we told them to each other, together."

Perhaps it was a bleached radish with a disk of black olive pasted on one end with cream cheese. The surface of the liquid barely rippled. No turbulence there. Patrice spun a seamless tale about his dyslexic mother, or maybe it was something else, he was never sure, but she was of course a beautiful, soft, delicate woman, and he her champion from birth. Amy listened closely, more closely than she had ever read anything, and she heard that some of it was false, but in the way that mattered it was all true. Patrice, child and man, was the real storyteller, and she admired the choices he made now, describing his ingenious strategies for anticipating and thwarting his mother's panic spells, laying them out matter-of-factly, injecting neither pathos nor hilarity, letting them stand alone. She pushed him for details, making him name the children's books, recount the alternative stories. He was up to it. In Mother Garrotte's version of Wanda Gag's *Millions of Cats*, an old woman drove away her son with her incessant nagging, and when he came back armed with millions of cats, she was so afraid that she let him in and stopped complaining. All the cats save one went back home, their mission accomplished.

Though he never said, he must have lived with his mother until she died. No summer camp for Patrice Garrotte, no dormitory life, no fifth-floor walkup in a strange new city. No dangerous lovers, no wife and child. He was too busy glazing her windows, monitoring her television access, vetting her visitors. He taught himself internal medicine so she wouldn't have to deal with physicians. "Not literally," he demurred, "I just collected a long shelf of medical reference books," but clearly—after all, he had identified Amy's Klonopin from an impressive distance—he had used his PDR as more than a doorstop.

Had Amy been the sort of person who scoured the perceptible world for signs, who believed in cosmic zoning, she would have recognized Patrice Garrotte as some sort of messenger sent to usher her safely through the skies. That she and Max and his mother had shared a fear of doctors would glisten with meaning. That both Amy and Patrice had in youth closed the door on risk and adventure, opting out of their own lives, would make them star-twins, would have foreordained their meeting. But their meeting was a happy accident. That was all, and that was enough.

We tell stories to fashion sense out of chaos: we crave order and achieve it with narrative. As long as she had been writing, Amy had taken this as an article of faith. Until this moment, though, she had not realized how urgent this need could be. Patrice was saving her with a story. Outside her window, beneath her shoes, the accidental universe howled and buffeted without sentiment or purpose. Inside, Patrice wrapped her snugly in a blanket of narrative threads. Amy, who had never enjoyed being read to, just let herself sink down and away.

She was with Max and Patrice and Maxine and other people and millions of cats in a great airy cottage on the banks of Lake George, where she and Max had summered once. It was some kind of rooming house now. Apparently it was hers. Catamarans and sunfish skimmed the diamond surface of the glacial lake. On the porch, Max was grilling scallops on the double hibachi, and also asleep, smiling, on the bamboo couch in the living room, and then pulling up to the cottage in their old Volvo, loaded down with groceries. "You're everywhere," she said. "I keep running into you," and they were going to play charades later. They both smelled of coconut oil and Marlboros and cedar. The cottage wheezed and bumped and danced and settled down like Baba Yaga's house on stilts. Patrice's mother gripped a lace handkerchief and whimpered softly. "It's just a little earthquake," Amy said. "We get them all the time." The rooms were countless, warm, and full of morning light, and underneath the quiet she could hear the muffled scolding of a million tiny birds. "Birds my ass," said Maxine, looking well and rested. "That's typewriters. Everybody's typing. Look what you've gone and done." Amy laughed. "We're here," said Max. "I know that," said Amy. "Give us a minute," he said. "Stop saying that," said Amy. "It's time to go," he whispered. *Stop saying that.* "Leave us alone for a bit longer," he said, but they wouldn't, and she opened her eyes to the sight of an annoyed flight attendant bending over her. "As you can plainly see," said Patrice Garrotte, "she's awake. Give us room." She had landed. She was down. She was alive. He walked her out of the empty cabin.

"Was your mother afraid of earthquakes?" she asked him.

"She was afraid of everything."

"We have them all the time," said Amy. I dreamed about her, she thought to say, but they didn't know each other that well. He wanted to stay and help with the bags. If she'd let him, he would have taken her to the hotel and run a bath. She waved him off. "I'll see you at the conference," she said. She watched him disappear behind a throng of reunited families, and while she waited at the carousel she took out her notebook. "The Storyteller," she wrote. Of course she would sell him her book rights, and of course Maxine would kick and scream. But Amy owed him. She could still see, almost, the lake from her long white porch, the Mohican Steamboat turning around midwater, heading back to Bolton Landing. Remembered light suffused the terminal, and beneath the echoes of arrival and departure the white noise, the happy sound, of typing.

CHAPTER TWENTY-FIVE

Veal Piccata

Amy hadn't been to Manhattan since 1965, when she came on a whim with her college roommate. They had trudged through the public library and the Met, attended a Fugs concert on Christopher Street, and for some forgotten reason eaten exclusively at automats. Although she read the online *Times* regularly, Amy, a true child of New England, had on some level expected everything to be more or less the same. She remembered now how much she loved the reckless belligerence of New York cabs. From her window, Manhattan looked and sounded reassuringly familiar, tall and bright and boisterous, but when she reached her hotel, she recoiled from sensory overload. This was not New York. It wasn't even America. Times Square looked like Tokyo, or how she had imagined Tokyo on the basis of disinterested glimpses on TV. The whole neighborhood was a colossal arcade, and the hotel lobby was featureless—nothing like the Taft, which she remembered as white-tiled, candelabraed, and within hailing distance of seedy. This lobby was unnecessarily huge and aggressively rectangular.

After Amy spent twenty minutes dawdling in her room, showered, and changed clothes for the conference, she still had plenty of time to eat dessert with her fellows. She knew this because Jenny Marzen had texted her ("come whenever u can we're saving a seat for u!!!") while she was still in the cab. Because the restaurant, like the Whither event room, was somewhere in this vast hotel, she slipped through a side door in search of a corned beef sandwich and ended up standing on 45th Street eating a pretty decent bowl of tomato bisque from a soup cart. Apparently Horn & Hardart had gone out of business.

When she got there, the "event room" was free of writers and full of people cleaning up after the last crowd, which had apparently gathered to hear from a murder of agents. Just now, the conference crew was taking down the signs for the "Agent Round Table" and replacing them with signs for the writers. There were, Amy estimated, two hundred audience seats. From the back where she sat, the writers' table on stage was reassuringly tiny. Of course it was not round at all, but a long table set up so that four pseudo-luminaries could face the crowd. She lifted her feet for a young woman running a carpet sweeper and scanned a program abandoned on the seat nearby. Yesterday morning's Bookseller Round Table—"Depending on the Kindles of Strangers"—had apparently focused on the rise of the electronic book. Perhaps that was supposed to be the focus of the whole Whither thing. Amy, who knew nothing about electronic books, took the time now to open up the event packet Maxine had express-FedExed to her two days ago.

Apparently the conference was designed to "give the book-reading public a better understanding of ongoing upheavals in the publishing industry," at which point, try as she might, Amy could not stay focused. Why should people who read books give a damn about the "industry"? For that matter, why should writers? She could see why publishers, booksellers, and agents needed to hash out this stuff, but writers weren't *industrialized* in the first place. They weren't on salary, they didn't have benefits and pensions, they lived by their wits. That without them the "industry" would collapse would be certain, except that if today's novelists went on strike, the MFA mills would replace them, overnight, with tomorrow's. Every hundredth human in America had a manuscript on his hard drive.

She saw that the tickets for tonight's discussion were the most expensive: fifty dollars for the privilege of sitting through two hours of baloney from Amy & Peers. They had paid half that to see the other three groups, including the agents. This surprised her. In San Diego and elsewhere, roving bands of agents routinely charged good money for five-minute pitch sessions with literary hopefuls. Today's session hadn't involved any pitching at all, just bloviating, but Amy was sure that aspirants had swelled the ranks of the agent audience anyway, if only to be within hoping distance. Was this also why they were paying to see the writers? Amy scribbled "Hoping Distance" in her notebook.

"Excuse me, madam, you'll have to leave," said a young man with a WPC pin on his shirt front.

"Why?" asked Amy.

"The doors don't open for another twenty minutes."

"I'm not an audience person," said Amy. "I'm—"

"You'll also need a different ticket, for the Writers' event." He was glowering at her. He must think she had tried to sneak in on an Agents ticket, like some high school kid theater-hopping in a multiplex.

Amy gathered up her belongings. "Is there some sort of green room?" she asked him. Milling around outside the magic door with *hoi polloi* wouldn't have offended her sense of status, which was nonexistent, but she thought she might not be able to resist the impulse to bolt for a cab to Anywhere Else.

The young man blanched. Amy had of course read about this phenomenon—in the 1920s, fictional characters blanched all over the place—but until now she'd never seen a real person turn this alarming shade of white. White people, of course, were really pink, but not this kid.

"Yes," she said, "I'm one of *them*"—airily dismissing the faraway stage—"but don't worry about it. Just tell me where I belong."

He led her up onstage. "We don't have a green room. There's no backstage area. I'm so sorry," he said more than once. He pulled out her chair, seated her at the table, and ran away before she could assure him that he had just been doing his job.

There was a personalized event packet in front of each chair like a place card. She had been seated between Jenny Marzen and Davy Goonan, and to his left was somebody named Jasmine White-Banerjee. Marzen had to be the designated heavy-hitter. Goonan should be, except he was old and out of fashion. Goonan she knew—not personally, but from his early books.

When Amy was in high school, Davy Goonan had been white-hot, a National Book Award contender, a hard-drinking Irishman with lethal charm whose brilliant, caustic, and often misogynist novels excited a largely female readership. Amy had enjoyed his books. He was the postwar Dreiser, his novels huge and lumbering, but she had loved Dreiser too. During the seventies, he was the go-to bull's-eye of feminist critics. He might have weathered the political sea change, except that he was also a bad-boy celebrity at a time when simultaneous public infidelities and fistfights actually harmed sales. Amy hadn't thought of him in years. Still, she was sorry now to read that he was presently toiling as an adjunct writing teacher at the New School. He was still in print but broke. He'd probably spent his fortune on fines, booze, and alimony. He must be at least eighty.

Amy took out her laptop and did a search on Jasmine White-Banerjee. Indian-American novelists had been *hot* (as the Industry would have it) for a while, but she was unfamiliar with this particular name. On a Burdock Press website, she found White-Banerjee, or rather a "book trailer" for her recent novel *Justine's Tale*. Amy, who had avoided looking at book trailers until now, clicked on the video, which opened with a woman's dark silhouette against a background of scarlet damask drapes. "I am Justine Moritz," she was saying, in a vaguely Nordic accent. "We were children together. He loved me like a sister. I loved him like . . ." Cut to a zag of lightning and a blast of bass trombones, then back to the silhouette, illuminated this time, revealing a youngish blond woman, who slowly turned toward the camera and resumed speaking. "We were children together," she said again. "Often he would show me his . . . experiments." Again with the lightning, then quick shots of cages, frogs, surgical tools. "They frightened me, but I loved that look in his eyes, that passion, and hoped that some day he would come to me . . ." A piano began to play the same five notes over and over, as a young man's face, scowling at something off to the side, appeared next to the blonde. This really didn't look like a novel about the Indian diaspora. The camera zoomed in on the girl's lips. She whispered: "And one day he did." The music stopped. "As a . . . monster." Instantly a quick-cut montage, accompanied by tom-toms, of screaming faces, spurting and dripping blood, a noose, and a creature who looked like Boris Karloff. Oh my god, thought Amy. This idiot had written a novel about Frankenstein's housekeeper.

"It is kind of over the top, but that's what you get when the publicity budget's for shit."

Amy looked up and almost screamed, for there stood the woman in the video.

"Yes," she sighed, "I did my own acting. This time, I won't have a cheap-ass publisher." She stuck out a cold little hand for Amy to shake. In back of her, trudging up the steps to the stage, were Jenny Marzen and Davy Goonan.

"We missed you!" sang Jenny. She handed Amy an ornate foil box. "We brought you a Frangelico brownie!"

Goonan was the first to settle in. The fit was rather tight, as Goonan and Jenny were considerably fatter than their author pictures. Amy was not, since her hideous photo was not a glamorized head shot. Only Jasmine White-Banerjee was fashionably slender. Also the youngest by at least twenty years. "What's that?" Goonan asked, pointing toward the video. Amy pressed "play" and slid the laptop in front of him. To her right, Jenny leaned into her and said, "I'm such a fan! We meet at last!" and so on, and the next few minutes were lost as the women engaged in rote fawning and the man stayed silent, glued to the screen. "What are you going to talk about?" asked Jenny.

"I have no idea," said Amy, just then recollecting something Maxine had said about her not being keynote. Keynotes were speakers. Was she supposed to get up and say something? She really should have read the material Maxine sent her. But she had been too busy preparing for death, and now the hall was beginning to fill. Amy tried to empty her mind and just watch people take their seats and the camera crew—there were just two TV cameras—fiddle with machinery and wires.

"Did the bastards force you to do this?" Goonan asked Jasmine White-Banerjee, pointing to the laptop screen. "It this what it's come to?" She laughed and shrugged and all but rolled her eyes at Amy and Jenny. Apparently they had had enough of Goonan during dinner, although Amy couldn't see that he was all that hard to take.

Jenny reached around Amy and put a hand on his shoulder. "Nobody forces us, Davy," she shouted, splitting Amy's right eardrum. "Book trailers are a new marketing tool."

"Here's the deal," Jenny said in a lower tone to Amy. "Jazz is going to talk about the writer's marketing responsibilities in the new millennium. She knows a lot more about this stuff than we do!" Apparently Jenny and Amy were "we." "I'm going to do my usual rags to niches shtick." She lowered her voice. "God only knows what *he*'s going to talk about."

Why did she think Goonan was deaf? His voice was low, husky, lilting. If he could hear himself talk, he couldn't be very hard of hearing. Out of the corner of her eye she watched him fool around with her laptop. This didn't worry her. She had put her stories on there, but they were on her home computer too, so even if he wiped the hard drive she'd be okay.

"Tom!" shrieked Jenny Marzen, at a portly middle-aged man in sports jacket and dungarees who approached the stage.

"Who the hell is that?" asked Davy Goonan.

"Tom Maudine, we told you, remember? He's from NPR. He's going to be moderator. Amy, you know Tom, right?"

"I know his voice," said Amy, who after a panicked second realized he was the NPR guy. She'd done at least ten "Just Us" radio shows with him and had assumed he was much younger, with dark hair and horn-rims, like Ellery Queen.

He shook hands all around, told Amy he was happy to meet her after all their hours together on the air, and then made his announcement. "We're trying something new this time, and I hope you'll all get behind it. I've prepared a number of questions for you, of course, but we're also going to invite viewers, listeners, and audience members to tweet questions of their own. I'll keep an eye on the tweets, and if they're better than mine, I'll—"

"Say again?" said Davy Goonan.

"It's a new system," said Tom. "If audience members want to come to the mike for questions, of course we'll let them, but we're hoping they'll be sending their questions electronically."

Goonan turned to Amy and muttered, "I could swear he said they were going to *tweet*."

"Yes, Davy, they're tweeting!" yelled Jenny Marzen, "It's the latest craze."

Amy had come to this conference prepared to learn that Jenny Marzen, who had somehow become her nemesis, was a perfectly likeable, intelligent woman. "Would you like to trade places?" Amy asked her. "You'd be closer to Mr. Goonan that way," but Goonan—for it must have been he—clamped an iron hand on her knee. Clearly he preferred a buffer between himself and the helpful harpy.

"This isn't half bad," Goonan said to Amy, pointing at the screen, where he had summoned up "True Caller," one of her recent stories. "It's a bit lightweight for you, isn't it? But it's nice."

Amy didn't know what to say. Davy Goonan read her stuff?

"Oh yes," he said, "I've stopped writing, but I still read the occasional story." He pronounced *occasional* with a long *O*, a charming remnant of his old brogue, or at least it charmed Amy, who felt for just a moment as though she were twenty again. Davy Goonan liked her stuff! He inclined toward her. "You know, those SOBs only paid for one drink at dinner. I thought this creature was just trying to manage my drinking, but no, she showed me the voucher, and it was one drink apiece! After that we were on our own."

"Do you mind my asking," said Amy, "why you're here?" Under other circumstances, with a different person, this would have been a rude question, but Amy was certain he would know what she meant.

"Could ask you the same," he said. "Fact is, thought I missed it." He took a drink of water. "Spotlights. Dancing girls. Never again, though. Cheap bastards."

When the room filled, the TV guys hit the camera lights and the show got underway. First to speak was Jazz W-B, who explained why all writers should participate in the marketing of their own books. She opened with a book trailer—not the horrible *Justine* thing, but one in the works for her upcoming novel, *Spielvogel's Complaint*. Since C-SPAN Books was low-tech TV, the video trailer was projected onto an old-fashioned white screen and ended up washed-out and hard to see. Still, it was watchable, as this time her new publisher had sprung for a real actor, a vaguely familiar goateed man who regarded the camera with unease as another man, off-screen, reeled off a monotone list of sexual disappointments. The audience tittered politely while Amy tried to identify the actor and also figure out why the name Spielvogel was so familiar. Both answers came simultaneously: the actor was Hal Hockman, who had been lynched twice in a memorable *Deadwood* episode, and Spielvogel was Portnoy's psychiatrist.

That this Wasp hyphenated her husband's name in order to garner reviewer attention was, Amy supposed, a forgivable all's-fair strategy, but Whitebread-Banerjee was also the kind of writer who, either lazy or simply unoriginal, kidnapped characters created by her betters and impressed them into her own second-rate books. This practice had been going on for some time now. Amy associated it with the flourishing population of young writers who didn't have anything to write about yet but thought they *had to write something,* and so they commandeered the lives of minor characters in famous novels. Scarlett O'Hara's mother, Squire Western's mistress, Sidney Carton's tobacconist. Great fiction can be fashioned out of anything, including hand-me-downs, but for every Jean Rhys there were a hundred Jasmine White-Banerjees.

Who spoke of promoting sales through blogging, of virtual book launch parties, of swooping in on book club meetings via Skype and answering questions for a fee. "Readers," she reminded them, "always want to know where we get our ideas!" She claimed that fiction writers could promote their books in much the same way as nonfiction writers do.

If Davy G hadn't swiped her laptop, Amy would have amused herself looking up these practices. What was a virtual book launch party? She suspected that whatever it was, it would produce virtual readers and virtual sales. Amy had attended two actual book launches, both for the first novels of students, and noticed that when you get people to leave their homes and drive to a bookstore, chances are they'll buy the book.

It was like bassets. If you take a basset out for a ride in the car, you must always buy or otherwise obtain something—a hamburger, preferably, but non-food works too. Otherwise the basset views you as an inept hunter and loses whatever respect he had for you in the first place. A virtual party is not a hunt and does not require a kill.

By the time Jazz had gotten halfway through her marketing tips, the crowd was restive, and Amy was meanly glad to see that when she wrapped up and announced, "Let the tweets begin!" the applause was perfunctory and nobody rose to ask a question. Tom

Maudine stood almost immediately and told everyone, including the tweeters, to hold their questions until after all four had spoken. Doubtless he had planned to do this, but it came off as a tactful ploy. The tweets might not have begun. Belatedly, Amy wondered if she was next. "Who's keynote?" she whispered to Davy G, just as his name was called. "Not I, evidently," he said, rising to his feet.

He began with a series of literary anecdotes having nothing to do with "Whither Publishing" and everything to do with what it had been like to be "young and full of it and mentioned in the same breath as Mailer and Bellow, as Shaw and Yates. That's Irwin Shaw and Richard Yates, to the likes of you. Do you read them? Do you remember them?" He slid his glasses down to the end of his nose and regarded the crowd for a half minute, silently asking *Do you remember me?* Jenny Marzen sighed theatrically, whispering, "Here we go, folks." And how long did Jenny Marzen plan to be remembered?

Out of the corner of her mouth, Amy whispered to her. "You're keynote, right?"

"There's no keynote," said Jenny.

"Well, I must be next, though." Amy was beginning to get nervous. She really ought to think of something to say.

"I'm sure you're right," said Jenny. "They just forgot to give us the order."

Well, Jazz W-B had given Amy plenty of material. Amy would be the anti-Jazz, the querulous oldster who railed against all these newfangled apps and tweets and for whom a trailer was something you were forced to watch while you waited for your movie to start. She could do this, and she could do it without directly insulting Jazz and her brainless advice. Amy had been a teacher for decades. Teachers who couldn't simultaneously praise a precocious student while showing why everything she had just written was lousy didn't have a calling. She could then scorn the very notion of writers having any responsibilities beyond simply writing as well as they can. She could go on and on about this subject practically in her sleep, since she'd done it before, often on the radio, so all she had to worry about was boring herself to death. She relaxed and tuned in to Davy G.

But Davy Goonan was no longer reminiscing about his young lion days. Davy Goonan was inveighing against tweets, apps, blogs, book trailers, book launches, and the very notion that writing and marketing should be accomplished by the same person. "But this is the world we live in," he said. "This is what it's come to." He reached into his jacket and removed a wrinkled sheaf of paper, which he opened with a palsied hand and from which he began to read. It was a copy (Davy said "mimeograph") of a marketing plan his agent had recently sent him. "Why, I don't know," he said, "as I have not written a novel in fifteen years. My agent is my agent's granddaughter. She is not yet thirty." The marketing plan was a bulleted list of ideas, patterned after marketing strategies for nonfiction. "'First,'" he read, "'identify your readers. Who are they?'" Again he regarded his audience for a long moment. The audience, who had peppered his lion tales with coughs and shuffles, went quiet. Davy put the paper back in his jacket pocket. "Let's say you've written a lovely first novel about, oh, a gay young thing of about forty, who adores hideous shoes and casual sex and who wouldn't dream of leaving the Big City, but then she falls in love with a visiting country singer from Oklahoma, you know, and against all reason she hops on to his tour bus and they light out for the territories. It's a romantic comedy, you see, and a rollicking adventure, and a musical if they make a movie out of it, and of course they get a flat tire in the middle of the Texas desert, and she finds a Gila monster in her shoe, and so on. Well, now, if you break it down, your readers will be: desperate spinsters of a certain age, country singers, bus devotees, lizard aficionados, shoe fetishists, and what have you. This is your *demo-graphic*." He chewed up the word and spat it out. "This is your *customer*.

"Now you do your research. How many bus devotees are out there, and where do they live? Do they blog? Do they have a union? Where do their children go to school?" A man in the audience laughed, provoking answering laughs—not titters—from the crowd. "You do the same for all the other demographics. You get it all down. This is serious business. This is the writing life." His sarcasm was exquisite. Max would have loved Davy Goonan, who could have, without an irony klaxon, communicated all his despair and contempt to a roomful of children. "This list, you see, is the beginning of your marketing plan. But it doesn't end there. No, no, it doesn't.

"Think again about these readers. Who else do they like to read? Do your research again. Find celebrity novelists who write about shoes, public transportation, Oklahoma, and reptiles. Jot down their names. This is very important. This is your second list, the 'In the tradition of . . .' list.

"Finally, it's come time for your platform. What is that, you ask? Well, are you famous as something other than a novelist? Have you walked on the moon? Are you at least plugged into a large group of people with money? Do you have access to a mailing list? Do you at least have your own website, you slacker, you *pretender*? Find your platform. If you haven't got one, build one. You *are* a carpenter, aren't you?

"Now you're ready to get published. You've got your platform, your customers, your list of popular writers of whom you'll re-

mind those customers, your blog and mailing lists. All you have
to do is put them all together in one beribboned package. You're
ready to market yourself. You have a brand. You're a Keebler Elf.
Your brand is Mature-Urban-Chic-Lit-Tex/Mex-Bus-Tour, and
you write in the tradition of Jack Kerouac, Zane Grey, and Jenny
Marzen."

The crowd, which had been giggling happily, drew its breath
at Davy's use of Jenny Marzen's name. This wasn't a comedy club,
and there she was, right up there in front of everybody. Amy
could hear her hearty, false laughter, could see out of the corner of
her eye that she was pretending to take his insult as good-natured
ribbing, and Amy was torn between two reactions. First, he had
been doing so well, and now he'd, as they say, shot himself in the
foot, daring the crowd to turn against him, because it's one thing
to make a point, but this just wasn't nice. Before her eyes he had
risen from the great pile of obsolete geniuses and awakened the
multitudes, and now he was shrinking just as quickly, staining all
he had just said with the sullen green of his own resentments. She
wanted him to stand his ground now, to defend himself or at least
his position, but he turned from the mike and shuffled back to his
seat to scattered applause. Jenny Marzen made a show of reaching
out and squeezing his arm and smiling at him for a job well done.
He didn't even acknowledge her. He looked like he needed a nap.

Amy's second reaction, which should have been her first, was
that now that Davy G had stolen all her thunder she was about to
face that confused crowd with absolutely nothing to say. She was
rising to her feet to do this—to say nothing—when Tom Maudine announced that Jenny Marzen would be the next speaker.

Jenny got up and conferred with Maudine, both of them looking flustered. He stepped back to the mike. "Change in plans," he

said. "We're going on a bit longer than we thought, so we're going to have a very brief intermission. We'll be back in ten minutes." Jenny and Jazz exited stage right, leaving Amy and Davy G alone. "That was almost brilliant," Amy told him.

"I was going to say 'Zane Grey and *Henrietta Mant*,'" he said. Amy laughed. "No, I was," said Davy, "and then I couldn't remember her goddamn name, and I had to say somebody. I don't know who the gal writers are nowadays." He leaned close. "I've never even read this Marzen woman. I've never even read *about* her. It wasn't personal, for Christ's sake."

Jenny returned and fiddled with her own laptop, calling up her speech. Her face was flushed. "Tom's saving you for last," she told Amy.

"Why?"

"Something to do with the tweets." Davy either hiccuped or snorted. "Also, Jazz isn't coming back."

"What?"

"She's got thinner skin than I do. Didn't you notice? It's practically blue."

Amy realized she'd forgotten all about Jasmine White-Banerjee, whose speech, after all, had been Davy's dartboard. If anyone should have taken offense it was she, and apparently she had. Amy would have felt sorry for her, except that it was silly to run off like that. On the other hand, Jenny Marzen, whatever her faults, was being manful about the whole thing, although she was clearly put out, probably because she had believed herself the biggest name at the table—well, she was—and so expected to be the climactic speaker. "Jenny," said Amy. "Would you like me to talk him out of it, so we can switch? I'm sure he's wrong about this." It really wouldn't matter whether she spoke next or last. She was screwed anyway.

"Nonsense," said Jenny, touching up her lipstick. "No worries," she said to Amy. "I just can't believe Jazz ditched us. What a child!" She sighed. "This is exactly the kind of stunt that makes all of us look bad." Amy guessed that by "us" she meant "women," and she had to agree. "*We* roll with the punches!" she said in a raised voice. "Don't we, Davy?"

"I went two rounds with Virgil Akins once," he said.

"I have no idea who that is, Davy," said Jenny, and Amy decided she wasn't really so bad.

Ten minutes later Jenny Marzen was at the podium. True to her word, her topic was "rags to niches." "They used to call it 'genre,'" she began, "and now they call it 'niche,' and what's interesting is that these are both French words, which we occasionally try to pronounce in the French way." She wondered why there were no homegrown English words for the concept, and Amy wondered a little too and was sitting back for a possibly interesting speech, except that Jenny just abandoned the point and pressed on. She brought up the notion of niche as marketing tool but dropped it almost immediately, no doubt because to argue for it straight-faced would just remind her audience of the Irishman's still-ringing sermon. Instead, she just talked about niches and how promiscuously they'd proliferated. She noted that there used to be a few: mysteries, westerns, romances, gothics, and that everything else was considered serious fiction. Now serious fiction—what they called lit-fic—was itself a niche, and all niches including lit-fic themselves had niches, and so on. Most of her speech was taken up just this way: she simply read off a list of fiction niches, making asides about each. It was an entertaining enough list. Romance had begotten First Love, Doctor-Nurse, Second Time

Around (where the heroine was divorced), and so on. Among Romance's grandchildren were Heaving Bosoms, Loins and Groins, paranormal romances, along with a huge subset of religious love stories, including Pentacostal, Sister-Wife, and Bonnet. The Bonnet novel, she had to explain, was Amish Courtship. She did the same for the genealogy of the serial killer novel, the school bus thriller, splatterpunk, steampunk, and preteen zombies.

It was entertaining enough for a while, but soon her audience began to disengage, at which point she switched attention to the lit-fic genre and its descendants. Apparently there was no such thing anymore as just a novel. Among today's serious fiction categories were metafiction, philosophical fiction, neuro-novels, magical realism, hyperrealism, hyporealism, antinovels, and she went on and on, to no discernible point.

Amy tried to tune Jenny out and plan her speech but was overwhelmed with the sheer fall of words. God, she hated lists. And she was suddenly and utterly exhausted. She had slept on the plane, but it hadn't been a real sleep, more of a coma, and hers had been a long and way too eventful day. She felt a bit light-headed too, probably because she hadn't eaten anything but half a styrofoam bowl of tomato bisque. Maybe when her turn came she'd just stand up there and faint. And then, too soon, Jenny Marzen wound up her talk, and it was Amy's turn. Davy poked her arm. "Akins was a welterweight," he said.

Tom Maudine gave her a long introduction, to which Amy could not fully attend. She heard him say "Rip van Winkle" and that the American reading public was about to be hit with a wave of "brand-new stories." *Something will occur to me,* she told herself as she took her place at the podium. This extremely rare coin was

minted in 1949. Tom's arm snaked around her as he placed bot-
tled water next to the mike. When, she wondered, did we become
so obsessed with hydration? Walkabout aborigines sucked mois-
ture from the roots of trees, and they did all right. The television
lights seemed brighter from here—not strong enough to overheat,
but enough to blind her to the audience. I will address, she
thought, not the invisible audience, not the camera's eye, but the
blinding light.

"My grandmother," she began.

What about her grandmother? Amy had no idea. She had said
"my grandmother," the first thing that popped into her head, and
basically assumed she would know what to say next. Maybe she
should just sit back down. That would actually be pretty damn
funny, but she owed something to Maxine. "Excuse me," she said,
and turned to Jenny. "What is a school bus thriller?" Big laughs,
during which she figured out why she had said "my grandmother."

"My grandmother loved *Photoplay* magazine. Also *Modern
Screen* and some others I can't name, all movie magazines. When
I would visit I would read them cover to cover. I had no idea
who Jeanne Crain was, but I knew her dress size and what Janet
Leigh cooked to please handsome hubby Tony Curtis. It was
veal piccata.

"My grandmother was a tireless reader. She had bookshelves
crammed with Pearl Buck and Erle Stanley Gardner and *Good
News for Modern Man.* She was the finest Scrabble player I ever
knew. And while she'd probably gone to the movies a lot when
she was young—she used to play piano for the silents—by the
time I knew her, she seldom bothered. Still, she read *Photoplay*
like a bible. One of the last times I saw her, she was complaining
about Linda Cristal again, that hussy, who this time was stealing Bobby Darin away from Sandra Dee. By then, of course, I

was all grown up. Who cared about Linda Cristal? We were bombing Cambodia.

"In the late sixties and early seventies, that terrible time, when I thought about my grandmother I would inevitably think about those magazines, and how quaint they were. Imagine, I would think, how naive my country *used* to be, when bright citizens would waste brain cells on the antics of movie stars! All because of the Great Depression, I thought. That escapist need to gossip about beautiful strangers as though they lived right next door.

"Gossip stopped in the seventies, the terrible seventies. We were serious people now.

"And then sometime later—it must have been the eighties—I began to notice that gossip was back. Only this time it wasn't movie *stars*. It was producers. Money men. I, who had once worried about who Pier Angeli was, was now supposed to recognize names like Bruckheimer, Evans, Lucas, and Simpson. And not just the producers. The directors, the screenwriters, the agents. The Business. The Industry. Magazines with the heft of telephone books devoted buckets of gloss to their faces, clothes, antics, the interior design of their houses. I noticed this and actually thought it amusing, and that it would eventually blow over. But as always, I was wrong." Out there, on the other side of the white, somebody coughed.

Amy stared back at the light until the coughing stopped. "Why are you here?" she asked. To herself, she sounded like the Great Wazoo, the stern character she had played sitting upon Carla's ridiculous wooden throne, so she played it up and *became* the Great Wazoo. "Not that it isn't nice to see you, but what does this Industry, the publishing Industry, have to do with you? Well, maybe some of you actually draw salary in that Industry, but what about the rest of you?

"Are you writers? Then this is the last place you should be.

Nothing's going to rub off on you. Writing is not a communal enterprise. There is no community of writers, any more than there is a community of spiders. We don't work in hives. We work alone. When we marry other writers, one of us gets eaten.

"Are you readers? Then this is the last place you should be. We're just talking here. We're not gifted *speakers*. We're not *performers*. We're not, most of us, particularly wonderful to look at. Why seek out the men and women behind the page, when the best of us is *on* it?"

Amy was fresh out. She had been working toward some point about business, about how they used to say that show business was everybody's business, which was nonsense, and now the book business was supposed to be everybody's business, and it had something to do with the malignant, apocalyptic rise of the corporation-state. Amy was sure there was some twinkle of truth in that tangle of just-formed ideas but had no hope of getting to it now. It was the stuff of smarter writers than she, and it belonged on the page anyway, not here. She was going to have to apologize and slink off. She would have felt worse, except that the entire event had pretty much been a bust. If it got written up anywhere, they would all look like crackpots and posers.

"Why are *you* here?" shouted a woman on the other side of the light. Without a mike, she sounded like a heckler. Her voice was familiar.

Tom Maudine appeared next to Amy, prepared to intervene, and Amy shooed him away.

"Is that you, Hester?" Amy asked.

"Yes," said Hester Lipp.

Amy wished she could see her. Did she actually look like Kate Hepburn with a giant mole on her nose? "I'm glad you asked," she said.

God bless Hester Lipp.

"I am here because earlier this year I fell down and hit my head on a birdbath."

"I asked you a serious question," shouted Hester Lipp.

"You asked me an excellent question, and I gave you a serious answer."

Tom Maudine spoke into Amy's mike. "There will be time for questions when the speaker is through."

"Which is now," said Amy. She reassured him with a pat on the shoulder. He nodded and motioned to somebody, probably the person with the walking mike. Her fingertips had not touched a man's jacketed shoulder in at least thirty years. She had never been much of a toucher, but when you danced, that's where you put your left hand, and she'd forgotten how lovely that sensation was, the otherness of that sturdy, padded shelf.

"The fall knocked me out and did some short-term damage to my memory," she said, "and then I gave a rather eccentric inter-view—"

"So that story you gave Chaz Molloy was true?" This from some invisible guy who had grabbed the mike.

"Exactly," said Amy. She went on to give them the whole story. She told about the horrifying sight of a total stranger waving and backing out of her driveway, the panicked flight to the emergency room, the old bag lady with the newspaper story, the noticing of that story by someone in the book business, the trickle of interest that grew from a few newspaper columns and blogs to a series of radio interviews and shows and finally to her appearance right here at this mildly televised event. She told them that as a result of all this she had begun writing stories again, and that when collected between hard covers, they would be called *Birdbath Stories*. She said that of all these absurd and, to her, mostly entertaining consequences, the happiest was the reappearance into her life of Maxine Grabow, and she ended by describing Maxine's exasperated, tireless work on her behalf, unacknowledged until now. She did this for Maxine, who surely was watching. Amy looked right at her in the blinding light. "I am here accidentally and just for the moment," she said. She smiled, waved good-bye, and took her seat. It was over.

Possibly forever, since she had given up her secrets, and happily too. Something was finished now. She didn't know what it was, but finishing it felt wonderful.

Amy had left the audience in some disarray, with Hester Lipp yelling, or maybe it was some other woman, some anti-accident Christian, and somebody else spoke into the mike, and poor Tom tried to mop up, and then applause started, at first timid, but it kept going and started to build. "Let's hear it for our writers," said Tom, and it rose to a level which, while not literally thunderous, was a modest roar, a long one, embellished with shouts and whistles.

"They love you," said Jenny Marzen.

"No," said Amy, "they just love that I shut up and sat down." Already she was picturing that silver morning train, the Chicago Limited, that wonderful three-day lie-down as her bed clicked and swayed west past cities and farmland and through scrub and desert and mountain all the way back home to her dog and her house and her own life. She was done.

"And now," said Tom Maudine, "let the tweets begin!"

"Goddamn it all to hell," said Davy Goonan.

CHAPTER TWENTY-SIX

⸎

Dead Zone

Amy loved trains just as much as she hated planes. For long-distance travel, a train was a great chugging cradle and the only mode that was at once civilized and somehow natural. Monet lived long enough to paint airplanes but didn't. And even today, when trains no longer puffed sensuous clouds of smoke and steam, their grave and mournful essence remained. Hearing their night cries, whether from within or afar, Amy couldn't shake the sense that, alone of all machines, they were sentient, tragic creatures. When they called out, they weren't warning human beings, who paid increasingly less attention to them no matter what they did; they were singing to one another and themselves. *I'm still here. Not gone yet.*

She napped from New York to the middle of Ohio, waking now and then to jot a dream in her notebook, a silly thing about dinosaurs, and how a few of the larger ones actually had coexisted with people for a brief time, only the people didn't take them seriously. Their scale was just too outlandish: they were too big to be

killed, and anyway they were inedible. Their hides were impene-
trable. Also they were no fun to look at. You couldn't take them
in, really, unless you spied one from a great distance, in a valley or
something, and then you saw that, take away their size, and they
weren't all that impressive. They lacked color, speed, variety. There
were just a few different shapes, that was all, so you could classify
them without effort. They weren't *interesting*. The world was such
a buzzing, dangerous, riotous place. Dinosaurs weren't worth
thinking about. You couldn't *learn* from dinosaurs. As people
lost interest in dinosaurs, they stopped seeing them, and hardly a
month went by when somebody didn't wander stupidly in front
of one and get himself obliterated. Parents warned their children
to watch out, to look both ways, but the lessons were forgotten,
like the dinosaurs themselves. You couldn't very well watch out
for something you had ignored into transparency. In the end the
dinosaurs died, not from a comet or an epidemic or a long drought,
but of heartbreak and humiliation.

Amy's dream read like the idiot child of Ray Bradbury and
Italo Calvino. She continued for a while picturing dinosaurs
thundering sedately through the cornfields of Indiana and Illi-
nois. She hated symbols, literary and non, especially her own, the
ones projected on her private movie screen during dreamtime.
They were always embarrassingly obvious. She was willing to concede that her antic projectionist knew what he was doing—that
every little symbol had a meaning all its own—but would have
enjoyed, just once, a bit of mystery. Well, those dream-spiders
who had transformed into disembodied hands had been mysterious, but she had given up on what they meant. She didn't dream
about them anymore—although whenever she mentioned spiders, as she had done in her Whither speech, she would flash on
that nightmare afterimage from her childhood, that hand perched

like a Hieronymus Bosch animal on her bedside table as though posing for the cameras.

Anyway the dinosaurs were trains. Or the trains were dinosaurs. Either way, she was not about to write a story for them. She fell back asleep, waking only for the changeover in Chicago.

The Southwest Chief crossed the Mississippi at suppertime, rolling through Fort Madison, Iowa, on its way to Missouri and Kansas. Amy sat in the observation car, messing with her laptop. The New York–Chicago train had boasted wireless Internet access, but Amy had been sleepy then. Now she figured she should email Maxine, maybe even do something with her blog, but evidently there would be no wireless access until she reached the coast. "The entire Southwest is a dead zone," said the conductor, "except for Albuquerque." So she leaned back to watch her country roll out to the west, which was much better than blogging.

Amy had never really seen America before. Though she and "Bob," newly and horribly wed, had driven to California three months after Max's death, she had paid scant attention to the changing scenery, instead focusing all her energies on pretending to be alone in the car. That she was sharing intimate space with a person who revolted her on every level was something that she simply accepted as part of her afterlife, the details of which hardly mattered. She had believed herself old and cast in stone. Amy gazed now at that forty-year-old child in frank amazement. What had been wrong with her? At the time, and throughout that whole marriage, she had anesthetized herself with food, wine, and bourbon but had hardly suffered blackouts. It was as though she had been self-abducted and brainwashed.

For instance, had the newlyweds crossed the big river at Fort Madison, Memphis, or St. Louis? She really ought to remember that. Had she seen the Gateway Arch firsthand? She thought so but wasn't sure. She seemed, sort of, to recall "Bob" making some lame wisecrack about it—but then that was his response to everything, so she might be making it up. She had always made "Bob" self-conscious. Everything he said to her was painstakingly rehearsed in his mind, then presented to her as an offering, as though at an altar. As though she were the Great Wazoo.

Until now, Amy had avoided thinking about him, and she'd always assumed this was because she was ashamed of the whole three-year episode, the cretinous marriage, the contemptuous way she had treated him. He had brought out the very worst in her. She had no respect for him and even less for herself for having married him, and she certainly didn't need to torment herself with the whole sordid episode at this stage of her life.

She closed her eyes and switched focus to the Whither conference, specifically the tweet brouhaha which had begun just at the point she had gathered up her belongings and which had raged for a full hour and would have gone on all night if the hotel people hadn't thrown them out. Virtually every comment and question had been directed at her. "It's a Battle of the Tweets!" Jenny kept announcing, and now, as Amy tried to recall specifics, all she saw in her mind's eye was the cover of a Dr. Seuss (*Tweeter Bitter Battle!!*) featuring the vacuous leering faces of all three panelists perched on top of feathered, grotesquely elongated necks. She couldn't remember the tweets themselves because she hadn't actually seen them in print—they'd been read aloud by Tom Maudine—although she had been mildly impressed by how quickly the cyberwarriors had formed opposing armies, the (bare) majority supporting Amy's position, most without understanding it, and the haters uniting in dudgeon over Amy's various presumptions (about the worthlessness of literary conferences and the arachnoid tendencies of writers and so on). She remembered that for a while the tweets were statements rather than questions, so she could let her mind wander off, but that eventually she had been forced to engage. She could not recall her answers, just that they had provoked laughter from the crowd, so that by the time it was all over she had felt like a performing seal. Jenny had kept on about how much everybody loved her. Goonan, to whom she looked for a minty blast of self-absorption, had leaned close and told her that she was "a fine girl," which would have pleased Amy no end forty years ago. The conference itself and the tweets, all of it, was markedly forgettable, and try as she might Amy could not sink into recollection or otherwise distract herself from "Bob," who kept bobbing up before her like a cork.

Her projectionist, who usually confined his antics to REM-sleep dreams, wasn't going to let her change the subject. Amy waited, emptying her mind as best she could—she had never been good at that, but here she was, between two coasts, nowhere, un-ensconced, and just like that, she saw it, bobbing along beside "Bob": the real reason she'd avoided confronting the whole cretin-ous three-year Bobisode was simply that "Bob" had been Max's idea, and to contemplate that, to face that, was to recognize that Max had been wrong.

She had never been able to pinpoint just when "Bob" became part of the scenery in the Augusta house. While Max was alive, the house was always full, of friends, lovers, hangers-on. Most of them came for Max the charmer, but some came for Amy, and "Bob" was one of those. She noticed him here and there, mainly because he looked uncomfortable in blue jeans, as though he were trying to blend in, but also because he was always bringing her ashtrays and wine. She had initially assumed he was one of Max's guys, some weird Middle American experiment. He was easily ten years older than they were, good-looking in a Tony Randall sort of way. But by the time Max was dying, she understood that "Bob" was there for her.

"Why is *he* here?" she had asked Max one night, after everyone had gone home. She hadn't needed to name "Bob" the odd man out.

"He's in love with you. He wants to marry you when I'm gone."

"That's not funny."

"You could do a whole lot worse."

She had turned away shuddering, wondering if his meds were doing something to his mind. Max must know she had no plans to "do" anything after he was dead. After his death lay the Unthinkable.

"He has money," said Max, "and you won't," thus occasioning the only serious argument they ever had. Why, she had asked him, do you want me to have money? You know I don't care about money, and he said that was why she should marry "Bob," because she'd never made a plan in her life and she wasn't getting any younger and she needed one, and it escalated from there, because they had been living an unplanned life, a *wonderful unplanned life,* that was the whole point, and when she had raised her voice and said that he had just looked back at her with raised eyebrows and an expression of what it took her days to admit was cold pity.

They froze each other out for a while and then didn't refer to the matter until the day before he died.

"I *had* to live an unplanned life," he said. "You didn't. That's all I meant."

She remembered that moment exactly. They were in the rescue truck on the way to the hospital because he had been too weak to walk to the car, but he was lucid, even animated. He took her hand; his eyes were bright. Agitated, she thought, recoiling from the disloyalty of a word used exclusively to describe pitiful old people. "It's all right," she told him. She kept saying that until he relaxed. No, that wasn't true. She kept saying that to shut him up. Had she really believed he was agitated? No, she actually shut him down, knowing that he had only so many words left.

Two and a half numb years later, sixty pounds heavier, and three thousand miles west of Augusta, she discovered what Max had tried to tell her. She had run out of paper clips and was fishing around in one of "Bob's" desk drawers when she found the old viatical settlement papers and graded life insurance policies, all taken out on Max, the majority payable to "Bob." She looked at them for a few seconds and returned them, and then took them out again. She did this numerous times. It took her most of the night to make herself read them and she still didn't understand, beyond the stark fact that Max and "Bob" had had a complicated arrangement whereby "Bob" would profit greatly from Max's death. Within twenty-four hours of the discovery, she had sent him packing. He hadn't argued. When the divorce went through, she saw he had mismanaged and lost all that ugly money and hadn't asked for half of the house, their only remaining asset. He just shuffled off, leaving no footprints, the only trace of his time with her the occasional waft of his undead cologne. She would be washing her face or making tea or rummaging through the garage looking for a screwdriver and there it would be, the zombie vapor of Brut, instantly summoning "Bob"—not his face or body but the Brut fact of him, irrefutable proof that he had once lived there. She would spray and scrub and throw things out and imagine for a few months that she had finally erased him, but eventually it would pop up again, *Eau de Bob,* an unnerving mix of vanilla, old moss, and what the CSI shows called decomp. To a premier scent hound like Alphonse, "Bob" must still be present everywhere, at all times. No wonder Alphonse was such a sardonic dog.

Now, rolling through Topeka, alone in an observation car in the middle of the night, she allowed herself to dwell on those complicated financial arrangements. Max had tried to talk to her about life insurance more than once. Something about bets. The Wagers of Fear, he called them, trying to prod her into a smile. If you were terminally ill you could still buy insurance, but it wouldn't pay off unless you lived a certain number of years. At the time he was pretty hale and was obsessed with this and up to his elbows in brochures and policy correspondence, all furnished by various brokers, one of whom apparently was "Bob." He told her the premiums were high, and when he went to show her the figures she said it was a grotesque idea, and why did they have to talk about this now, and it was none of his business what she did after his death, she could take care of herself, thank you so much.

From the time of diagnosis, she had declined to dwell on a future without him, not even in the form of what philosophers called a thought experiment. She did research medical and pharmacological treatments, anecdotes about miracle cures, and the typical progress of the disease, none of that was off-limits to Amy. She saw herself as his shining guardian. But money was taboo. Money meant the future, and Amy hated the future. She had hated it before he got sick, and then, she hated it even more. The future was an abomination.

"Like every other animal on earth," she used to boast, "I live in the present." What a crock. She had said this for the first time at a party, a year or so before they got married. She must have been very young and very drunk. How pompous to make such a pronouncement anywhere, let alone at a party, for God's sake. Had Max rolled his eyes? She couldn't remember the people, the faces, just the flocked, bubbling wallpaper in his old apartment, *bordello chic* he called it, and the background music. Dylan singing "Country Pie." Imagine comparing herself to other animals. She wouldn't last five minutes in a forest. *Surely* he had rolled his eyes. What had he thought of her then, before their life together? She had no idea.

Now she understood that this sort of thing—not fear of death, but dread of waking—was why she never left home. Away from home, surrounded by everything foreign, she could not numb herself, to memory, to truth. There was no escape here.

What had he thought of her at the end, that he should entrust her future to a total stranger? Why, if he was so concerned about her *future*, hadn't he made *her* the beneficiary of all those damn policies? He'd done this dumb thing with forethought, set her up with a caretaker, a man neither of them even liked, as though even *he*, even Blob, could do a better job of looking out for her than she could herself. Never mind the fact that he was spectacularly wrong about "Bob." He had been wrong about *her*.

The lights in the observation car dimmed. Amy moved to a swivel chair on the north side and leaned her forehead against the glass, canceling her own reflection. The stars were out in force all over the huge Kansas sky, brightening as she watched. She kept her eye on them through Wichita, Hutchinson, Dodge City. Until he died, she had never paid much attention to the night sky. Afterward, she had taken to scanning it regularly. She still did. Alphonse would be somewhere in the yard, skulking behind a bush or investigating spoors, and she would look up without planning to, without meaning to, and her thoughts would fall away, and she would make herself very still, alert to any sign, however tiny, of his presence there. As though he were hiding.

The heaven of her childhood had been all sky blue and creamy cumulus, a place where sunny days blazed on inexorably. This nightmare of unending daylight had soon led her to the terrifying, inhuman idea of infinity itself. She would lie awake trying to make peace with the idea, to accept it, world without end, as a good thing. By the time she was ten, she had lost her religion. If heaven had been described like *this,* like the night sky, black, implacable, perhaps she could have hung on to some remnant of it.

Where did they go, the dead? Nowhere! crow the atheists, and she could respect the conviction but not the swagger. Had they ever seen a person die? Had they ever seen a body subside, abandoned like an old suit by its departing spirit? They ditch us, the dead, they shrug us off and leave us with nothing. Memories were worthless. At least to Amy, who remembered words and sounds, not images. No sooner had he left than she began to forget his face. She could describe it in detail, build it feature by feature, sentence by sentence, but he had taken all the pictures with him. And he had taken more. He had taken his memories of her, his knowledge of her, leaving her unknown. And now she had to wonder if he had known her at all.

Here was grief. The ongoing erosion of faith. The dead do not simply leave. They go on leaving forever, and what they leave behind stirs, shifts, fades. Amy almost cried. Then she took out her notebook and began to write. The dinosaurs weren't trains. They were writers.

❦

CHAPTER TWENTY-SEVEN

Star

Amy had been home for three days before she listened to her answering machine messages or read any email, logging on only to check the dates when messages were sent, so she could verify that Maxine hadn't died. Her phone lines, of course, were unjacked from the wall. She fed and communed with her dog. She began three new stories and finished one. "Storyteller" transformed Patrice Garrotte, his mother, and herself into a single person, a twelve-year-old girl diagnosed with a terminal illness. The girl has never had an active imagination, but now, confined to a hospital bed, plagued with pain, terror, and the anguish of her family, she weaves a narrative populated at first by movie stars and TV detectives, men to whom she is intensely sexually attracted without knowing what this means, and then, as she nears death, the narrative turns into a mystery about a lost ring or a cryptic entry from her own diary or the murder of an unknown woman, and the engine of the mystery perpetually stalls and restarts, but all the while its population grows, new characters strolling out of rooms, rooms telescoping into more rooms, so that no sooner is one question resolved than two more bloom in its place. The narrative, which begins as an act of will, slowly rises, weightless, and her with it, not toward a white light, but into chains of possibility, a web of paper chains extending not forever but to a perfect vanishing point. She liked the story, although not as much as she had the original, the story Patrice had used to save her life.

She should invite him to join Carla's retreat workshop. As promised, she had taught the Birdhouse Six (Ricky, Surtees, Tiffany, Robetussien, Brie, and Yoga Pants) once a month since the workshop started up. Actually, they were down to five, as Yoga Pants had left in a huff over Amy's "negativity" during the second group critique of *Skinny White Chick*. In all fairness, the session had been unusually brutal, but with Kurt Robetussien and Brie Spangler leading the charge and Amy being forced to mop up after them. Since people new to workshops usually tread lightly, Kurt and Brie had surprised Amy with their frank distaste for the novel's narcissistic protagonist. "We are all the heroes of our own stories," said Brie, "but all that means, as Mary McCarthy said, is that we live in suspense from day to day." "The trick," said Kurt, "would be to make us heroes in the imaginations of other people." Amy wondered about Kurt's patients. Did he give them his full medical attention, or did he let his mind wander, to literary matters? It seemed almost unfair that he could do both. While Yoga Pants sputtered that her central character wasn't *her* at all, that she was a wholly fictional character ("Who looks like you," sniped Tiffany, "is divorced like you, and lives in a condo in La Costa"), Amy wondered why she was needed here. She'd made a halfhearted attempt to placate Yoga Pants and rehabilitate her stupid manuscript but was relieved when the skinny white hero actually grabbed copies of it out of everybody's hands and slammed out of the Birdhouse.

Amy dropped Patrice Garrotte a line extending an invitation, copying in Carla and Harry B. Then, feeling good about "Story-teller" and virtuous about devoting a few minutes to her work-shop duties, she decided to glance through her emails.

At once it became apparent that in order to make sense of what people were writing to her, she'd have to backtrack a full week and begin reading the letters sent during and immediately after the Whither C-SPAN thing, which apparently people had actually watched on TV. Maxine was the first: her subject line, *What did I tell you?*, was the message itself. Amy guessed this was an affirmation, since the next twenty messages were forwards from senior editors and agents, some of whose names she actually recognized, along with literary columnists from the *Times,* the *ARB,* and *The New Republic.* The only forwarded message she could bring herself to read was from Lex Munster, and that only because he was the one who had started the ball rolling in the first place. Lex Munster, whom she pictured as a cross between Fred Gwynne and Philip Seymour Hoffman, was the Perkins/*ARB* editor who had read Holly Antoon's article last New Year's. The guy Maxine said had Asperger's and a nose for literary news. Now he was asking Maxine if Amy would join some ungodly rolling panel of lit-fic writers whose mission it was to sprinkle enlighten-ment dust on bookstores and college campuses throughout North America. "Stars like Morrison and Roth (we hope) will join at some of the larger venues, but we're looking for a core of six whom we can count on week-to-week. Amy would be perfect." Surely Maxine didn't expect Amy to do this. Unless they could do it in a tour bus, like Loretta Lynn.

Amy plugged in her phone and called Maxine, who picked up on the eighth ring and sounded like she had just run a marathon. "I gave already," she said.

"I'm sorry," said Amy. "I've been writing since I got back. I meant to call you yesterday."

"Bullshit," said Maxine. "What do you think about Charlie Rose?"

"He seems like a nice man," said Amy.

"Call me when you've read your damn mail. Ten minutes, max. I haven't got all day, if you know what I mean." Maxine hung up.

Maxine was apparently going to play the terminal illness card at every opportunity. The hell with Maxine. As Amy waited for Maxine to call back, she looked at all the forwarded emails, one of which was from some woman connected with Charlie Rose. It looked like a feeler. It didn't come out with an invitation to be on his show; it just inquired about her availability. In addition to the Munster Traveling Litfic Show, there were enquiries from book chains, local radio and TV shows, and publishers. The language used in most of these emails was identical: people claimed to be "excited" by Amy's behavior on C-SPAN. Terms like "voice of reason" and "no-nonsense" cropped up a lot. The phone rang before Amy could begin to think about any of these offers, if indeed they were actual offers. It was no longer as easy to say "no" as it had been before. Before what? Before Maxine. Before the birdbath.

Amy leaned back in her chair. "You know what I'm going to say," she said.

"Suit yourself," said Maxine. She hung up.

* * *

The phone, at which Amy was staring, went off immediately, and the calling number wasn't Maxine's. "Holy crap," shrieked Carla, "I thought you were gone for good! How are you? Amy, you were so awesome! We're on for next Thursday, right?"

"Did you get my note about Patrice Garrotte?"

"Done and done," said Carla.

"I've got to go," said Amy. "See you then."

She stared at the phone some more. Amy didn't have Call Waiting. Maxine had probably tried to call back while Carla was on the horn.

After five minutes, Amy actually shrugged her shoulders a little, as though someone other than Alphonse was watching. Alphonse was not impressed. She closed out her email program and clicked on her blog. Perhaps it was time to post something on the "I KNOW YOU ARE, BUT WHAT AM I?" page that Ricky Buzza had set up for her. And what a wonderful night that had been, luxuriating in her old books, drinking the last of her good wine, enjoying the company of a fellow human being. And what a long time ago it seemed, although, now that she thought of it, it had been only a few months. She missed Ricky and wondered how he was doing with his ridiculous serial killer book. For that matter, she missed Harry B and his bemused legal advice. She even missed Dr. Surtees. Eventually, as Holden Caulfield said, you miss everybody, even that goddamn Maurice.

Ricky had set up this page so that commenters could weigh in on various Amy-related controversies. Amy was humbled to see that in the past week alone he had been forced to set up five different pro-con topics. She could see in parentheses the number of comments for each so far.

- The Deal with Jasmine White-Banerjee (10)
- The Deal with Jenny Marzen (2)
- The Deal with Davy Goonan (26)
- Amy's Big Reveal (196)
- Haters (305)
- Stand-up (10)

There wasn't much of a deal with Jenny Marzen—the two commenters liked her books, sort of—and even less of one with Jazz White-Banerjee, who had either leaned on people to post raves about her performance and books or written each of the comments herself. Amy was glad to see a renewal of interest in Davy Goonan. Few of these people had actually read him, but on the strength of his spellbinding conference speech they were planning to run out and track down his novels. Unlike the live audience, these people had not minded his apparent slam of Jenny Marzen, calling it "brilliant" and "ninja."

In spite of her speech and her repeated insistence during the tweetathon, virtually all commenters refused to believe that the birdbath story was anything but a clever fiction, or a not so clever one, and that's how the pro-con debate played out. Amy was disheartened by this, and even more so by the silly arguments offered in support of her side-splitting antics, referred to by Prince Spaghettiday as a "meta-stunt." At least the people who disapproved of her theatrics were coherent about it. "I have better things to do," complained Sarge Entwistle, "than spend my remaining minutes parsing the cryptic asides of this dim literary light. She needs to either write something or shut the hell up." Amen, said Amy.

The Haters didn't hate Amy—they hated each other, along with individual tweeters and live audience members. Reading through some of their posts, Amy realized how little attention she had actually paid to what was going on during that time. The live audience questions, especially those of Hester Lipp, had registered with her, and she winced now as she saw poor Hester being torn apart on the page by a bestial mob. It wasn't enough that they thought she was strident and unpleasant. They ridiculed her face and body. Apparently Amy's mental picture of Hester had been dead wrong: she was a "shrieking battleaxe" with "the body of a Humvee and the face of Pete Postlethwaite." Amy spent a half hour deleting the nastiest of these comments.

"Stand-up" was not a roster of remarks but a list of links, all to YouTube. Taken together, Amy saw that she could watch her entire "stand-up comedy" performance in ten-minute chunks. To avoid this she hibernated her computer and dragged Alphonse out of the house for his first evening walkies since the Night of the Coyotes.

The July sun wasn't quite down, but already the air was cooling. Alphonse was slower than usual, or perhaps Amy was a bit speedier. She had lost some weight over the last few months, enough so that her shirt and jeans were pleasantly baggy, and while she didn't have a spring in her step, she wasn't breathing hard as she came to the top of the drive and sat on the big rock there. She hadn't been trying to lose, but jumping through hoops for Maxine had probably boosted her metabolism, effecting an anxiety diet.

The big flat rock where they always rested sat in front of the most expensive house on Jacaranda, a three-story house made of actual wood, reputed to have an actual cellar, though Amy had always been skeptical. She had never met the owners, though she had often admired their Japanese maples, which reminded her of home. Quite plentiful in the East, they required too much water for most inland residents. Their leaves were desiccated now, mostly mulch at the base of each tree, perfect camouflage for rattlers. The maples had fallen on hard times, as had the house itself, which according to the sign out front was now owned by Wells Fargo. Amy slipped Alphonse off his leash, shut him behind the low stucco wall, and watched him over the gate as he patrolled the perimeter. He flushed a cottontail out of a crimson hibiscus bush; the rabbit shot through dry grass into a pile of firewood, but Alphonse paid it no mind. He was too busy savoring its scent, unraveling its recent itinerary. Scent hounds were true scholars. Like Amy, Alphonse lived in his head. If he had to kill his meat, he would probably be a vegetarian.

Amy jotted "Anxiety Diet" in her notebook and pondered the metaphysics of scents. Aside from apes, corvines, and parrots, most animals did not engage in symbolic thinking, perhaps because they couldn't, perhaps because they didn't wish to. Why name things when they were right there and you knew what they were for and whether you needed them? Who had time to philosophize? Still, the basset took in everything and cataloged it, and how was that possible without signs or symbols? She had no doubt that he was now exploring the recent and not-so-recent lives of all this property's residents, from the humans who had built the place and lost it, to the gophers, lizards, raccoons, and mice to whom it was an ancestral manse. He could if he wished reconstruct whole scenes, plots, stories of sexual conquest and frustration, of sickness and misery, tales of violent death and hairbreadth survival. Here a trespassing cat ran afoul of two coyotes. Here in winter a human pup dropped a Frito, which fed a tree rat, who fed a redtail. How did he handle these narrative spoors? His dreams must be far richer and more detailed than her own.

She let him stay as long as he wanted, which turned out to be the better part of an hour, and as they walked back home he looked more thoughtful than usual, less hell-bent on getting back to his sofa cushion throne. He strolled, distracted, like a recent theatergoer working out the significance of a second-act monologue.

There were no new emails, no blinking numbers on her answering machine. It was ten o'clock in New York. Amy poured herself two fingers of bourbon and watched herself on YouTube.

She had always resisted the idea of herself as a perceptible, memorable object. Of course she knew she was more or less visible, that her corpus could be sensed by human and animal alike, but from childhood she had found it difficult to believe that she lingered in memory when she wasn't in the room. When a neighbor child or teacher or classmate would say, "We were just talking about you" or "I thought of you the other day when . . . ," she would be startled and put off. Why would they think or talk about her? What was wrong with them, that they were reduced to filling up head space with Amy? She wasn't offended or paranoid, just mystified. She once made the mistake of mentioning this to a boyfriend, the son of an Augusta psychiatrist, and been mauled with sympathy. "Don't you know how special you are?" he asked. What an idiot. Amy, not the boyfriend, Francis Pangloss, who didn't know any better and couldn't be expected to anyway, not at the age of twenty. But she should have known better. Why had she shared with him? Pan*coast*. She'd been only baffled, not driven by loneliness. Amy had never been lonely in her life.

Of course she knew she was special. Everybody was special in his own head, which was the only place that counted. It was way too much to expect being special to other people. The very thought was repellent. This attitude had contributed to Amy's childhood reputation as a stuck-up snot, which hurt her feelings a bit since it was untrue, at least at the outset, at least until she grew tired of being misconstrued and decided that most people really weren't very bright. Children are never seen as eccentric, only abnormal. You didn't get to be eccentric until you aged, which was why it was now almost impossible to alienate any of these people, no matter what she did. Not that she was trying to, but she was alarmed at how dense her commenters, her viewers, had been. They thought she was cute.

And now, looking at the first ten-minute installment of her Manhattan stand-up debut, she was forced to see why. This woman, a complete stranger to her, had a kindly face, her own mother's face. She peered out at the audience (or rather into the white light, but you'd never know it) over the tops of her reading glasses like Aunt Bee. The disconnect between her benevolent demeanor and her dry, understated delivery made for riveting TV, according to the YouTube posters, who seemed more illiterate than those on her own page. According to them, she was a "hoot" and a "roit" and "beyond gay," whatever that meant. Did they think she was gay? No matter.

Audience members, or perhaps C-SPAN, had included multiple videos of Amy prattling about her grandmother's movie magazine habit. In vain Amy searched her own face for some hint of the woman she had once been, the one who had loved mirrors so much that she'd slapped them up on every wall in the house and in the first year of their marriage encouraged Max to invest in an overpriced antique cheval glass. "It opens up the space," she had parroted, and he said she had the spatial sophistication of an infant and grumbled about opening up his wallet and teased her about her vanity. She said she didn't have a vain bone in her body.

"Okay, but your face is over the moon about itself." She said she wasn't *socially* vain. He snorted. She said she didn't care what other people saw when they looked at her, but yes, all right, she did love her own reflection, the blatant fact of it. There she was, everywhere she looked, right there, surrounded by solid, familiar objects. This made her a solid, familiar object. "You're a very strange person," he had said. A few nights later they had risen after midnight from their respective beds, their respective lovers, she to use the bathroom, he to do some late-night reading, and encountered each other naked in the dark connecting hallway, and they had stood still, looking, and Max had taken her hand, and Amy had caught sight of them both in the long mirror, and together they had turned and regarded themselves there. Amy had caught her breath. "We are beautiful," she said. "Yes, we are," he said. And they were. Just astonishingly beautiful. Young, strong, perfectly made. Undeniably corporeal. Amy, whose sense-memories were never plentiful and who learned to be skeptical of the few she had, never doubted the accuracy of this one. True to form, she was not able later to recapture the image itself, nor would she have wanted to, since the truth was sharp enough. The moment had been enchanted, as sublime as their visible selves but sorrowful in recollection. She could never look back at it without awareness of her own mortality and his. Somehow she knew the moment itself had triggered their decay, imperceptible for a while but still relentless. And there, on her computer screen, was the proof, a face and body he would never have recognized and which she barely recognized herself, since the only mirror in her house was on the bathroom medicine cabinet.

There was a famous problem in philosophy called Identity Through Time. Amy, who had majored in philosophy as an un-

dergraduate, had found it, along with most problems in philosophy, intriguing but not very. Let's say on Monday you have a car
and on Tuesday you replace the muffler. Is it the same car on
Tuesday as it was on Monday? Well, obviously. But what if, over
time, you replace every part of the car, from the chassis to the engine to the horn. Is it now the identical car? Well, no. So, at what
point did it lose its identity? This was where Amy always nodded
off. At some point, she would think, to be discovered by someone
with a more persistent intellect than hers. Still the underlying issue entertained. What does it mean to say *the same car, the same
house, the same woman*? Was the woman she looked at now identical to the child who had read Krafft-Ebing that rainy day? She
scoured her own pale, tired eyes for evidence, but there was none.
Like all strangers, like all visible corporeal human beings, this
woman was an utter mystery. Looking at her from the outside was
nothing at all like looking in a mirror. Unless we happen on them
without warning, we control what we see in mirrors. This was
beyond her control. For a short while, Amy was disturbed by not
being disturbed: she felt she ought to be horrified and wondered
why she wasn't. But soon she relaxed into the experience, the
brand-new experience of seeing herself from the outside.

The woman looked uncomfortable in her skin and not particularly happy to be where she was but otherwise calm. When
she asked the audience why they had bothered to come to the conference, she managed to look both exasperated and sympathetic,
as though she'd just been interrupted by doorbell-ringing tots
selling band candy. And as the tweets began, while she made her
way back to her seat at the long table, she fielded three in a row
over her shoulder with short-phrase answers, each getting bigger
laughs than the one before, all without cracking a smile herself or

(thank God) twinkling. What advice did she have for young writers? *Take notes.* What was her favorite novel? *Buccaneer Governess.* Seriously? *No.*

The hourlong Battle of the Tweets was also posted in ten-minute increments, all with over ten thousand views. Tom Maudine or somebody had thought it would be a great idea, in addition to reading hand-picked tweets aloud to the panel, to show all the rest of the tweets onscreen. C-SPAN's clumsy attempt to do this below the writers' faces had backfired spectacularly. Amy guessed that someone had weeded out obvious tweet-spam and then someone *else* had accidentally fed the weeds into the onscreen caption queue, with results that even Amy found hilarious. Under a snoozing Davy Goonan, electronic ticker-tape read ***Magugah OOH MY OOH MY OOH MY>>>#TEEN SEX CHAT VIDS.*** As Jenny Marzen gamely attempted to address an incoherent tweet about the crying need for a *"Very* Young Adult niche," all-too-coherent messages crawled beneath her earnest, animated face, ***Horndoggie1998*** *HEY HOTTIE MCHOOTTIE CHECK OUT MY #GARDEN WEASEL **Tw9lv_C8pcakes** OGLALA SIOUX EMERGNC PLS HEALP **PlumpF4nt45y** NHANCE UR SEXUAL ORGANS IN KENYA NO JOKE **bl00dynylons** LOL!! U SMELL!!* Because the messages were formatted exactly like news-crawl banners, they were impossible to ignore and lent a whiff of global crisis to this least critical of proceedings. Amy watched herself slice and dice a tweeter who had objected to her "community of spiders" remark.

"Bloomsbury," read Tom Maudine, "was hardly a community of spiders!"

"Does this," responded Amy, gesturing minimally, "look like Bloomsbury to you? Bloomsbury was the coming together of artists, novelists, poets, philosophers, economists, historians, critics.

It wasn't a guild of memoirists. It wasn't a mystery writers confab. If Bloomsbury was half as influential in the development of twentieth-century art and thought as it is supposed to have been—which is probably the case—it wasn't because they were all up to the same damn thing," while underneath that motherly smile crawled *fstophell666 OBVIOUS DAY AT CAMP STUPID Nojoke911 TARD ALERT mnsterm$sh DID YOU SEE THAT!! LMFAO,* and she was forced to admit that the whole spectacle, including what her own talking head was saying, really *was* Obvious Day at Camp Stupid, and yet undeniably, as the blurbists have it, *compelling.* It was the riotous coming together of a million tiny minds and three slightly less tiny minds over a bubbling cauldron of words and letters.

Entranced, Amy watched them all, then moused through other sites, Epic Fail and the Onion, where the funniest of the bunch were included, and watched again as Tom Maudine read, "Why do you think you're here just for the moment and by accident?" and Amy sighed, opened her mouth—she was going to say, "Why do you think you're not?" which would have been a Camp Stupid riposte—and Davy's sleeping head slid off the heel of his hand and knocked over three open bottles of smartwater, which cascaded the length of the table, thus allowing Amy to answer the question with a deadpan Jack Benny stare into the white light while the hall erupted in laughter and applause and underneath it all **sarge_entwistle** tweeted *ASK ME ABOUT OWL POOP.*

Amy picked up the ringing phone. "It's two in the morning," she said.

"I don't sleep much anymore."

"I was going to call you first thing."

"Sure you were."

"You know I was."

"What's the deal, babe?"

Alphonse had given up on Amy ever going to bed and was dreaming about cottontails and coyotes on the rug beneath her computer desk, his stubby legs jerking adorably. "The deal is I don't fly and I don't go anywhere without my dog. Otherwise, I'm yours." ·

"Back at you," said Maxine, and hung up.

"I'm a shining star," whispered Amy, waking Alphonse, and together they toddled off to bed.

CHAPTER TWENTY-EIGHT

There's Your Story

Amy began the next morning with the assumption that a first-class Amtrak roomette would provide room for both of them, then learned that dogs were not allowed on trains. Unless there actually *were* a Loretta Lynn lit-fic tour bus, she would have to subject him—and herself and the Crown Vic—to an extended road trip. She was trying to imagine how to manage this when Maxine called.

"How would you feel about being bipolar?" asked Maxine.

"Happy and sad. Listen—"

"It's either that or clinically depressed or—*bad idea*—schizophrenic."

"Look, they won't let my dog on the train."

"Way ahead of you. Here's the deal. Alphonse can travel with you everywhere *if* he's what they call a service dog. Unless you want to wear dark glasses and bang into walls, which would be fraud anyway, your best bet is some sort of *mental* disability.

You'll have to get certified, and so will your dog. We can do the whole thing in three weeks. Two. I know people. It'll cost you a little, though."

While Maxine rattled off the Service Dog Plan, Amy watched through her back door as Alphonse rooted around at the base of the birdbath. He did not look particularly excited about the investigation; still, this was his yard, his birdbath, and she felt a stab of guilt about her whimsical decision to drag him across the country. He was aging, like Amy. He needed his rest.

"Of course, you've got *phobias* up the wazoo," Maxine was saying, "but those are iffy when it comes to certification. Phobias could get him certified as what they call an Emotional Support Dog, but those aren't Service and they won't get him on the train and in the hotel. How about clinical depression, babe?"

"Look," said Amy. "I really appreciate it, and I'm sorry, but I don't think this is going to work out."

"I'm emailing you some material right now. Look it over." She coughed elaborately and hung up.

Maxine's first attachment was a color photo of a malamute gazing serenely out a train window. He was sitting on a narrow bed, his owner's wizened hand resting on the crown of his noble head, and he looked fulfilled. The caption read, "Aurelius guides his partner, a one-hundred-year-old woman suffering from bipolar antisocial personality disorder, across Canada on the fabled Rocky Mountaineer." Damn Maxine, who knew this would make Amy laugh and weaken her resolve. Amy skimmed electronic brochures. Apparently the basset would have to wear a natty vest of cobalt blue with "Hands Off, I'm On the Job" printed on it in marigold-yellow. There were patches, tags, wallet ID cards, and a certificate suitable for framing. Squinting, she noted that the certificate did not specify the owner's disability. She called Maxine.

"Seriously," she said. "I'm not disabled. This is fraud any way you look at it."

"Now we're talking," said Maxine.

"How would I obtain this thing, this proof that I'm unable to function without him, except by lying my head off to some official?"

"I know some people," said Maxine.

"Mobsters?"

"Give me a couple weeks. You don't have to do a thing. Meanwhile, I've got you ten bookings already, beginning the third week in August, so bye."

Within a week, Maxine had set her up as a certified victim of HPD. Hypervigilant Personality Disorder sufferers were asocial types who upset their fellows and distracted themselves by "constantly searching for hidden meanings in ordinary things." Apparently this so-called disorder involved both excessive sensory overload, which was silly since Amy had been able to blink away most sensory stimuli since childhood, along with an "unhealthy preoccupation with the inner lives of other people," which instantly neuroticized every novelist who ever lived. "A typical afflictee is prone to imagine the most outlandish possibilities. *Does the man sitting next to me on the commuter train have a bomb in his briefcase? Will the truck I'm passing blow a tire, swerve in front of my car, and kill me?*" How was this an affliction? Anyway, wondering wasn't the same as *obsessing*. What the websites described was more along the lines of a benign thought experiment, the sort of thing she routinely engaged in to keep from getting bored. To the HPD brigade, it was a symptom of malignant creativity.

"You're a natural, babe," said Maxine, and Amy agreed that if called upon she could probably fake it.

*   *   *

She spent two weeks packing and preparing. The vet pronounced Alphonse hale and in remarkably good shape for a nine-year-old basset, "especially the spine," which looked youthful on the x-ray. There were no shadows there, no fog either, she was pleased to see. She thought about closing down the house but decided instead to hire a sitter. Ricky Buzza, only fitfully employed and still living with his dad, was delighted. On the strength of five chapters and an outline, he had attracted the curiosity of an agent (a good one, Maxine said) to flog his serial killer novel. "She's not on board yet. She says *Caligula's Scalpel* is a mouthful, and I can see that. Plus nobody would name their kid Caligula anyway. I'm calling it *Tiberius*."

Carla and the gang wanted to throw her a bon voyage party, but she put them off, dealing with their latest submissions electronically. Patrice Garrotte, she was happy to see, had been welcomed into the Birdhouse Retreat—he was actually living on the premises and writing fiction, not memoir. He wrote a story not about his mother, not quite, but about aging sisters, one a writer who lives in a Nantucket beach house with a long white porch. The architectural similarity to her plane-dream, the one at the Lake George cottage, was startling. Not much happened in the story, which was mostly atmospheric, but the women were sharply drawn. She could not see herself full-on in either of them, but she was somehow there in it. When she was young, she had taught graduate students in Orono and had watched workshop writers cannibalize one another in their fiction, stealing names, faces, biographies, social quirks, ostensibly all in fun, but really to diminish their competitors, to pin them to the page, and she had found this an ugly practice, particularly as most of them had no idea of their real motives. Now here was Patrice, and she did not feel pinned. Only taken in. Good for him.

On the 12th of August, Amy and Alphonse set off in a stretch limo for Union Station, Los Angeles. Amy didn't even argue about the limo this time, which was free anyway, directly paid for by somebody, not Maxine. She had hoped he would snooze on the floor, but car travel had always made him uneasy, and he spent most of the trip pacing the long floor in desperate search for a scent other than artificial new car. Once again she became anxious. How would he survive two full days on a train to Chicago? But five minutes after the Chief began its eastward slide, he clambered up on the opposite seat in their little roomette and, after a cursory glance out the window, fell fast asleep. The rocking of the train was as soothing to him as to Amy.

She did wonder at the outset whether her HPD would cause conductors and porters (now for some reason called "car attendants") to look at her funny, readying themselves for outbursts of irrational vigilance, but they did not seem apprehensive, and they all smiled at Alphonse. Apparently all the world loved a basset.

Next she fretted about his bathroom breaks, which would require leaping off the train at various stops (she had packed a box of ziplock bags) and frantically searching for a patch of green. The Amtrak people had warned that stops were of an unpredictable length. But the porters looked out for her, letting her know the best stations and longest stops, and the procedure was much less fraught that she had anticipated. By the time they got to Kansas, two Japanese teens in the next roomette, having discovered Alphonse, were attending to his every whim. Before she reached Chicago, Amy realized that she had run out of anxiety triggers.

288 @ Jincy Willett

She had nothing to worry about, and for the first time in her life found herself enjoying a journey.

She was having an adventure. She was at home on the road.

Within three days she had done a radio interview, two bookstore appearances, and the first lit-fic panel, joining Jenny M, some poet, and a Booker longlister with a terrible head cold. Amy tuned out of most of it, a series of cliché lamentations on the general illiteracy. Late in the hour, when prodded by the student moderator, she launched into a defense of libraries real and virtual, reassuring the audience that whether books are read or not, they are no longer in danger of disappearing forever. The only way the modern-day Library of Alexandria could burn was if the world ended, in which case illiteracy would be the least of our problems. The poet, who had been silent for the whole hour, countered with something cryptic about the looming Age of Darkness, at which point they all congratulated themselves and broke for prosecco and brie.

This was to be the default script of the traveling lit-fic show as they hopscotched through the heartland through late summer and into the fall, most of the panel discussions set down in university commons rooms, lecture halls, and libraries. They hit De-Paul, Case Western, Ohio State, Beloit, and everything in between. All the campuses were green, all of the older buildings Early American Greek. On Columbus Day they crossed the border into Ontario and did York in Toronto, then on to McGill in Montreal. The panel personnel were as interchangeable as the undergraduates who ushered them around.

Maxine had arranged for Amy to speak at Colby, where she had earned her undergraduate degree, and in Waterville they were joined at dinner by an old beau of Max's whom Amy could neither recall nor recognize, who welcomed her "home" and then embraced her, sobbing. She was surprised, even as she extricated herself, at how little this upset her. Six months ago she would have retracted like a turtle. Now she patted his back, murmured the requisite clichés, sent him off, and enjoyed the curious glances of panelists and faculty, who waited in vain for a backstory. She was the featured speaker that night, to a packed audience in Lorimer Chapel. As had become her custom, she talked for a quarter hour and then threw the discussion open to the crowd. They asked questions about her old novels, half of which she couldn't answer because she had not looked at the books for decades. Apparently she was beginning to be taught.

An improbably tall girl introduced herself as president of the Maine chapter of the American Ephemera Association, and Amy, thinking this was a brilliant put-on, drew her out at great length. One minute she was talking about ticket stubs, 7-11 receipts, and toddlers using magnet letters to spell out immortal gibberish on refrigerator doors, and then next she was asking Amy a paragraph-length question about the role of ephemera in twenty-first-century writing. Apparently the question was serious, so Amy tried to answer without laughing.

Everything everybody wrote was ephemeral as far as anyone knew. Future scholars might regard the whole of all their works— Amy gestured to include her lit-fic colleagues—as no more significant than unearthed pottery shards. Jenny M sprang to her feet, ostensibly to second Amy, but really to burnish her own future shards, allowing Amy to tune out long enough to remember that here, in this place, she and Max had wed. The event had been low-key and last-minute, just the chaplain and a few friends, and she could remember almost nothing of it—not the weather, or what she wore, or whether Max's hair was still long, or even who the friends were. They had gone to Augusta that morning for the license and planned to marry on the weekend, but then said what the hell. It was a what-the-hell wedding in every sense, and the chapel interior had surely been repainted and updated many times since that day, yet she could suddenly see the chaplain's sad face as though he stood before her right now, pronouncing them man and wife. How odd memory, to house such tiny drawers, spring-loaded like Chinese puzzle boxes. She had not seen Max clearly in her mind's eye even once since his death, and here was this man she had not thought of in forty years, sharp as a Kodachrome slide, his long face lined and gray. He had been distracted with grief. His son had just been killed at Quang Tri.

She fled the chapel as soon as she could and took Alphonse for a stroll around Johnson Pond. He liked fresh water. Before the trip neither had known this, since the one time she took him to Moonlight Beach he had been outraged by the surf, the way the water snuck up on him when he was investigating marine curios. He had gotten his big feet wet and blamed it on her. Ponds were different. They probably smelled a lot better without all that decomposing seaweed. Almost every college campus had one, its honest shoreline teeming with items of interest—sushi wrappers, beer cans, neon-colored condoms like radioactive jellyfish. He surely had a stronger sense of the history of this place than Amy did. But for the ghost of Pastor Swanson, the campus stirred up no memories for her. She could vaguely recall her old dormitory sitting room and the library coffee lounge; she remembered ten-foot snowdrifts, beer keg races, panty raids, and one drunken sophomore night when everybody, even Amy, sledded on cafeteria trays down the icy terraced hill in center campus. She could, if she tried hard enough, recall the scent of wet wool, the awful stab of chilblains on her exposed fingers. But she could not recall a single person or conversation, or indeed any significant event. Her life had certainly not begun here. If anywhere.

She sank down in the grass, fished out her cell, and called Maxine. "This is getting old," she said.

"As soon as you do Manhattan, you can dump the panel and go wherever you want."

"Are you sure you don't mind? Is this going to make you look bad?"

"What do I care? Anyway, you lasted longer than I thought you would. Where do you want to go? I can book you straight home from Penn Station."

Amy imagined trudging through her front door. She saw the waiting computer, the blinking answering machine. "I've never been to the Great Northwest," she said.

"I'm on it," said Maxine. Her voice was stronger than usual. Maybe she was taking some new meds.

"No more colleges," said Amy. "No more kids."

Maxine promised bookstores and libraries, and hung up.

"We're going to take Manhattan," she said to him.

Alphonse loved the Spalding, an eccentric hotel near the West Village catering to creative types and their pets. Per its brochure, from the minute he swept through its old-fashioned revolving doors, he was home. Here he didn't need to be a service dog, nor did Amy have to pretend to be unusually vigilant. He was walked, fed, and massaged, all on someone else's dime. The brochure also offered psychic basset readings for an extra charge, which didn't sound at all East Coast to Amy, but apparently California was winning in certain culture skirmishes.

She spent three days without him, being shuttled between radio and TV stations. She met too many people and stared into too many white lights. Everyone was courteous and friendly—she did not have a single Chaz Molloy moment—but she was never able to figure out what any of these people wanted from her.

Really, her whole life had been like that.

Because of Arab uprisings and the tanking economy there was no room for her on Charlie Rose, but she had no time to be grateful because she was instantly booked on four talk shows as well as another C-SPAN snooze festival, this time an interview with a man she probably should have recognized, who spent most of his on-screen time with her fielding telephone questions. Apparently C-SPAN had learned not to tweet.

The talk shows were marginally more interesting. She met some famous actors and actresses, most tiny and thin with outsize heads. They looked like beautiful balloons on sticks, and they were mostly quite pleasant. She met a nasty comedian with terrible manners and a handler who circled him in a cartoon whirlwind, supplying coffee and drugs; she met an old woman from Tallahassee who crocheted with her feet. "I learned when I was a kid," she told Amy while they were waiting in the green room. "My sister had no hands and could do everything with her feet. I was very competitive." Amy watched her performance on the monitor. The audience loved her, not so much for the crocheting, which was impressive but grotesque, but for her offhand explanation: "I was bored," she said, when asked why she cultivated this talent, then shrugged elaborately and twinkled for the cameras. She did not mention her handless sister, whose mention would surely have dampened the crowd's enjoyment of the trick. She really *was* competitive.

Amy wrote "handless" in her notebook but expected nothing

from it. Her story ideas were drying up, not because she was fresh out, but because she wasn't built for writing on the road. She missed her dog. She yanked him from the canine masseuse and brought him with her to the last show; they let him out onstage with her, where he amused everyone inordinately. You would think they had never seen a basset hound in their lives.

Three days later Amy and Alphonse bridged the Mississippi at LaCrosse, Wisconsin, racketing toward the Northern Pacific through farmland and forest and the long, somber prairies of North Dakota and Montana. After a dutiful trudge through megastores in Minneapolis and St. Paul, they visited only little independent bookstores. Portage, Winona, Devil's Lake, Minot. They took their time, disembarking for a day or two at each stop, staying at Motel 6s and local B and Bs. Finally all Maxine's preparations were paying off: Amy actually had to explain about her HPD more than once to justify rooming with her service dog. In the big city hotels, they knew, more or less, who she was and never asked. In the heartland, she was mostly unknown. Amy liked it here.

She autographed her old out-of-prints but read from her new stories, all scheduled for publication, but this was the first time she had shared them. Though crowds were small, she never spoke to an empty house. The most alert, intelligent audience for the whole trip was in a tiny store and coffee stop in Wolf Point, Montana, where it seemed every member was anxious and ready to argue either with her or with one another over the issues raised in her fiction. They listened closely, seriously, and they related what they heard to their own experiences and perceptions. They were better than sophisticated. They showed no interest in her private life; they wanted no writing tips or publication advice. One elderly woman hated "Shadow," the one about the hospital chapel and the river of suffering; another, who seemed to be her older sister, defended it with passion. The first, Betty, said the story made the suffering man out to be some kind of martyr. "What he's going through is nothing unusual," she said, and her sister said, "That's exactly the point." They all disliked the bus plunge story. She could tell, not because any of them said so, but because of their tolerant smiles. She decided she didn't much like it either.

After the reading, the older sister came up to Amy to apologize. "Betty always looks at the sunny side," she said. "It's a religion with her. With all of us up here, really. The nights are so long. Throw shadows at your peril." They talked about *The Old Curiosity Shop* and *Vanity Fair,* and she admired Alphonse, who snored beneath the signing table. "He's wearing some sort of outfit," she said delicately. "He's a service dog," said Amy. She opened her mouth to explain about the HPD and how of course she didn't really have it, then decided not to waste the lady's time. Her name was Emily. Emily waved good-bye at the door. It was snowing, a full two weeks before Halloween. "Never seen anything like it," said Emily, and went out to join Betty on the cold sidewalk.

On the train, most evenings Amy had eaten with Alphonse in the roomette, but since that energized crowd at Wolf Point had habituated her to conversation, she missed, just a little, the company of her own kind. That evening Amy decided to take supper in the dining car. The maître d', a magenta-coiffed young woman whose job it apparently was to segregate diners according to age, seated her with Thelma Schoon, a hearty old dame who hailed from Lincoln, Nebraska, and was thinking of writing a book about it. She recognized Amy from TV and asked where she got her ideas, but soon turned the conversation to her own story.

Thelma could still remember things that had happened when she was barely two years old. She must have been born in the middle of the Depression, as she had clear memories of men coming to the back door of her house, asking her mother if she had any old shirts. "They were trying to get jobs, and they needed white shirts. We never threw out any of Daddy's, in case someone could use them." Thelma's parents had been academics, teaching "at the U." Tenure had fed and housed them. She talked about family sabbaticals, summers in Puget and Long Island Sound, and about her mother teaching Arapaho children before she got married. It was the mother who told Thelma she was a "born storyteller." This was false. She had phenomenal recollection of detail—what any true writer could have done with that!—but no sense of what made a story worth telling. As they waded through baked trout, artichoke hearts, and a not-bad Chablis, Thelma rambled through a childhood recorded but not really taken in. Listening to her was like viewing someone's vacation slides. Of course, Thelma had a story—everyone has a story—but she did not seem to know what it was, and didn't know she didn't know. Knowing what your story is, Amy was fond of telling her classes, was what separated writers from everybody else.

Amy prodded her now again with questions. *Did you ever attend your father's lectures? Did your mother miss the Arapaho?* But none touched off a true narrative. Amy found her mildly interesting despite the chaos, the one-damn-thing-after-anotherness, of her memory stores. Her hair was iron gray and collected at her nape in an intricate bun. She wore no wedding ring and never mentioned children, and as she spoke, her eyes took in the dining car, the diners, Amy, the crossing lights outside their window, filing it all away with care. When they finished, Thelma headed off to the observation deck and Amy back to her roomette. Perhaps, said Thelma, they could breakfast together. She was a hoarder, Amy thought as she bedded down. She never threw anything away. Amy would have suffocated in all that clutter. "Hoarding," she wrote in her notebook, and instantly slept.

The crash impact did not wake her. Rather the sharp pain in her right side, pinned against the wall as she was by some fixture that had come loose and lodged in her ribcage. In the pitch dark, she knew she was no longer in bed but couldn't tell where she was. The basset's toenails clicked frantically—not a walking rhythm, but as though he were fumbling with some metal object, and then he slid into her lap. He was shivering. She felt him all over for bumps and wounds but could find none, and at her touch he quieted down and licked her hand, so assiduously that she wondered if *she* were bleeding, but no. Outside was dead quiet and then shouts, screams, and, from some distance, an explosion, and her window lit up yellow, so she could see the compartment interior and find the door latch. She stood, leashed Alphonse, and opened the door, expecting smoke and flames, but the narrow corridor was silent, the air still, and they found their way outside without incident.

The second she stepped off the train Amy came to herself, fully understanding that they had somehow crashed, and she turned to go back in, to check the other roomettes, to call out to anybody trapped inside, but three men were already ahead of her. She recognized a porter; the other two looked like passengers. Again she checked Alphonse. He was fine, quite chipper, straining at the leash to move down the line, to follow the jumble of cars, a few, like hers, still more or less on the rails, others jack-knifed, and one far up ahead horribly mounting the trailer of a semi which apparently had crossed its path. She could tell it was a semi only because the cab was not on fire. The rest of the truck and surrounding train was engulfed. She could not see beyond the fire to the front passenger cars and engines.

People ran frantically from car to car, looking for a way back in, or huddled in clusters, or wandered along the embankment which sloped steeply down from the rails. They were in high frosted grass; she could not see beyond the firelight farther down. For all she knew they were hard by forest, farmland, water, or some life-threatening precipice. They were someplace in Montana. She really hadn't been paying attention. Compared to this endless unknown, the mangled, burning train seemed the safer bet, marginally more hospitable. Alphonse yanked her on past quiet children and yelling adults. Her right side hurt—she had maybe broken a rib—but she was otherwise all right, certainly in better shape than the people being dragged from the cars now. A grown man struggled with his rescuers, called for his mama. "Poor man, he's delirious," she heard a woman say, and another answered, "No, he's not. I saw him in the dining car. He's traveling with his mother." Everywhere she wandered, people called out names. *Timothy! Carol-Ann! Daddy! Mrs. Carmen Lopez!* Casualties were laid out in rows near enough to the fire so that those attending to them could see their injuries, which ranged from burns to head wounds to amputated limbs. The rows looked inordinately neat, as though someone had measured, trying to achieve a tidy grid. She knelt and pressed down hard on a silent man's thigh while the magenta maître d' tried to tighten a tourniquet, but beneath Amy's palms she could feel the pump empty him out and quit. "He's gone," she said, and the young woman said, "We can't know that," and kept at it. Amy choked back a laugh. I must be hysterical, she thought, and then the idea of having this thought struck her as even more hilarious, and she had to turn away and pretend to cough and choke. *We can't know that.* There was an article of faith for you.

The sky to her right lit up as three helicopters landed in what turned out to be a rocky field, so there went *that* mystery, and rescue personnel streamed toward them. Some of them set up a command post next to the injury grid. She knew this because the apparent leader, who looked no older than Ricky Buzza, actually used the words "command post." Amy and the other passengers who had been trying to help were supplanted by people who knew what they were doing, and after watching for a while she was about to wander away when a young man adorned with fluorescent straps and badges asked to borrow her dog.

"There's a missing child," he said.

Amy glanced at the nearby car, folded in on itself, flames dancing in the windows. Alphonse would die in that car. He would get himself pinned or blown up. "You want to take him in there?" she asked, pointing. Already she was frantically trying to imagine a decent excuse for not allowing them to do this. Already she knew there was none.

"The kid isn't on the train," the man said. "She must have been thrown clear or wandered off."

Amy still hated the idea, although Alphonse had not stopped pulling on her since they disembarked. "He's not a bloodhound," she said, but she let him take her dog away, because how could she not. She watched Alphonse trot past the helicopters and into the darkness of the field. He certainly looked purposeful. His long ears brushed the tops of the frosted grass. They were bred that way, to keep the scent in front of the nose. What would she do if they lost him? She started out after them but was interfered with by an officious young rescuer who shone a blinding flashlight in her face and took her elbow. "Why don't you come over this way, ma'am?" he said, attempting to guide her back to the injury grid, and she said, "Because I have other plans." She shook him off. "If you'll excuse me, I have someplace to go." "Ma'am," he said, "who is the president of the United States?" "John Quincy Adams," she said, and just then a naked man ran up, grabbed the rescuer, and demanded to talk to someone in authority. Amy slipped away.

When she got beyond the helicopters and out and down into the field, all noise and light receded together. She felt her way forward until she could begin to see the moon and then the brighter stars emerge in a sky that was a perfect bowl of dark. Her feet were bare. Well, that was probably a good thing, she thought, or else she'd be tripping all over the place. She was beginning to be cold, the dark silence was waking up her senses, but she still had a little feeling in the soles of her feet, and she marveled at the relative smoothness of the rocks out there, Montana rocks, nothing like the sharp, unwelcoming rocks of Maine, and she dwelled on that hopeful thought as long as she could, all the while listening intently, and sure enough she heard him, very far off, woofing happily. Good. He was safe. She was trying to decide whether to stay there and wait or make her way back, and then she heard a ragged moan not far away, too low-pitched for a child, and then she found someone, a woman, Thelma Schoon, lying on her back, her face and hair shiny with thick blood, her eyes bright and darting, her remaining arm stretched out on the ground, her hand raised and waving like a metronome.

"Thelma," Amy said. "Here I am," and tried to shrug off her coat and cover her, then realized she was wearing only a nightgown. "Over here!" she shouted back at the faraway lights. Thelma's other arm had been torn away at the shoulder. Amy could not imagine how she might be saved. She called out again and then lay down beside Thelma and, resting most of her weight on one elbow, covered her with her body, her flannel gown instantly drenched. The smell of blood was almost intoxicating. "Here I am," she kept saying. "It's Amy." "There you are," said Thelma. "Dinner's ready." Her body pulsed, its rhythm regular but so faint. "Am I hurting you?" Amy asked. Thelma said she hadn't stolen the candy, no matter what Janie said. Janie was a great big liar. Amy lifted her head and shouted again, "Over here!" but Thelma said *hush-hush-hush*. "Talk to me, Thelma," Amy said. "I'm here." Max had died without her, sending her down the hospital hall for a glass of milk. Now she attended hard to this dying stranger's gasps and murmurs, at once conversational and unintelligible, and plainly narrative. She heard *Harold* and *of course* and *never, I never did that*. She said this over and over. "I know," Amy said. "All the doors were wide open when I left them," Thelma said, "and I laughed and you were right there rising." The light left Thelma's eyes.

Amy kissed her forehead. "There's your story, Thelma," she said.

After that she got lost trying to find Alphonse and then a huge fluorescent man walked up and threw a blanket on her. She explained that the blood wasn't hers, that there was a dead woman on the ground someplace, and that she had to find her dog.

"You're the lady with the dog?" asked the man, and then yelled toward the light, "Hey, I got the dog lady!"

"Where have you taken him? What have you done with him?" She was so cold and shaking terribly. She couldn't feel her feet.

The man wrapped the blanket tight around her and picked her up as easily as if she were a child.

"This is ridiculous," said Amy. "I can walk, thank you very much."

"Your feet are all torn up, ma'am," he said, trotting uphill toward the light, the train, the carnage.

"I told you, that is not my blood."

"Yes it is."

"No it is not. Listen to me. I want my dog."

"Your dog's a hero, ma'am. Hold on a minute and I'll show you."

Amy was perilously close to crying with frustration and probably something deeper. Also, she was peeved. In her girlhood, she had daydreamed about moments just like this, being carried off by some brute in the woods. It wasn't sexy at all. It was stupid. Now they were back in the light, ten times brighter than before, and he set her down gently on a gray blanket. The radiance began to warm her. "That was a total waste of energy on your part. I'm just going to get back up," she said, but she couldn't see him, the light was searing her eyes. "Back off," he yelled. "Leave this woman alone! Have some respect!" She heard him ask someone for a hot washcloth, and then she felt it on her face, warm and rough, as he scrubbed at her mouth and cheeks. "Sorry," he said, "but you look like hell, and I can't keep these creeps away forever." Why did this lummox care what she looked like? His familiarity was breathtaking. Had they known each other in an earlier life?

When she managed to shield her eyes with a blanket corner, she saw she was in some infernal media arena, with two TV cameras right there in front of her and a hovering news helicopter shining down like God's flashlight on all of them, the quick and the dead and Amy.

She tried to rise and escape and found she could not. The

lummox had been right about her feet—they were all scraped up raw and would have to be bandaged before she could walk. She tried to at least turn her back, but the news people were everywhere. One of them knelt down beside her and stuck a microphone in her face. "Amy Gallup—" he began.

"How do you know my name? Buzz off! People are dying! Shame on you!"

"It's on your dog, ma'am," said the lummox, somewhere to her left. He sounded like he was enjoying himself.

"Where is my dog?"

Someone thrust a leash into her hand, and at the end of it, there was the basset, safe and sound, in his brilliant blue-and-gold service dog outfit, which did, she now remembered, have her name embroidered on it, followed by "HPD." Alphonse, not Amy, was the cynosure of all media. Apparently he had found a toddler freezing in a ditch. On either side of her, TV reporters broadcast identical fables about little miracles, answered prayers, and single rays of hope. Someone had given him a soup bone on which he crunched happily, stretched out on the ground and propped up on his elbows like a sphinx, holding it upright in his great front paws, his profile dancing in the strobe of flashing cameras. "Bassets are never used for search and rescue," some expert was explaining. "This is most unusual." Amy couldn't figure it out either, unless the child had cookies in her pocket. That was probably it.

She was still cold, deep in her bones, so she rolled herself tight in the blanket and curled up on her side, facing away from the commotion. After a long while it died down. She called him to her and folded him into the blanket and nestled against him. He smelled like smoke and earth, and he warmed her. She had never been in shock before, and assumed that soon it would either set in or wear off. She waited for it, listening to cries and chatter and far-off wails and sirens and the rumble and whine of machines. Already she was losing Thelma's bright eyes, her upturned face in the moonlight, already Thelma's dying moments were turning into words, she could feel them slip away to join the rest of her own chaotic memory stores. What a shame that all of Thelma's hoarded data, all those images she had categorized, dusted, and polished, every one of them was gone.

A hand grabbed her shoulder. "Take me last," she said, "it's just a broken rib." The lummox handed her a cell phone. "Somebody wants to talk to you," he said.

"Babe," said Maxine.

It must be at least three in the morning. How had she found her?

"You look like something out of *Titus Andronicus*."

"Oh, for God's sake. Am I *on the TV*?"

"Not at the moment. Look, I booked you a flight from Helena."

"Why would you do that? You know I don't fly."

"Seriously? What are you afraid of now?"

"Flying!"

"Amy," Maxine said. Amy could not remember Maxine ever calling her by name. "You've just gotten yourself into a mass-fatality accident. It's all over the news. They're saying twenty-three dead. *You're alive.* You got past it. Just fly the hell home and call me, because we've got a lot to talk about, let me tell you."

Amy noticed something odd: Maxine hadn't coughed once during this speech. In fact, she hadn't coughed, at least on the phone, for a while now. Was she really dying? Did she even have emphysema? Amy was afraid to ask. "You've seen too much bad TV. Knock it off with the profiling."

"See, you're Captain Hook," said Maxine, who just wouldn't quit. "The crocodile just bit into your other leg, but then *he let go*. What are you afraid of now?"

"I'm not afraid of dying in some generic accident. I'm not phobic about tornados, banana peels, or freak gardening mishaps. I'm afraid of dying on a plane." She told her she'd get herself checked out somewhere, get her ribs taped or whatever, and keep going. "I've heard good things," she lied, "about Spokane." She handed the phone back to the lummox. "If she calls back," she told him, "hang up."

A little while later he came back. The sky was beginning to lighten. "Ma'am, we still haven't found that dead individual you told us about. Are you sure about what you saw?"

Amy sat up. "Look at me! I'm covered with blood that's not my own. Of course I'm sure. She's out there somewhere. I might have lost track of time. I might have wandered farther than I thought. Keep looking. Her name is Thelma Schoon, and she comes from Lincoln, Nebraska, and she's writing a book about it." Amy's eyes watered up. She really needed a decent stretch of sleep. "And she's dead and she deserves to be found and buried, so keep looking."

"No, I'm not!" came a voice behind her. Amy looked around and Thelma Schoon hobbled toward her, covered with dirt and ash and no blood. She still had two arms, one in a sling, and her hair had not escaped its bun. "What a night!" she said, kneeling down beside Amy.

Amy stared at Thelma Schoon. She had not felt so unmoored since New Year's, when she had watched Holly Antoon back out of her driveway, waving like an old friend and shouting nonsensical thanks. Had she finally had some kind of cerebral event? She closed her eyes tightly and opened them again, just to make sure that she was really here on the hard ground next to a smoking train wreck in northern Montana: that the past year had actually happened; that she hadn't stumbled into a birdbath and dreamed up three full seasons. Thelma Schoon took her hand. "I've been looking all over for you! There you are."

"There we are," said Amy. She looked down at herself. The length of her gown, neck to hem, was truly encrusted with somebody's dark blood. Thank god. "I'll admit," she told the lummox, "I was wrong about the name, but I'm not wrong about the dead woman. You need to keep looking."

Thelma didn't shut up until the last batch of ambulances came. She told Amy and everybody else about all she had seen and heard during the long night, the people she'd met, the amazing, terrible, memorable sights. She regurgitated names of passengers and crew; she knew how many train cars had been completely destroyed and how many were still on the rails. She knew what freight the truck was carrying and that the driver, who was apparently at fault, had died on impact. If Thelma had found that woman in the field, she would have learned her full name and Social Security number and been able to lead rescuers to her precise location. Thelma was nice enough but tiresome, and she took too much pleasure in all the excitement. Amy decided she really didn't like Thelma all that much.

Yet she had loved the dying woman. She might tell herself she hadn't: that it had been a moment of insanity, of shock, that she had not been herself. She might claim that she had embraced the woman and seen her through to the end because she had been denied that privilege with Max. But she knew this wasn't exactly true. Not fully. The moment had been both mysterious and transcendant. Amy went to take out her notebook, but of course it was gone, abandoned in what was left of her roomette.

She pulled the lummox aside. "I feel as though we almost know each other by now," she said. This was true. He had been a constant through an endless and tumultuous night.

"I know what you mean," he said, smiling. She could make out his features now: he was older than she had thought, and balding. She wondered if he were a lumberjack. Were there still lumberjacks?

"What is your name?"

"Franklin, ma'am."

"Franklin, would you do me a favor?" Amy lowered her voice. "Would you make sure Miss Schoon and I are put on different ambulances? She's tiring me out."

"She is pretty chatty, isn't she?"

They made her lie down on a stretcher, and they were going to kick out Alphonse, but Franklin interceded and helped load them both in. "By the way," he said as they closed the doors, "we found her. Her name was Harriet Johnston."

In exchange for a pencil and some sheets of paper, Amy let the medics check her pulse and stick an IV in her arm. She wrote *Harriet Johnston*. Had she actually used Thelma's name on Harriet Johnston? How horrible. She imagined herself on her own deathbed, surrounded by weeping strangers, calling her *Shirley, Veronica, Grammaw, Thelma Schoon*. She hoped Harriet Johnston had had a sense of humor. She wrote *All the doors were wide open when I left them*. She was losing the words already. She wrote *and you were rising*. She wrote *never, I never did*. When the ambulance got to the highway, they turned the siren on.

She had been wondering when she was going to take in all that had happened. She had been expecting some sort of shift in perspective, perhaps a falling away of denial, an inrush of horrific detail, but she was beginning to understand that this would not happen, because there had been no denial, no resistance at all. She could remember the evening in an unbroken string, from waking up against the wall of her compartment to right now. When she was young, when she was middle-aged, the taking in of bad news had been arduous. She never subscribed to the seven stages theory; rather she had felt like a great amoeba having to deform itself around an object as big as she or bigger in order to ingest it and make it part of herself, and of course be changed to her core by the process. This time, though, none of that had been required. One damn thing after another had happened, she had been witness to and participant in catastrophe, and she had accepted it all without struggle, as though it were somehow old hat. Perhaps she had been rehearsing for it all her life. Perhaps she was over-rehearsed.

Her only aberration during that whole night was jumping to the absurd conclusion that an unrecognizable mortally injured woman was the only other passenger on the train whom she actually knew. How cheap, how convenient that had been. Poor storytelling on her part. She would have to remember it for use as an object lesson, should the topic of oh-so-handy coincidence arise in her next workshop session at the Birdhouse. "Do you see what I did there?" she would ask them. "I tried to make sense out of chaos, which is of course our job, but I got lazy." They must have put something in the IV, because she was very sleepy. She jotted down some titles:

"You Were Rising"
"Great Big Liar"
"Lumberjack"

She folded up the paper, stuck it in the sleeve of her gown, and slept.

CHAPTER TWENTY-NINE

How I Write

They got back home before Thanksgiving but lay low throughout most of December. Ricky had taken great care of the place and asked no questions about the tour or the accident when he met her at the station. "We all kept up with your thrilling adventures," he said, but didn't say what that meant or prod her for thrilling details. He warned her that Carla planned to throw her a welcome-home bash. "I'll put her off as long as I can," he said, handing her the keys to car and house. "But you know it's going to happen."

A full week went by before she lost the sensation of being on a rocking, clacketing train. After a brief recuperation in a Montana hospital, they had explored Wyoming, Washington, and Oregon. Sometimes they had stopped in towns with no bookings, no bookstores, just to be alone. She had gotten her phone back from the Amtrak people, along with all of her miraculously unincinerated luggage, but she kept the phone off most days. "Text only," she texted to Maxine, and that's how they kept in touch during those weeks. At night, in motels and IHOPS, she wrote three stories, start to finish, and began a novel. Once home she continued writing and dealing with proofs of the new story collection. She changed the title from *Birdbath Stories* to *Malignant Creativity*.

After they'd been home for a week or so, Amy noticed strange cars cruising past her house, the drivers peering into her backyard. Some of them leaned out their windows with cameras. She wondered if they were desperate real estate agents, but the Blaines explained that Alphonse was a local celebrity now, that a TV station had actually called them for anecdotes about the heroic basset, and that, to their credit, they had refused. Amy worried that he might be stolen, but after a couple of weeks the excitement died down. The heroic basset himself was happy to be home. Ricky had planted some winter squash in the raised garden, and for some reason Alphonse liked to take the afternoon sun amid the pumpkins and butternuts.

She put Carla off as long as possible, which turned out to be easier than she had imagined since the Birdhouse had apparently gotten along just fine without her. In her prolonged absence they had not hired any life coaches or gurus but had learned to function independently. Carla told her they had exciting news but that she'd have to come to the Christmas party to hear it. "We'll do a party and dinner and last class, all in one," she said. Amy said she didn't have time to read any of their work.

"Not that kind of class," said Carla. "Just, you know, a seriously last class." She cleared her throat. "We know you're busy now," she said. "We know everything's changed."

No, it hasn't, Amy wanted to say. I still have time to teach you once in a while. But then she understood that everything had changed for *them*. Carla wasn't as gushy as her old self: she sounded her age; she sounded busy, distracted by the demands of her own life. Maybe she was growing up.

Though Carla instructed her not to bring presents, at the last minute Amy decided to take them the Norfolk pine they had bought her last year, the one she had been carrying on the day she fell. That it still lived was a miracle: its lower branches had fallen off months before, but it was taller than she remembered. Ricky had rescued it from the full sun of the raised garden where she had abandoned it, and through the fall he must have fed and watered it back from the dead. It deserved a decent home. She stopped on the way to La Jolla to buy tinsel, a star, and two blue glass ornaments, and decorated the tree on Carla's doorstep before knocking. It looked exactly like the tree in *A Charlie Brown Christmas*. Amy was just thinking this when Harry B opened the door and said it.

Carla's interior décor had changed dramatically. Amy had expected as much, and had amused herself on the way down trying to imagine which Disneyland theme she'd have embraced this time. Would there be waterfalls? Mine shafts? Would she have hung vines from the beams so people could swing from room to room? Not quite. The living room had been transformed from an enchanted Tiki cave to what looked rather like an airport lounge. All the boulders, brooks, and carnivorous plants had vanished, and in their place were clusters of contemporary sectionals, all the color of weathered bone, and banks of computer stations against the two inner walls. The stations were defined by acoustic partitions. There were coffee machines and a water cooler. "Is this Tomorrowland?" she asked Harry B.

"That was my first thought also," he said, handing her a drink, "but it's actually a functioning writing space."

"They look like office cubicles," she said. "Do people actually use them?"

"Honest to god," said Harry under his breath. "They sign up for blocks of time. There's even a faction that wants full cubicles, so no one can see in."

"Like a job!"

"Like a corporate job. Carla's the office manager in spades. She's got it set up so they can get online, but anybody caught playing Angry Birds loses the space for a week."

Amy opened her mouth to say, "That's insane," and then realized that it wasn't. It was brilliant. Carla had come up with an anti-retreat, where writing was not an ascetic calling but a white-collar task measurable in logged hours. "I'll bet they're producing like mad," she said, and Harry held his palms apart as if describing a huge fish.

Carla swept up, tailored and beige, followed by caterers with trays of hors d'oeuvres. "There you are!" she said. "I have so much to tell you!" Carla and Harry B walked Amy to a chair in a nest of sectionals, and without so much as a snap of her fingers people gathered around her, pushing furniture from all corners of the room, and in minutes everyone was seated comfortably before her. Patrice Garrotte startled her with his presence: she had known he was working with them, but it was so odd to see him here. In her mind he was always on a plane. Kurt Robetussien, Ricky, Tiffany, Dr. Surtees, and Brie Spangler were all present, and there were six or seven strangers, each of whom Carla introduced and Amy instantly forgot, so stunned was she by Carla's self-assurance, the ease with which she commanded the room. She had dropped a ton of weight and her helmet of hair was of a color found in nature. Was this a good thing?

"First of all," Carla said, "Harry's getting us incorporated. Also we've decided to go with a different name."

"Different from what?"

"Well, you'll remember that—see, Harry, I told you!"

"Carla wanted to do a PowerPoint presentation," Harry said, "and I talked her out of it."

"It would have shown the original name, Croatoan, the Missing Writer's Colony, and the steps by which we came to realize that a less . . . *ironic* . . . name would garner more positive attention."

"Carla, this is your business. I don't have anything to do with it."

"Well, but you came up with the name, and I didn't want to offend you."

And yet you have, thought Amy, with your ridiculous corporateness. What have you done with Carla Karolak? " 'Croatoan' was an ironic suggestion on my part," she said. "At any rate it's your retreat."

"But it's not a retreat," Carla said, leaning forward, and in her eyes Amy finally got a glimpse of Carla's old abandon, that endearing willingness to take an idea and run off a cliff with it. "See, that's what got me thinking. You know, how you always make fun of solitary, windswept writers?"

"I do?"

"Yeah, you know, with their oak tables and their, I don't know, hurricane lamps and handmade foolscap—"

"And their precious little rituals," said Tiffany, "and their special pencils."

"I don't think she said 'handmade foolscap,' " said Dr. Surtees. "It was 'homemade foolscap *notebooks*.' "

"Same difference," said Tiffany.

"World of difference," said Dr. Surtees. "If you made your own paper, you'd stink up the whole house with pulp."

"Excuse me," said Amy, "if I ever said anything like that, it wasn't for posterity. Good lord, were you guys taking notes?"

"We don't have to," said Ricky. "We've got podcasts."

She did sort of remember riffing on writing rituals and monastic cells, just variations on what she had already said during that first NPR gig, but had thought that because nothing was written down it would instantly vaporize. But they had podcasts and YouTube and they knew how to use them. Still, wasn't it less onerous to glance back over a page than to force yourself to listen to it or watch it more than once? How did they have time to memorize her foolishness? Were they multitasking? Did these people—did *other* people—listen to her droning on pretentiously about literary pretensions while journaling, tweeting, and shucking sugar peas?

"We're calling it Inspiration Point," Carla said, slipping a card out of the pocket of her silk blouse. It read *Inspiration Point!*

"Wouldn't *Exclamation Point!* be catchier?"

"See," said Ricky to Carla, "I told you."

"Well," said Carla, blushing, trying not to look devastated, "we have a number of other promising alternatives." She lowered her head and fished out some more cards.

"*Inspiration Point* is just fine," Amy said. It wasn't, but she was anxious to make amends for trying to bring Carla to heel, as though she had no right to take her place in the world. Amy despised bullies, and here she was, being one. "I'd leave off the punctuation if it were me, but you have to do what you think is best."

"Really?"

"Absolutely," said Amy. "Now, tell me more. Tell me everything."

*   *   *

Everything was a lot. Inspiration Point—IP—had thirty members, six living on premises, all of whom paid plenty for the right to commit themselves to twenty cubicle hours per week, minimum. At first, Carla wanted a weekly page quota, but Harry B talked her out of it, so that the only requirement was what Carla called "butts in seats" twenty hours per. Failure to log these hours or to obey rules against time-wasting computer games meant instant one-week suspension; two failures meant a year-length expulsion with no refunds. During the first weeks two paying members were drummed out, and the rest, seeing that Carla wasn't kidding, knuckled under, and in no time word of mouth brought in four more, and soon there was a long waiting list. "We considered expanding," Harry said, "but decided on a limit of thirty for the time being, until we see the results."

The results so far were impressive. Kurt R had finished his cancer nurse novel. He thought it was pretty good for a first novel ("It's wonderful," said Brie Spangler, sitting beside him, her hand on his shoulder), but he figured he'd never find an agent for it unless he wrote something cheerier, so he had started a comic novel about a small-town emergency room. Brie Spangler said it was hilarious.

Brie had abandoned her working-class car-thief novel and was "working on short fiction" and mum about her progress, which Amy guessed was nil, though she was "loving the atmosphere" of Inspiration Point and talking it up on the radio. Amy hoped Kurt R appreciated that she was paying, both in money and in time, to be his besotted cheerleader.

Patrice was working on a new story, "not about my mother," so good for him.

The biggest surprise of all was Surtees, who had miraculously quit doing those horrible medical thrillers and was writing a weekly advice column for the *Reader*. "It's actually worthwhile," Harry whispered. "He answers questions and keeps everybody up-to-date on local infections and contagions. He's like the measles weatherman. The Measleman. The *Times* is putting out feelers."

Amy was torn between admiration and despair. Whether deliberately or accidentally, Carla had applied something like a Weight Watchers model to the huge consumer base of lit-wannabes, basically getting them to pay her to do something they ought to be doing on their own, and of course it was chugging right along, and even with no business sense Amy could easily imagine a nationwide IP franchise annually contributing tens of thousands of publishable manuscripts to the Matterhorn stack of books nobody reads. Yet she liked the idea of the anti-retreat: the unmagical workstations, the unglamorous time clock. What they were describing came much closer to her own experience of writing than any "How I Write" account she had ever read.

Ricky Buzza cleared his throat and stood up. "I have news," he said.

"You got the agent," said Amy.

"Who blabbed?" asked Carla. "Nobody was supposed to blab!"

"He's just got that look," Amy said. He did. Triumphant guilt, the unmistakable aura of the first writer in the pack to make good. Amy remembered how it had felt for her, when she was younger than Ricky, getting advice on her manuscripts from a guy in the English Department who had thirty years earlier had spectacular success with one short story—it was anthologized everywhere and made into a movie and a teleplay—and then gone dry. He'd put in a word for her with his old publisher, and she could still remember the unpleasant surprise on his face when she'd mentioned (off-the-cuff, by-the-by, like the insensitive young snot she had been) that they'd bought "the thing." He'd shifted expressions instantly, replacing the honest one with one of paternal pride. Had the shift been achieved deliberately behind the palm of a hand passing from top to bottom it would have been comical, but of course the moment was anything but funny, and neither was her own response, that ugly-feeling hybrid of sympathy and glee. Until that moment she had not thought about what she did in the privacy of her notebooks as a competitive undertaking, but of course it was, and here was Ricky, the first of the group to make good. He was red-faced, fidgety, ready to burst. "It's more than an agent, isn't it?" she asked him. Nobody, even today, could look that bursty about an agent.

"Well . . . sort of, yeah. She's talking with two publishers. They're—"

Carla leaped to her feet. "Bidding war! Bidding war!" she screamed, totally breaking character, jumping up and down like the performing toddler she had once been.

"Well, technically more of a skirmish," said Ricky. "But yeah."

Amy, happy to feel not a twinge of envy, scanned the faces before her. Only the new people looked less than overjoyed, but then they had no history with him. "*Tiberius,* I presume?" she asked.

"Yes," he said, over Carla's manic chanting, "but we've changed the name again."

"*Nero?*"

"Wow," said Ricky. "How did you guess? Also, it's his last name, not his first. I'm scrapping 'Denton.' My agent's idea. Turns out there used to be a kind of baby pajamas called Dr. Dentons."

"No kidding," said Amy. It would be mean to tell him she knew this. She probably shouldn't have guessed "Nero" either. If she had ever had children, she'd have had to practice feigning ignorance. What was that like? she wondered.

When the excitement died down, Carla told everyone it was time for Last Class. "I have nothing left to teach you," Amy said, meaning it, and Carla, yelling, "We knew you'd say that!" ran from the room and wheeled in an enormous flat-screen monstrosity. "Which is why we set this up."

"Tiffany did, actually," said Ricky. "She spent hours putting it together."

"It was fun," Tiffany said. "I took a film school extension class a couple of years ago. This was great practice."

"We also assumed," said Dr. Surtees, "that you were so busy making appearances that you probably missed most of this."

Amy had an awful idea what "this" was and lacked the heart to tell them that one can't very well miss what one has deliberately dodged. She sighed theatrically, snagged two drinks from a passing caterer, and settled back.

Tiffany had mashed together footage from both C-SPAN appearances, the Whither debacle and that interview she'd barely stayed awake for. There were amateur videos too of bookstore events, none of which she recognized. Tiffany alternated snippets from all that with audio clips from a hundred radio interviews playing beneath a montage, still pictures of trains, radio stations, and Alphonse, who had apparently been featured in magazines and on various blogs. On the cover of *Parade* he stared nobly to the left, *Hands Off, I'm On the Job* clearly legible on his blue service vest. He had also made the national newscasts: there he trudged, snuffling through the Montana grass, immortal against a backdrop of smoke and flame.

Then came the talk shows. Resisting the urge to blur and shield her eyes, she watched her oxymoronic self, a kindly wiseass, a seraphic scold, engage with entertainers, seeming to take every question seriously. She smiled often and never laughed, and when she wasn't smiling she was a little scary. She didn't do that corny peering-over-the-tops-of-glasses thing anymore; instead she inclined very slightly forward, adjusting her bifocals upward, studying the speaker's face intently. This made some people nervous, but that had not, she recalled, been her purpose. She had simply been trying to figure out why they were there and what they were doing. Most were much less lifelike in person than here on the screen, so armored they looked like androids. How did you get to this point? What's your story? she was wondering, though it looked as though she were cataloguing them like pinned moths.

On the talk shows, nobody asked her about her books or her opinions about writer/reader ratios, so they were spared her well-worn foolscap riffs. They all wanted to talk about was the birdbath accident and what had led to what and what it all meant. She watched herself reflect their questions back upon them, getting them to spill their own metaphysical theories, which, for most of the movie people, boiled down to everything happening for a reason. Twelve of them referenced their "journey" or their "path." She remembered wanting to write that down, and now took out her notebook and did. When had Americans started journeying? Was this some faux-Buddhist thing? A skeletal actress whose path looped between jail and rehab claimed to be her biggest fan, and then reeled off the titles of her favorite Amy books, all of which were in fact written by Jenny Marzen. She saw the host catch the mistake—he was a sharp guy, he furrowed his brow and glanced down at the note cards on his desk—and she saw herself catch his eye and shake her head, warning him off. She'd forgotten that moment: that exchange of looks, the subtlety with which they had negotiated, the grace with which he'd backed down, forgoing the easy laugh in deference to her. The girl was an idiot, but that didn't mean they had to embarrass her. She watched a coked-out comedian whose specialty was insult pretending to pretend outrage at having his segment cut short. Hers had run much longer than planned, so when he came on set he was furious. He alternated between roasting her age, body, and vocabulary and throwing himself at her, murmuring "Forgive me, darling, I'm not myself tonight," which was apparently one of his trademarks, a guaranteed laugh-generator, except that it didn't. She remembered wanting to bat him away, but only because he was touching her. Otherwise he was just pitiful. She watched herself watch him with what looked like kindly concern. The audience went silent; the unhappy host sat still; the miserable comic shut his mouth. This moment she remembered clearly, because of the hush.

This had been her first time on national television, and she just assumed the dead air meant they were on some sort of break and the mikes were off, which gave her leave to do what she did, which was to lean close to the comic and ask, in a low, gentle voice, "What is *wrong* with you?" The crowd's roar of approval shocked her as much as it did him. And until now, she hadn't known that the moment was actually *televised*. How horrible. Millions of people saw her humiliate this man.

"What is *wrong* with you!" Ricky was shouting now, and the others were chanting, "What is *wrong* with you!"

"Why are they doing that?" she asked Harry B.

"It's a meme," he said. "It's all over the Net. You're the new Where's the Beef Lady."

Tiffany's mashup went on for an hour. Amy was touched by the group's enthusiasm, the joy with which they greeted every memetic moment, their pleasure in being able to do this thing for her, and she made it through the rest of the hour by focusing on *that,* while tuning out as much of the display as possible. She hoped the smile on her face was as convincing to them as was the smiling countenance of the televised creature, a woman Amy thoroughly disliked.

She was the reason Amy never watched unscripted TV or listened to talk radio. The woman, like many of the hosts and a few of the guests, was bright, guarded, and possibly interesting, but her willingness to be on show like this, her comfort with it—and it was undeniably comfort, she never looked uneasy—canceled that all out. Who the hell were these people, who imagined the minutiae of their lives and thoughts could be of public interest? "You're a pro," one of the hosts had told her off-camera, "you could have been doing this all your life."

She saw he was right. She saw that this woman attracted attention by ignoring it, understanding that it was her due and that it was worthless. She made other people self-conscious. Her serenity was tactical. She saw that her gift was that, unlike most of these spotlit people, she didn't care. What a thing to put on your tombstone. *I never cared about anything.*

Well, except Max. And these people here. And getting some of it down right. And her dog, who wrapped up the show on a high note, sniffing the feet of cameramen, navigating rivers of cable, rooting in the couch cushions next to a Fox News blowhard and coming up with what looked like a strip of beef jerky, to the deafening delight of the crowd. "Another meme," said Harry. "Your dog is gonna bring this jerk down."

She stayed as long as she could stand to, answering questions about what this or that celebrity was like, and were any of the green rooms actually green, and how did it feel under the hot lights. At ten o'clock as she gathered herself to leave she realized that no one had asked her about the train wreck. Not one single question. Even Carla had refrained, and Amy was seized by a sudden impulse to embrace her, to embrace all of them, an impulse so sharp she almost gave in to it. How well these people knew her.

So she sat back down and stayed a little longer and gave them everything, the fire, the rocky field, the dark theater, the lumberjack who called her the lady with the dog, the dying woman. She gave them Harriet Johnston and Thelma Schoon. She gave them *and you were right there rising.* She gave it all away knowing that she would now be unable to use any of it herself, having told it, the richest of her tiny cache of life stories, and she did it gladly, without effort, as though she were an old hand at self-sacrifice.

She left them then, happy and waving, and drove home, all the while hearing *What's wrong with you?,* all the while answering, knowing, *I should have had children.* She could barely make out the freeway lane markers. She had to pull over in the breakdown lane just to get herself together. These days her night vision wasn't all that great, even when she wasn't crying.

The phone's last ring was echoing when she got inside. "I know you're awake, babe," said Maxine.

Amy picked it up. "Are you really dying?" she asked her.

"It's a Christmas Miracle," said Maxine. "I was, but now I'm not."

"Don't screw with me, Maxine. I'm not in the mood."

"What can I tell you? I had a real diagnosis, they said I'd be gone in a year, now they're saying I'm good for now. Honest. What's the deal?"

"A real diagnosis of what?"

"A fatal pulmonary whatsit, not cancer. My lungs are turning into glass, okay? They stopped, though. They're half-glassed."

"You don't cough anymore."

"I quit smoking. Thanks for reminding me."

Amy decided to believe her. She needed an undying Maxine. "Listen," she said. "I don't want to be a TV personality. I mean it. I hate the whole damn thing. I really do."

"Good," said Maxine. "You're a nine-day wonder and you've had maybe seven days. This is smart. Leave them wanting more. I was worried I'd have to talk you down."

"I thought you knew me."

"I do know you, but I've known a few others who got blinded by the headlights and lost their way. Remember Hetty Mant? She had another four-five bestsellers in her, but she flamed out on *The Match Game*. Hey, are you crying?"

"Not anymore," said Amy. She explained about Tiffany's mashup and how depressing it had all been. "I had a goddamn epiphany," she said. "I hate when that happens. It was grisly, Maxine, but I feel much better now." She did. Yes, her life was a poor stunted mess of missed chances, and yes, she had played to lose, and yes, there was nothing to be done about it now. She felt sad, but not numb. Hollow, but not empty.

Maxine talked books. Amy was going to make enough on the *Malignant Creativity* advance to support herself modestly for the next three years. They discussed what Amy was working on now, the new stuff, the possible novel, and she agreed in principle to another non-televised tour sometime in the distant future. "You keep writing, you won't have to do anything else unless you want to. You can quit the online gig if you like. Up to you. Gotta go."

"Maxine? Was all this worth it? For you, I mean. All the work, all the machinations, the reservations and the bookings and the plots and the Byzantine mind games and, well, putting up with me, let's face it—"

"You're kidding, right?" She sounded miffed. "That was the most fun I've had in thirty years. We're a goddamn team, babe!"

She went to fix herself a drink, then realized she was wide awake and not ready to wind down. She put on the coffee and joined Alphonse in the raised garden. For December the night was balmy. She sat down on the wall beside him and listened to him crunch on something. His brow was shiny in the moonlight and mostly white now. He had just about lost one of his three colors, the chestnut washed out with age. Basset hounds were not noted for longevity. The thought that he would die sooner rather than later was unbearable, except that it wasn't, because everything was bearable. We are built for suffering, she knew; we do it well. But to do it right now, when everything was excellent, would be silly. When Max got sick she had suffered strenuously, tormenting herself through sleepless nights as though grief could be prepaid in installments. But what if you could? she wondered. What if you could bank pain in some repository, like a Christmas Club, parceling it out in tidy packets while you're young and strong. This was a vapid idea for a story, but it stuck anyway. There was something usable in it, some tiny thing.

There was something too, much larger, in the shabby spectacle of her televised image, which had indeed been *she* but not *self.* There was a difference between the two, and it bore exploration. As did a lifetime spent not waiting in the wings but living there, refusing the light, finessing the drama. All about her, in the night sky, in the garden shadows, hid the children she had never had, the people she had never touched, mapping out a vast flickering network of missed connections. There was something in a life lived barely.

"We are willful creatures," she told her dog, surprising him into an upward glance. She could see the moon in both his eyes. "We have work to do," she told him. Together they rose and made their way through the dark to the back door of her bright little house.